THE
SPIRIT OF LIBERTY

Ted Allbeury

This title first published in Great Britain 2007 by
SEVERN HOUSE PUBLISHERS LTD of
9–15 High Street, Sutton, Surrey SM1 1DF.
Originally published 1995 in Great Britain only
under the title *Beyond the Silence*.
This title first published in the USA 2007 by
SEVERN HOUSE PUBLISHERS INC of
595 Madison Avenue, New York, N.Y. 10022.

British Library Cataloguing in Publication Data

Allbeury, Ted
   The spirit of liberty
   1.   Espionage, British - Fiction
   2.   Cold War - Fiction
   3.   Spy stories
   I.   Title II. Allbeury, Ted. Beyond the silence
   823.9'14 [F]

   ISBN-13: 978-0-7278-6458-1

All Severn House titles are printed on acid-free paper.

Printed and bound in Great Britain by
MPG Books Ltd., Bodmin, Cornwall.

Here richly, with ridiculous display,
The Politician's corpse was laid away.
While all of his acquaintance sneered and slanged
I wept: for I had longed to see him hanged.

Hilaire Belloc, Sonnets and Verse (1923)
'Epigraph on the Politician Himself'

The spirit of liberty is the spirit
which is not too sure that it is right
Judge Learned Hand

ONE

CHAPTER 1

Old habits die hard and Kennedy had paid off the taxi at Victoria Station and walked the rest of the way to Ebury Street. As he crossed the road to number 25b he wondered if it really was the chaos back at Century House with Facilities planning the move to the new HQ, or was it because he rather liked the pretty safe house itself, that had made him choose it for the meeting. It was no longer a safe house. Some joker at the Soviet Embassy had sent a 'Get well' card addressed to the Director-General 'care of' 25b Ebury Street. But the rent had been paid until the end of the year so they might as well use it until then.

He pressed the door-bell and when the door clicked open he walked slowly up the steep, narrow stairs, aware that security cameras had watched his progress from when he crossed the street, and that now the internal circuit had taken him over.

Maggie was waiting for him on the small landing at the top of the stairs.

'Mr Farmer and Mr Shelley are in the side room waiting for you, sir.' As he thanked her and turned she said, 'Will you sign the chit, sir, please?'

He sighed and read the card. It confirmed that Angus Roffey, Signals Section, had checked the whole house at 14.00 hours that day and it was electronically clean. He signed the card and Maggie said, 'I've told them it's either tea or coffee until after the meeting.'

He smiled and headed for the side room. It was bright, walls and ceiling Dulux Brilliant White and Venetian blinds at the windows overlooking the street. Farmer and Shelley looked bored already.

There was no tape recorder and no notepads. It was not a meeting of record. Kennedy had told them briefly already what he wanted to discuss. In fact he had already made his mind up about what to do, but a little support from other sections would do no harm; it might even spread the load if the whole thing went down the pan.

He took off his jacket, hung it over the back of the chair and sat down.

'Thanks for coming, both of you.' He paused. 'Let me just outline the problem.' He paused. 'Our old friend Carling. Lord Carling. Ex-SIS and suspected by several colleagues of having played footsie with the Russians during his time with us. Maybe even before.' He paused. 'And maybe even after he left us.'

'Why the sudden interest in him now, Freddie?'

Kennedy hesitated for a moment, then said, 'Two reasons. Maybe even more. The timing is because we have strong indications that one of the tabloids is considering one of its "investigatory" pieces on SIS. You know the stuff. They want to hang it on to the Carling business. Mole in the heart of SIS. Lax security. Who was protecting him? Heads must roll – and all the usual crap they dish up.'

Farmer said quietly, 'I gather you've got some scheme in mind—'

Shelley interrupted. 'First things first, Freddie. You say some of our people suspected him.' He paused. 'On what grounds? Where's the evidence?'

Kennedy shrugged. 'I've had long conversations with the DPP and he says we have nothing that would stand up in court. And we *could* end up with a libel writ.'

'So could the tabloid, Freddie.'

'Fair enough. But old Carling's in his late sixties. May even be seventy already. The tabloid could be waiting for him to kick the bucket. Just putting the bits together as they come in.'

Shelley said, 'It must be old stuff now. You say some people suspect that he's still playing footsie with the Russians. Glasnost and perestroika will have ended those games. He can't be important enough for them to risk running him now.'

Farmer shook his head. 'I'm always reading about him on trips to Berlin, Vienna, Prague and Budapest. He hasn't stopped those.'

Kennedy said, 'He'd claim that it's just his work for the Arts Council.' He smiled. 'Or could be.'

Shelley laughed softly. 'It's a bloody good cover anyway.' He looked at Kennedy. 'I gather you've got something in mind?'

'Well. The obvious alternative to prosecuting is to do a deal. He tells us all and we give him immunity from prosecution.'

Shelley nodded. 'So?'

Kennedy sighed. 'The snag is – we've got so little evidence that I wonder if what he's got to tell us is worth the immunity.'

'Go on.'

'I had in mind having a chat with Carling. Tell him about vague suspicions here and at the tabloid. Tell him that there's pressure building up to expose him and we'd be prepared to do a deal, but we need to know roughly what he's got to tell us before we can make a decision.'

Farmer frowned. 'And what if he just tells us to get stuffed?'

Kennedy shook his head. 'Put yourself in his place, Dickie. An aristocrat, a popular and well-known figure, an icon of the arts scene. He won't want to go through the mill of a court case or being done over by one of the tabloids. You know what they'd make of it.'

Shelley interposed. 'And what they'd make of us too. Nothing definite – "high-level sources suggest" – "a well-informed ex-officer says" – "who is protecting the traitors?" – it's all been done before, with far less to go on than in this case. Even now I ask myself: if our people had suspicions why the hell didn't they do something about it?'

Kennedy shrugged. 'First of all the suspicions are only with hindsight, and secondly – like I said – the DPP says we'd be out on our ears as soon as the judge had heard the opening statement and read the file.' He paused. 'It's going to take some time even if he co-operates. Whoever does it will have to decide whether Carling is telling us the full story or just a cover-up.'

'Who've you got in mind?'

'One of my own chaps. Name's Mathews. Wasn't even born when our friend could have first started playing games with the Russians. He can get alongside Carling without the luggage of prior knowledge or old prejudices.'

'How long's he been with us?'

'Five years officially, another three years before that on loan from the I.Corps.'

'Positively vetted?'

'Of course.'

Farmer shrugged. 'You seem to have got it all worked out.'

Kennedy smiled. 'Can you think of something better?'

'No. It just seems a bit – I don't know what – airy-fairy. We ask our friend to spill the beans but promise him nothing definite. Why should he trust us?'

Kennedy, still smiling, said, 'It isn't us he'll be trusting, it'll be Mathews.'

There was a long silence and then Kennedy said, 'Shall we vote on it?'

Farmer shook his head. 'No. I'll go with it for want of anything better.'

They had hung on, gossiping, for another ten minutes and then gone their different ways. Only Kennedy went back to Century House.

CHAPTER 2

Kennedy knew George Carling from Carling's last few years with SIS and had subsequently met him from time to time at meetings at the Foreign Office. He decided that he ought to meet His Lordship alone to get the thing moving, before briefing Mathews. There were ways of presenting the possible deal that he felt he could best put to Carling himself. He phoned him and arranged a dinner meeting at the Reform.

The conversation during the meal was amiable and amusing as Carling gave him the inside story on the fine-art forgeries that had recently been exposed. He obviously enjoyed the discomfiture of the so-called connoisseurs and experts. It seemed in character that Carling was so obviously on the side of the forger.

They took their coffee in the members' lounge in comfortable armchairs in a corner that gave them some privacy. Kennedy ordered malt whiskies for them both and as he lifted his glass to Carling, he said, 'I need your help, George.'

Carling was obviously surprised. 'Really. What sort of help?'

'We need your co-operation.'

'Who's we?'

'SIS.'

'Sounds ominous.'

Kennedy smiled. 'Not really.'

'What's it all about?'

'You.'

'Me? For God's sake. I've been away from that game for a decade. What help can I give you?'

Kennedy took a deep breath, then said, 'Would you be surprised if I told you that there are people in SIS and elsewhere who suggest that your loyalty was questionable?'

Carling laughed. 'Which particular loyalty?'

'Loyalty to this country.'

Carling smiled. 'Oh that. No, it wouldn't surprise me at all. Everybody from directors-general down has suffered unfounded stories about their loyalty. The likes of me are fair game.'

Kennedy said quietly, 'We have information that one of the tabloids is trying to put together a story that suggests you had contacts with the KGB over a number of years.'

Carling smiled, shaking his head. 'But they couldn't prove it.'

'They don't have to. They print the story and their sales go up. They can keep it on the boil for weeks and months. You've seen what they've done recently to quite insignificant politicians. And you're very well known to the public.'

'And you're afraid that SIS will be accused of being lax and inefficient.'

'That's part of the problem.'

'What's the other part.'

'We need to know the truth.'

'Go on.'

'We thought it might be prudent to go over the past with you.' He paused. 'And then, if it satisfies us, grant you immunity from prosecution in exchange for your co-operation.' He paused again. 'It would be done very discreetly and in confidence.'

'So what's the problem?'

'First, that you may not agree to co-operate, and secondly, that you give us a heavily doctored account of whatever happened.'

Carling smiled. 'Not get value for money, yes?'

'I suppose you could call it that.'

'And if you're not satisfied, what then?'

'We go back to square one. To the situation as it is today.'

'All bets off.'

Kennedy shrugged but said nothing.

'Who would I be talking to?'

'One of my best officers. Timothy Mathews. Mid-thirties, wide experience. I think you'd quite like him.'

'It sounds an interesting exercise. What is it you people used to call it? "Walking back the cat?" Seeing what really happened and how it had influenced your old colleagues when they'd made the wrong moves and wrong analysis.'

Kennedy, relieved, smiled. 'We call it damage limitation these days.'

'So when do you want to start?'

'As soon as possible and when it's convenient to you.'

'I'll have to go, Kennedy.' Carling stood up. 'I'm due at the Festival Hall. Tell him to phone me at home.' He smiled. 'I'm sure you know the number.'

Mathews put the tea bag in the mug with the sugar and reached for the bottle of milk, his hand hesitating before it grasped the bottle. He tried to remember what his father had always said about the only way to make a good cup of tea was to put the milk in last. Or was it first? He poured in the boiling water. As he stirred in the milk he realised how hopeless he was domestically, now he was on his own. His solicitor had said it would be easy. A 'no-fault' divorce. No lies about either party. Just an acceptance that she'd wanted out. Out for him and in for Roger Thomas, a local solicitor. A real creep of a man, self-satisfied and, as they say, with a reputation with the ladies. And, standing on the sidelines, trying to take it all in, eight-year-old Tony, the Mathewses' son. Care and custody to the mother, Pamela, reasonable access for the father. The court had said that as they seemed reasonable people access could be left for the parties and their solicitors to settle. His chap had said that the best he could get him was every other Saturday, 9 a.m. to 6 p.m. The first two Saturdays had been no problem but the third Saturday Pamela said the boy was going to a Cub camp and would have to miss out. And as he started to protest she had hung up.

When the phone rang he was careful not to give his name or the number.

'Yes?'

'The deputy would like to see you, Tim. Soon as possible. He suggests three this afternoon.'

'Where?'

'Do you know the Special Forces Club?'

'Yeah.'

'He's having lunch there. He'll be waiting for you.'

'Any idea what it's all about?'

'No idea. But I'm sure it's frightfully important.' And he heard her soft laugh cut off as she hung up.

He wondered what it could be. Kennedy was his immediate boss and had been for two years. Tough but fair and had been over all the same hurdles in his time.

He wouldn't call him back from his week's leave unless it was either urgent or important.

Mathews paid off the taxi at Harrods and walked the short distance to the Special Forces Club. Kennedy signed him in after the club steward had checked his ID and then took him upstairs to a private room. When they were sitting Kennedy looked across at Mathews.

'How's things?'

'Much as usual.'

'I've got a special assignment for you. It might help to keep your mind off the domestic problems.' He paused. 'What do you know about George Carling – Lord Carling to give him his proper title?'

'Is this the Arts Council guy? The one who's always on TV?'

'That's the one. He used to be SIS. Some years full time and then a kind of unofficial consultant on Eastern bloc intelligence.' He paused. 'We've always had our suspicions that he was playing games with the KGB. All circumstantial. Virtually nothing we could use in court.' Kennedy looked towards the windows and then back at Mathews. 'We've done a deal with him. We've formed a small committee to control it. Myself, Shelley and Farmer. Let me tell you what we want you to do.'

Kennedy spent ten minutes explaining the deal he had done with Carling and the background that had prompted it.

'He's actually agreed to do this?' Mathews said with obvious disbelief.

'Yes.'

'Maybe he'll just try and string me along. And we'll end up knowing no more than we know now.'

'Could be. But it'll be up to you to decide if he's just wasting our time.'

'Do you think he's guilty?'

'I'm sure he is but I not only couldn't prove it in court, I doubt if I could convince anyone who matters in SIS either. They don't like suspicion, most of them have been under suspicion for something or other at some stage in their careers. They only want facts.'

'How long have we got?'

'As long as you need. It's going to take time to get to know him well enough to judge whether he's telling the truth or not.'

'What about the newspaper?'

Kennedy shrugged. 'They'll be more cautious than we need be. Their lawyers will see to that. They'll probably wait until Carling dies.'

'How old is he?'

'Late sixties, could be seventy even.'

'Looks younger on TV. Who's got his "P" file?'

Kennedy reached in his briefcase and brought out two videotapes. 'I suggest you don't read his file unless you absolutely need to. These are videotapes of programmes he's been on and a few clips of black and white surveillance material. Most of it stills.' As he handed the tapes to Mathews he said, 'It's better to go in with a clean slate and no prejudices. Feel free to contact me any time you want.' He shrugged. 'Some sort of sitrep weekly will do, even if it's a nil report. OK?'

'OK.'

CHAPTER 3

———————

Despite Kennedy's warning about going in without prejudice, Mathews had a look at Carling's entry in *Who's Who*. There wasn't much. Born 1920, which meant he was about seventy. Not married. Served for five years in Intelligence Corps during the war. Rank, Captain. Foreign Office, which meant SIS, from 1945 to 1960. Then nothing but various consultancies. Arts Council, British Film Board, Tate Gallery, and the London Symphony Orchestra as fund-raiser. Hobbies listed as photography, ham radio and reading. Education, Harrow and Trinity, a 2:2 in modern languages, German and French.

The videotapes were mainly TV interviews. He was a frequent guest on programmes about the arts including a solo interview with Melvyn Bragg, where they seemed to get on well together. There was a slightly acerbic *Late Show* where Carling was amiably defending one of the London orchestra's performances at the Festival Hall against a reviewer who was angered by 'fluffed notes on the horns, mistimed entries by the brass and jagged string playing.'

The surveillance clips in black and white showed Carling and another man strolling around the lake in St James's Park, Carling getting out of a car at the Polish Embassy in Portland Place, Carling and what looked like a casual meeting but had all the signs of a contrived meeting, with a woman at Gatwick in the Burger King. There were a number of other photographs, none of them apparently significant unless you knew who the people and places were.

Mathews looked at the card that Kennedy had handed him giving Carling's home telephone number. It gave a code number that he didn't recognise and he phoned Facilities to check where it was. It was a Tunbridge Wells number. He rang three times before he got a reply and then it was Carling himself who picked up the phone.

'Carling.'

'My name's Mathews, sir. I was told to get in touch with you.'

'Who?'

'Mathews, sir.' When there was a long pause he added, 'Century House.'

'Ah yes. Of course. You want to see me, I suppose.'

'When would suit you, sir?'

'Come down tomorrow. Not before 9 a.m. I'm not an early riser. You know where my place is?'

'No, sir, I don't.'

'You car or train?'

'Car.'

'OK. Take the Frant road out of Tunbridge Wells but don't go to Frant, turn off left to the Bayham Road. Through Bells Yew Green and on to a sign for the trout farm. Turn left through the gates and go on about a mile and you'll find my house on the right-hand side of the road. There's a sign says Lake Cottage. You can't miss it.'

'I'll be there about ten, sir.'

'Good show.'

And Carling hung up.

    *   *   *

It was the last day of March, a Saturday, and the roads were busy as Mathews drove through Tunbridge Wells and turned off at the Pantiles. Fifteen minutes later he saw the sign for the trout farm and the wide open gates. Five minutes later he was at Lake Cottage. It wasn't Mathews' idea of a cottage. It looked as if it had once been at least four terraced cottages before they had been converted. Beautiful stone and large old-fashioned windows. A brick path led through a front garden with two magnolia trees already in bloom despite the weather, and masses of daffodils across the two lawns with primroses in flower each side of the path. The solid oak door was ajar but he rang the brass bell and waited.

A young woman came to the door and when he gave his name she smiled and said, 'His Lordship is in his study. I'll take you to him.'

Mathews barely had time to notice the rooms but he was conscious of antique furniture, a Steinway grand in the sitting room and walls everywhere lined with books. The girl knocked on a solid door and then opened it and ushered him inside. She smiled at the man in the leather armchair. 'Mr Mathews to see you, sir.'

Carling held out his hand without getting up and nodded to another chair facing him. 'Good journey?'

'No problems, thank you.'

'You need the loo or a cup of tea or anything?'

'Not at the moment, thank you, sir.'

'So. How do we start?'

'Can I ask you how I should address you?'

Carling smiled. 'You make me sound like an envelope. Not My Lord for heaven's sake. Let's start as you started, with 'sir' in deference to my age. When we've got to know one another it can be George.' He paused. 'Let me start, eh?'

'Of course, sir.'

'I gather you want to talk about my life, so I'd like to know a bit about you. Where you come from. Your background. What you've been up to in SIS. OK?'

'I'm thirty-five. Recently divorced—'

Carling intervened. Eyebrows raised in query. 'The job? Never around when you're needed and all that?'

'No. Not really. She met someone else, more successful. A solicitor.'

'Bastards. All of 'em. I wouldn't trust any one of them an inch. Go on.'

'A son. She has him. I'm fighting for access.' He paused. 'I was born in Erdington in Birmingham. Went to King Edward's and then St Antony's, Oxford. My father has a music shop. Sells instruments, pianos and sheet music. My mother gives piano lessons. He likes jazz and she likes Schubert and Chaminade. In SIS I did the usual two-year training and probation and I've had postings in Berlin, Paris and Vienna and a year in Washington.' He paused and shrugged. 'That's about it.'

'What a splendid summary. I assume that when you say Washington you mean Langley and the CIA?'

'Yes.'

'How did you get on with the Americans?'

'I liked them.'

'Why?'

'Oh. I found them generous and optimistic. They don't really understand Europeans but they mean well.'

'Interesting.' Carling shuffled around in his chair and tossed a cushion to the floor. 'And now. What do you want to know about me?' He paused and looked at Mathews.

'By the way, do you believe all those stories about me having a relationship with the KGB?'

'I've no idea, sir. I don't know much more than that there *were* rumours.'

'Fair enough.' He laughed quietly. 'This is going to be like a long version of *This Is Your Life*. They were planning to do me on that show but Julie stopped them. By the way, Julie looks after me. Supervises the cleaning and cooking and all that. She's very attractive but I don't sleep with her. She came from an orphanage and I'm very fond of her.' He paused looking at Mathews. 'You *did* wonder if I slept with her, didn't you?'

Mathews blushed and said hesitantly, 'I guess it passed through my mind. But only fleetingly,' he added.

His Lordship laughed heartily. 'Well done.' Then more seriously: 'How about you. Do you have a girl you sleep with?'

'Just girlfriends. One or two.'

'Good show. Always be discreet.' He sighed rather theatrically. 'Now me. Where shall I start?'

'How about you do your background as I did? Just briefly.'

'I inherited the title when my father died. We didn't get on well together but I admired him. He was brave and a great patriot. Was our ambassador in Vienna for a few years. He was also a snob, and what we would now call a racist. He didn't like foreigners and he didn't like Jews. He thought we made a great mistake not going along with Adolf Hitler. Despite all this he had great charm, that's why my mother married him. She was Austrian. A great singer. I don't know how she stood him. But she did. She loved him, poor woman.' He paused and sighed. 'She loved me too. Protected me. He thought I was a sissy. He caught me reading a Left Book Club book called *Guilty Men*, about Tory politicians who voted for rearmament because they had shares in the companies who made the arms. He burned the book in a kind of ceremony. Echoes of the Nazis. I hated him and I was frightened of him. And of course it made me what they'd nowadays call a typical left-winger. I think I would have been anyway but he made the idea even more attractive. I was about seventeen then.

'I was at Trinity when the war broke out. I joined up. The army. I went into the I.Corps because of my languages. I was bilingual German and had decent French. I served here in the UK and a short time in Italy and then in Germany. Denazification and all that. And then I was approached by SIS. With everybody being demobbed they were short of people. It was typical of their attitudes that they just looked for the sons of people they deemed loyal and trustworthy.' He smiled. 'The old-boy network, you know. Society had not got around to realising that sons sometimes want to be the opposite to their fathers.' He paused and sipped from a glass of water.

Mathews said, 'Were you positively vetted before they recruited you?'

Carling smiled. 'No. They hadn't even invented it in those days. For them my father was proof enough that I was the right kind.'

'Apart from your father, what was it that first made you decide you were left wing?'

'Well, I didn't know then that having those thoughts made me left wing. I'd never even heard the words.' He closed his eyes, thinking, for several moments and then said slowly, 'I guess it was a photograph that started it all.' He stood up. 'I've still got it. Let me show it to you.'

It was almost ten minutes before Carling came back with a file and a piece of a newspaper. He put the picture on the low table between them. 'It's from the *Daily Herald*. I've never got it out of my mind.'

The picture was brown round the edges with age. It showed row on row of ill-clad men with hopeless faces trudging through the rain in a grim street of some industrial town.

Mathews looked up at Carling. 'Who are they?'

'They were the Jarrow marchers, unemployed men from Tyneside who had been thrown out of work. The woman at the front was a Labour politician, Ellen Wilkinson. Later, somebody lent me a book she wrote called *The Town that was Murdered*. Very sad. Very disturbing.' He went on. 'A miner in those days, after long hours down the pit, took home two pounds and four shillings a week. Even the poorly paid workers in the cotton mills earned more.'

'And you wanted to do something about it?'

'I wish I *could* say that. It made me angry and sad but it didn't enter my mind that I could do anything about it.' He smiled. 'I showed the book to my father. He just said the marchers had been wasting their time. And that led to our first big bust-up. But in fact he was typical of most of his contemporaries.'

'So what did you do?'

Carling shrugged. 'Nothing. Absolutely nothing. Except be uneasy and unhappy about those men and others like them. And in less than a year I was in the army.'

'Well at least you were doing your bit against Hitler and fascism.'

Carling sank back into his chair, shaking his head. 'Not really. Nothing so rational. I just joined up, because that was what most of my university friends did.' He shrugged and smiled. 'Let's say I was aware of the human predicament but not of politics. I guess that didn't start for another couple of years.'

'How did it start?'

He laughed. 'This is where you'll prick up your ears. It started because I was terribly impressed by the tremendous sacrifices of the Russians. Rather naïvely I wrote a letter to the Soviet Embassy praising their resistance to the Nazis.' He smiled and looked at Mathews. 'I got a letter back almost immediately. Thanking me for my letter and inviting me to an official cocktail party they were giving for Allied officers. I was on leave after doing a training course at the depot in Winchester. I was a lieutenant then. The party seemed quite formal, interminable toasts and around forty officers, most of them Brits including two brigadiers and several colonels.

'There was a young Russian captain introduced himself to me and said he had heard my mother sing at a concert in Vienna. He was a pleasant chap and we arranged to have a meal together. We went to an Italian place in Frith Street. He had noticed my I.Corps cap-badge and green flashes on my arm and he asked me the usual questions about when I thought the war would end and if I was going to stay on in the army. He told me about his family in Kiev and he spoke about the terrible casualties and the brutalities of the Germans in the areas they had captured.'

'What was your job at that time?'

'I was part of a team at GHQ Home Forces covering the German Order of Battle.'

'Did he ask about your work?'

'I guess we'd had three or four meals together before he asked me for any information.'

'Can you remember what he asked you?'

'Not exactly, but he was mainly interested in the movement of German troops from France to the East Front.'

'So that they had ammunition to pressure Winston Churchill about mounting a Second Front?'

'I guess so.'

'You must have realised that you were committing an offence in passing military intelligence to a foreign national?'

'A foreign national who happened to be an ally. An ally who was actually fighting our mutual enemy. Doesn't that make a difference?'

'That's surely for other people to decide, not individuals who only have one small piece of the jigsaw?'

'To my mind our people should have been passing that information themselves to the Russians. How could it affect our forces for our allies to know what the enemy was doing?'

'That's not really the point. You were doing something that you knew was an offence just because *you* decided it was the right thing to do. Did it never strike you that you may be endangering the lives of our men?'

'Tell me how it could do that?'

'I don't know. No more did you.'

'Do you think it might have saved some Russians' lives to know where the Germans were moving up troops to attack them?'

'I suppose so.' Mathews paused. 'Did they pay you for the information?'

Carling looked shocked. 'Of course not.' He paused and looked across at Mathews. 'Haven't you ever broken the rules because you thought that the rules were stupid sometimes?'

It was several moments before Mathews replied. 'I don't think I have to answer that.'

Carling laughed softly. 'You're pleading the fifth, aren't you? That's the coward's way out.' He paused. 'Does the truth have to be only for me, my friend, but not for you?'

Mathews half smiled. 'OK. Yes, I have sometimes ignored orders or bent the rules when it seemed better to do that.'

'I rest my case, m'lord.'

Mathews laughed and then there was a knock on the door and the girl came in with sandwiches and coffee, placing them on a low table between them.

'Smoked salmon, beef and cheese. There's more if you want it,' she said.

'Thank you, Julie. How about you join us?'

For a moment she hesitated and then she said, 'I'd better not. There are things to do.'

Carling smiled at Mathews. 'She's going to make someone a wonderful wife.'

As she turned to go, Carling said, 'Hold on, my dear.' And turned to Mathews. 'Why don't you stay the night?'

'I didn't bring anything.'

Carling said to Julie, 'Give him my old study bedroom and find him a razor and the rest of it.'

'Right, sir.'

As she left Carling said, 'She's such a honey, that girl. Just does things. Nothing's too much trouble.'

'How long has she been with you?'

'Eat up. Help yourself.' He paused, thinking. 'I'd guess it must be – let me see – she was sixteen when she came here – must be five or six years.' He laughed. 'You don't remember dates and things too well at my age.' He paused. 'I say, she's given me some brie. I love brie.'

'How did you find her?'

24

'I often get asked to give talks. You know – Rotary and the WI. They insist on giving me a fee and think I'm being snobbish if I don't take it. There's an orphanage between Tunbridge Wells and Eastbourne and I get them to send the fee there.' He munched at his sandwich and then said, 'Saves all the bloody palaver with the Inland Revenue. It's seldom more than fifty quid.' He paused. 'Where was I? Why am I going on about all this?'

'The girl, Julie.'

'What about her?'

'How you found her?'

'Of course. What a fool.' He sighed. 'She was being a bit of a nuisance at the orphanage. I go there about once a month. They asked me to talk to her. Seemed reasonable enough to me. I don't think anyone had ever listened to her before. Been in care, fostered, the usual routine. But she was bright as a button. I fixed for her to have a tutor to get her a bit civilised. I gave her the job here about a year later. I had an old biddy who looked after me then. She was a motherly old soul and the girl loved her. Then the old lady died after about a couple of years and Julie has been on her own here ever since. She has a help two or three times a week and we've got a part-time gardener.' He looked at his watch. 'Let's have a break and Julie can show you your room.'

To Mathews the room seemed big. There were leaded windows along one wall and the other walls were lined with books. A comfortable-looking bed was under the windows and there was a hand-basin with a mirror and an electric razor on a glass shelf under the mirror. There was a white towelling bathrobe draped across the bed and a small table with a reading lamp at the head of the bed.

Mathews looked at a small pile of paperbacks on the bedside-table. There was Len Deighton's *The Ipcress File* and a couple of Linda Barneses, and Sue Grafton's *A is for Alibi*. At the bottom of the pile was an Ed McBain and John O'Hara's *A Rage to Live*. The books on the shelves were mainly reference books, dictionaries and a number of books in German. There was an old edition of *Encylopaedia Britannica* and a shelf of travel books and maps.

Mathews turned and walked to the windows. The late afternoon sun cast long shadows across the lawn from the budding fruit trees. Immediately below the windows was a paved area with a small formal pond already garnished with yellow marsh marigolds. Mathews opened one window and leaned with his arms on the stone window-sill. There were the sounds of sheep and lambs not far away. He wondered what he would have been doing if he had gone back to London. He'd probably have phoned Joanna or Mandy and taken her out to dinner at one of the Soho restaurants and then back to bed. They were both quite recent relationships. He hadn't messed about when he was married but he was determined now to make up for lost time but not be long-term committed. On the whole he decided that he was quite happy to be where he was. The house and its garden had a timeless air, a feeling that nothing would go wrong here. It reminded him of a painting by Monet, or was it Renoir?

He took off his jacket and stretched out on the bed. Somebody was playing the piano downstairs. Quiet, gentle, flowing music. The kind his mother loved so much. A few minutes later he was asleep.

CHAPTER 4

Carling had insisted, despite her protests, that Julie sat down to dinner with them. She was part of the family, he said. As they talked through the meal Mathews could see how Carling had built the young woman's self-confidence. His Lordship aired his views on *Coronation Street* and *EastEnders* but left it to the girl to point out the finer points of the characters and criticise where she thought *EastEnders* often went too far in its desire to be topical. They were both regular followers of *The Archers*. Mathews had listened with some amusement at the man who regularly appeared on TV arguing with great erudition the similarities of Satie's music with Picasso's painting.

When the meal was over, Julie discreetly disappeared and Carling had sat at the piano, thinking for a moment and then smiling, said, 'Let me play a piece of your mother's Chaminade. Is your mother a feminist by the way?'

'No. Far from it. Why do you ask?'

'Well, Chaminade is no longer popular and it wasn't until fairly recently that the feminists realised that she was a woman not a man. However . . . let me have a go at her. See if you recognise it.'

As Mathews listened he recognised the music. It was a song his mother often played, singing quietly as she smiled at his father. When Carling finished he turned to Mathews, smiling. 'I'm sure your mother will have played that for you.'

Mathews smiled back. 'I think she played it more for my father than for me.'

'Do you remember what it was called?'

'Was it "The Little Silver Ring"?'

'Well done, well done. Simple music but I like the words. The woman looking at the silver ring her lover gave her and thinking that the ring encircled all her life.' He smiled. 'They call it schmaltz but it's more than that.' Carling stood up. 'Anything more you want to know about what I've told you?'

'I'd like to know about your unit that covered the Order of Battle of the Germans. How did you get the information?'

Carling moved back to the armchair. 'SIS had agents in Europe and SOE had people in France and the Low Countries. We had people who read local newspapers – road accidents involving military vehicles, some sergeant in a unit who played football for a local team and then plays somewhere else when the unit moves elsewhere. Even radio request programmes of music for the Wehrmacht. Then there was photographic reconnaisance by the RAF. There was a continuous flow of small details that were analysed by our staff.'

'Did you ever ask your Russian friend about the Soviet forces?'

'A kind of quid pro quo, you mean?'

'Yes.'

'No.' He shrugged. 'It didn't seem likely to matter to our people where some Soviet tank brigade was stationed.' He paused. 'The war in Russia appeared to be in another world. It was a different war. We had enough of our own problems. We were glad that they were fighting the Germans but that was all.' He laughed softly. 'It was like my father and his friends who said you don't have to worry about the poor, they were used to being poor and you just let them get on with it.' He paused and looked at Mathews. 'Do you ever go to church?' He smiled and held up his hand as if to calm the surprise on Mathew's face. 'I ask because there's a performance of Fauré's Requiem at one of the churches in Tunbridge Wells tomorrow. It's one of my favourites. I chose the Kyrie when I did *Desert Island Discs*. I thought perhaps you might like to join me.' He smiled. 'You don't have to.'

Mathews hesitated for a moment and then said, 'I'd be glad to go with you.'

Carling looked at Mathews. 'Do you miss seeing your son?'

'Yes. A lot.'

'What's getting in the way?'

'My wife. I mean my ex-wife.' He paused and shrugged. 'It's just spite. A way of getting back at me.'

'Why should she do that?'

'God knows. It's probably Thomas, her solicitor and her intended new husband.' He paused. 'Everybody thinks he's very wealthy but he isn't. He's in debt up to his ears and he's also being looked at by the Law Society for misuse of clients' funds.'

'How do you know all that?'

'I've checked up on it myself.'

'You must have bent a few rules to do that.'

Mathews shrugged. He hadn't noticed Carling's half-smile. 'So what? It's my son who's going to suffer when it all goes wrong.'

'It must be a great worry for you.'

'It is.' He paused. 'That reminds me. That Left Book Club book you mentioned. Where did you get it?'

Carling laughed, softly. 'I was still at Harrow then and there were books passed around that could cause trouble if you were caught reading them. There were three or four circulating in my circle. The Left Book Club book was one of them, then there was *Lady Chatterley's Lover* and a lesbian novel called *The Well of Loneliness*. I can't remember the other one. They were all pretty innocuous by today's standards. I found them pretty boring even then. A few taboo words. Much ado about not very much.' He paused. 'Why did you ask?'

'It seemed that was really the start for you. The picture in the paper and then the book. I wondered how the spark was ignited.'

'Don't read too much into it. There were many young men who had similar thoughts to mine. Some were influenced enough to eventually become politicians.'

'But politics didn't interest you?'

'Not the slightest. I'd seen and heard them at home. My father's friends. I detested them.' Carling stood up. 'I think I'll get off to bed. Have a good night's sleep and breakfast's at about nine on Sundays.'

In his bedroom Mathews tried to collect his thoughts. Carling seemed a strange man but he had a lively mind despite his age. He wondered if Carling had ever been married. Apart from his title and possible wealth, he guessed he must be the kind of man that women would find very attractive. He wasn't handsome but his was a lived-in face and the features were the kind you saw on sculptured heads – a Roman face. But it was the eyes and mouth you would remember. Big, brown eyes and a full sensual mouth made wider by the smile creases each side of it. And above all you would remember his modesty. He listened intently when you spoke. Mathews felt in a way that Carling had been as much learning about him as the other way round, and he felt he had learned something from his talk with Carling but he wasn't sure what it was. He could understand now why Kennedy had briefed him not to rush things and not to leap to conclusions.

CHAPTER 5

They drove to the church in Carling's beautifully preserved Rover 3-litre, vintage 1963. When they were leaving after the service, Mathews realised how well-known His Lordship really was. It was slow progress back to where the car was parked as Carling had to stop at several groups of obviously admiring ladies. There were a bold few who even asked him to autograph hymn sheets and New Testament fly leaves. And Carling chatted amiably to all of them as if they were old friends.

Julie had put out an array of drinks for them in the conservatory where, as the back of the house faced due south, it was both warm and sunny despite it being barely the start of spring.

Carling sat with a glass of red wine and Mathews had a sherry.

'Well, Mr Mathews, what did you think of poor Fauré's Requiem?'

'I thought it wasn't bad for amateurs.' He paused. 'Why *poor* Fauré?'

'He never heard it sung. I think the first time it was performed was at his funeral.' He smiled. 'The French never like new ideas. But great on monuments to politicians.' He laughed. 'Just think of what they did for poor old Pompidou.' He paused. 'But they never take to new boys until they've become world famous. But at least they pretend to be civilised, which is more than our lot do.' He put his glass down on the white table-top, turning to look at Mathews. 'But I wouldn't trust that bloody parson with a fiver.' He emphasised his point with an extended finger. 'Never trust a man who uses words like "whomsoever". They hide behind words like some men hide behind beards. It's a sure sign of deviousness.'

'What were you doing when you were in Germany?'

'That was mainly counterintelligence. And, of course, denazification.'

'Did you keep in touch with your Russian friend in those days?'

Carling reached for his glass and turned it slowly, watching the wine swirling in the glass. Then he looked up at Mathews. 'In the last year of the war my contact was somebody else. Somebody more senior. I kept that contact when I was in Germany.'

'What information did you pass to them at that time?'

'In the last year of the war I was still in London and I kept them informed on what we and the Americans were planning about post-war Europe. And in Germany I passed them any evidence that came my way about Nazi war crimes against Soviet citizens, mainly civilians. Sometimes I could identify Russians and Ukrainians who had collaborated with the Nazis.' He paused and looked at Mathews. 'And no. They didn't pay me. They did give me a Leica IIIb, but that was, I believed, a genuine gift, not a reward. I could have got one myself in those days for a carton of cigarettes.'

'How did you pass the information to them?'

'In London it was the normal rigmarole of dead-letter drops and chalk marks on park benches for meetings in different places.' He smiled. 'They rather liked the James Bond bit. I suppose it was necessary. Our people had them under surveillance most of the time. Not always the right people, of course.'

'What sort of places did you use for meetings?'

Carling sighed, closing his eyes, thinking before he replied. 'It's hard to remember. It was a long time ago.' He paused, obviously trying to recall. 'There was a place in Frith Street, a printing place. A house in Finchley, the house of a Party member, a Scot.' He sighed. 'A prostitute's pad in Shepherd Market. A Joe Lyons café in Leicester Square. A shed on an allotment on Hackney Marshes.'

'You must have been a high-grade informant to rate that sort of treatment.'

'Yeah. I think I was. What I gave them was very useful to them. But it didn't harm us, their knowing.' He paused. 'You've got to remember, these people were our allies. Churchill presented Stalin with the Sword of Stalingrad on behalf of the British nation. What I passed to them ought to have been given to them by us as a matter of routine. It maybe saved thousands of lives, but what did Whitehall care?' He shrugged. 'The Russians were used to dying. It was a national pastime.'

'And in Germany?'

'No problem. I was in Hamburg and Berlin. In both cities there were Russian liaison units. The British Army treated them like genuine allies. They respected them. They were all serving soldiers. There were pretty wild parties every night of the week. Good food, lots of booze, and lots of pretty girls. Of course, SIS and Whitehall didn't feel the same way about our gallant allies and it was barely a year before the Cold War set in on both sides.'

'Who was your contact?'

'There were three or four depending on the material concerned. They were all military officers so far as I could tell.' He smiled wryly. 'Maybe they were NKVD but I don't think so.' Carling stood up. 'Let's have a bite to eat.'

'Is there any reason why you haven't named any of your contacts?'

Carling shook his head slowly. 'No reason at all except that on the one hand I don't remember their names and on the other hand it's not likely that the names they used were real.'

After they had eaten Carling said that he was going to take a nap.

'Meantime, my friend, make yourself at home.'

Mathews drove to the nearby village of Lamberhurst and tried to phone Kennedy but there was no answer. Knowing as he did it that it was stupid, he dialled what had once been his home number and it was Pamela who answered.

'Hello.'

'Hi. I just wanted to know how Tony is.'

'You've got a bloody nerve. You know you're not supposed to contact me except to make arrangements for having Tony.'

'So is it OK for next Saturday?'

'Your solicitor wrote to Roger complaining that I was trying to stop you seeing Tony. Roger's advised me to withdraw our voluntary agreement and get it settled formally by the court. And until it's been heard there's no access.'

'Do we really need to make a dogfight out of me seeing my son?'

'It was your solicitor who set the ball rolling, not mine.'

'What about Tony's interests?'

'He's got to get used to new circumstances. Roger has

36

explained it all to him.' She paused. 'After all, Roger will soon be his father.'

'You really are a bitch.' And he hung up, trembling with anger at the thought of Roger Thomas working hard to alienate his son from him. For a moment he touched his forehead to the coolness of the glass panel of the phone box until an old lady knocked on the door of the kiosk, gesticulating that she wanted to use the phone. As he held the door open for her she looked at him. 'Are you all right, young man?'

Confused, he said, 'I'm fine, thank you. It's a bit hot in there.'

He walked to his car trying to keep back the tears in his eyes because it was the first time in many months that somebody had shown even the slightest interest in how he felt.

The three of them had dinner together but Julie had taken out the dishes and left the two men together, still sitting at the table, with a bottle of Marks and Spencer's '91 Margaux between them.

Carling looked across at Mathews and said, 'I think it's time you called me George, and it's Tim, isn't it?'

'Yes, sir.' Then he laughed. 'It'll take me time to get used to it.'

Carling shrugged. 'A lot of nonsense anyway.' He paused. 'What's your next question?'

'You said you were never interested in politics because of the politicians you saw at your father's house. Does that mean you don't ever vote?'

'I voted Labour in 1945 like everybody else in the forces. Time for a change and all that. I felt they had the right ideas.'

'What made you stop voting Labour?'

'Well, Labour did a good job – in my opinion – for about six years. But they became, for me, the proof that our kind of politics in ridiculous.'

Mathews smiled. 'I don't follow the reasoning.'

'They made election promises about what they'd do if they were elected. They were elected. And they did what they promised to do.' Carling laughed softly. 'And then they had to get on governing the country and it was no longer a plan. Just responding to events. A bandage here and a Band-Aid there.' He shrugged. 'So they did stupid things, the bigots and extremists muddied the waters, and that for me was the end of Labour. They were just men desperate for power like all the others.' He paused. 'I don't think I've ever met a politician I'd really trust. To me they're suspect right from the start. Why do they want to be in politics? Not to do the rest of us good but to have the power to control our lives. I suspect all men who have power over people's lives. Judges, lawyers, priests, prison-warders, police, bosses of any kind. People who can sack a man just to save money or because they don't like him. Power is the corruption, not money. Remember the old adage – "money is the root of all evil"? It's always misquoted – First Epistle of Paul to Timothy – it's "*love* of money is the root of all evil". And the same applies to power. It's the love, the lust for power that is evil.' Carling laughed. 'My God, I'd better shut up. I'm beginning to sound like Billy Graham. Forgive me, my friend, but when the subject is politicians I tend to let rip.'

For Mathews it had been very revealing, an oldish man with such intolerance in one area where otherwise his character was so easy-going.

'I found it interesting. What are your views on lords?'

Carling thought for a moment. 'For those like me who

inherit the title – we're just stuck with it. But we generally have an advantage. We're either rich or fools. Seldom both – they tend to be self-cancelling. They've got enough money not to grind an axe for reward and a good many have been trained from childhood to responsibility for others who work for them.

'You can see it in the House of Lords. When some party egoist is given a life peerage he begins to relax. You'll hear more good sense spoken in the Lords than in the Commons. Even the front benches avoid the open lies and deceit that go on in the Commons.'

'What would you have liked to be if you weren't born to be a lord?'

Carling leaned back in his chair. 'What an interesting question.' He closed his eyes for long moments. When he opened them, he said, 'It's impossible to answer. All the bits and pieces contradict one another.' He shrugged. 'And I have no skills, no qualifications. Or at least, the only qualifications that I have are what everybody has but few people use.'

'What does that mean?'

'Most people look without seeing, listen without hearing and have only enough love to love themselves. I think for some reason I'm not like that. But such talents as I have are not virtues but just how I was born.'

'So where are the contradictions you spoke of?'

'Contradictions?' Carling looked puzzled. Then, 'Ah yes, contradictions.' He smiled. 'I've often wished I was a Jew. A member of a community that never had a square deal from the world in general. I've got a need to fight for oppressed people.' He laughed. 'And I'd hope that being a Jew would have made me a great musician.' He paused. 'The contradiction is that I'd also

like to be an Italian.' He looked at Mathews. 'That's
surely contradiction enough?'

'Tell me. Why Italian?'

'I just like Italians. They're alive, they wear their hearts
on their sleeves, they love music and art and all things
artistic. Not just the upper classes but working classes
too.' He smiled. 'And they like old people and kids.' He
reached for the bottle. 'One last glass, Tim?'

'I've had enough, thanks. Thanks for making it easy to
talk to you.'

Carling smiled. 'We've got a long way to go, my friend.'

CHAPTER 6

Mathews was buttering his last piece of toast when Carling joined him for breakfast. There were untouched copies of *The Times* and the *Daily Mail* at the side of Carling's place.

'Which do you want?' Carling said. 'The *Mail* or *The Times*?'

'Neither thank you. I'm going to London for the day, is it OK if I come back tomorrow?'

'Of course. I never move from here if I can avoid it.'

'Is there anything I could get you in London?'

'Let me think.' He paused for a moment. 'They've just issued a new CD of Korngold's fiddle concerto. I'd be grateful if you could get me a copy. Do you know Korngold's music?'

'Didn't he write film music?'

'Well done. Yes. So the poor man is despised by all the cognoscenti. But in fact he was a fine musician.' Carling grinned. 'Could be me, my alter ego, despised because I make good money writing popular music and ostracised because I'm a Jew.'

Mathews said quietly, 'What kind of friends do you have?'

'Friends?' Carling was silent for a moment. 'Good friends – none. Pleasant, interesting contacts and acquaintances –

scores of them. All over Europe. But not friends. That's too much responsibility. Sometimes you let friends down.'

'Have you ever let a friend down?'

It seemed a long time before Carling answered. Then he said quietly, 'I can think of two occasions when I let a friend down. I still regret it.'

'Who were they? What happened?'

Carling shook his head. 'I wouldn't want to talk about it.'

As he reached for the marmalade Carling said, 'You know music makes strange bedfellows. Did you know that when he was a young man Nye Bevan was madly in love with a young woman cellist?'

'No. I didn't know that. Seems out of character. Both the loving and the cello.'

'They're very popular, lady cellists. They all seem so very beautiful.' Then as a seeming afterthought Carling said, 'And it *is* a lovely instrument. Beautiful to listen to and lovely to look at.' He smiled at Mathews. 'We do go on, us old fogeys.'

Mathews laughed. 'You'll never be an old fogey, that's for sure.'

For a moment Mathews thought that Carling looked surprised, or sad. He wasn't sure which.

Mathews stopped in Sevenoaks and made three phone calls, all to London numbers.

His meeting with Kennedy was relaxed and Kennedy smiled from time to time as Mathews reported on his stay with Carling.

When he finished, Kennedy said, 'You seem to have laid out the foundations of a relationship. What did you think of him?'

Mathews shrugged. 'Hard to describe. Definitely left wing although he claims he doesn't know what left wing means. Seems too easy-going to be playing games with the Russians.'

'He's admitted to you that he passed restricted information to a Soviet contact during the war?'

'But the onus in court would be on us to prove it. Anyway, most people today would probably approve of what he did.' He paused. 'You said at my briefing that he was suspected of other things. What were they?'

For a few moments Kennedy seemed absorbed in checking the date and time on his digital desk clock, and then he said, 'Remember way back when the media were always going on about the so-called Fourth Man? And in the end poor old Blunt was left with no chair to sit on when the music stopped?'

'I remember it vaguely.'

'The media decided that whoever the Fourth Man was he had tipped off Burgess that we were closing in on him. In fact we knew exactly who had tipped off Burgess and it certainly wasn't Blunt. Nor was it anyone in SIS. It was a politician's stupidity. Anyway it was obvious that Blunt was going to carry the can as the Fourth Man so we did a deal with him. Trading what he had been up to in exchange for immunity. A bit like you're doing with friend Carling. Except that in Blunt's case there was virtually nothing to tell us that was significant. But we knew all along that Burgess, Philby and Maclean weren't the only ones working for the Soviets. We reckoned there were at least three others. Blunt was one of them. There was an academic of sorts and there was Carling.

'We had enough to take both Burgess and Maclean to court and know we would win and they'd get long sentences. But they had done a bolt to Moscow and were no longer in our jurisdiction, so they were out. The DPP and the Attorney-General himself said that despite all the stuff we had on Philby it wouldn't stick in the High Court. Philby wasn't sure how much we'd got on him so he didn't resist when we quietly moved him out. After SIS he worked as a journalist in the Middle East for *The Economist* and one or two newspapers. There were hard feelings in high quarters in SIS about Philby, and Nick Elliott was sent out to pressure Kim in Beirut to get a confession that would stand up in court. Philby admitted everything but lit out for Moscow a few days later.' He paused. 'There are still people in SIS or who have retired who think we should be looking much harder at Carling.'

'Are you one of those people?'

Kennedy hesitated and then said, 'I guess I'd like to know what *did* happen way back. And, if I'm truthful I'd like to know if friend Carling carried on after the Philby gang had been dealt with. But I don't go all the way with some of them when they talk of prosecution.' He smiled. 'That's why I was glad to get approval for my suggestion that you carry out this little exercise to test the water before anybody starts splashing around.' He looked at his watch. 'I've got to go, Tim. Next year's departmental budgets.'

Mathews' meeting with Latham, his solicitor, was in Hampstead and as he drove there he went over in his mind his talk with Kennedy. Kennedy had seemed satisfied with the rather disjointed and inconclusive report on his time with Carling. It still sounded a bit of a wild-goose chase, but if that's what they wanted, so be it. As he parked his car and walked up to the High Street, he wondered what Latham would have to say. It always seemed to him as if

Latham had more sympathy with the other side. It had been an easy ride so far. No great conflict over the divorce and the financial settlement. But now she was playing games about access he needed somebody who was totally on his side.

When Mathews was settled in the visitor's chair, Latham said, 'I'm sorry you're having problems about access to the child. How often has it happened?'

'Three times so far.'

'In what period?'

'Ten weeks.'

'Any idea why she's playing up?'

'I assume she gets a kick out of being bloody-minded.'

'What reasons has she given?'

'A Cub camp, a cold, and some other engagement.'

'Any offer of an alternative access?'

'No. She just hangs up on me when I protest.'

'I've had a letter from her chap suggesting that it should be settled by the court and meantime that there should be no access. What do you feel about that?'

'How long before it could be heard?'

'Ten to twelve weeks at the moment.'

'What alternatives do I have?'

'I had an unofficial word with the other party's solicitor but there was no joy there. He said his client had given him firm instructions to go back to the court. Not very co-operative, I'm afraid.'

'Why should he be co-operative?' Mathews said angrily. 'He gets his costs out of my pocket and screws her into the bargain. And they both get a kick out of harassing me.'

'Don't make comments like that elsewhere, Mr Mathews, or we shall be facing a writ for slander and we couldn't prove a thing.'

'I've checked a dozen times in the last three months. His car was in the drive all night.'

'You mean you checked on them yourself?'

'Yes.'

'Mr Mathews, I must advise you very earnestly not to pursue this – this matter. We should be on very thin ice. Very thin ice indeed.' He paused. 'Remember, in the eyes of the court she is entitled to have a relationship with anyone she chooses. She's a free woman now.'

'She told me that she will be marrying him shortly and to remember that the bastard will then be Tony's father.'

'You mean she intends marrying Roger Thomas?'

'So she says.'

Latham took a deep breath. 'It's best I make no comment on that but she's talking nonsense about your son. You're his father and always will be. Even if she does marry him, which I very much doubt, they couldn't have Thomas adopt him without your agreement.'

'Which they'd never get.'

'Quite. I'd still like to suggest a policy of wait and see – for at least a few weeks. There's little else we can do.' He stood up, holding out his hand. 'Sorry to seem so negative but I want the court to see that we have kept to the rules. I'll write a pressing note to Thomas, just for the record.'

'Do you know him personally?'

'Yes, I do. Off the record I can assure you he won't be marrying your ex-wife. That's for sure.'

'Is this because of the Law Society enquiry?'

Latham turned his head quickly to look at Mathews. 'How on earth do you know about that?'

'I checked up on him.'

'You or a private investigator?'

'Me.'

'Well, for Chrissake don't tell me. I don't want to know.'
He shrugged. 'I'll send you a copy of my letter to Thomas.'

The estate agent had described the flat as being in Chelsea but in fact it was well into Pimlico. Nevertheless, it was pleasant, with a distant view of the Thames. It had two rooms with kitchen and bathroom, newly decorated and with fitted carpets supplied by the landlord.

There were half a dozen letters in the box. The one Mathews opened first was his bank statement and for once he had more in his account than he expected. There was an offer for double-glazing, two insurance offers and a brochure from BUPA. The last letter was from his parents. Nothing startling. He smiled to himself as it went through his mind that letters from his mother were what would be classed as nil reports in Century House.

When the phone rang he picked it up as he went on reading his parents' letter.

'Hello.'

'Hi, Tim, Joanna. Do you still want to see that stuff from our morgue?'

'Yes, please. Are you OK?'

'Yeah. If you could come round now you could have an hour with it.'

'Where?'

'*Daily Mail*, you eejit. Northcliffe House. Yes or no?'

'Yes, please. I'll get a taxi. Will you be there?'

'Of course. And you'll owe me a decent dinner. See you.' And she hung up.

He had only known Joanna for about three months. She was twenty-five, exceptionally pretty and worked as a researcher for the gossip and showbusiness sections of the *Daily Mail*. Her aim was a column of her own, which almost certainly meant a move to another paper. She was modest but slightly bossy, which he put down as part of her job specification. They had met at the wedding of mutual friends and she had slept with him that first night. She made it seem rather like being awarded the *Good Housekeeping* seal of approval.

She was waiting for him in the entrance hall of the newspaper offices, giving him a peck on the cheek as she took him to stairs leading down to the basement.

'I've had a quick look through the file in the morgue. Why are you interested in this old boy? He looks quite intriguing. A milord who seems to be permanently agin all kinds of authority is a rare bird.'

'I just need a bit of background, honey. And I've booked us a table at Jardin des Gourmets for eight. By the way – am I allowed to make notes from the cuttings?'

'Of course. It's all run-of-the-mill stuff.' She opened a door. 'Here we are. The files are on the table with the reading lamp. I'll be back in an hour. If anyone asks you what you're doing, you're working on some research for me. OK?'

'That's fine.'

'Any problem, my extension number's in the internal directory by the phone.'

The Carling records were housed in three old-fashioned box-files labelled with the periods they covered. He started going through the latest material.

As Mathews riffled through the cuttings it was obvious that until recently Carling had been an avid writer of letters to editors, mainly to *The Times* and the *Guardian*. They were usually provocative and against the grain, defending some writer or painter or performer who had been the victim of some excoriating review. What was interesting was that Carling's letter always evoked a torrent of letters in support of his views.

One of his recent letter campaigns had been his suggestion that what the country needed was another Festival of Britain to remind the world and the country of all the successes in science and the arts that the nation had achieved in the last three decades. The correspondence had gone on for weeks and *The Times* had eventually not only supported the idea but had subtly taken it over as if it had been their original thought.

The harassment by the media of politicians and public figures for their alleged sexual or financial indiscretions had been another of Carling's targets. We are all sinners, was his theme, but most of us don't get found out. There was an unusually sharp letter about the behaviour of Lord Wigg and the part he had played in the Profumo affair. It was clear that George Carling was always on the side of the losers and victims of media or political hypocrisy. Despite this he seemed to be admired by the very people he criticised.

There were brief pieces about two different betrothals over the years. One to a distant relation when he was in his early twenties, and the other in his mid-forties to a Polish film actress. From the grainy pictures the only thing they appeared to have in common was that they were both exceptionally beautiful. From the typed chronology on the cover of the files it was clear that there had been no marriage in either case.

There were dozens of photographs with brief captions of Carling at first nights of plays and films, standing in line to be spoken to by the Queen or some other member of the royal family. Almost half of the photographs were of Carling at similar functions in other European capitals,

Warsaw, Prague, Budapest, Vienna and Berlin, where his status seemed to be as an unofficial representative of the Arts Council or as a guest of the government concerned.

There were a few interviews for women's magazines by women journalists who mainly asked questions about what it was like to be an earl. The tone was always friendly and only one interviewer had asked him about his time in intelligence. He had, it seemed, laughingly dismissed it as the mistaken patriotism of a rather naïf young man. It was obvious that the ladies had taken to His Lordship. One of them had suggested that he looked rather like Peter Finch in the Oscar Wilde film.

There was nothing worth copying and when his hour was up and Joanna came for him, the box-files were already closed and put to one side.

They had a long, pleasant meal at Jardin des Gourmets and then took a taxi back to her flat in Chelsea.

As she poured them drinks and handed him a glass, she said, 'Why are you interested in Lord Carling?'

He shrugged. 'Just a routine check-up. Why do you ask?'

'There has been talk about one of the papers doing some sort of exposé on SIS and Carling's name was mentioned.'

'Which paper was it?'

'I'm not sure but I think it's the *Sun*. It came up at our own editorial meeting last week. They didn't give the name of the paper or the source of the rumour. But I think it was being taken seriously.'

He smiled. 'Let's go to bed.'

As they sat at the table after dinner, Carling said, 'What are you reading at the moment?'

Julie smiled. 'You're just checking on whether I'm reading that paperback you gave me.'

'Which one's that?'

'*Aristotle on Ethics.*'

'Ah yes. What d'you make of it?'

'A load of rubbish for people who've got nothing better to do than sit around nit-picking about what is courage or happiness.'

'You don't feel it helps to analyse the various types of courage or happiness?'

'No way. We all know what courage is and we all know what happiness is. It's like when you take me to posh restaurants and the waiter asks me whether I want it on or off the bone. What does it matter? Either way it's just a piece of fish.'

He smiled. 'I like that, my dear. Courage – on or off the bone.' He paused. 'Speaking of virtues, what do you think of our young man?'

She shrugged. 'He doesn't trust anyone. And I don't trust him either.'

'Give me an example.'

'I can't. I just know it. Feminine intuition.'

'He's very bright.'

'But not much heart.' She paused and looked at him. 'Don't trust him, Georgie. I don't know what you and he are up to but he's not as innocent as he looks.'

He smiled and reached over, covering her hand with his as he said, 'Don't worry, my dear. We'll make him human between us.' He paused. 'By the way. Do you think he's handsome?'

She nodded. 'Yeah. Very. That's his only virtue in my book. He's very attractive especially as he doesn't seem to realise it.'

He laughed. 'There's philosophy for you. Who needs Aristotle?'

CHAPTER 7

They were sitting on the trunk of a tree that had come down in the long-forgotten hurricane. It was on the edge of the woodland and warm from the spring sunshine.

'How did you get transferred from Field Security in Germany to SIS?' Mathews asked.

'Well, when the war was over there were lots of officers who wanted to get back to civilian life as soon as possible before all the jobs had been taken,' said Carling. 'I was interviewed by a couple of chaps, one who knew me well, and we had three or four meetings and then they offered me a job in SIS.'

'Doing what?'

'They didn't specify my duties but I was put on the German desk with special responsibility for the Russian Zone that eventually became East Germany. Then for several years I was a kind of interface, as they called it, between the German section both West and East, and the Soviet desk.'

'You must have had contact with Philby at that stage?'

'I already knew Philby. We had met when we were visiting lecturers at Beaulieu for SOE.'

'What did you lecture on?'

'The war was still on then, of course. Philby dealt with the structure of the Nazi Party and its organisation, and

I talked on the German intelligence services. The Abwehr, the Gestapo, the SD and Gehlen's organisation, Foreign Armies East.'

'How did you get on with Philby?'

'I liked him. He was sociable and he played the piano very well – Jerome Kern, Irving Berlin, Gershwin – that sort of thing. But I didn't spend much time with him. I wasn't, as they say, "into" drinking and the party games.' Carling shrugged. 'Most people liked him. He was very charming. Except to his women, of course. He treated them very shabbily. Not, perhaps, a man to admire.'

'How often did you come into contact with him?'

'Three or four times for SOE and fairly regular brief contacts at meetings at Broadway. Much later I saw him a couple of times in Washington when he was at our embassy and I was visiting Langley.'

'Were you surprised when he turned out to be a traitor?'

'Nobody was ever able to substantiate that he was a traitor. Only he knows what he did or didn't do.'

'Him and Nick Elliott, of course.'

'All that Nick ever got was what Kim Philby told him. Who knows what the actual truth was. Senior SIS men, including at least two directors-general, have been accused of treason by the media.' He smiled. 'But only after they were dead.'

'If that suggestion was made in the press about you, what would you do? Would you sue them?'

Carling said quietly, 'Let's wait and see, shall we?' They walked over to the ornamental pond and stood looking at the fish. 'I used to have plenty of koi but the herons from Bewl Water take them. Maybe I should just keep to the goldfish and frogs.'

Mathews hesitated and then said, 'Do you mind me continuously asking questions?'

It was a moment before Carling replied. 'I think you've been very diplomatic, dear boy. It could easily have slipped into an interrogation rather than a stroll down memory lane.' He laughed. 'It's a bit like our old friend Proust and *A la recherche du temps perdu*. No. You carry on asking. The only thing you have to bear in mind is that that was then and this is now. It was a long time ago. And the world was very different then.'

'You said you didn't like politics because of the politicians you met at your father's house. Was that the only reason?'

'If I said I didn't like politics that was a mistake. It's politicians I don't like. Not just ours but all politicians. It angers me that a quite small group of power-hungry men can decide the fate of millions of young men.' He paused and then said, 'OK. Let them decide on war but on one condition – that the next day they will all be shot or hanged.' He laughed softly. 'We old boys can be terribly bloodthirsty under our Marks and Spencer's woolly sweaters.'

After sandwiches for lunch, Carling went up to his study bedroom and pulled the leather chair to the windows that ran from ceiling height to floor level.

Mathews had shown him the picture of him with Oleg in Shepherd Market. As always with surveillance pictures it was taken on 35mm fast film and the print was hopelessly grainy. His own face was only just identifiable. Mathews had said that they thought the shot was taken somewhere near Broadcasting House. He had said that he didn't recognise the other man in the picture. Poor Oleg. He was a born loser and his compatriots had used him ruthlessly, swearing that they valued his contribution to the war effort. But all they had wanted was to establish a working relationship so that they could insert Panov. Panov was more sophisticated. He had worked for them in Paris before the war and for a time in Australia. He understood how to use the idealism of foreign sympathisers. Never wanting more than was reasonable, and trading the gossip of NKVD intelligence headquarters in return. Not averse to a sly joke about Stalin or some lesser Kremlin figure. Never an offer of money or valuables but just building the feeling of being comrades in a cause that was going to liberate the poor and oppressed, the workers who created the world's wealth. Carling wondered how far up the ladder of Soviet life you had to go to find the men who actually knew that it was all no more than a dream.

The problem was that it was a highly desirable dream. It's not easy to abandon a dream. The indications that it was all a myth could perhaps be mistaken. Analyse it how you will, the men who created that dream had had good intentions. There were simpler ways just to grab power. Why such an elaborate scenario? It was no more than a variation of those loving words on the Statue of Liberty – 'Give me your tired, your poor, Your huddled masses yearning to breathe free . . .' Maybe the Americans hadn't lived up to those generous sentiments, but way back they must have meant them and that was a similar dream. These days, with the benefit of hindsight, people said it had all been nothing but a dream. But they were wrong. Underneath it all was that longing for a better life for everyone. Why should that be just a dream? Why let it all go? Perestroika and glasnost mustn't wipe out the dream.

The young man Mathews was sharp and observant, but Carling wondered what sort of life he led. Mathews seemed too controlled, lacking in enthusiasm for being alive. A man without a goal to reach for. Earthly but not worldly. Hard-working but not creative. He'd have to work on him. How could he explain to a man like that what had motivated people like Philby? In the end, of course, Philby had gone too far and arrogance had taken over.

Poor Philby had always dreaded the thought of ending up in Moscow. He spoke no Russian and he knew all too well that once you were no longer in a position to supply them with intelligence you would be of no use to them. They'd treat you well. A decent flat and even, perhaps, a dacha at Peredelkino. A life status equivalent to that of a general, but stuck with Burgess and Maclean and a few KGB 'friends' involved in your interminable debriefing. For a defecting double agent could even be a triple agent. And Kim was, in any case, a dyed-in-the-wool Brit. Even in Washington he had to know the latest Test match score. He had avoided Moscow for so long and taken such risks in so doing that Moscow had wondered about his commitment. The SIS conclusion was that a drunken evening and his confession to Nick Elliott had left him no choice. He didn't even return to the dinner party he had left. The Order of Lenin would be no consolation for Kim Philby. And with the boredom and monotony of his useless life he ended up ruining the lives of a few more women. Somebody had once described Kim Philby as a romantic shit. But Kim was never really romantic. Charming yes, but romantic no.

Carling sighed as he wondered how long the business with Mathews would have to go on. Kennedy obviously wanted to make sure that he was going to get his pound of flesh before he did a deal, so the longer he himself could drag it out the better. And the longer he could keep them in the past the safer he would be. He could choose his own cut-off point. Give them enough to see it as a confession for past deeds and do a deal and Kennedy would be satisfied. He smiled to himself at the thought of using them instead of them using him.

CHAPTER 8

'Julie and I are going over to the orphanage. Would you like to come with us? It's all very informal.' Carling smiled. 'It gets them a couple of inches in the local rag and that helps donations.'

'Are you sure I won't be in the way?' asked Mathews.

'Of course not. It's just a flying visit.'

As they drove down the Eastbourne road, Carling related how the orphanage had been given the big house in an old lady's will and £500,000 for its upkeep as an orphanage for girls. The money had been wisely invested and they now had a reliable regular income. He said that the director of the orphanage was a very Christian woman and Julie had laughed and said, 'That's how he always describes people he doesn't like. She ought to be running a prison. She's a great believer in retribution.'

Carling smiled. 'I think it would be fair to say that she runs a very tight ship. But she has her problems. Not every girl is like our Julie.'

As the car crunched to a standstill on the gravel drive, the massive oak doors of the house stood open and a young girl waved to them from the steps. As they approached she gave a little curtsey to His Lordship and said, 'Madam's compliments, m'lord, and she's waiting for you in her room.'

In her comfortable room, Madam, a grey-haired woman in her late fifties, welcomed them and invited them to sit. There were sponge cakes and glasses of milk on a low table placed strategically between them. Mathews had been introduced as a friend. Proceedings followed what was obviously a well-tried formula. She related and detailed new donations and details of girls who were receiving instruction in domestic and commercial skills and finally a few details of problem girls. Problems ranging from disobedience to defiance, from promiscuity to pregnancy.

There was, it seemed, one special problem. Her name was Gabriella, surname not yet established. Parents unknown both as to names and circumstances. Intelligent guess said that she was part West Indian and part Spanish or Italian. She had been in institutions since being left in a cardboard box on the steps of a police station in Liverpool. She had been passed from one foster parent to another. None of the relationships had been successful and now, aged sixteen, she had a six-month-old child. Girls with babies or children were not accepted at the orphanage and Madam was at her wit's end. The girl refused to go into the Council hostel. Madam described her as both feckless and irresponsible, and blamed the West Indian blood. She accepted that the girl loved the baby but she had to go where the authority decided was suitable. Would His Lordship persuade her to do as she was told. His Lordship said he would talk to the girl. The last item of news was that three of her girls now had full-time jobs locally and were soon to leave the orphanage for their own places. There were a dozen names on the Council list for three new girls to fill the vacancies at the orphanage. There was a touch of Miss Jean Brodie about Madam.

*   *   *

In the small room with its cot and single bed the young girl was sitting watching the sleeping baby. She stood up as Madam introduced them all before she left. Mathews was amazed. The young girl was so beautiful, with a mane of black hair, big dark eyes and a wonderful, dazzling smile.

Carling sat beside her on the edge of the bed. She talked animatedly with delicate movements of her hands as he chatted to her. The baby's name was Carlotta. No, that wasn't anything to do with the father's name. She spoke as if the father were of no importance.

When Carling said gently, 'You obviously very much wanted this baby, am I right?' she beamed.

'She's all I shall ever want.' And her hand went between the bars of the cot to touch the sleeping baby.

'Why is she so important to you?' Carling said quietly.

For a moment she looked at the baby and then she turned to look at Carling. 'All my life I've longed for somebody to love me and to have somebody to love myself. That's why.'

Mathews saw Julie looking at Carling's face. For a moment they were all silent and then Carling said, 'You know Julie, don't you? She used to be here. Now she looks after my home for me. She needs some help. There is a small flat over my garage that was meant for a chauffeur. You could have that and a small wage for helping Julie. Would you like that?'

There was a long silence and then she said softly, 'Do you really mean that?'

'Yes. If you want it.'

'When? When could I come?'

Carling looked at Julie, eyebrows raised in query. She laughed and shrugged as she nodded. And Carling said, 'I'll have a word with Madam, Gabriella. You and Julie collect up all your things and the baby's things. I'm sure Madam will let us borrow the cot until we get one of your own.'

She flung her arms around his neck, kissing him like small children kiss people who have just given them a highly desirable present. His Lordship seemed to enjoy it.

When they arrived back at Lake Cottage there was a large black limousine parked in the lane and as they turned into the drive there was a uniformed chauffeur.

'Good afternoon, milord. BBC.'

'BBC?' Carling said. 'I don't understand.'

'The arts discussion show.'

'But that's not until the thirtieth.'

'It's the thirtieth today, sir. But we've got plenty of time. No hurry at all.'

Carling stood transfixed and then turned to Mathews. 'My God, Tim, I'll have to go. Can't let them down. How about you come with me?'

Mathews grinned. 'I'd enjoy it.'

Carling turned to Julie. 'Can you make our new young lady at home, my dear?'

She smiled. 'Of course I can. But have a cuppa before you go.'

It was over an hour before they both left for the drive to London. Carling had insisted on checking out the rooms over the garage himself and had gone over with Julie the things to be brought from the house that Gabriella and her baby daughter might need that night.

There were four participants in the discussion programme and the producer, a woman in her early thirties, briefed them all after they had been to make-up.

'As you all know, the subject for this evening is government funding of the Arts.' She smiled a professional smile. 'Is it enough? Is it distributed effectively? And does the taxpayer get value for money? As much controversy as you want. No holds barred. Let the chips fall where they will.' She handed over to another woman who said, 'Cars have been laid on immediately after the show for those who have asked for them but there's a meal available for those who can stay.' She smiled. 'Best of luck. Enjoy the show.'

One member of the group was a senior spokesman for the Arts Council, a man who knew exactly how much money had gone where from government funding. His opposite number was a musician from an orchestra whose funding and future existence were in doubt. The third participant was a left-wing journalist whose carping criticism of the government was too obviously political. The programme had followed its expected course. The Arts Council man and the orchestral musician were at loggerheads from the start. And Carling intervened from time to time in support of either argument.

It was in the last five minutes of a diatribe by the journalist that Carling took him on.

'Do you seriously suggest that there should be no funding of the Arts in this country? The second biggest earner of tourist currency?'

The journalist sneered. 'I should have thought that I had already made that clear. The answer to your question is yes. Not a penny. The prices of theatre tickets, concert tickets, opera tickets make them an entertainment for the rich not the man in the street.'

'And what would you suggest the money be spent on instead?'

His face suffused with anger, the man said, 'Have you

seen the disgracefully poor figures of our aid to Third World countries?'

Carling smiled. 'My friend, I have a definition of aid to poor countries – aid is poor people in rich countries giving money to rich people in poor countries.'

The producer recognised the perfect ending that could hit tomorrow's headlines and signalled to the presenter to close the show.

In the hospitality room, the man sitting next to Mathews said, 'He's a real bastard, that man.'

Mathews shrugged. 'He's just a journalist grinding his axe.'

'I don't mean him,' the man said. 'I mean that stupid old fart Carling.'

They didn't stay for a meal. Carling said he was tired and wanted to get back home.

It was after midnight and there wasn't much traffic but they were held up by a garbage truck. Carling looked out of the window and suddenly said, 'My God.' He spoke to the driver. 'Is this Drayton Gardens?'

'Yes, milord. It is.'

Carling turned to Mathews. 'That house across the street there. That is where Kim Philby's mother's flat was. That's where he gave the press conference after Macmillan had cleared him in a statement to Parliament.'

Mathews followed Carling's gaze. It was just beginning to rain and the old Victorian house looked grim and forbidding with its bay windows and net curtains. It passed through his mind that Carling must have known it very well to have recognised it. Carling was still looking at the house as the garbage truck moved on to release them.

Mathews saw the tiredness on Carling's face as he sat

with his head back, the streetlights turning his big hand-some features into the face of a Roman statue. Then Carling said quietly, 'Do you think she'd have settled in all right?'

'I'm afraid I never knew her.'

Carling opened his eyes and turned his face to look at Mathews. 'Never knew who?'

'Philby's mother.'

'I meant the little girl – Gabriella. One more strange place after a life of being shunted from one ghastly place to another.' He sighed. 'And you have a baby so that you've got somebody who'll love you and who you can love.'

'She seemed pleased enough with her new home.'

'Poor soul,' Carling said. He gave a deep sigh as if for the whole of humanity. 'I'm going to take a nap, old chap.'

As he lay back in his seat with his eyes closed he could still see the house and he wondered why Kim had always lived in such gloomy places. The place that was now the orphanage had been the training school for radio operators in the war and it had been chosen because it was handy for Philby's house at Crowborough. Another grim building. He'd seen a photograph of it when *The Times* was doing one of its pieces on Philby, years ago. He could remember when Philby was so much at odds with Aileen, his wife, that he was living in a tent in the back garden of that wretched house.

CHAPTER 9

It was a bright sunny day and they had walked down to the ruins of an old abbey, Bayham Abbey, about a mile from the cottage. Julie had given them each a Mars bar and as Mathews unwrapped his he said, 'How did Philby get to know Burgess and Maclean?'

'Do you know about Litzi?'

'No.'

'I'll have to go back a bit to Cambridge. Philby was first spotted as having either extreme socialist or mild communist leanings by a don at Trinity named Maurice Dobb. He was a more or less open communist and on his last day at Trinity, Philby spoke to him about joining the Party. Dobb realised that he was too potentially useful to have as a mere member.

'Dobb gave him a lead to a group of communists in Paris who passed him on to Vienna. There was a lot of trouble there with Nazi sympathisers eager to integrate with Germany. Philby threw himself into the fight against them, acting as a courier and getting hunted communists over the border into Czechoslovakia. He was sent to stay with a chap named Israel Kohlman who was a committed Party worker. Kohlman had a young daughter in her early twenties. Her name was Alice. Alice Friedmann. Everybody called her Litzi. She'd already been married and divorced.

'In the end she was on the Nazis' wanted list and the simplest way to get her out of the country was for Philby to marry her. They were lovers already, but I think the marriage was equally a marriage of convenience.' Carling smiled. 'Hugh Gaitskell and his wife were the witnesses at the marriage in Vienna.

'They came back to England and Kim started a fund to raise money for Austrian workers who by then had been totally defeated by the Nazis. He gave a fund-raising talk at Trinity and that was when he first had contact with Guy Burgess who was on a fourth-year research scholarship.

'For a short time Philby was quite openly a communist. People just accepted it.'

'So why was he recruited for SIS with a background like that?'

Carling shook his head. 'With hindsight it's incredible. But it's the old, old story. With a war coming or actually started you had to recruit new people in a hurry. There's no litmus paper for loyalty, so you turn to the old-boy network. The old boys themselves are too old and they've all got other responsible positions. So you go for their sons. Philby's father was a well-respected man. An explorer, an Arabist and all the rest of it. His son, Kim, had been a first-class games player and a very successful scholar. What more do you want?' He paused. 'Nobody looked into his background at that stage. And by the time they started looking, he had created himself a right-wing background. Reporting from the Franco side for *The Times* when Franco was killing socialism and socialists in his own country in a dress rehearsal for World War Two.' Carling smiled and went on, 'Forgetting any suspicions of helping the Russians, I still wouldn't be recruited by SIS today. I'm not good enough by any standards.'

'What happened to Philby's wife?'

'Litzi? They divorced and she just faded out of sight. She got into films in East Germany. Was disappointed in their lack of progress towards communism. Moved to West Berlin and then to France where, as far as I know, she lives today.'

'Who actually recruited Philby for the Russians?'

Carling turned his head, looking at the distant hills for long moments before he looked at Mathews again.

'Let me just say that it wasn't a Russian who recruited him. He's still alive. Never been under any suspicion. He's near the end of his days. He deserves to die in peace.'

'Why?'

'Why what?'

'Why should he die in peace?'

'Dear boy, you're doing what they all do. You're looking down the wrong end of the telescope.'

'I don't understand.'

Carling reached down to pick a daisy, looking at it carefully and Mathews saw for the first time a look of anger on the old man's face. It went quite quickly as he turned back to Mathews.

'If you ignore Philby's contacts with the Russians, he had the kind of war record that would have got anyone else at least a medal, maybe a knighthood. His work to defeat the Germans was incredibly effective. Long hours, great energy and consistently good planning and execution of everything he handled. That was the core of his work during the war and it can't be just swept under the carpet.' He wagged his finger at Mathews. 'And remember what I said, the Russians were our allies. He wasn't helping our enemy.'

Mathews half smiled. 'I'm sorry. I've obviously annoyed you.'

'I wouldn't say that.' Then he smiled. 'Yes, you have annoyed me. But you weren't there at the time. You can be forgiven. But there are people who were there who still distort the facts for their own reasons.'

'What reasons?'

'Who knows, Tim? Who knows? If you ever discover them, please do tell me.' He paused. 'Jealousy, maybe. Just look at what they did to poor old Blunt. Offered him immunity in exchange for a full confession and then let it leak to the press. And then, the shameless muck-raking by the media – like sharks with a piece of meat. And what was he, for God's sake? Just a messenger boy. Nothing more. But away from his so-called treason he had risen to an important position by his own skills. Loses his title, his job and his character.' He shook his head like a dog coming out of water. 'Hypocrisy is our national vice these days. And . . .' he said bitterly, '. . . They'll do the same to me if they get half a chance.'

'That's not my impression.'

'Tell me.'

'I've nothing to tell. It's just instinct.'

'Tell me. Tell me more.'

'There really is nothing more. I just have the feeling that there's some game on the chessboard but you're only one of the pieces. An important one but not the king anyway.'

Carling looked thoughtful, pursing his lips, then saying, 'Let's walk back and have some lunch.'

Mathews felt that Carling had had enough for one day and he drove up to London after lunch. He stopped at Sevenoaks to telephone Century House and make an appointment to see Kennedy.

*　　*　　*

Mathews got the impression that Kennedy wasn't very interested in what he had to report. His comments were brief and he looked at his watch several times.

'The way he talks about Blunt sounds as if he's a bit wary about doing a deal.'

'I think he'd have thrown me out by now if he was totally against it.'

'Maybe. Anyway, keep plugging away. There's no hurry.'

'What about the tabloid?'

Kennedy smiled. 'We took the editor out for lunch and I think they'll put it on the back burner for a bit.' He paused. 'His proprietor's going to have some problems himself if they go ahead.'

'Any particular phase you'd like me to concentrate on?'

'Not really, Tim. You're on a fishing expedition and it means dipping in where you can.'

'You think it's worth it?'

Kennedy looked surprised. 'Don't get me wrong. It's worth it all right. Keep going, fella.'

Kennedy had just agreed to having his mail redirected to a Post Office Box at the main Tunbridge Wells post office but Mathews went back to the flat to check that all was OK and to collect his recent letters.

It smelled dusty and stale and he opened all the windows to let in some fresh air and then looked through his post.

There was the usual letter from his parents, a TV licence reminder, a quarterly service charge from the landlord and an official-looking foolscap envelope. He opened it carefully and took out the folded document and a letter from his solicitor. The letter was brief.

Dear Mr Mathews,

I enclose a statement by the petitioner regarding access to your son Anthony James. I shall need to take a statement from you in response. Please contact me to make an appointment. The hearing is not until September so there is plenty of time but we may also need to have statements from witnesses to support your statement.

Yours sincerely,

P. Latham.

The folded statement was eight pages long and on the outside it said,

IN THE MATTER OF THE CHILDREN ACT 1989

IN THE MATTER OF ANTHONY JAMES MATHEWS

BETWEEN

PAMELA JOAN BAILEY   PETITIONER

AND

TIMOTHY MATHEWS   RESPONDENT

This is the statement of the oral evidence of Pamela Joan Bailey to be at the hearing of the above mentioned matter.

He wondered why she had gone back to her maiden name but he read on slowly, growing more angry and frustrated by the minute. It had all the vitriol that legal terms would find acceptable and was obviously concocted by Roger Thomas.

Mathews had, apparently, taken little interest in his son during the marriage and had pressed her to have an abortion when she found she was pregnant. He had been violent and abusive to her in front of the child. On the occasions when he had had access he had not kept to the agreed time for his return and the child had been seriously disturbed after each visit to him.

Shaking with anger, Mathews phoned Latham who was busy, but sensing Mathews' pent-up anger he agreed to see him as soon as he could get up to Hampstead.

Latham leaned back in his swivel chair until it creaked as he listened to Mathews' diatribe about his ex-wife's statement.

When it eventually came to an end, he said, 'Let me give you some advice, Mr Mathews. These statements fly around before a case is heard. They annoy whoever's on the receiving end but that's about all they do. They don't impress the judge because he's heard it all before. Divorce cases and custody cases are about the only occasions when a person's character can be kicked around in the court as a means of stating a case.' He pointed at the copy of the offending statement on his desk. 'I've seen hundreds of statements like that in my time. They don't cut any ice with a court unless the plaintiff can produce witnesses or evidence to back up the statements.

'Now even if everything that she says was proved, the court operates on the basis that a father should have access to his children. He can have a criminal record as long as your arm, he can have been a violent husband but that alone doesn't make him a bad father. At the very worst your wife will have to agree to regular access. Bearing in mind the unproven facts she relies on, I think that you will be given reasonable access. One day, Saturday or Sunday, every two, or maybe three weeks.

'So I strongly recommend that you play it very cool, Mr

Mathews. If the other side do indulge in spite, it's not much fun for them if you don't rise to the bait. So do me a statement. There's no hurry. End of next week would be fine.'

'I'm sorry if I overreacted. I'll do as you say.'

Latham smiled. 'I'm on your side, Mr Mathews, even if it doesn't always look like it. I've been through it all hundreds of times. I've seen what happens if it's done the wrong way.'

Back at his flat, Mathews took his cellphone and spare battery and battery charger and then went down to his car. He wondered what Carling was doing. It was getting late. He looked at his watch, it was almost nine o'clock and the moon was already up.

Carling, Julie and Gabriella had eaten together in the big old-fashioned kitchen with its copper pots and pans, the thick oak beams and an Aga cooker. The baby was asleep in her carrycot near to the warmth of the cooker.

'So,' he said, 'tell me what you've been doing today, the two of you.'

Julie had a list beside her plate. 'Fixed Gabby a TV and one of your old radios but we'd like you to look at the aerial. We got some baby clothes from Oxfam in Tunbridge Wells and some clothes for Gabby.' She looked at him, smiling. 'That's about it. And Gabby's cleaned all the inside windows.'

He looked at Gabriella, smiling. 'Are you happy, young woman?'

She smiled shyly. 'I love it. I can't really believe it.' She paused for a moment. 'When will I have to leave?'

'Never, girl. This is your home now as much as it's Julie's and mine.'

There were tears on her cheeks and her voice quavered as she said, 'You don't know how happy I am.'

74

He turned to Julie. 'Let's try that lovely Pavlova I saw in the refrigerator. Let's celebrate. Then we'll clear up and I'll play you a bit of music.'

When the crockery and cutlery were in the dishwasher and the kitchen table smooth and bare again except for a small glass vase with four or five dandelions, they all went into the sitting room.

He put a CD on the Technics hi-fi without telling them what it was. It was Nigel Kennedy playing the Mendelssohn fiddle concerto. He played them only the first movement but they had sat entranced by the lush and loving music.

After that he sat at the piano and started to play, singing the words in German. And then he stopped and looked at them, smiling.

'I don't know if you know it but my dear, dear mother was Austrian. From Vienna. And she was a concert singer. But there was one of those lovely romantic old Viennese ballads she really loved. She used to sing it to me . . . It's about a Viennese word – *Servus* – which means "goodbye" but not really goodbye . . .' He played softly and sang the words

> *'Sag beim Abschied leise Servus*
> *Nicht Leb' wohl und nicht adieu*
> *Diese Worte tun nur Weh . . .'*

He sang a couple of verses then closed the piano lid carefully and stood up.

'I'll walk you home, Gabby, and carry Carlotta for you.'

He shone the torch ahead of them as they walked through the small orchard to the garage and he lit the way for her up the wooden staircase to the flat.

Inside he switched on the light and looked around to check that all was well. He put the carrycot on the sofa and took Gabby's hand. 'You won't ever have to leave, my dear, so just relax and enjoy it. Everybody loves you.'

As he walked back threading his way through the fruit trees there was a carpet of pink petals on the grass from the wind-blown blossom. He stopped, and switched off the torch, standing in the darkness, his eyes closed.

The little girl was so like her. The long mane of black hair, the big brown eyes, the neat, upturned nose and the full sensual mouth. She could have been their daughter. He wouldn't ever forget her. Not a day passed without thinking of her. 'Dear, lovely Rachel, I wish you were here.' Despite everything they could have the rest of his life for just a day with her again.

He realised that he was talking to himself aloud, and he switched on the torch and walked slowly back to the house. He shouldn't have played them the Mendelssohn. It was unbearable but it was so beautiful that he wanted them to hear it. Like splashing them with holy water. Despite his dark mood he smiled to himself at the thought. You don't splash nice Jewish girls with holy water.

CHAPTER 10

Mathews had hesitated between Robertson's Golden
Shred and Tiptree coarse-cut marmalade. He reverted
back to childhood and took a spoonful of Golden Shred
to spread on his toast. Carling was leaning across to see
the headlines on *The Times* front page.

He turned to Mathews. 'I liked it better in the old days
when they had classifieds all over the front page. All sorts
of stuff. Wonder cures for anything you could think of.
Offers to make you a millionaire for a fiver. Even the
sleaze was nicely done. Beautiful young girl needing help
with fees for art studies. Anything considered.' He smiled.
'We need a bit of sleaze to keep us lively. You don't have
to do anything. Just use your imagination.'

'Kennedy said that I ought to arrange some payment
they can make you for my keep while I'm here.'

Carling laughed. 'You know why he said that, don't
you?'

Mathews shook his head. 'No. Only the obvious reason
that it would be at least a gesture.'

Carling smiled. 'And if the chips are ever down he can't
be accused of abusing my hospitality.' He paused. 'You
look a bit down this morning. Something to do with that
laddie of yours?'

Mathews told him the latest chapter from the saga and

Carling listened intently. When Mathews finished his tale, Carling said, 'Tell me about the lady. What's she like? Pretend you've only just met her.'

Mathews laughed. 'I wish I had. She's very pretty. Blonde, blue eyes, nice shape. It was our temperaments and attitudes that weren't right. We married too young to realise the differences. She was real middle class. Like her parents. You go by the book. You do what the rules say. You read the *Daily Mail*, not the *Mirror*. You wear Barbours and pearls. You play tennis, or cricket if you're a chap. You like musicals but not opera.' He stopped and shrugged. 'That's about it.'

'And your side of the trouble?'

'Well, I wasn't definable. Part working class. Don't leave the lights on when you're not in the room. Taxis are for crises or coming home from a week at Rhyl. Repairing clothes not chucking them away. Home cooking not microwave. And on top of that a strange outlook on life. Money doesn't really matter nor does doing the right thing by other people's rules. Liking classical music. Liking Lloyd Webber songs but liking Puccini even more.'

'An interesting analysis. What's her name? And where does she live?'

'Her name's Pamela, she uses her maiden name apparently – Bailey. And she lives in what was our house in Esher in Surrey.'

'You miss seeing the little boy, don't you?'

'I do. It's crazy. When it rains I wonder if he's got his mac. But when I did see him I didn't use the time sensibly. You can't, you know. You can't ask how his mother is or it's prying. And you don't have a background. So it's the Science Museum, the National History Museum and the cinema. I take him from a real life with a constant background and give him a few hours of what seems like a temporary and phoney life. Mine.'

It was several minutes before Carling spoke. What he had just heard had changed his mind about Timothy Mathews.

'We must talk about this. See if we can't work out something better.' He smiled. 'What do you want to talk about today?'

'Shall we go in the garden. You like it there, don't you?'

'I do, my boy. How perceptive of you. The garden gives me a better perspective. Not just the view. But the feeling of things going on from year to year. Trees that were here before I was born and will be here long after I've gone. Wondering if the daisies on the lawn aren't really more beautiful than those fine Dutch tulips.'

He stood up and walked to the open French windows and Mathews followed him to the wooden bench by the pond. When they were both comfortable, Mathews said, 'In the last days of the war what was your actual job?'

Carling smiled. 'Some people saw me as just a messenger boy and that suited me quite well. Philby's section was based at St Albans and then it was moved to Ryder Street. The place was torn down after the war and it's now *The Economist* offices. I was a kind of liaison between Philby and our old headquarters in Broadway. There was a lot of office politics by then, with people trying to make sure that they were kept on when it was all over. Philby was determined to stake his claim for a senior position and there was a lot of information in HQ that would help Philby and the Russians. It was my official job to look for what might be of use to Philby's team.'

'And what were you doing for the Russians at that time?'

'You have to realise that this group – Philby, Burgess, Maclean, Blunt and, I guess, Cairncross too, were all committed to communism. Each knew that the others were committed but didn't know how much and in what way they served the Russians, if at all. I was the only person who knew what was going on. I was there to keep an eye on them all for the Russians and report on them to my control.'

'Why you and not one of the others?'

'Because they trusted me more than they trusted the others.' He smiled. 'And strangely enough because they knew I wasn't a committed communist.'

'You mean they didn't even trust Philby?

'They didn't trust any of them. Not completely.'

'Why did they trust you?'

Carling was silent for a few moments and then he said, quietly, 'It was something that happened. I can't tell you what it was. Maybe later, when I know you better, but not right now.'

'And Philby obviously came out top in the reshuffle after the war.'

'Yes. He certainly did. Underneath all that charm was a born conspirator and it worked in offices just as well as in his work. But what actually made certain he'd be kept on was a genuine piece of intelligence evaluation on Philby's part. He bothered just that bit extra and it paid off.' He paused. 'I don't want to bore you with the details.'

'I'd like to hear them. They sound interesting.'

Carling sighed. 'On your head be it. I'll make it as brief as I can.' He closed his eyes for a moment before he started speaking. 'There was a lot of pressure on Philby from the Soviet side to make sure that he consolidated his position in SIS.'

'How do you know that?'

'It was I who passed their comments to him.' Carling shook his head impatiently. 'Anyway. A German Foreign Office Ministry official named Kolbe, walked into the British Legation in Berne, in Switzerland. Said he was an anti-Nazi and offered to provide copies of secret documents. He even brought some samples. Our chap was so stupid that he didn't even read them, so the German went to the Americans, Allen Dulles, OSS. He proved to be a real find for them. The Americans said he was the best agent they'd ever had.

'OSS routinely passed copies of the documents to SIS, but Dansey was sure they were a plant and passed them to Cowgill and I mentioned their existence to Kim. He asked the cypher people to check the documents against the Ultra intercepts of German Foreign Office messages and they matched. They were genuine. The cypher people, the army, the navy and the RAF were desperate for all they could get. Kim passed it all to the Foreign Office, by-passing his boss, Cowgill, who, when he found out, was furious. So when it came to who was going to head up Section Nine it lay between Cowgill and his assistant, Philby. Well, Kim got the job and Cowgill, who was an avid anti-communist, resigned in a huff. It was incredible. Philby was safe, he'd got to be head of the section that covered all anti-Soviet operations and he'd got rid of a potential trouble-maker.'

'The Russians must have been very grateful for your part in it.'

Carling smiled. 'You don't understand how Russians think.'

'What's that mean?'

'The KGB, or the NKVD as it was then, like treason but they don't like traitors. You must have found this,

Tim. All espionage organisations are the same. They use traitors but they neither admire them nor trust them.'

'Did they see you as a traitor?'

Carling shrugged. 'It's hard to say. I was different from the others and that was always a problem for the Russians.'

'In what way were you different in their eyes?'

'Well, the others had all been members of the Party. They were traitors by conviction. But I'd never been a communist and was never interested in communism. And on top of that my father was an earl.' He smiled. 'I think they were rather impressed by the earl bit.'

'Was it a calculated decision never to join the Party, to give you better cover?'

'No. I told you earlier that communism never appealed to me. I helped the Soviets in the first place because they were fighting our war and I slowly got to feel that their attitudes to people were better than ours.'

'In what way?'

'The capitalist world works on the basis that we must all look out for ourselves. Get rich so that the world can't get you. The Russians never lived up to their constitution of brotherhood but at least it was what they set out to do.'

'Did you really prefer a dictatorship to democracy?'

'Now you're talking politics again. For me, all political systems are useless.' He paused. 'How can you have democracy? Why should what the majority want always be right? There are countless thousands of people in this country who can neither read nor write a sentence and who never give a moment's thought to politics or ethics but they still have a vote and influence the way you and I live.'

Mathews smiled. 'You're better at arguing a case than I am.'

'You're making my point, my friend. A man may win

an argument or a debate but that doesn't necessarily make him right. Maybe he's just a better debater.'

'When did you stop your contact with the KGB?'

Carling laughed. 'Why not ask me – when did I stop beating my wife?' He paused, still smiling. 'Let's say I'm pleading the Fifth, and maybe the Fourth too.' Carling stood up. 'Let's go and find Julie and some drinks.'

They all had lunch on the patio at the back of the house, with Julie and Gabriella, and the baby asleep in her carrycot in the shadow under the circular table. Joe, the gardener, was eating a cheese sandwich as he sat in the sun with his backside ruining a spread of aubretia on the rock garden.

'How's the vine this year, Joe?'

'Gonna be a record year, milord. I've done a bit of thinning out.'

'Any problems?'

'Yeah. Two. Those damned herons have taken the last of our koi. I think you ought to have one of them plastic herons to keep 'em away.'

'I talked to Sir John about that. He says they don't work after a couple of weeks. Says we need wire all round the edge of the pond. But I'd rather have no fish than that. You said two problems, what's the other?'

'That there aerial on top of your radio shack as you calls it. The pole's getting covered with lichen on the weather side. I don't know if it makes any difference. I can have a go at cleaning it if you wants.'

'No. It's not a problem, Joe. It's only the bits at the top of the pole that matter. And they're aluminium.'

'I'll be off then, milord.' Joe pointed at Gabriella. 'That one's been helpin' me with the weeding. Cleared out all the forget-me-nots. They was beginning to get mildew.'

Carling looked at the girl, smiling as he said, 'Well done, Gabby. You've made a conquest there.'

As Joe hobbled away, Julie said, 'At least he didn't call you Your Worship.'

Carling laughed. 'He used to call the judges at the County Court Your Grace.' He turned to Mathews. 'Let me show you my shack.'

The radio shack was about fifty yards beyond the garage and Gabby's new home.

'At one time it was a pigsty and then it was a storage place for apples. We give the apples away these days and I had it tidied up so that I could use it.' He smiled. 'Julie calls it my playroom. I suppose it is in a way.'

There were heavy locks on the door and it was dark inside. There were no windows but when Carling switched on the lights the interior was bright and spotlessly clean. Walls and ceiling were painted white and the floor was terracotta tiles.

There was a bench along the facing wall with the usual pieces of equipment that ham radio people go in for. Two ICOM transceivers, microphones, extension speakers. Shelves with rows of audiotapes and a pegboard with carefully laid out cable connections with different plugs and each properly labelled.

Carling pointed at the right-hand end of the bench. 'That's what they call an M-7000. A communications terminal. I can plug it into a short-wave radio and it takes Morse or other codes and converts them into normal alphabet characters. Covers ship-to-shore – aircraft – press agencies, embassies, all sorts of things.'

'How often do you come here?'

'Most days I have a play around. All amateurs have networks. Radio fanatics arguing about equipment and antennae, the latest discovery of some amateur in Thailand or the Yukon. There are magazines about the hobby.'

'What's the attraction?'

Carling grimaced. 'For some it's the technicalities, the chaps who build their own equipment . . .' he laughed '. . . they believe in valves, not transistors and chips. For some, I suppose it's the kick you get out of listening to something that's nothing to do with you.' He shrugged. 'For me I know nothing about the technicalities. I just buy the equipment and have fun with it.' He paused. 'Did you ever do a radio course?'

'We had a couple of days in the course on radio and communication generally but nothing technical.'

Carling smiled. 'I can remember doing my course. The Morse training school was on the top floor of Dickens & Jones, the department store. Gave perfect cover in wartime for us walking in and out. We each had our own instructor. Mine was an ATS girl. First class. She went to get me a cup of tea one day and I had a quick look in my "P" file. On the radio form it said, "Describe characteristics of operator when sending Morse under stress," and she'd written: "This officer always transmits as if he's under stress." ' He laughed. 'I never mastered Morse, I'm afraid.'

'Did you ever need to use Morse?'

'No.' He laughed. 'The main attraction to Morse was that you got extra pay if you passed the tests. But it was considered rather infra dig. Morse was for trades-men rather than us brainy types.'

Mathews pointed out an aerosol can marked 'Blower'. 'What's that for?'

'It's air under pressure. Photographers use it a lot to keep dust off negatives. I use it to keep the radios clean. All those knobs and switches seem to attract the dust and dust can ruin electronics in no time.' He smiled. 'I've got a similar aerosol in my bathroom and I use it to clean the head of my electric shaver.'

As Mathews made his way downstairs for the evening meal he realised that it was Carling who had been questioning him as they sat out on the patio in the afternoon sun. Asking him about his life with Pamela and about their son. He seemed to listen carefully but he made no comment and offered no advice. Which was at least a change.

Carling and Mathews took their coffees out to sit in the last of the sun on the patio and it was Carling who got them back to what it was really all about.

'You know, one thing always puzzles me. You and all the others. Even those who were around in the old days always seem to take for granted that Philby was the one who mattered to the Russians.'

'Who *was* the one who mattered if it wasn't Philby?'

'Have you ever heard anyone mention the codename "Orphan"?'

'No. Who was Orphan?'

'He was the one who mattered. Orphan was Maclean.'

Mathews was genuinely surprised. 'Why Maclean?'

'Well, he was the first of the Cambridge crowd that they recruited. Apart from that he had several virtues so far as the Russians were concerned. First of all he hated America and Americans, and secondly he moved and worked in much more delicate areas than Kim Philby. Philby on his own was useful inside SIS. He could abort actions against KGB agents and he could inform the Russians on the internal workings of SIS, including any agents SIS managed to run inside the Soviet structure.

'But the espionage that really matters is only one level.

It's what governments do or are thinking of doing that really matters. Maclean was a top Foreign Office man. He saw all the papers crossing an ambassador's desk wherever he might be. When Maclean was in Washington, Stalin himself read everything from Maclean.'

'What about his drunkenness and his crazy behaviour?'

Carling smiled. 'No Russian has ever thought ill of a man who drinks too much. They do themselves. From the Kremlin itself down to the beggars in the backstreets. It's a national pastime. They don't see it as a vice. And the behaviour . . .' Carling shrugged. 'Inside the Kremlin walls their behaviour was just as outrageous. And in any case they saw that our people both tolerated Maclean's behaviour and covered up for him.'

'Why *did* our people tolerate him? All those drunken and violent exhibitions in public and all that stuff?'

'The old-boy network, my friend. Good backgrounds. Officer fathers, public schools, Cambridge and so on. You have to remember that when they were starting in life, they were all very bright. Good at sports, excellent scholars and lots of charm. Charm counted for a lot in those days, no matter how spurious it might be. Kim Philby never drank when he was a young man. Lived very abstemiously. They made their way because they all had genuine talent.

'Philby didn't get to be a Section Head in SIS by anything other than talent. Nobody pulled any strings for him. Maclean didn't get to be First Secretary at our embassy in Washington without being a very clever chap. Even poor Burgess. He won the Roseberry and Gladstone history prizes at Eton and he won his scholarship in history to Trinity. But they were all human beings. They just happened to have flaws in their characters.'

'What were the flaws?'

'In the case of Burgess and Maclean they had the burdens of being alcoholics and homosexuals.' He paused. 'But Philby was different. His flaw was a lust for power and an incredible arrogance. He was not just efficient, he was ruthless. Ready to sacrifice other people's lives if it suited his plans. And of course they were all flawed by their passion for a political system that was nothing like they thought it was.' He shrugged. 'But plenty of so-called intellectuals fell for the same myth. We even had a "red" Dean of Canterbury, a man who openly avowed his communism.'

'But you seem to have rather liked them.'

'What makes you think that?'

'The way you speak about them. You try to emphasise their good points.'

Carling sighed, the deep sigh of contained exasperation. 'My dear Tim, what you've heard about these people is a one-sided view. If it had been like it's retold now, SIS would have had these men in court.' He paused. 'Just imagine what it would have looked like if it did get into court. Prosecuting men for treason whose crime was to pass on information to our then allies. Information that could maybe save tens of thousands of lives. The media would have a field day and the public would be on the side of the accused. Put it back down all those years when it was happening and the pro-Soviet feelings would have been overwhelming. There was no Cold War then.' He paused. 'They broke the rules, they were disreputable in their private lives but they took risks in what they thought was a righteous cause. Only one of them did us harm.'

'Was that Philby?'

'Yes. Read up the records on the Albanian operation. At least fifty men walked into a trap that Philby and the Soviets had contrived. They were all executed on the beaches where they landed. I have no respect for Philby, he *was* a traitor, by any standards. The others – in my opinion – were not.'

'And you?'

Carling shrugged, unsmiling. 'You must make up your own mind on that score.' He looked at his watch. 'I'm going over to have a chat with Gabby. I'll see you tomorrow.'

Up in his room Mathews undressed slowly by the light of the bedside reading light. It suddenly seemed crazy to be spending his days talking to a man about things that had happened before he himself was born. There was something wrong about it. Maybe not wrong, but at least it was strange. It was time he had another meeting with Kennedy.

CHAPTER 11

Kennedy's secretary had shown Mathews into his office and told him that Kennedy was on his way. He'd just called in on his cellphone from somewhere around Victoria Station. He wouldn't be more than five or ten minutes.

The strict internal security at Century House made his invitation to wait for Kennedy in his office a small sign of privilege and approval. And that same security-mindedness made him wonder what he'd done, or would have to do, to warrant the *Good Housekeeping* seal of approval.

Kennedy came in fifteen minutes later. Full of energy, jacket slung over one shoulder, tie loosened, pointing to one of the visitors' chairs as he sat down at the other side of his desk.

He leaned forward, elbows on the desk. 'How's it going?'

For about ten minutes Mathews detailed the various episodes that Carling had talked about. At the end Kennedy leaned back in his chair and Mathews wondered if it was a sign of disappointment or just a need to think about what had been said.

Then Kennedy leaned forward again. 'Did he actually admit to tipping off Philby about the German stuff from Switzerland?'

'Well, I wouldn't say *admit*. I didn't force it out of

him – he just said it in the course of talking about Philby being ambitious for the top job.'

'That's very interesting.' He paused. 'Has he ever asked you if you were wired?'

'No. He seems to trust me as – I was going to say as a friend – but that's probably going too far. Let's say that he treats me as a neutral.'

'You say he despises Philby because of the Albanian business. How does he feel about the others?'

Mathews shrugged. 'Tolerant, I guess. But quite sure that it was Maclean the Russians valued, not Philby.'

'D'you think he's gay?'

'Who? Carling? No. I'm sure he's not.' He hesitated. 'Well, maybe not sure, but my instincts tell me he's not.'

'There are two areas I'd like you to move on to if you can. Details of his KGB controllers and then his contacts with them after the war. Later on I'd like you to fish around what happened when he broke off with them. Indeed, did he ever break off with them? I can't believe all those trips to the Warsaw Pact countries were just for the Arts Council. Why just those countries? There were no visits to South America, Asia, the Middle East. But dozens of visits to Prague, Moscow, Budapest and Berlin.' He paused. 'Anything I can do for you?'

'Just one thing. I'd like to meet somebody who was in SIS when Carling was in. Just to get another angle. Somebody near his age.'

Kennedy closed his eyes, thinking for a moment and then he reached for the internal phone and pressed a button.

'It's me. Have you got a current address for an old boy named Powell – no, not him. This one's – let's see – Arthur, a major. Must be retired. No. I'll hold.'

Kennedy tucked the receiver under his chin and said,

'I've sent a decent cheque to His Lordship.' Then he turned back to the phone. 'Yeah – that's the one – write out his address and phone number and give it to Tim.'

Kennedy hung up. 'Carling must have been a pretty good operator when you look back on it. He wasn't suspected like the others. In fact nobody raised even the vaguest suspicion until about five or six years ago.'

'Why then?'

'There was a report from our chap in Prague. Seems that Carling had been seen at some reception at the Soviet Embassy. Seemed very much at home and had left with a known KGB man in a KGB car. After that people started remembering odd things and it looked very suspicious. There have been other reports of contacts that we don't like.' He shrugged. 'Nothing you could rely on.'

Kennedy stood up to end the meeting and walked Mathews to the door. Mathews picked up the slip of paper from the secretary.

CHAPTER 12

The address was in Chichester. One of those small but beautiful houses in The Pallants. The woman who opened the door was trying to calm a German shepherd dog that was barking aggressively.

'Quiet, Tessa.' She smiled faintly at Mathews. 'She won't do anything. Just doesn't like strangers. Can I help you?'

'I was hoping to have a word with Major Powell.'

'He's in the garden. If you'll wait I'll get him for you.'

She left the door open as she led the dog away and a few minutes later a man appeared. Tall and thin, wearing a panama hat and a cream-coloured linen suit.

'I'm Powell. What is it you want? If it's British Legion Tubby's looking after that these days.'

'Freddie Kennedy gave me your address.'

'Kennedy, Kennedy. Who's he?'

'He works at Century House.'

Powell seemed to hesitate and then said reluctantly, 'I see. You'd better come in. We'll go in the garden.'

It was a small garden, but carefully laid out to give both privacy and a feeling of space.

They sat in wicker chairs under a lilac still in bloom.

'And how is Freddie these days? Still screwing everything that moves?'

'He's fine, but I don't know him as well as you obviously do.'

'Don't know how he got away with it. Part of his training, I guess.' He paused. 'And what can I do for you, young man?'

'I wanted to ask you about George Carling. Lord Carling. Freddie said you knew him in the old days.'

'George, eh? And what's he been up to?'

'Nothing so far as I know. I just wanted to get somebody else's view of his background.'

'Most of the time when I knew him was in Washington. I was at the embassy. Passport Officer or some such bloody title. And George was liaison with Langley.' He peered at Mathews. 'You been to Langley?'

'Yes.'

'Well, Georgie boy was our liaison chap with the CIA.' He shrugged. 'Did a good job as far as I know. Seemed to get on with them better than his predecessors.'

'Was Philby in Washington when you were there?'

'The whole bunch of 'em were there. Maclean, First Secretary at the embassy. Then Burgess came as Second or Third Secretary, I've forgotten which. It seemed he didn't want to come. Hated Americans but he'd caused so much embarrassment in London that it was Washington or the boot.'

'How did the others get on with the Americans?'

'The Americans detested Burgess from the start. He was openly anti-American and his drinking and sexual habits were outrageous. He stayed at Philby's house when he first came over. Aileen, Philby's wife, loathed him. Philby was a smoothie and a dedicated traitor. Angleton, the head of counterintelligence at the CIA, rumbled him right from the start. Didn't trust him an inch. Maclean . . .'

he shrugged '. . . he covered himself publicly, but in private he was anti-American.'

'What was your role?'

'When London realised that Angleton was gunning for Philby, they sent me in as official CIA/SIS liaison.'

'So what was Carling doing?'

Powell shrugged. 'I never knew. But whatever it was he wasn't part of the embassy staff. He had his own place in town. He was working with the CIA but I don't know any details.' He smiled. 'The Americans were a bit cagey about him at the start but he soon got his feet under the table and they loved him.'

'What did you think of Carling yourself?'

Powell hesitated. 'Why are you asking me?'

'Just to get an impression of the man from someone who knew him in the old days.'

Powell was silent for a few moments and then he said, 'You're doing some sort of check on him, aren't you?' He paused. 'I suppose if Kennedy gave you my name and address it must be official.' He paused again. 'They've left it a bit late, haven't they?'

'Who knows?'

'OK. Back to business. I liked Carling. He was generous. I don't mean money. He was generous about people. He didn't rush to judgement. And whatever he was doing I always reckoned that he did it well. But there was something odd about him. He was extrovert but a loner at the same time. He listened but you never knew what he was thinking.' He paused. 'What did he say about me?'

'I haven't asked him anything about you.'

'Does Kennedy think Carling was playing games?'

'I think some people have some doubts.'

'If he was playing games, then you can take it from me

that he was much more dangerous than Philby and his gang.'

'What makes you think that?'

'Just instinct. No flaws that I could see. But if he put his mind to something he'd make it work.'

'What kind of thing? You mean like Philby and the others?'

Powell shrugged. 'Could be. I've no idea. Not a clue. But I've been in the business a long time.'

'Would you trust him?'

Powell smiled. 'I don't trust anybody. Twenty years in SIS puts you off trusting people. Let's say I'd trust him with my wife, with my money, maybe even with my life but I still wouldn't trust him. There's something odd there but I've no idea what it is.' He turned to look at Mathews. 'Somewhere inside that man there's conviction. Not of politics or religion. It's as if he worked it all out a long time ago. And he's stuck to it ever since.' Powell wagged a finger at Mathews. 'I've always thought he ought to have been a priest, but not belonging to any religion. They made martyrs of that kind of man in the old days. Broke their bones on the rack. Burned 'em at the stake.' He smiled and shrugged. 'And nowadays, all over the world, we put them in prison and leave them to rot.'

'Did Carling have any particular friends when he was in Washington?'

'He didn't have much to do with the Brits. His main contact was – Jesus, one of those American names, Chuck or something.'

'Hank?'

'Yeah, that's it, Hank, Hank Henney. He was CIA. The CIA was quite new, came out of OSS, and I think Carling was there to help them organise recruitment and define targets. When he eventually went back to London I know the Americans raised hell to get him back, but London wouldn't play. A mistake in my opinion.' Powell looked at his watch. 'Let's have a cup of tea before you go. My Muriel makes wonderful sponge cakes.'

It was a Friday evening and by the time Mathews had followed the coast road past Arundel, the weekend traffic from London was already building up. Couples off for a weekend in the sun, families with tents and barbecues, buckets and spades. He envied them the set patterns of their lives. He wondered what Tony was doing for the weekend. He must get down to writing that bloody statement for his solicitor. Maybe he should buy a boat and moor it down at Chichester. Have something that the boy enjoyed so much he'd raise hell if she tried to cancel his outing with his father. His mind went to his ex-wife and he wondered what the hell she saw in that creep Thomas. There was a time when he could do no wrong so far as she was concerned. There must have been something that changed it all. But he had no idea what it was. He could remember it now. Another sunny day, and he'd parked his car in the drive because they were having a baby-sitter and going out for dinner. She was sitting there in the living room and he knew from her face that something was wrong. Tony had had an accident? He'd been hurt? He was in hospital? And then she'd told him. No reasons, no discussion. Not even a row. She was moving out to her sister's for a week so that he could collect his things. She was divorcing him. She was going to marry Thomas.

Mathews had stood there like an idiot. Dumbstruck. Watching it like some episode in *Neighbours* as she picked up her handbag and coat and swept from the room. He could remember that she was trembling as she sat there saying her piece and his instinct had been to comfort her but it was as if he were paralysed. It seemed so unreal.

The house was scrupulously clean and tidy and she had left him a meal on the kitchen table. Ham and a dish of salad. The next few days had been like a bad dream. A mixture of lethargy and bursts of angry activity. Finding a lawyer, closing bank accounts, packing his belongings, sure that he could leave most of them as she would never be allowed to take over the house and throw him out after having walked out on him without any excuse or reason. Three weeks later she was back in what was now referred to as 'the matrimonial home' and he was required by law to continue paying the mortgage and the bills. There was little that he could put in his counterstatement. He had no complaints about her that were worth recording. He'd have gone on with her happily enough and he would have tried to put right anything that she complained of. But she hadn't complained.

Back at Lake Cottage Mathews had chatted for a few minutes to Julie and then gone to his room. Carling was on the train back from London where he had been on a TV programme discussing the exhibition of Bill Brandt's black and white pictures at the Photographers Gallery.

He had almost finished his legal statement when Julie came in with a tray. Sausages and mash, half a Gallia melon steeped in brown sugar, and a pot of coffee. She was surprised when she noticed the trace of tears at the edge of his eyes as he thanked her for bothering to get him a meal.

*   *   *

It was midnight when Carling got back to the cottage. A side window had been smashed on his much-loved Rover and the radio stolen.

'You know, Julie,' he said 'it would be more sensible and less expensive to leave the car unlocked with a notice saying, "The car's not locked so don't break a window but the radio's ten years old." '

She smiled. 'I've poured you a whisky. A Glenfiddich. There's ice and water if you want it.'

As he sipped his whisky she said, 'The boy's back. Looks very miserable. I made him supper and his light went out half an hour ago.'

'He's upset about not seeing his son.' He shook his head. 'I'll have to do something about that. It's crazy. Always remember: never get in the hands of lawyers. They'll cause more troubles than they solve and they'll rob you blind while they're doing it.' He sighed. 'My God, I'm tired. I shouldn't have to do all this running around at my age.'

She smiled. 'Go on, you know you love it.'

CHAPTER 13

As she brought in the coffee-pot Julie announced that His Lordship was having a long lie-in. Mathews drove to the village and posted his statement to his lawyer. By the time he got back to the cottage Carling was sitting at the table in his dressing gown, going through his mail. He looked up as Mathews sat down opposite him.

'I'm going to be away for three or four days next week. I'm on the panel for the young musician of the year competition in Prague. You're welcome to come along but Century House would have to fund your travel and subsistence.' He smiled. 'My favourite city, Prague. So beautiful, like all Europe used to be. Even under the communists it was a city of culture. Great orchestras and queues for every concert.' He smiled. 'Mahler and Dvořák – the local boys who made good. What more could you want?'

Mathews smiled. 'I'll speak to Kennedy but I don't think he'll feel it's necessary.'

'What's the position with your boy?'

Mathews told him about his statement and Carling frowned. 'Doesn't make sense. It's got locked into a crazy situation. We'll have to think of some way of getting it back to normal.'

Carling and Mathews were in the garden when Julie came out and said that there was a phone call for Mathews.

The call was from Kennedy, who wanted to see him as soon as possible. They settled for lunch at the Special Forces Club.

They talked cricket and the Derby as they ate and took their coffees out into the main room at a table by one of the windows.

'Tell me about your meeting with Powell.'

When Mathews had said his piece about Powell, he raised the possibility of a trip to Prague with Carling. Kennedy had turned it down out of hand. Their man in Prague could cover Carling's movements and contacts. Mathews then raised the possibility of a quick trip to Washington to talk to the man who Powell had said was Carling's CIA associate.

Kennedy thought about it for several minutes and then he said, 'Why not? How are you going to trace him, he'll have been out of the game years ago?'

'I was thinking of contacting Maguire, who was my opposite number when I was in Langley.'

'OK. But not longer than three days. Check with Maguire that he can actually locate Carling's guy. What was his name?'

'Hank Henney.'

Kennedy looked surprised. 'I've heard of Hank Henney. I think I attended a lecture by him at Langley on running non-national agents in overseas countries. Something like that anyway. Looked like Walter Matthau but sounded more like a drug-runner. OK, I'll get Facilities to fix you up.'

'Any chance of saving time by flying Concorde?'

Kennedy laughed. 'You must be joking. And Economy, not even Business Class.'

Mathews looked at his watch. It was midday Washington time and he put through a fast-track call to Langley. When he got through it seemed Maguire was now based in New York but the CIA operator was able to transfer the call. It was a secretary who answered and when he asked for Maguire she asked his name, which he gave, but when she asked his business, he told her frostily just to put him through. A few seconds later Maguire came on the line.

'Maguire. What can I do for you?'

'It's Tim Mathews, Joe.'

'I'm sorry, I don't . . . Jesus, where are you calling from? I thought it was a local call and I didn't recognise the name out of context. How are you?'

'I'm OK. I'm coming over in the next few days. Just a quick trip. I wanted to contact a guy named Henney. Hank Henney.'

'Official or unofficial?'

'Official, but nothing desperate.'

'You're lucky. He's been retired for years. He's no longer in Washington. He lives here with his daughter in Queens. When are you coming?'

'Is tomorrow OK? I'll change my flight from Washington to New York.'

'Fine. Send me a fax of your flight number and I'll meet you in.'

'Thanks.'

High winds had delayed the landing for an hour but Maguire was waiting for him at the luggage carousel and had taken him through Immigration and Passport Control and then on to the car park.

The rain was beating down as Maguire headed for the city.

'It's a bit late to contact Hank today but I'll take you over tomorrow morning and leave you with him. You can phone me at the office for a lift back. Or get a cab. Where did you book in?'

'There's a dump I used to stay at near Madison Square Garden. I've booked in there for a couple of nights.'

'OK. We'll drop your bag there and then head for the clubs.'

'Does your old lady let you go to clubs?'

Maguire grinned. 'My old lady's somebody else's old lady now. Took a fancy to an insurance guy and I didn't stop her. How's yours?'

'Same as yours but mine went for a lawyer.'

'Fuck 'em all, Timmy boy. We're well rid of 'em.' He laughed. 'We'll celebrate tonight.' He paused. 'Here's your hotel. Hop out, take your bag and I'll find somewhere to park. No, I tell you what, I'll go back to my place and freshen up and I'll come back to you in a couple of hours and we'll hit the town, OK?'

Mathews smiled. 'Anything you say, Joe.'

Mathews signed in and took his bag up to his room on the tenth floor. He had slept on the flight but he needed a bath and a shave.

Room service had brought him orange juice and a beef sandwich and as he towelled himself dry he walked over to the TV to switch it on. There was a short, sharp shock as he touched the switch. He had had a similar shock when he closed the door to the bathroom. He phoned down to the housekeeper and asked for an electrician.

The big black man tried the TV and the door handle but there was no shock. Mathews insisted, and when he touched the switch again himself the shock was obvious. There was even a small burst of blue light. As he looked at the electrician, the big man shrugged. 'It's just static, buddy. That's all.'

'So what can you do about it?'

The man looked at him and shrugged. 'Maybe you need to get laid.'

Maguire obviously shared the electrician's diagnosis and they had done the rounds of a dozen bars and clubs before going back to Mathews' room at the hotel with two girls in tow. Mathews had no idea the next morning as to what time his companions had left but Maguire had turned up in time for breakfast looking alert and at ease as they talked about Hank Henney.

It seemed that Hank Henney was a bit of a mystery man even inside the CIA, but that wasn't abnormal. Gossip and some informed guessing suggested that he had been responsible for communications with CIA field agents in Europe and the Middle East. He had been an officer in OSS when it was being dissolved and had been recruited into the newly formed CIA a few months later.

'I can't tell you much about him. We don't ask other employees what they do. I expect it's the same with your lot.'

'You're right.'

'Shall we go?'

'OK. Are you sure he'll be there?'

Maguire sighed. 'He's got a bad hip joint, so he doesn't get around much. He's due to have a replacement any day now. They've got a small balcony at the back. He sits there in the sun. When there is any sun.'

As they drove over the bridge to Queens, Maguire said, 'I'll leave you with him and come back in half an hour. You can have another session with him this afternoon or tomorrow. See how it goes. Don't wear the old boy out.'

Hank Henney was in his mid-sixties but he looked younger. He was handsome and there were only streaks of grey in his thick black hair. When Maguire had introduced Mathews to Henney and his daughter, Anna, he then left.

'Would you like to see my ID, Mr Henney?'

Henney smiled. 'No. Joe Maguire says it's OK. And that's enough for me. What can I do for you?'

'Arthur Powell gave me your name. He spoke very fondly of you.'

Henney smiled. 'Fondly, eh. A nice English word. And how is Arthur?'

'He's fine. He's got a nice house in Sussex. Not far from the sea and he seems to be a keen gardener.'

'And how did my name come up?'

'He said you were a good friend of George Carling – Lord Carling – when he was working with the CIA in Washington.'

'D'you know George Carling?'

'Yes. I've been staying with him for several weeks.'

Henney grinned. 'A lovely man. Wants to put the world right all on his own.' He paused. 'But he must be long retired by now.'

'He is but he still lives a very busy life on TV and radio, and in the newspapers.'

'Has he got over the girl?'

Mathews looked surprised. 'What girl d'you mean?'

Henney shook his head. 'Doesn't matter. Shouldn't be talking about it anyway.' He paused. 'So. How can I help you?'

'I was interested in what Carling was doing when he was over here.'

Henney's bushy eyebrows went up. 'But he was an SIS man.' He paused. 'How come an SIS man is asking *me* what another SIS man was doing? Your people must know what he was doing.'

'There doesn't appear to be any official record of what he was doing.'

'Has all this been cleared by the brass?'

'You could check with London if you want.'

'I mean has it been cleared by Langley?'

'Why should Langley need to clear information about an SIS officer?'

For long moments Henney was silent and then he shook his head and said, 'How long have you known Joe Maguire?'

'I met him about five years ago when I was posted over here to Washington as junior liaison with Langley.'

'How long were you here?'

'Just short of two years.'

'And what were you working on?'

'I was controlled by the Deputy Director for Operations.'

'Go on.'

'I was at the HUMINT Requirements Tasking Center.'

'You'd better level with me, boy. Why are you checking on George Carling?'

'It's just routine.'

'Don't give me that bullshit. Routine what? Checking on a guy who retired – what was it – fifteen, sixteen years ago?' He paused. 'Those bastards in London are trying to pin something on him, aren't they?'

Mathews heard the door-bell and prayed that it was Maguire. It was, and five minutes later they had left with a further session arranged for the afternoon. Mathews said nothing about his conversation with Henney and they went for a sandwich at a café near the local police precinct.

They had got to the hot chocolate when Maguire's bleep went. He stood up, still sipping his drink.

'Won't be long. I'll use the house phone.'

He put down the empty mug and wiped his mouth with the back of his hand, looking around for the phone. He walked to the counter and the girl pointed down a short passage. Mathews watched Maguire press the buttons for the number and then called the waiter for the bill.

It was nearly fifteen minutes before Maguire came back, lowering himself slowly into his seat before he looked at Mathews, frowning.

'What the hell were you talking about with Henney, for Christ's sake?'

'Nothing special. I just asked him about a man who used to work with him.'

'A Brit?'

'Yes.'

'SIS?'

'Yes.'

'I am in deep shit, boyo.' He stared at Mathews. 'I've got orders to escort you to Kennedy and check that you board the plane.'

'When?'

'Right now. Somebody's gone to your hotel to pick up your stuff and a driver will bring it here. And off we go.'

'Can I phone London?'

'No. My guy said if you make any difficulty and don't co-operate you'll not just be sent off, you'll be handed over to Immigration for your visa to be cancelled.'

'On what grounds, Joe? What the hell is going on?'

'I've no idea, but according to them you're stamping around on some very thin ice.'

'Have they contacted London?'

'Not yet. But I'm sure they will. They're really doing their nuts. Hollering about your people going behind their backs and God knows what else.' He paused. 'There's the driver now. Give me a couple of minutes with him and then come over. And don't, repeat don't, say anything in front of him.'

'Did they tell you why they were doing this?'

'No. They just wanted to make sure that whatever it was, it was all my fault. If anything happened I was going to be the fall guy.'

'Who did Henney speak to at Langley, do you know?'

'No idea. It was my boss who talked to me. Asked what the hell I thought I was doing.' He paused. 'And believe me, he was shaking in his shoes.' He turned and looked hard at Mathews. 'Who was this guy you asked Henney about?'

Mathews, still surprised and angered, said softly, 'Let's leave it, Joe. I'll get London to assure Langley that you know nothing about any of it.'

Maguire sighed. 'Thanks. Maybe it's better for me to just be righteously indignant and ignorant and ride it out.' Maguire looked towards the driver standing by the bar. 'Let's get on our way. We've paid your hotel bill. Your seat's booked already.' He laughed softly. 'The airline had to chuck off some crappy pop star to get you on so you're going First Class.'

They sat in silence as the driver made his way to JFK. The driver handed over Mathews' case and the flight ticket to Maguire, who walked with him to check-in and escorted him past passport control and on to the flight assembly waiting room.

Fifteen minutes later they were put through the final checkpoint and Maguire went with him to his seat at the front end of the plane. They shook hands without speaking and Mathews saw Maguire speaking to the chief cabin steward before he left the plane.

As he settled back in his seat after they were airborne, Mathews closed his eyes and tried to make some sense out of what had happened in less than a day. On the surface it was legitimate enough for the Americans to stop him from talking with a retired CIA man. What made it extraordinary was the speed and crudity with which they had reacted. And the fact that Maguire had told him originally that his section head had seen no problem. It was all in the business, whatever it was. And Hank Henney was long out of the business. He guessed it must be just the CIA resenting not being put in the picture. It would be interesting to hear what Kennedy had to say about one of his senior men being escorted out of the USA. It was just as well that he'd cleared his trip with Kennedy. And because the CIA had arranged his return flight at least SIS could cash in his return ticket.

CHAPTER 14

Dickie Farmer was waiting for him at the end of the tunnel from the plane. He looked amiable enough.

'Kennedy wants to see you at Century House. I've got a car.'

'How did you know what flight I was on?'

Farmer grinned. 'I understand Freddie got a call from the States. What the hell's going on?'

'I've no idea. I got the bum's rush. Escorted on to a plane. I was there less than a day.'

'What did you do, for Chrissake?'

'I just talked to a CIA guy. He was a friend of a Brit who worked in Washington way back. They both retired years ago.'

'I'm on Freddie's committee dealing with Carling. You've no need to talk in code.' He paused. 'What did you uncover?'

'Nothing. Absolutely nothing.'

As they got to the Hammersmith flyover Farmer concentrated on the driving. The early morning traffic was already causing long tailbacks and it was forty minutes before he dropped Mathews at Century House.

'Go on up. He's waiting for you. Take your kit. I'm not signing in today.'

'Thanks for the lift.'

'You're welcome.'

It was only when Mathews saw that Kennedy was wearing an open-necked blue denim shirt and blue jeans that he remembered it was Saturday.

'Well,' said Kennedy. 'sit down. Glad to see you got back. Seemed you might have ended up in Rykers.' He paused. 'Tell me what happened.'

'There's not much to tell you.'

'So tell me what there is.'

It took only ten minutes for Mathews to cover everything that had happened in New York but he could see from Kennedy's face that he was taking it very seriously.

'Let me get this quite clear. You told Maguire that you wanted to meet this guy Henney who'd been mentioned by Powell when you interviewed him. But you didn't say why you wanted to meet him?'

'That's right.'

'You didn't mention Carling's name to Maguire?'

'No. I didn't even mention it after the meeting and when they were throwing me out.'

'And Maguire's boss had OK'd your contact with Henney.'

'That's what Maguire told me.'

'But when you raised the subject of Carling with Hank Henney he seemed suspicious. Asked if we were trying to pin something on him, or words to that effect?'

'Yeah.'

'In the café before Maguire got the phone call he was normal and co-operative, yes?'

'He was just his usual self. I wouldn't say he was co-operative because there was no co-operation asked for.'

'Then they didn't even let you go back to the hotel. Said you were already booked by them on a flight and that if you didn't co-operate they'd hand you over to Immigration to cancel your visa and make you an undesirable.'

'They didn't mention making me an undesirable but that's what it would have meant. I'd have been barred from any future visit to the States.'

Kennedy sighed and leaned back in his chair. 'So what do you think it was all about?'

'The only thought I had was that they thought I'd gone behind their backs in contacting Henney.'

'Rubbish. You'd contacted Maguire. No objection from him about protocol. The blessing of Maguire's boss, yes?'

'So he said.'

'So the only problem was raising the subject of Carling?'

'Seems like it.'

'There's something very odd here, Tim. I've looked up his record and at the time he was in Washington he was responsible for smoothing out routine problems between SIS and the CIA. Their assessments always gave him the highest rating and when he was brought back to London they made strong representations that he be left there for another tour of duty.'

'It's really crazy, isn't it? What did they say when they phoned you that I was on my way back?'

'That's what worries me. The man who spoke to me wasn't CIA and all he said was that they objected to our clandestine approach.'

'What rubbish.' Mathews paused. 'If he wasn't CIA I suppose he must have been some goon from Foreign Affairs.'

'I wish he had been that.'

'What was he then?'

'I asked him who he was speaking for and he refused to answer. He just hung up. That in itself made me very suspicious and I asked Cheltenham to trace the origin of the call.' He looked at Mathews. 'Guess where it was from?'

'Washington? New York?'

'Neither. It was a Maryland number. Fort George Meade, the National Security Agency. It was the direct line to the NSA's chief of security.'

'My God. What's going on? Was Carling ever at NSA?'

'No. Neither did he have anything to do with Cheltenham and GCHQ.'

'It's crazy. It doesn't make sense. What interest can NSA have in Carling?'

'That's gonna be for you to find out, my friend.'

'What do you want me to do?'

'Go on exactly as you have been doing. Don't, whatever you do, confront him. But just bear in mind that there's more to George Carling than we thought.'

'He's been so open and friendly.'

'Fine. Keep it that way. But keep a small doubt at the back of your mind.'

'Maybe the Yanks have warned him about me contacting Henney.'

Kennedy shrugged. 'Who knows? See what you think. D'you want me to take you to lunch?'

'No thanks. I want to be back at his place before he gets back himself.'

'He's due back Monday. I'll let you see a copy of our chap's report on his visit.'

'Could be interesting now.'

'I doubt it. Whatever he's up to he's been in the business a long time.' As Mathews turned to leave, Kennedy said, 'It surprised me that GCHQ didn't try and conceal the source of the call. They just treated it as a routine SIS enquiry.'

'Why's that significant?'

'Because it means that GCHQ aren't covering up anything for the benefit of NSA. They normally work hand in glove with one another.' He went on as he saw that Mathews hadn't grasped the point he was making. 'It means that whatever Carling's connection was with NSA, Cheltenham didn't know about it.'

'But what could Carling do for NSA? They're only concerned with telephone and radio surveillance.'

'Those guys in Fort George Meade cover everything that moves. They can listen to a Soviet tank commander giving orders to his men as they head up the main highway to Smolensk or Kiev. They can record every telephone conversation in the world. Military, espionage, civilian, political and economical. They know more about what's going on in the world than the President of the USA himself, and the heads of every government that exists, plus anyone who's trying to overthrow them.'

'I still can't see the Carling connection.'

'Neither can I, but it means that there's more to Carling than his connection with Philby and his mates.' He paused and shrugged. 'Just bear it in mind, Tim. That's all I'm saying.'

CHAPTER 15

Swanson was talking on the phone when Newman walked into his office. He nodded to his visitor and pointed to a chair. When he put down the phone he said, 'I thought we'd better have a word together about this cock-up by Hasset.'

'Has any damage been done?'

'From what I've been told so far, no. But it's far too important to take any risks at all.'

'Why did Hasset give the OK to his guy Maguire in the first place?'

Swanson sighed. 'Ignorance. The standard problem of too much security, I guess. There are only three people who know about the operation. You, me, and our friend at Fort George Meade. And as far as I know it's worked. We're completely watertight. Even if it had been a normal top-secret operation Hasset would not have been in the picture.' He shrugged. 'Why should he be? It's not his area. Maguire is a trusted officer and the request for Hasset's approval for the Brit to meet Hank Henney was more a courtesy request than asking for official approval.

'Hank's long out of the business. A Brit from SIS wants to meet a retired operator. So why not? If the Brit hadn't been a pal of Maguire he could have ferreted out Henney's location independently with very little trouble. The SIS offices in New York and Washington could have trawled around for Henney without us even knowing.' He shrugged. 'Let's face it, if it wasn't for Henney's suspicions we would never have known what the Brit was after.'

'Who did Henney speak to here at Langley?'

'He contacted Delaney, who hit the panic button and set the Brit on his way home.'

'Why was Delaney so hasty?'

'Treated it as the Brit and Maguire and Hasset going behind his back. More a status thing than anything to do with security.'

'The Brit didn't protest – threaten to ring London or call the SIS office in New York?'

'No. I gather from Maguire that the poor bastard's feet didn't touch. He was on a plane two hours after Henney called in.' He smiled. 'Cost us his hotel bill and plane fare.'

'Any complaints from London?'

'That's the main problem, Vic. The call was made to Kennedy who's a pretty laid-back guy. Said he thought we had been over-reacting. Mountains out of molehills, et cetera. Said we owed him one and I agree.'

'So how's that the main problem?'

'When it all blew up somebody here at Langley had done a quick check on Carling and saw that he had been liaison between SIS London and the NSA at Fort George Meade. So they contacted NSA Security and Bauer took the whole thing over. It was Bauer who phoned Kennedy in London. He didn't say who he was, his name or his status and Kennedy wasn't hunting bear and just accepted the call as being from Langley.'

'Bauer's an arrogant bastard. A pity he had to be brought into the operation in the first place. But again, what's the problem?'

'The problem is, did Kennedy really accept the call as a routine apology for precipitate action by juniors in our setup? Or did he check where the call came from and start wondering what was going on?'

'Who would he have checked with?'

'He will have tried British Telecom, who would have referred it lock, stock and barrel to GCHQ.'

'Could they have traced it?'

'No problem at all.'

'And they wouldn't have protected the security of our operation because they don't know anything about it?'

'Exactly. There's no way I can find out what Kennedy thinks without stirring the pot and raising even more suspicions in London. We'll just have to ride with it. But I thought you ought to know.'

'What exactly did the Brit ask Henney about Carling?'

'I didn't want to show too much interest but what alerted Henney was two things. First, why was a Brit from SIS checking up on another SIS man who was long out of the business? And secondly, why, when challenged, did the Brit insist that it was just a routine check? Apart from all that, it seems that old Hank was a great buddy of Carling's,' he smiled, 'and thought the Brits might be trying to do him out of his pension.'

'Where do we go from here?'

'I feel that unless it blows up in London it's best to let it go. Do nothing, unless we're forced to.'

'Any back-up plans in case it all falls apart?'

'No.' He looked very serious as he said, 'I'd be prepared to break a lot of rules to keep this on the road.'

CHAPTER 16

A phone call from the embassy in Prague had been a message from His Lordship, who would be most grateful if someone could pick him up from Gatwick. Monday evening from Berlin. The scheduled British Airways flight.

Mathews drove the ancient Rover 3-litre and had an hour to wait before the delayed flight was due in. He cashed in on his passenger's title and used the VIP lounge. He took the opportunity to phone Kennedy. It was an insecure line so they talked in the limited but translatable jargon of intelligence and Kennedy said that he already had the report from their colleagues in Prague and Kennedy was sending a copy to him care of the Central Post Office in Tunbridge Wells. No names were mentioned, nor was there any reference to the shambles in New York.

As he sat sipping coffee and barely aware of the garbled announcements of landings, takeoffs and delays, his mind was sorting the pros and cons of raising his abortive New York trip with Carling. It was either confrontation or saying nothing. He decided that silence was truly golden in the circumstances. Confrontation would ruin his established good relationship with Carling and could even offend him enough for Carling to send him packing.

His Lordship was escorted to the VIP lounge by a senior airport official and a BA stewardess. He was all smiles and bonhomie and all Mathews's instincts told him that Carling had not heard of his furtive trip to New York.

They all sat around with sandwiches and Napa Valley wine discussing the possibilities of Gatwick setting aside the space for a gallery of British paintings and photographs. The Tate and Kodak had already promised co-operation and hinted at a possible subsidy if the Arts Council matched it. It seemed amazing that a seventy-year-old man could always create such an atmosphere of enthusiasm and new thinking no matter what was being discussed, whether it was young girls with babies or a commemorative concert for some previously unappreciated composer.

'And what have you chaps been up to?' Carling said as he headed them back down the M25.

'I was away for a couple of days and yesterday I took the girls and the baby down to Bexhill.' He laughed. 'We actually paddled, and made sandcastles.'

'Now there was a nice thought.' He paused and, as if he had been considering it, he said, 'Well done, my boy, well done.' He paused. 'You know. That's the only way we can save the world. Take care of one another. What we ought to do is each one of us take responsibility for one other human being.' He waved a hand from the wheel. 'We hear of thousands of people somewhere killed by floods or famine or war and it's too much to absorb. But see one small Colombian baby on TV yelling its head off as they stick in a syringe, we can't wait to send off a fiver. We're very soft-hearted you know, we Brits. Good people.' He said, 'Nice people underneath.'

His Lordship's dialectic wandered over the Samaritans, the Salvation Army, Barnardos, Oxfam, Save the Children and finally Mother Theresa. Not the slightest sign that anything had changed in their relationship.

Carling had finished his breakfast and was reading *The Times* as Mathews poured himself another coffee.

'This is interesting, Tim.' He looked across at Mathews. 'Your ex-wife's solicitor. What did you say his name was?'

'Thomas. Roger Thomas.'

'Where's he live?'

'In Esher. Lives in a flat over his offices. Why do you ask?'

Carling folded back the unwieldy pages of the newspaper, and folded it again, handing it to Mathews.

'Read that. Top right-hand corner.'

It was only three column inches but the headline was enough – 'Surrey solicitor arrested by Fraud Squad.' Mr Roger Thomas, a solicitor in the commuter suburb of Esher, Surrey, had been arrested late the previous evening and charged with offences related to the fraudulent misuse of clients' funds and of making false returns to both the Inland Revenue and Customs and Excise. He had denied all charges and would come before local magistrates in two days' time.

Mathews put the paper to one side. 'It was only a question of time.'

'You think it's true?'

'I'm sure it is. From what I gathered he's been at it for years.'

'You must be delighted.'

Mathews shrugged. 'I'd like to have seen her face when she heard the news. We all have our lessons to learn.'

'And what lessons have you learned out of this, my boy?'

Mathews thought for a moment. Then, with a quizzical look on his face he said, 'I guess I spend too much time looking at other people and fail to look at myself. I thought – and still think – I was a reasonable husband and father.' He shrugged. 'But I obviously wasn't.'

'Will it make any difference with this chap out of the way?'

'I've no idea.'

'Have you ever seen a trout farm?'

'No.'

'There's one about a mile up the road. Let's take a walk and have a look at it.'

There were two large lakes and on the hill behind them was the big house that had been converted into apartments that all had magnificent views across the valley. There were half a dozen anglers around the larger lake, and a clubhouse with several expensive cars parked alongside it.

Carling led Mathews along a narrow pathway at the edge of the lake to what had once been a boathouse with a wooden jetty. They sat in the sunshine watching the anglers on the far bank casting their flies on to the smooth surface of the water. After a few minutes Carling said, 'What do you want to talk about next?'

'What did you do in SIS after the war was over?'

'Because of my German and the experience I had on the denazification programme I was posted to Berlin.'

'When was this?'

'About 1957.'

'Was George Blake in Berlin then?'

'He was there about a year before me.'

'Did you know that he was a KGB agent?'

'No. I knew from hints from my Russian contacts that

there was somebody in SIS Berlin who was passing them information but they were always very careful not to break an agent's security.'

'What was your role with the Russians?'

Carling smiled. 'It wasn't a role. But we were well into the Cold War by then and I did what I could to calm them down.' He paused and shrugged. 'And to calm our people too.'

'What was your SIS job at that time?'

'I was responsible for getting information on what they called the Russian Zone, which became East Germany.'

'What sort of information?'

'The influence of German communists, their relationship with Moscow and the general population's attitude to the Russian occupying forces.'

'And what did you give the Russians?'

'Mainly my opinion on the various moves they were making. At the time they were sure that the West was going to invade the Russian Zone and they built up huge forces on the borders between the zones. And that made our people sure that the Soviets were going to come over the border and smash through to the Channel.' He sighed. 'It was typical of the whole Cold War period. Suspicion, rumour, false information and neither side understanding the other side. It was a nightmare, believe me.' He shrugged. 'I did my best for them and us to sort out the rumours from the facts. I can remember when our staff in border cities like Brunswick, Göttingen and Hamburg were issued orders to destroy all their records in twenty-four hours as a Soviet invasion was imminent.

'The Russians had moved in troops around Magdeburg. Mainly to make the local population pay for their keep. When I warned them how it was seen in our camp they were amazed and reluctantly dispersed half their divisions to other parts of their zone. It was like keeping two wild animals from one another's throats. The intelligence on both sides was appalling. Inaccurate, misconstrued and looking for trouble. I'm not sure how my situation assessments to either side made any difference but I did my best.'

'How long were you in Berlin?'

'Eight or nine years with a two-month break when London called me back for a temporary assignment.'

'What was the assignment?'

'When they closed down Bletchley they kept on some of the cryptographers who were breaking down top security codes, especially those used by the Russians. It was the group who first gave the clues that eventually identified Maclean as "Homer", the Russian codename of a British diplomat working for the KGB. They were all experts at their jobs and like most experts they were bad administrators, politically naïve and resentful of any civil service attempt to organise them. I had got to know them well at Bletchley when they were working on Enigma and Ultra; SIS suggested me as a co-ordinator and everybody was surprised when they agreed.'

'Where did they work after Bletchley?'

'They had a place in a London suburb, Eastcote, and I had a couple of rooms on the top floor of the building.' He smiled. 'It worked quite well. They got on with their work, which was all they cared about, and I kept SIS, the Foreign Office and the Civil Services at bay.' He smiled. 'In the end they all finished up as a special section of GCHQ.'

'Were you ever at GCHQ?'

'No. I had quite a lot to do with them but I was always SIS, or Foreign Office on secondment from SIS.'

'Were you ever PV'd at some later stage in SIS?'

'Like I told you, there was no such thing as positive vetting when I first joined, but I was PV'd before I was sent to Berlin as a matter of routine. And I was PV'd again in the late sixties.' He smiled. 'I think that was because somebody had suggested way back that I was gay because I wasn't married.'

'But being gay wouldn't have automatically affected your career.'

'Agreed. But that's not what matters. If you have never disguised or hidden that you're gay, that's one thing. But if you are revealed or exposed as being gay, it means that you told lies when you were recruited and in subsequent checks. And under those circumstances you'll certainly be sacked.' Carling stood up. 'Time we were getting back.'

As they walked back together Carling, seemingly apropos of nothing obvious, said, 'Never, never, trust politicians or bureaucrats. They live on lies.'

When Mathews woke in the night he switched on the bedside lamp and looked at his watch. It was 2.30 a.m. and he knew there was something that he should be thinking about. The little warning bells in his mind had rung as they walked back together from the trout farm. It was something that Carling had said. But he couldn't isolate it.

CHAPTER 17

There was a brown envelope for him at the post office in Tunbridge Wells and Mathews went for a coffee at Importers.

The contents were mostly junk mail but there was one envelope with a red wax seal. In it was the report from the SIS in Prague.

Surveillance: 1096
Subject: Earlybird
Operator: Cooper

Subject arrived at RUZYNE airport Thursday noon. Was driven with other members of the delegation to ADRIA HOTEL at VACLAVSKE NAMESTI 26. Subject allotted suite. Others to rooms, some sharing.

Ascertained that subject was not part of ARTS COUNCIL party but guest of CZ government.

Thursday evening subject attended PART ONE of Young Musician of Year Competition at NATIONAL THEATRE. Later attended buffet at BRITISH CULTURAL CENTRE at NARODNI 10.

Friday. Subject spent whole day and evening with Czech cultural officials at MINISTRY OF CULTURE. Ate in evening at SHALOM, MAISELOVA 18, in Jewish quarter. Was with six others. All nationals, two were senior members of former Czech Comm. Party now in govt employ as diplomats.

Saturday. Subject had visitors in his suite all day. Mainly actors, musicians and artists. In evening attended PART TWO of competition and was on judging panel. Later with mixed party from competition at CAFE SAVOY, VITEZNA 1.

Sunday. Walked in old town with unidentified young woman approx mid-twenties. Seen with subject and others on other occasions. Evening was interviewed on TV on subject of 'Acting as a Visual Art'. Ate with same young woman at SHALOM in evening.

Monday. Subject paid courtesy call to BRIT EMBASSY. Mid-day accompanied delegation to airport but did not board booked flight back to Gatwick. Lost contact at airport with subject but was able to ascertain that subject took LUFTHANSA flight to BERLIN, TEGEL. Arrived BERLIN approx 14.00 hours. Left TEGEL on BRITISH AIRWAYS late evening flight to GATWICK but have no information on subject's movements in BERLIN. Flight details solely from bookings clerk.

ENDS

Mathews read it through a second time and then slid the two pages back into the envelope. He knew Cooper, an ex-policeman who had been recruited into SIS from Special Branch much to MI5's annoyance. The codename Earlybird for Carling was typical schoolboy humour and words like 'ascertain' were giveaway echoes of long ago police statements. He wondered who the young woman was. Mid-twenties was a bit young as a seventy-year-old's companion.

The rest of the mail was junk except for a couple of letters, one from his mother and the other a postscript to the surveillance report.

Subject: Earlybird
Operator: Cooper
Subsequent to my report I have been able to ascertain that the previously unidentified young woman seen with subject was

not local. Her name was given to me as RACHEL MARIA AARONS and her nationality as GERMAN. Other background unknown but speaks fluent ENGLISH, GERMAN and RUSSIAN.
ENDS

Back at Lake Cottage, Julie gave Mathews a cup of tea in the kitchen and as he helped himself to sugar he said, 'Where is he?'

'He said he was going away for a couple of days.' She hesitated, then said, 'He seemed upset, I heard him moving around in the night. Have you two had a row about anything?'

'Not that I know of, Julie.' He smiled. 'We don't go in for rows. Anyway, there's nothing for us to have rows about.'

'What do you talk about with him?'

He shrugged. 'Just old times. The way things were a long time ago. Long before you were born. Long before I was born for that matter.' He paused. 'What made you think he was upset?'

'He didn't talk at all. It was as if his mind was far away. He didn't hear what I said when I spoke to him, tried to jolly him along. He always chats away at breakfast.'

'Did he ask where I was?'

'No. He didn't mention you.'

'Any idea where he was going?'

'No. Just gave me a list of people to phone to cancel things and say he was indisposed.'

'If he phones I'd like to talk to him. Maybe I could cheer him up.'

'I don't think so, Tim. I'll tell him but I think he wants to get away from all of us.'

'How much luggage did he take?'

'A travel bag and a holdall.'

'Don't worry, Julie. He's a very wise man. He'll be OK.'

'I hope you're right.'

Carling avoided all the VIP stuff at Gatwick but nevertheless travelled Business Class. He read a paperback version of Cyril Connelly's *The Unquiet Grave* and refused the offered tray of food and courtesy drinks. At Tegel he took a taxi into the city and signed in at The Savoy in Fasanenstrasse. The city was full of conventions but his title got him a suite on the first floor.

He sat in the comfortable armchair, his case and holdall on one of the single beds. He needed time to think. Talking day after day to Mathews had brought back memories that he hoped had long been buried. For them it was a matter of possible treason. For him it was a reminder of what had been the happiest days of his life. Maybe the only happy days of his life.

As he walked down the Kurfürstendamm later that evening it seemed strange that the burnt out Tiger tank was no longer half buried in the huge shell hole in front of Kempinski's.

TWO

CHAPTER 18

Even after the ruins of Hamburg, Berlin had been a shock. The Soviet tanks and artillery had systematically reduced every street, every building, to mountains of rubble, which were still there fifteen years after the war ended.

They'd allocated him a small apartment, two rooms, a kitchen and bathroom in one of the side streets of Savigny Platz, over what had been a fruit shop. The building had been saved from the blast by the taller buildings on either side that were now just a shell. There was electricity for Allied services four hours a day. Unfortunately there was no way of discovering which four hours it would be but the offices at the Olympiad had a permanent supply of both electricity and water and the officers' mess had reasonable supplies of food, but it was forbidden to buy locally produced food. There was little enough for the surviving Germans.

It was 1960 and nearly five years after he left Hamburg when Carling first saw Yuri again. There was still a pretence of co-operation between the occupying forces. It had been at a cocktail party given by the French. Yuri was wearing a well-cut olive-brown uniform with black riding boots and the three gold stars of a full colonel.

They avoided each other until they were in a group

of people waiting to claim their hats and coats from the tables that were serving as a cloakroom. As they stood shoulder to shoulder Yuri smiled and said softly, ' "*Zur letzten Instanz*" in an hour. Yes?' Carling nodded but didn't speak. The meeting place was a beer-house that had escaped the shells and the bombs. It was just inside the Russian Zone.

Yuri had changed into a civilian shirt and was waiting for him at a table in the garden at the side of the pub. He smiled as Carling sat down at the table.

'Nice to see you again, Georgi. How are you?'

'I'm OK. Congratulations on the double promotion.'

Yuri smiled. 'Just dressing up for the occasion. I'm still a major.'

'And still KGB?'

'Yes,' he smiled.

'What are you doing in Berlin?'

Yuri shrugged. 'I'm posted here in the hope that you'll go on helping us.'

'Helping you do what?'

'Helping us survive.'

'You won the war, Yuri.'

'But our cities all look like this.' He waved a hand at the city around them. 'The Americans want to break us economically and our old allies are wondering if it isn't a good time to wipe us off the map.' He paused. 'Twenty million Soviet people killed, our money spent on the war. It's a grim time. Believe me.'

'But how could I help you?'

'Just keep us informed.'

'About what?'

'Anything you learn about Western moves that are aggressive towards us. Economically, politically or militarily.'

Carling shook his head slowly. 'The war's over, Yuri. Without the war as the background I can't help you.'

'The war's not over. It's a cold war now.' He paused. 'The Soviet Union is the target of the most powerful government in the world. Not that long ago the American public were raising funds to support us, and Western governments were sending us guns and tanks. Today an American can be hounded out of his job – not for being a communist, but just for being suspected of being a member of the Party. Even knowing a communist can cause you to be ostracised by your friends or fellow workers. Nobody is free from suspicion. We were heroes and now, a few months' later, we are criminals. The American government took a long time before they put down McCarthy.'

'You haven't convinced me, Yuri.'

'We've always had a two-way deal, Georgi. You helped me and I helped you. I can still help you.'

'How do you know you can help me?'

Yuri smiled. 'We know that you are responsible for intelligence about the so-called Russian Zone. We don't have any love for our East German colleagues.'

For long moments Carling looked at Yuri. It was not just a handsome face but gentle, with smile creases at the eyes and an incipient dimple when he laughed.

'Ask me one thing that's really important to your people. Not to you but to your members.'

'No problem, Georgi. Are the West intending to invade our zone or our homeland?'

Carling looked surprised and shocked. 'Absolutely not. I've never heard even the most tentative suggestion of any aggressive action.' He smiled. 'But I have heard our people wondering why you have so many Red Army divisions around Magdeburg. There are those who wonder if your people might be thinking of coming over the border.'

It was Yuri's turn to look shocked. 'That's crazy. We moved troops from Leipzig and Dresden because the Magdeburg area is mainly farming. The big cities couldn't support our troops with food and accommodation. We didn't even send their tactical units with them.'

'Where are those units?'

'Still back in Leipzig and Dresden.' He paused. 'Maybe this is going too far but if you check carefully you'll find that there are no tanks or armoured cars with our troops. They are all in a vehicle park at Halle.' He paused. 'How did your people react?'

'They made contingency plans for if you came over the border.'

'Did you move troops?'

'No. We don't have enough fighting units to move around.' He shrugged. 'We demobilised most of our troops years ago. Our soldiers had had enough of the war.'

'Can I use what you've told me?'

'I guess so. Maybe you're right. Maybe we *should* keep in touch.'

Yuri leaned back, seemingly relieved. 'I won't go too far, Georgi. And it'll be a fair exchange, I promise you.' He waved his hand around at the tables. 'We can meet here or at my place, any time.' He reached in his pocket for a pen and scribbled two numbers on a piece torn off the bar menu. 'The top phone number's for my place, the bottom number will contact me twenty-four hours a day.' He paused and pushed forward his pen. 'Write down where I can contact you.'

Carling smiled. 'Let's leave it that I contact you.'

Yuri shrugged. 'Doesn't have to be business, Georgi. I always enjoyed your company.' He paused. 'I've just realised. Music, you're fond of music. I've got a few musician friends coming to eat with me tomorrow.' He smiled. 'Two local Germans, and two Czechs.' He laughed. 'All glad of a meal. Why don't you come?'

Carling shrugged. 'Why not? Where and when?'

'Seven o'clock.' He reached for the piece of paper with his telephone numbers and wrote his address and pushed it back across the table. Carling didn't recognise the street. 'Where is it?'

'It's off Alexanderplatz. The north-east corner. It was a block of flats. Mostly ruined but better than nothing.' He smiled. 'I'll look forward to that.'

Carling relaxed. 'So will I.'

The others were already there when Carling arrived. They were all a little younger than both he and Yuri. But from the moment he was introduced to Rachel Aarons he could barely speak. It took a glass of vodka to loosen his tongue. She wasn't just pretty, she was beautiful. Jet-black hair below her shoulders, heavy-lidded dark eyes, a neat nose and a full soft mouth. She was wearing a black silk dress that she said one of her aunts had given her. And she played the violin in a quartet that sometimes had to be a trio when the viola player was on duty as a policeman.

They ate sausages and bread, on plates on their laps, and Carling had brought a jar of coffee. Yuri had 'liberated' a banana each for the two girls. The talk was all of music and performers and they listened intently to Carling's picture of the music scene in London. None of them had either a radio or a gramophone; all they had was the usual musicians' gossip and the music they made themselves, even if it was no more than a piano transcription of some symphony. There was much talk of Wagner and Furtwängler.

It was Jan, one of the Czechs, who turned to Rachel Aarons. 'You're a Jew, Rachel. Should former Nazi musicians be allowed to perform in public now?'

'Of course. They're musicians first, and if they hadn't joined the Party Hitler or Goebbels would have probably had them thrown in jail.' She smiled. 'Being a musician is what matters, not whether you are a Party member . . .' she laughed '. . . or a Jew.'

Yuri joined in. 'The Furtwängler row is nothing to do with him or his membership of the Party. It's a public contest between the Soviet Kommandatura in Berlin, who want him to be the conductor of the Berlin Philharmonic which is now "ours" and the British and American Control Commissions, who insist on sticking by the rules. Furtwängler accepted the title of Prussian State Counsellor way back and that means it is mandatory that he has to go before the Denazification Commission.'

Carling said, 'Does that mean that you agree with our attitude, Yuri?'

'Of course. So do most Soviets in Berlin except for the bureaucrats.'

'And bureaucrats in the British and American sectors who want to apply the rules to annoy the Soviet authorities.' Rachel Aarons was at least smiling as she said it, but Yuri avoided looking at Carling, whom he had introduced just as a British officer.

Back in his apartment Carling tried to recall what Yuri's place was like, but all he could remember was the girl. It was almost midnight but he phoned Yuri's home number and arranged to see him at his rooms the next day.

Yuri's place was in a narrow alleyway not far from

the police station. The buildings on either side had been completely destroyed and Yuri's building was held up by massive wooden struts at an angle, cemented into the ground. In daylight it looked totally unsafe. Yuri's rooms were on the ground floor and the other rooms in the house were also occupied by Soviet officers of middle rank. In the bombed area at the side, a wooden hut had been constructed to house a diesel generator that supplied electricity for the whole house.

Carling could see the setting sun through the skeleton of a ruined building. It was big and glowing against the pale, misty blue of the sky. It reminded him of sunsets at the family home in Scotland. Sunsets that others saw as beautiful but for him always looked ominous and angry.

Yuri was at the open door, leaning, relaxed and smiling, his shoulder against the door frame. When they were in Yuri's room the Russian poured them both a fruit drink, passing a glass to Carling and raising his own, smiling as he said, 'Na zdrovia.'

Carling smiled and said, 'Slaintye.' When Yuri frowned, Carling laughed and said, 'It's Irish.' He paused. 'Who is she, Yuri?'

Yuri frowned. 'Who is who?'

'The girl who looks like Audrey Hepburn – Rachel Aarons.'

'You mean you've risked coming into our zone just to find out about a girl?'

'Not just a girl. A special girl.'

Yuri shook his head, smiling. 'I can't believe it. You had girlfriends in London and even more in Hamburg. I'm sure you slept with many of them but I can't think of one of them you'd have done this for.'

'So tell me about her.'

'Sit down, for God's sake, while I collect my thoughts.' As he sat down himself, Yuri said, 'Can I take it that your interest in the girl is personal, not professional?'

'Entirely personal.'

'You won't use her or involve her in any way in your work?'

'No. Never.'

'Well. Let's see. She's nineteen or twenty, I'm not sure which. Her father was German, her mother was Russian. She's now a resident of East Berlin. Speaks fluent German, Russian, English and French. Can get by in Czech and Hungarian.' He paused, thinking, and then he said, 'If she didn't live here she'd be playing violin for some major orchestra. She's had offers from America and England already.'

'Why didn't she take them?'

'Our East German colleagues wouldn't allow her to leave, even for one concert.' He smiled. 'They prefer athletes and gymnasts to musicians.'

'Tell me about her parents.'

Yuri sighed. 'A great example of the stupidity of politics. Her German father died from the effects of being in a concentration camp because he was a Jew. Her Russian mother died way back, worn out by worry and ill health. She gave music lessons to disabled people, Germans, here in Berlin. Rachel's father had been deputy chief of the main Berlin library. Neither of them belonged to or were interested in any political party. Educated and talented, they lived for their only child – your Rachel.'

'Why *my* Rachel?'

Yuri laughed softly. 'She asked me about you, so I guess I'll be right in the end.'

'What did she want to know about me?'

'Just background.'

'What did you tell her?'

'Nothing much. Son of an earl. British officer. Intelligent. Well off. Liked girls and music and all the other arts. Not formally political but had views on how the world should be run. Hopelessly sentimental views that would not work.' He smiled. 'Do you want to see her again?'

'Yes. Of course. Will she meet me?'

'I'm sure she will. But you'd have to use this place. She lives in a hostel and it's controlled by the local Party officials. Mean, puritanical bastards.' He shrugged. 'So when do you want to see her?'

'Tomorrow OK?'

'Sure. Let's make it early. Say six and then you can take her back into your zone and give her a meal somewhere.'

'That's great.' He paused. 'There's something I want to ask you, Yuri. Why did Moscow refuse Marshall Aid from the Americans? It was a generous gesture by the Americans and it looks aggressive to the rest of the world to refuse it.'

Yuri smiled. 'A condition of receiving payouts under Marshall Aid was that the country concerned would not claim reparations from the Germans. We are determined to make them pay for what they did to us. The conditions for Marshall Aid were insulting to the Soviet people.'

Carling shook his head slowly. 'Good old Virgil. "I fear the Greeks even when they bring gifts." '

Yuri laughed. 'An American said it better.'

'Who?'

'Tennessee Williams. "We have to distrust each other. It is our only defence against betrayal".'

'Sounds like Camino Real.'

'It is.'

'Are you sure she'll let me see her?'

Yuri shrugged. 'Pretty sure. It was obvious that she liked you from the way she asked about you and talked about you last night after you had gone.'

'Do I have any rivals?'

'She's very attractive so she has lots of men friends. But none of them is more than that.' He paused. 'So far as I know.'

'Thanks for letting me use your place.'

'You're welcome.'

CHAPTER 19

She was there, alone, when he got to Yuri's place. He had bought a small Blaupunkt radio for her on the black market; it had cost him two packets of Woodbines.

'Just so that you can hear some music,' he said as he gave it to her.

She looked at it carefully, turning it on and tuning it to different stations. Then she looked up at him, obviously delighted.

'What a wonderful gift. I'll be the envy of everyone at the hostel.' She smiled. 'I'll think of you when I'm listening to music.'

Despite the many ruined buildings still acting as grim reminders of the war, by 1960 Berliners had begun to build both industry and commerce. In the Western Zones there were reasonably well-stocked shops and several cinemas were showing American films. In the basements of ruined buildings there were dance-halls and a wide variety of restaurants and cafés. It was to one of these that Carling took Rachel Aarons that first evening. It was run by a Viennese couple and Carling was a favourite, not only as a regular customer who sometimes provided luxuries like real coffee, and sugar for their cakes, but because he could slip naturally into a Viennese accent and vocabulary. Earlier that day he had brought in candles for their table.

He had asked her about her family and she had told him of the pleasant civilised life they had recounted to her of before the war, and the turmoil of the war and after, when she was growing up. And Carling had told her about his parents, especially his mother from whom he had absorbed his love and knowledge of music. It had been an extraordinary evening. It was as if they had known each other for years. He tried not to use his training to probe about possible relationships with other men and he had been ridiculously pleased when she challenged him.

She laughed as she said, 'You're trying to find out if I have a steady boyfriend, aren't you?'

He smiled back. 'Yes. Was it so obvious?'

'Yes.' She laughed. 'I'm flattered.'

'Can I see you again tomorrow?'

'The quartet are playing at a local hall. You could come and hear us.'

'And I can see you afterwards?'

She smiled. 'Of course.' She paused. 'By the way, I expect you guessed from my name that I'm Jewish.'

He shrugged. 'I didn't, actually.' He smiled. 'It makes me wish I was Jewish.'

She laughed. 'I'm not religious. My father was, but my mother was a lapsed Catholic. Music was their religion. Jewish music sometimes affected my father, especially when I played Max Bruch's *Kol Nidrei*.' She smiled. 'It made him cry but he loved it.' She paused. 'With your Scottish connections I'll have to play you Bruch's *Scottish Fantasia*. That's quite sad music too.'

'Where were you when the war started?'

She laughed. 'I wasn't born when the war started. I came along in 1940. It was 1947 before we were together as a family again. My father was still in bad health when he was released from being in a concentration camp. My mother had moved from Dresden to Berlin a few months after the surrender so that she could be near where the camp prisoners were released. He was already in a hospital. When Mama died, father's sister came to look after us both. And father died last year.'

'Do you miss them?'

'Yes. But conditions have been so bad and there were always so many problems that there hasn't really been time to think about anything much except just surviving.'

He reached out to touch her hand. 'I'll try and make it better for you from now on.'

'You have already. This is the first time I've ever eaten at a restaurant.' She smiled across at him. 'I'm glad you asked me out. And I'm glad you want to see me again.'

'I'm a very lucky man starting tonight. No . . .' he said '. . . starting last night.'

He walked her back to her hostel and made arrangements for the next evening. He kissed her cheek and she was standing on the steps when he turned back to see if she was there. They waved to each other and he was the happiest man in Berlin.

The old man facing Carling across the small table had once been a member of the SPD, the left-wing party that had been taken over by the Communists in the Russian Zone but still functioned in West Germany. He was seventy-two years old, one of Carling's most useful informants. In 1953 the Russians had opened fire on workers protesting against the conditions in East Berlin and so far as Kurt Lang was concerned it was unforgivable. He had no family that could be used as hostages for pressure on him. Carling had persuaded him to join the Communist Party and act as an informant, and the old man was a shrewd observer of what was going on.

'They've created a new committee. They call it the Committee for Conserving Labour. It's run by a chap from Moscow but the rest are locals.' The old man looked at Carling. 'You need to watch that committee, my friend.'

'Why?'

'The Party's worried about all the skilled people who are slipping over to the West. It's getting to be a real embarrassment politically and economically. There's companies ready to pay a fortune to get hold of a skilled electrician, and toolmakers can get a flat thrown in. There's a lot of real criticism from Moscow. Threats of dismissals and worse. I was told there had been hints of jail sentences – enemies of the State and all that stuff.'

'Is it likely to affect us?'

'Who knows? I just wanted to warn you that they'll do something sooner or later to stop the flow of people into the West.'

Carling nodded in acknowledgement. 'My people have asked me for an opinion on what the ordinary people feel about the Berlin communists, and what they feel about their standard of living.'

The old man smiled. 'You got all day?'

They talked for three hours and Carling asked his man to come back with all the detail he could uncover about acts of nepotism and corruption by Party administrators. The Foreign Office information section was planning to mount a radio series on abuses by the Party in East Berlin.

Carling had informants in all walks of life in East Berlin and although he realised that he was witnessing and recording the skirmishes of the Cold War, he found it grindingly boring. He longed for someone, even someone on the other side, to show a spark of imagination, a gesture of faith in human beings. But as always in politics every day was given to moves and countermoves in the struggle to command people's minds and lives. If it had not been for Rachel he would have pressed for a posting to some more rewarding area. Not that he knew where that could be. Maybe he should consider resigning from SIS altogether. But what would he do for a living? He had not been raised or trained to oversee the family's assets.

All his free time was spent with Rachel Aarons and his work for SIS gave him every excuse and opportunity to spend his time in East Berlin. She knew now what his work was, but by a kind of osmosis rather than being told by him. He had never used her as a source of information. Amongst her circle of friends they were seen now as a couple. A few wondered why they didn't marry despite the administrative difficulties that would be raised by both sides' bureaucracies. But Carling was cautious about disturbing her life by what would amount to open defiance of both sides' tensions in the uneasy city. He believed that the Good Lord would send a sign when it was right to take that step. That they would marry was never in doubt for either of them. Life went on and they were happy enough.

At the year-end meeting in London to summarise the year 1960, it was agreed that it was not a good year for Western intelligence. Both in political terms and espionage, the Soviet's shooting down of the American U-2 plane well inside Soviet territories was the significant feature of the year. The sequence of events left both the White House and the CIA exposed to the world as both liars and inept fumblers in the intelligence business. There was no doubt that 1960 was Khrushchev's year.

Carling's report on personalities and conditions in East Berlin was praised for its information but criticised for not indicating what would happen in the next twelve months. They agreed with his view that Moscow was angry and frustrated that all their attempts to make the Western Allies withdraw from Berlin had failed. But what would Moscow's next move be? There had been long and indecisive discussions about using Carling's contacts for counterpropaganda but he had refused to allow his informants to be involved in any kind of direct espionage. They were informants, not agents, and most of his sources would dry up if they were asked to do anything even bordering on espionage. Their dislike or even hatred of the system didn't go as far as treason.

CHAPTER 20

On New Year's Day 1961 Rachel, thanks to some string-pulling by Yuri, moved into the luxury of a two-roomed apartment near St Nicholas' church. The Nikolaiviertel had been rebuilt to reflect, as near as the authorities could afford, the beautiful old buildings that had been ruined in just one half-hour midday raid by American Flying Fortresses. The new buildings housed shops and cafés as well as people, but in a harmony that satisfied those locals who could remember the historic quarter before the war.

With Rachel now independently accommodated they spent even more time together and on Easter Sunday he asked her to marry him. She had laughed, kissed him and said – 'When?'

'We'll have to do a bit of investigating.' He looked at her. 'It will mean you moving to our zone. Is that OK?'

She smiled. 'Like it says in the Bible – "Whither thou goest, I will go; and where thou lodgest, I will lodge." '

'Have you got any kind of passport?'

'No. Just my birth certificate.'

'I'll have to do some trading with Yuri. You'll need to have an identity card at least. And it will mean getting married in the British Zone.'

'Do your people know about me?'

He shook his head. 'No. So far as they are concerned, I just come over here to do research.'

She looked up at his face and said softly, 'Are you a spy?'

He sighed. 'There are no such things as spies. I'm an intelligence officer.'

'And Yuri?'

'He's the same as me. But he's KGB.'

'So why are you such good friends?'

He shrugged. 'We've known each other a long time. From the war. The Russians were our allies then. We helped each other.' He smiled. 'We kid ourselves that we can help keep the Cold War cold and not hot.'

She put up her lips and they kissed and then she said softly, 'I'll always remember today, Georgi. It's the best day of my life.'

'So far. There will be better days.' He smiled. 'Where shall we go to eat? How about our old friends at Mutter Hoppe?'

She slid her arms around his neck, looking up at him, smiling and happy. 'I love you so much, Georgi.'

He smiled and kissed her nose. 'I love you too, my dear.'

Her face looked solemn as she said, 'Shall we have children, Georgi?'

'Of course.' He hesitated. 'I mean if you want to.'

'Would you want to?'

He laughed. 'It would be great. I can't wait.'

'I'm two months' pregnant. I wasn't going to tell you.'

'Why not?'

'In case it was not what you wanted.'

'Don't be silly. Of course I want us to have a child. Are you OK? Have you been checked over properly?'

'Yes. I'm having another check in two weeks' time. Are you sure it's OK with you?'

His arms went round her and she knew that he meant what he said as he kissed her avidly.

CHAPTER 21

The meeting was in a room at Karlshorst, the Russians' command HQ in East Berlin and when Yuri was shown into the room he didn't recognise either of the officers sitting at the table.

They were both colonels, one with infantry insignia and one an artillery officer. Yuri guessed that the insignia were probably spurious. Just used to conceal their real status.

The older man introduced himself as Litvak and the other man as Panov.

'Tell me about this man Carling.'

'I've been working with him since our days in Hamburg. He has always been reliable.'

'How much do you pay him?'

'He's never been paid.'

'So what is it? Girls, young boys or what? Don't tell me he's a communist.'

'He first contacted our London embassy during the war to express his appreciation of our struggle against the Germans. Since I took him over we have just exchanged general information.'

'About what?'

'My reports are all on file, comrade colonel.'

'About what? You tell me. I don't ever trust reports. For

me reports are there to cover the writer's arse if anything goes wrong, meantime a bit of publicity in the hope of promotion.'

Yuri was tempted to point out that they were not KGB officers and he wasn't ready to accept casual insults from unknown men. But he held his tongue.

'We discuss the reality of things in the media that are attempts to stir up tensions between our two countries.'

'You mean all you do is no more than gossip about gossip?'

'No, comrade. I mean exactly what I said.'

'Can you tell him what you want him to find out for you?'

'No.'

'Why not?'

'Because that's not the way we work. He is not my agent and I am a contact not his controller. And the same applies to me.'

'Is he worth the time you spend on him?'

'I leave that to my senior officers to decide. I've been under instructions to keep a close relationship with him.'

'Does he make critical comments on our regime?'

'About the same as I do about his government. We aren't political.' He half smiled. 'No dialectic from me and no *Daily Telegraph* from him.'

He saw a quick smile on Panov's face and then Litvak said, 'I'll contact Belinkov. It's up to him but I like to get my own impression face-to-face of what's going on.'

Yuri drove back slowly to KGB HQ in Normannenallee where Belinkov was waiting for him.

Pointing to a chair, Belinkov said, 'I've just had Litvak on the phone, shitting his pants about Carling's problems.'

'Did he oppose my proposals?'

Belinkov shrugged. 'Just putting down a marker to protect himself if anything went wrong.'

'He controls the police and the local politicians. Could be a nuisance if he chose to be.'

Belinkov shook his head dismissively. 'I'll deal with him.' He paused. 'It's too good an opportunity for us to miss, Yuri. He'd *have* to co-operate.'

'I still don't like it. It seems a poor reward for his help and goodwill towards us.'

'D'you want somebody else to handle it?'

'He wouldn't go along with any of it if it was somebody else.' He paused and hesitated before he said quietly, 'We are good friends with years of proven trustworthiness behind us. It's more than just an informer contact. Are we ready to lose that?'

'Of course not, but Moscow are involved now. They see this as an incredible opportunity.'

'Opportunity for what?'

'To have our own man right inside SIS.'

'Even hint at that and we'll lose him for good.'

'It's a risk worth taking, Yuri. And the success will all be down to you.'

'And if it fails? Who carries the can then?'

'You won't fail, Yuri. You won't fail.'

'I shall need co-operation from a lot of officials.'

'You'd get it but you must string him along for at least three months.' He shrugged. 'After that we'll see.'

By the end of May Yuri was telling Carling that he was having no success with the East German authorities. They were raising difficulties about issuing Rachel with an identity card and they had said that any application to be allowed to leave their zone would have to go before a commission that met very infrequently.

As they moved into June, Carling decided that he would have to try alternative ways of arranging their marriage. It was at that point that he started listing Rachel Aarons as an informant on his official list. He had told none of his colleagues of his love affair and because he operated virtually independently of the SIS setup in Berlin there was little on the record of any of his informants. But there might soon be a time when he would need to use his official status to get things done. Helping an informant could be seen as a reasonable reward for past co-operation.

He was uncertain too about the wisdom of letting it be known that he was proposing to marry a German. Especially a German from the Russian Zone. And who could he get to officiate at their marriage? There were padres attached to several British units but they would probably want to check that his marriage to a German was authorised, especially as he was an SIS officer. He would have to check if a marriage performed by a German pastor was equally valid in the UK.

What worried him most was his feeling that Yuri's attitude was changing. He seemed uneasy about something. They still met regularly and exchanged information but he sensed that Yuri was now looking for information that he must know Carling was not going to reveal.

Carling had past favours he could cash in on in both zones and he reluctantly decided that he should go ahead and deal with his problems with his own resources.

It was the end of June when he received notification of his promotion to the SIS grade equivalent to a lieutenant-colonel in recognition of the work he was doing in the Russian Zone.

Pastor Franks was in his sixties. He had been cleared by a denazification panel. He had been a padre to a Wehrmacht artillery unit but had never, despite a lot of pressure, become a member of the Nazi Party. At the end of his second meeting with Pastor Franks, Carling's instinct was that the priest was both sympathetic and unconventional enough to be told most of the truth. On the third visit the pastor listened in silence to Carling's story.

When he had finished Pastor Franks said, 'Why go to all this trouble when you could tell your superiors exactly what you have just told me?'

Carling shrugged. 'Because I know they would never give me permission to marry a German because of my job. Especially a girl from the other side.'

'How could they stop you?'

'First of all I would be posted to some other country. Probably South America or an Arab country.' He sighed. 'They are powerful people, there are a lot of other things that they could do.'

'Like what?'

Carling shrugged. 'Harassment of the girl maybe.'

'Sounds like the Gestapo.'

Carling shook his head. 'These are the means that all intelligence organisations have at their disposal. They don't always do anything. The threat or the expectation is usually enough.'

Pastor Franks nodded. 'You must love this girl a lot. Does she love you as much herself?'

'Yes. Absolutely.'

'Well, let's look at some of the facts. First of all, a marriage in Berlin or anywhere else by a genuine priest is valid anywhere in Europe. I have married several British soldiers to German girls because that was what the girls' parents wished. But, of course, the soldiers concerned have had permission from their commanding officers to both marry and to marry here in Germany. It's over fifteen years since the war ended.' He smiled. 'We Germans are being allowed to be part of Europe again. So the ceremony itself is no problem.

'However, there are other problems. I should need some official identification for your girl and a permit for her leaving the Russian Zone. And, of course, a permit from the British for her to be a resident of the British Zone for seven days before the marriage.'

Carling was silent for long moments and then he said, 'One way or another I could fix all those things.' He paused. 'Would the marriage still be valid if it were found at some later date that some document was not genuine?'

Pastor Franks smiled. 'I thought you might ask me that. Let us say that provided the documents concerned looked genuine to me when I was shown them, that would be enough. And once you two are married not even the joint efforts of the Kremlin and Whitehall could invalidate it. You will be married in the eyes of the Good Lord and that is all that matters, even in these ungodly times.'

'Will you marry us then?'

'Yes. Of course.'

They had talked for over an hour and Kurt Lang had said it again and again.

'They're up to something. I don't know what it is but they're having secret meetings. Some of them seem scared of whatever it is. But mark my words, my friend, they're going to do something that scares them, and that scares me too.'

'Is it going to mean another Berlin airlift, d'you think?' asked Carling.

Kurt Lang shrugged. 'I just don't know.'

'There's something I wanted to ask you, Kurt. Can you get me a blank identity card and a permit to leave the Russian Zone?'

'The ID card I can get you for cash.'

'How much?'

'Forty dollars last time I heard.'

'And the permit?'

'I've never ever seen one but I'll ask around. Would a photocopy do?'

'Better than nothing. How long would it take?'

'The ID I could get you in a week. The other I just don't know.'

'I've got a Leica IIIb, if that would help.'

'I'll come back to you on that.'

The French had their usual party for 14 July and Carling had used it to talk to Yuri. They stood in the evening sunshine of the garden identifying the guests one by one.

Yuri frowned. 'Who's the girl with Barrault?'

'She's his mistress. I can't remember her name. She's a nurse at their military hospital.'

'But I thought that young German girl, Ursula, was his mistress.'

'Yuri, you bring your French mistress to Bastille Day parties, not your German one – even if she is prettier.'

'Are you going back to Rachel's place after this?'

'Yeah.'

'I can give you a lift if you want.'

'OK. About half an hour after the speeches, yes?'

'Suits me, comrade.'

Carling laughed. 'Don't comrade me. I'm not a bloody comrade and never will be.'

'Aren't we heroes any more, Georgi?'

Carling smiled. 'Just people, Yuri. Same as the rest of us.'

On their way back in Yuri's battered BMW, Carling said, 'You know that Rachel's pregnant, don't you?'

'I guessed she was. She didn't tell me. When's it due?'

'Round about October.'

'I still haven't had any luck with the Identity Card.'

Carling shrugged and said nothing. But he knew then that something was wrong. It wouldn't have taken even a day for Yuri to arrange for an ID card for Rachel. But it didn't matter any longer. Kurt Lang had come up with one, and Hermann Stahl who used to forge documents for the *Sicherheitsdienst* was completing it for him including the official stamp and a beautiful forgery of the correct signature. It was back-dated a month and valid for two years. But why wasn't Yuri co-operating? Maybe Yuri was out of favour and didn't want to take even small risks. Or maybe their contact was no longer considered useful by Moscow.

As he walked back later that night through the Brandenburg Gate to his place after seeing Rachel, he decided to put in for some of his overdue leave. When they had fixed the date for her to come over to the British Zone he'd claim leave from two days before. He'd been given two dates by the pastor for the wedding. Saturdays, 19 and 26 August. He would book a flight for them for the same night and they would spend a few days in London. When a specialist had checked her over they'd rent an apartment and she would stay there until the baby was due. And he would stay as long as he could. If he had to go back to Berlin before the baby arrived, he would claim more leave and get back to her.

Kurt Lang had not only got a genuine blank exit permit but also a photocopy of a cancelled copy that Hermann Stahl could use as a reference. Carling looked at the old man. 'I'm very grateful, Kurt. Will the Leica be enough?'

The old man smiled. 'You can keep your Leica, my friend. It cost nothing.'

'I don't understand.'

He rolled up his sleeve and pointed. 'There are still people who count this as something that matters.' He was pointing at the tattooed numbers on the inside of his thin, pale wrist.

There were tears in Carling's eyes as he looked back to the old man's face.

'I don't know how to thank you, Kurt. I really don't.' He paused. 'There must be something.'

The old man smiled. 'You remember Kurt Schumacher, ex-Reichstag deputy for the SPD, ex-concentration camp victim and now head of the West German SPD?'

'Yes, of course. I met him once. He was living near Hanover then.'

'He still does.' He nodded. 'So get me a signed photo of him.'

'That's dangerous for you to have, Kurt. You know that.'

'I'm too old to care about those bastards. I just want to have it. I won't put it up on the wall.'

'OK. I'll get it for you. It may take a couple of weeks to make contact.'

'No problem.' He shrugged. 'Time is what I've got.'

'I'm in your debt, Kurt. I won't forget it.'

CHAPTER 22

Carling began to wonder if he was becoming slightly paranoid. He had seen the man on the motorcycle so many times in the last few days. Always in East Berlin. But the man and the girl he had seen only in the British Zone. The number on the motorcycle had been changed several times but Carling knew enough about motorcycles to be sure that it was always the same 350 cc BMW. A model made just before the war, when BMW held the world's motorcycle speed record. The rider was a man in his late twenties and whoever had instructed him on how to carry out surveillance from a motorcycle had been singularly inexpert.

The couple were about his own age. The man was well-built, balding at the front, with red hair. The shoes he wore weren't German, neither were his clothes. The jacket was a good tweed and the chinos looked new. The girl wasn't pretty but she wore quite modish clothes and what looked like an expensive wristwatch. Carling tried dodging them on a couple of occasions and although he lost them he saw them again ten minutes or so later. They spent too much time looking in the windows of shops that were closed.

Yuri and he had always had an unwritten deal. Neither of them would put the other under surveillance. And if their colleagues arranged a surveillance the other man would be warned. There had been no such warning from Yuri.

Perhaps it was just a coincidence. The sightings weren't all that frequent but from the instincts that came from his training Carling sensed that something was wrong. Or different. Even Yuri's rather distant attitude seemed like a warning.

But none of it really mattered. He saw Rachel every day and he had never been so happy. He had bought her a ring from an old Polish woman who dealt in fine jewellery from the back of a junk shop near the zoo. It was a single diamond with a beautiful claw setting.

All the occupiers of the city of Berlin insisted on exercising their free rights of access to all zones including the Russian Zone. Mainly these rights were exercised formally and without deliberate provocation. Allied officers in uniform were seldom challenged and then only by the Russians. German civilians frequently lived in the Russian Zone and worked in one of the Western zones. Carling seldom wore uniform.

Twice he had phoned both of Yuri's numbers but there was no response and he decided to go to his place to see if there was some problem.

The main door at the top of the steps was open and he rang the bell on Yuri's door, the first inside the hallway. But there were no sounds from inside. Almost without thinking he put his hand on the door-knob and turned it. The door opened and he called out, 'You there, Yuri?'

There was no reply and he walked into the room, closing the door behind him. As he looked around he saw that the room was not only empty but it had been stripped. Even the single naked lightbulb had gone. He could hear the sounds of children playing in the street and he knew something was wrong. Very wrong.

It seemed a long walk to Rachel's place and he decided not to tell her about what had happened. Why worry her? In another week she would be with him on the other side. Everything was arranged. On 19 August they would be married and that was all that mattered. He took her across to the British Zone for a meal and then to a showing of Antonioni's *La Notte*. He had half a mind to take her to his place for the night but decided against it. Keep to the routine. Take no risks. His leave had been agreed and left open for him to decide when to take it. In two days' time he would warn his main informants that he would not be around for a week or more.

He used an official car from the pool to take her home and on the way back he told the driver to drop him at the Brandenburg Gate and, despite the rain, he walked the rest of the way.

As Carling opened the door of his flat he saw an envelope on the mat inside. It was addressed to 'C'. He opened it slowly and took out the slip of paper inside. It just said, '*Sonntag – Mauer*': 'Sunday – wall'. He didn't understand it and he crumpled it in his hand and tossed it into the metal basket by his desk as he reached for the phone and dialled Yuri's numbers. There was still no answer at either of them. He took the crumpled paper from the basket and smoothed it as flat as it would go. It was handwritten in ink, in old-fashioned German script. For long minutes he looked at it, even slanting it against the light to check if there was a microdot. But there was nothing. And it meant nothing to him. It must have been delivered by hand, there was no stamp and no postmark. It reminded him of a note written by a suspect KGB line-crosser caught in Göttingen. He'd said he had information that he was afraid to talk about. He'd offered to write it down. The message said,

'Die Russen sind im besitz ein halbes Litre von schweres Wasser': 'The Russians are in possession of half a litre of heavy water.' He had assumed the man was mentally ill until a month later when he had heard on the BBC news that heavy water was used in making atom bombs. It was revealed that the German plant for manufacturing heavy water had been the target of a commando raid in Norway. The suspect line-crosser had long been released. But the possibilities that he had let go by still haunted him.

The next day, Saturday, he had picked up Rachel from her place mid-morning and they had spent the afternoon at Grunewald on the banks of the Havel river. An enterprising woman had set up a stall selling coffee and sandwiches near the Kaiser Wilhelm Tower and they had stayed until late afternoon. In the evening the quartet were playing at a student concert at the university building. Schubert and Beethoven.

After the concert, which was a great success, Carling took Rachel for dinner at the Austrian place where she was now as welcome a customer as he. It was a day of sunshine and music and when they kissed goodbye he said, 'It's going to be like this every day of our lives.' They were to be married the following Saturday.

At midnight on Saturday, 12 August 1961 all the S-Bahn trains travelling from East to West Berlin stopped running. East German police and Stasi men were checking the papers of all passengers. West Berliners were allowed to continue their journey on foot and East Berliners were told to go back home. The confused passengers, as they walked out of the various stations, were alarmed when they saw the streets full of troop carriers and armoured cars along the sector boundary. And behind the armoured vehicles were Soviet tanks.

There were workmen working under floodlights tearing up cobblestones and paving slabs and manoeuvring tank traps to block off the streets. Those who ventured as far as the Brandenburg Gate watched jackhammers digging holes for concrete posts to carry barbed wire. It was obviously a well-planned operation being implemented with military precision.

When the phone rang he switched on the bedside light and glanced at his watch, 02.50 hours. He picked up the phone.

'Carling.'

'It's MacIntyre, George. You'd better get down to the Brandenburg Gate. Your people over the other side have gone amuck.'

'What are you on about, Mac. What people?'

'The East Germans. They've closed the Gate. They're building a bloody great wall. Tanks, guns, the lot. They say they're closing the whole border of their zone.'

'Have we got anyone there?'

'Who knows? It's chaotic here. London are raising hell. I'm just manning the phones.'

There were lights everywhere and it was as bright as day. There were Russian tanks lined up with guns levelled and pointing straight down Strasse des 17 Juni, the former Charlottenburg Chaussee renamed as a memorial to the East German workers killed by Soviet troops when they protested against conditions in East Berlin. There were other tanks fanning out to cover the Tiergarten, and hundreds of men and dozens of cranes laying huge concrete blocks along Ebert Strasse as far as the eye could see.

He could see Soviet officers moving from group to group and long lines of lorries all the way down Unter den Linden to beyond the university block. The noise of generators, the engines of lorries and the building machinery was deafening but beyond the lights West Berlin police and British military police were pushing back the crowds of civilians who were beginning to arrive as the word spread of what was happening.

As Carling pushed aside one of the metal barriers that had been put up, he was stopped by a Military Police major who asked for his ID. As he handed it back the major said, 'They've told me they have orders to fire on anyone who goes beyond the barriers.'

'What's the idea of closing the Gate?'

'Their liaison chap told me they're doing this along the whole of their zone border with us. No movement is going to be allowed in or out either way.'

'You mean permanently?'

'Seems like it. The wall here could take anything we could throw at it except for artillery.'

'What are we doing about it?'

'They've called a meeting of the Control Commission later today but from the way they're talking over the other side they won't budge an inch. The Red Army officers I talked to said if we attacked the wall in any way it would be treated as an attack on the Soviet Union.'

'D'you think they mean it?'

'I'm bloody sure they do. They were shit-scared, I tell you. They think the East Germans might turn on them if there was any fighting.' He shrugged. 'Anyway, don't go near them.'

By then the crowd numbered thousands. Shouting, jeering and booing the men working on the wall. From time to time a Russian officer used a loud-hailer, speaking in rough German, warning that anyone coming beyond the barriers would be shot. And whenever he spoke the gunners on the machine-guns that were now in place under the Tower would fan the barrels of their weapons in arcs across the crowds.

And as he stood there Carling remembered Kurt Lang's constant warning that the Russians and their East German stooges were going to do something to stop the flow of workers to the West. And he knew now what the note meant. It must have been a last-minute attempt by old Kurt to warn him.

There was no point in waiting around. He needed to find out what was going to happen. It was a deliberate provocation by the Russians and it wasn't going to be easy to ignore it. The Western allies could lose face with the Germans if they backed down. But nobody in the West would relish starting World War Three. Sunday, 13 August 1961 was going to be a milestone in many people's lives. For Carling only one person mattered and no matter how he would do it he was going to get her into West Berlin.

At SIS's offices at the Olympiad Stadium Carling had been congratulated for the warnings he had given about some impending action by the East Germans to stop the flow of skilled people to the West, but his mind was on what to do about Rachel.

In the evening he went again to the Brandenburg Gate. There were groups of people still watching the work going on but the big crowds had gone, afraid of what they saw and afraid of what might be about to happen.

There were tanks and armoured vehicles on both sides now and there was a group of senior officers, British, American, French and Soviet talking at a spot where one of the barriers had been removed. Both the War Office and

Whitehall had decided to take no retaliatory action. Let the West Germans see what the Soviets were really like, with their East German puppets ready to turn East Berlin into a prison camp for their citizens.

At a meeting of the Occupying Powers in the afternoon, an agreement had been reached by threats and counterthreats from both sides on a rough and ready *modus vivendi*. The memorial to the Red Army soldiers who had lost their lives in the battle for Berlin was in the British Zone. A Soviet honour guard, changed twice daily, would be allowed to mount guard on the memorial. Two Soviet Jeeps would be allowed access to the Western Zone daily on a prescribed route and after a formal check at a checkpoint to be erected that night. Soldiers of the three Western occupiers would be given unchecked access to East Berlin in uniform but only in vehicles, without stopping, and with no contact with civilians. This protocol would be observed until further meetings at top level could decide on future access and restrictions. For two weeks no civilians from either side would be allowed access to the other zone. After that time, access would be by certain agreed checkpoints, with identities and reasons for movement subject to a check and interrogation. Civilian access would be strictly limited.

For no particular reason Carling walked back to the Olympiad, just because the activity there gave him a feeling of security. There were things that could be done but he would have to think about it carefully.

The phone was ringing as he opened the door of his place and when he lifted it there was silence at the other end. He hung up and seconds later it rang again. When he picked it up the voice was familiar.

'If you recognise my voice don't mention my name.'

'Go on.'

It was Yuri Porenski.

'We should meet.'

'Where? And when?'

'At the barrier at the Gate. In an hour. But in civilian clothes.'

'OK.'

He hung up without waiting for an answer. He knew then why Porenski had been avoiding him. He would have known about the wall that was going up. And that meant he was no longer to be trusted. But maybe he could be used.

Carling saw Yuri straightaway. He was standing on the fringe of a TV camera crew right up against one of the metal barriers. As he approached Yuri he heard the Russian say softly, 'Where in your zone? Say it quickly.'

'Back entrance to Kempinski's. When?'

'About half an hour. Move away. Now.'

There were two taxis parked on the rank outside the rear entrance to Kempinski's and Carling stood between the two cabs watching for Yuri. He came five minutes later, hurrying round the corner from the Kudamm and walking through the open doors to the reception area in the hotel. Carling waited for another five minutes to make sure that Yuri was alone.

Inside, Yuri was sitting in an armchair, half rising as he saw Carling come in and walk over to him. Carling sat on a leather couch facing the Russian.

'What is it you want, Porenski?'

'Can we talk somewhere else? Somewhere less public.'

'About what?'

'About you and me. And the girl.'

'You knew about the barbed wire and the wall, didn't you?'

'Yes. But there was no way I could warn you.'

'Don't give me that bullshit. You phoned me tonight. You could have phoned me days ago.'

'I've been a virtual prisoner.'

'Did you put me under surveillance?'

'Not me. That was people above me. I had no part in it.'

'Did you tell them about our deal? No shadowing on either side?'

'Yes. I told them.'

'And?'

Yuri shrugged and looked at him. 'They don't care about such things.'

'Was it the young couple?'

'I don't understand?'

'The surveillance team. Was it a young couple?'

'No. Our man was on a BMW motorcycle.'

'So how did you get to be a prisoner?'

'Because of my relationship with you.'

'Tell me more.'

'They see you as a great catch. They want you to go much further with them.'

'Further? What's that mean?'

'They want you committed to us. Hard information.'

'They must be crazy. Didn't you tell them I'd never go along with that?'

Yuri looked away for several moments and then looked back at Carling. 'Yes. I told them. But they said you would have no choice.'

'Go on.'

'First they could threaten that if you didn't co-operate they would make an anonymous call to your people at the Olympiad and tell them you were spying for us and had been for years.'

Carling shook his head. 'The information you gave to me and the opinions I passed on to you are all in my reports. It was my job to talk to you. I told you nothing you couldn't have worked out for yourselves if your people only bothered to learn about the West.' He paused. 'You said first – let's hear secondly.'

Yuri shook his head. 'I couldn't bring myself to say it, my friend. I'd rather you met them and heard it for yourself.'

'Who is "them"?'

'The head of the KGB in East Berlin.'

'Why should it make any difference who says whatever it is you people want to say to me?'

'Because you probably won't believe it if it's just me telling you.' He looked at Carling. 'Don't you understand? They're not playing games. They mean what they say and they'll do it, believe me, they'll do it.'

Yuri's voice was shrill and he put his hands to his face, his head bent, his body rocking backwards and forwards as if he were in pain.

There were passing people, waiters and guests, who looked at the strange figure in the armchair. Carling leaned forward and said, 'You'd better come back to my place. Come on.'

He stood up, lifting Yuri by his arm, to his feet, then leading him out into Fasanenstrasse heading back towards Savigny Platz. As they walked through the almost empty streets, Carling tried to put aside in his mind the thoughts that were gathering there. Thoughts that didn't bear thinking about but wouldn't go away.

Yuri had never been to Carling's place before and he looked uncomfortable as he sat at the kitchen table facing Carling.

'Did your people order you to contact me?'

'Yes.'

'To do what?'

Yuri sighed. 'To give you a message.'

'From whom?'

'From the KGB in East Berlin.'

'But who? What's his name?'

'Does that really matter?'

'Yes.'

'He's my boss. His name's Belinkov. Nikolai. He's a full colonel.'

Carling nodded. 'And you're going to make things difficult for me and Rachel if I don't co-operate the way you want. Yes?'

'Something like that.'

'Go on.'

'They've put her under protective custody.' As he saw the anger on Carling's face he said hurriedly. 'She's not in jail. They've moved her to a house under guard.'

'You won't leave here, Yuri, until she's been released.'

'Georgi, if you arrest me and shove me in jail they wouldn't give a damn. I'm expendable. And it would mean that they'd just apply more pressure to you through the girl.' He paused. 'Remember she's pregnant. Due to have the child in late October. She'll be well cared for if you co-operate.'

'And if I don't?'

Yuri shrugged helplessly. 'You know what they're like. The only way they can get at you is through the girl. They'll give her a hard time. She'd be in prison. Enemy of the State and all that stuff. And they'd put the child in a State orphanage.'

For long moments Carling was silent and then he said, 'When can I see Belinkov?'

Yuri fumbled at the inside pocket of his jacket and pulled out a card, checking it before he handed it to Carling.

'You can contact me twenty-four hours a day on that number. He'll see you any time you want. It's that important.'

'How do I get past all the barbed wire?'

'From tomorrow morning there'll be a checkpoint at Friedrichstrasse. It won't be in use for a week but it will be manned. You'll have to come in civilian clothes and on foot. I'd be there every day with a car.'

Carling stood up. 'I'll think about it.'

Yuri looked relieved. 'I hate all this, Georgi, I really do.'

'You don't hate it enough, my friend. You can always refuse to go along with it.'

'And then they'd shoot me.'

'Yuri, they'll shoot you in the end when they've got no more use for you. Just so you can't talk about what they've been up to.' He paused. 'Can you make your own way back to the barbed wire?'

'I guess so.'

Willy Brandt, the mayor of Berlin, was on a train between Nuremberg and Kiel when he got the news of what had happened and he flew back to Berlin immediately. He was angered by the complete confusion of the Allied military authorities and even more angered that the Federal Government in Bonn was just avoiding any reaction. All his calls to Adenauer went unanswered. His public statements were forceful and emotional, but only he spoke up. It was as if those responsible were paralysed into inaction. Meantime the Wall was growing higher and longer by the hour.

One of Carling's most valuable talents in his work with SIS had always been his ability to get to the heart of any problem. Cutting away the inessentials to identify what really mattered. Then deciding what had to be done. But faced with this personal problem it was not so easy. He knew from the start that he'd have to go along with their demands until he could find a better solution, but he also knew that he would demand certain conditions no matter how hard they pressured him. He spent all of one day deciding what those conditions would be and they gradually became clear.

Twice he was called to meetings at the Olympiad about the situation concerning the Wall. He had given his comments on both long-term and short-term reactions to the Soviet moves. He emphasised, and his was a lone voice, that the Wall must have been approved by Moscow and that Khrushchev himself must have given his own approval. It was East German thinking but done with Soviet blessing. He stressed that in his opinion Moscow would certainly not back down and that all Allied retaliation should be aimed at the East Germans.

CHAPTER 23

The checkpoint was a builder's asbestos cabin and there were steel rods sticking up from the road to prevent any vehicle short of a tank from forcing its way through.

Yuri was there as arranged but the car was parked a couple of hundred yards away. It was a Russian Zil with no number plates and a civilian driver. After a few minutes Carling realised that they were headed for the Soviet military HQ in Karlshorst.

When they arrived Carling was checked at two guard boxes and it was obvious that he was expected. He was treated politely but the body searches were efficient.

A pleasant young woman in uniform escorted them to Belinkov's office. It was a large room with a long table with seven chairs each side. Belinkov was waiting at the door. He smiled amiably as he led them to where several chairs were placed around a low, circular coffee table.

Carling had been in the intelligence game too long to imagine that all KGB officers looked like the villains in American gangster films. They were just men. Some good, some bad. But you shouldn't trust even the good ones.

Belinkov waited until they were all seated and then smiled as he said, 'You must forgive me, I looked you up in *Who's Who* but I don't know whether I should address you as Lord, Earl or Viscount. Which should it be?'

Carling shrugged. 'My name is Carling and I'm a lieutenant-colonel in the Intelligence Corps.'

Belinkov nodded, still smiling. 'OK. Let's get down to business. As you can imagine, Yuri Porenski has kept me informed about your mutual chats. They have been useful, I think, to both sides.' He waved his arms. 'Preventing unnecessary friction, explaining another point of view. And I've been much impressed by your basic thinking. I know you are not an admirer of our Soviet system but you seem to have a balanced eye.' He paused. 'And we don't forget that kind letter you sent to our Ambassador in London way back in the war. It was a generous gesture. Much appreciated. As I think Yuri has explained, we want to ask you to go just a step further with us.' He smiled. 'To help us avoid making silly mistakes—'

Carling interrupted. 'Colonel, we don't need to go into motives and justification. We are both in the same business. We all do things that make us ashamed of the business we're in. We all do things that would make us look like criminals to a normal person. What you are doing so far as I am concerned is blackmail. Let us not pretend otherwise. If I don't do what you want you will make the life of my fiancée a misery. Harassment, prison, who knows what depths you would sink to? So let us cut out the bullshit and find out what is left.'

Belinkov nodded. Not smiling now. 'Agreed. So how do we go about it?'

'I've made a list of my demands but there is one thing that you have to understand right from the start.' He paused. 'I will not – repeat not – ever supply information that could cost one of our men his life. Do you accept that?'

'Who would be the judge of that?'

'Me.'

'OK. I understand your attitude. Please go on.'

Carling reached into his jacket pocket and pulled out a sheet of paper and handed it to Belinkov.

'My typing is not very good but please ask me if there is anything you don't understand.'

Belinkov nodded as he unfolded the typed sheet. The room was silent for several minutes before he looked up at Carling.

'Tell me. What would you do if I said that these conditions were not acceptable?'

'Nothing?'

'Really? But we could just hold you here as a prisoner. You could be in the Lubyanka in Moscow by this time tomorrow.'

Carling smiled, shaking his head. 'That would be very stupid, Colonel. Before I went to the checkpoint I posted a letter to my home, addressed to me. To await my arrival. In it I have given details of all my dealings with Yuri and the details of this meeting. If I was absent from my room in West Berlin and my office for two days they would start looking for me. As the days went by they would widen the search to my home and they would find the letter.' He paused. 'You might end up in the Lubyanka with me.'

Belinkov raised his eyebrows. 'I don't think so, my friend. But you have a point.' He paused and then said briskly, tapping the typed paper he was still holding, 'I accept your conditions.'

'All of them?'

'Yes. I'm not sure about the marriage but I'll check on it.'

'It has to be before the child is born.'

'Of course.'

'So tell me your first enquiry of me.'

'I would like details of all people serving SIS in West Berlin. Names and responsibilities.'

'That will take about a week.' He paused. 'When do I see my girl?'

Belinkov looked quizzically at Yuri who shrugged. Belinkov said, 'How about you arrange an afternoon meeting here next week? You bring the details and Yuri takes you to see the girl.'

'No. That won't do.'

'Why not?'

'I have asked for a weekly meeting with my girl. It's one of the conditions you agreed to. I don't want my meetings to be related to when I provide information. It may take weeks sometimes to get you what you want.'

The Russian shrugged. 'OK. When do you want to see her?'

'Tomorrow.'

'OK. Fix it with Yuri on your way back in the car.' He stood up. 'We have both been in this business for a long time. I think we can have a friendly relationship.'

Carling nodded. 'Let's see how it goes.' He paused. 'When can you let me know about the marriage?'

Again Belinkov looked at Yuri.

Yuri said, 'It'll only take a few days. Some time next week.'

Carling nodded at Belinkov and then followed Yuri out of the office.

As they walked together down the corridor Carling made the arrangements with Yuri to see Rachel the next day. They were to meet at the checkpoint at 6 p.m. It had been one of Carling's conditions that he saw her once a week for a minimum of two hours, and alone.

There was a TV crew taking shots of the temporary checkpoint and Carling had stood in the checkpoint cabin with Yuri until they had packed up their gear and gone. As he waited his mind was on the information that Belinkov wanted. The names and status of the SIS detachment in West Berlin could have been put together in a week by any intelligence organisation that knew its business. Just the gossip at diplomatic cocktail parties would do it. He knew who all his opposite numbers were in the CIA, French intelligence and the German station of the BND in Berlin. The KGB problem was that most of them were such obvious thugs that nobody ever invited them to semi-official parties. They didn't understand the West. They didn't even understand their own East Germans.

It was dark when Carling finally strolled through the gate avoiding the tangle of barbed wire on each side. He thought about having coffee and a sandwich at the Austrian place on the way back, but decided not to. They would ask why Rachel wasn't with him and he didn't want to be reminded of that. He looked up at the sky. It was dark blue with no clouds and the moon was full, gentle, glowing and peaceful. It made him think of Puccini's aria, 'O Silver Moon'. And that too made him think of Rachel.

CHAPTER 24

'She's got a small house actually in the Tierpark. It used to be the head keeper's house. It's quite pleasant and I think she likes it.'

'It doesn't worry you, that, Yuri? Making a prisoner out of a friend?'

Yuri shrugged. 'I carry out my orders just like anyone else.' He paused. 'What did you think of Belinkov?'

'No comment.'

'Just off the record.'

'Nothing's off the record from now on.'

'When had you planned to marry her?'

'This Saturday or the following Saturday.'

'I can arrange it for the second Saturday if you want.'

'Well done. Tell me more.'

'You don't mind it being at a Catholic church?'

'It can be at a Muslim mosque just so long as it's a legal marriage, recognised in any country.'

'It's at St Hedwig's.'

'The Cathedral?'

'Yes.' Yuri smiled. 'Even an organist.' He could see that Carling was impressed by what he had done in less than a day.

'Have you told Rachel?'

'I've told her about your visit but not about the wedding.'

The gates of the small zoo were open and Yuri drove the car along a narrow drive to a small house with a garden.

She was standing at the open door, smiling and waving to him.

Yuri said, 'I'll come back for you about ten. OK?'

'Yeah.'

They had talked for half an hour. She seemed to have been treated quite well but obviously didn't understand what it was all about. He told her everything. About his work and what he had agreed with the KGB.

When she said, 'Do you trust them?' he put his hand to his mouth and shook his head. He winked as he said, 'I'm sure they'll stick to our bargain.' He paused. 'Let's walk in the garden while there's still some sunshine.'

In the garden he said, 'They'll have the whole place bugged. Never say anything that really matters.

Then he told her about the wedding. At first she couldn't believe it.

'But it's a Catholic cathedral. The most important in Berlin. And I'm Jewish.'

'Do you mind?'

'No.'

'So no problem. And it's a proper marriage. Recognised everywhere.' He laughed and kissed her, then drew back his head to look at her. 'And an organist too.' He paused. 'With the deal I've done I can be with you every Saturday. I'll try and persuade them to increase that.'

'I'm so happy now I've seen you.'

When they opened the double gates of the park as he and Yuri left, Carling noticed that the two guards were in Red Army infantry uniforms. A sergeant and a private.

When they were parked away from the checkpoint, Carling handed Yuri an envelope.

'That's the stuff Belinkov wanted. I wasn't intending to hand it over until you'd fixed the marriage arrangements.'

'He pulled a lot of strings with the Bishop.'

'Good for him.'

'Do you want another visit on Saturday?'

'You bet. Can you arrange it?'

'Yes. Same time as today.'

That Saturday was a busy day for Allied personnel in West Berlin. Vice-President Lyndon Johnson flew in accompanied by General Lucius Clay, who had once been US military commander in Germany. The hero of the airlift that had saved Berliners from starving and had broken the Soviet's attempt at blockading the city and forcing the Western allies to withdraw from Berlin.

It had poured with rain most of the day but despite that, thousands of Berliners had assembled to hear the speeches by the Americans and Willy Brandt. In a cosmetic gesture to the locals there had been a march past of the newly arrived US Army reinforcements.

Late on the Friday evening he had a phone call from Yuri saying that their 'mutual friend' would like to see him, so could he make it an hour earlier for their meeting the next day? Wondering what it was all about, Carling agreed.

On the way to Karlshorst Yuri had said that Belinkov had been much impressed by Carling's report.

They had gone through the usual rituals at the Soviet HQ and Belinkov had taken them to a small room near his office. It was more a room for socialising than an office, and Belinkov had asked Yuri to leave them alone.

When Yuri had gone Belinkov said, 'That first request was a test, Colonel Carling.' He smiled. 'We already had the information concerned. Although your report was more up to date.' He shrugged. 'People move on in our business. The co-operation I really wanted from you lies in another direction. I hope you'll forgive my little test but you'll understand why it was necessary when I say that you might find my actual requirements more acceptable than our previous arrangements.' He shrugged and smiled. 'Let me jump in feet first.' He paused. 'We lack information on our most important target – the CIA. You will not be offended, I hope, if I say that the Americans are more important to us than the British.' He sighed. 'We know almost nothing of our adversaries in the CIA in West Berlin. We hope that you will help us to rectify that.' He leaned back in his chair, his eyes intent on trying to read the reaction on Carling's face.

After a few moments of silence Carling said, 'I must say, you people never fail to surprise me.'

'I don't believe that, my friend. Maybe in this case you are surprised.'

'The idea of asking an SIS officer to act as your mole inside the CIA is certainly novel.'

'I have to confess that it was a brain in Moscow that designed this scenario. How do you feel about it?' He leaned forward. 'Just a quick reaction.'

Carling smiled. 'My first reaction is that you're crazy. Why not use a Soviet national?'

'Very simple. We don't have a Soviet national capable of getting alongside an American.' He smiled. 'We're beginning to realise that. We are looking at the young men and women of the Bolshoi for training. You must know very well that we don't fit in to a sophisticated Western background. Some day it will be better but that will be too late for the likes of me.'

'What do you want to know about them?'

Belinkov spread his arms wide. 'Anything. Who they are, what they are doing and what they are planning against us.'

'Let's give it a try. But I shall want better conditions with my girl.'

'We'll find a way of living together.' He looked at Carling, pointing his finger to emphasise the point. 'Remember, these CIA people spy on your country too. It's not just us.'

Carling laughed softly, recognising the truth in the thinking of that cunning mind.

Belinkov said, 'Contact me through Yuri but from now on it's you and me. Yuri's just a messenger.'

CHAPTER 25

St Hedwig's Cathedral behind the newly renamed Französische Strasse had been heavily damaged during the war but had since been lovingly restored, combining the classical features of the old church with creative innovations. Like a theatre-in-the-round, the congregation faced the altar on three sides. Even the East German government had provided substantial finance for the restoration.

The Cathedral was normally open to the public every day, but on that Saturday it was closed for an hour to accommodate an unusual marriage ceremony.

The bride, Rachel Aarons, in a white silk dress, was formally made the wife of a man in a dark blue suit whose name appeared on the marriage certificate as George Carling, occupation: civil servant. The best man was wearing the uniform of the Volkspolizei although his witness signature said 'musician'. The bride's supporter was the organist's wife. The music played was the traditional 'Wedding March' by Mendelssohn and a piece by Dr Thalben Ball called simply 'Elegy'. This latter at the request of the bridegroom, who had previously played it on a piano to the organist who had never heard it before although it had been specially written for church organs.

The party enjoyed a lunch at the Metropol Hotel in Friedrichstrasse and the bridal couple spent the early evening together on one of the Weisse Flotte excursion boat-trips on the river. They spent the night and the following day at the house in the zoo park at Friedrichsfelde.

It was midday on the following Monday when Carling got the phone call. It was a voice he didn't recognise.

'Hello.'

'Carling? George Carling?'

'Who's speaking?'

'Maybe you won't remember me but I'd like to meet you.' It was an American accent.

'What's it all about?'

'Let's say it's about your current situation. I think I could help you.'

'I don't know what you mean.'

There was a brief laugh at the other end and then the voice said, 'I think you do, Colonel. I think you do.'

'Tell me more.'

'Not on the phone. That wouldn't be wise. Could be tapped.' A pause. 'I know you know Kempinski's. We could meet there in about half an hour.'

'How will I know you?'

Carling could hear the smile in the man's voice as he said, 'I know you, Colonel. I'll wait for you near the reception area. Yes?'

'If that's what you want, OK.'

There were several people sitting around in the small lounge space between the reception desk and the rear entrance but Carling knew who the man was as soon as he saw him. He was reading a book – Salinger's *Franny and Zooey*. It was the male half of the pair he had thought were watching him for the KGB. The man looked up, smiling as he patted the space beside him on the leather sofa. As Carling sat down the man closed the book and put it beside him. He said quietly, 'Hi. You're Hank Henney. I've got a room upstairs. Shall we go?'

'Where's your girlfriend?'

'I don't understand.'

'The girl you were with when you were tailing me around Berlin.'

The man smiled. 'You just made me ten bucks. She swore you hadn't spotted us.'

'D'you stay here at the hotel permanently?'

'No. The room's just so you and I can talk and not be seen together in public. Right now we're just casual strangers chatting in a hotel lounge. I'll go first. It's on the second floor. Room 390.' He stood up, smiling, and said quite loudly. 'Glad to have met you.'

Carling waited for five minutes before he headed for the elevator. The man was younger than he had seemed in the streets and the accent was unmistakably American. Almost certainly New York.

It was a bright, pleasant room with modern furniture and the man who called himself Henney was standing at a small bar checking over the bottles. He half turned.

'What d'you fancy? There's everything here.'

'A tomato juice if you've got one. No angostura and no Worcester sauce.'

'My, my. A guy who knows exactly what he wants.' He lifted a bottle, eased off the cap and poured the contents into a long glass. Picking up a glass already filled he walked across to where Carling was sitting and put both drinks on a glass coffee table between them.

'There you are.' He held up his glass. *'Na zdrovia.'*

'Cheers.'

'I guess everybody asks you this but what do I call you – Lord, Viscount, Earl or what?'

Carling sighed. 'They do. Just call me Carling.'

'OK. Carling. Let's face it. You got problems, pal. Lots of problems. I think you need some help.' He paused. 'Am I right?'

'I don't know. Maybe you should tell me what problems I've got.'

Henney grinned. 'You wanna list?'

'Anyway you like, Mr Henney.'

'Hank.' He sighed. 'Brooklyn, New York.' He paused and looked at Carling over the top of his raised glass. 'So. Back to your problems. I guess the root of your problems is that little gal of yours. She's a honey but she's a problem all the same. Am I right?'

'Who are you, Henney?'

Henney smiled. 'You've guessed already who I am, haven't you?' He paused. 'I'm CIA. The new boys.'

'Is this an official contact?'

'Let's just say it ain't an official contact between CIA and SIS. My contact's only with you.'

'Do others in CIA know you're contacting me?'

'Only two, and only one of them knows why.'

'Why was I being followed?'

'Like I said, we're the new boys. We haven't had your people's experience in operating in Europe, especially into an area controlled by the Soviets. We wanted to know what was going on over the other side. So we checked on who was doing it for the French.' He shrugged. 'We weren't impressed. So we had a look at what the Brits were doing about it. And we came up with your name.'

'We thought maybe it would be good to – what shall

I call it? – follow in your footsteps. That was quite an eye-opener. Your friend Yuri and all that. We did a bit of research on him too. And in the course of all this we discovered that the mighty dollar worked even more wonders over the other side. We made a bit of a run at them, just a small team of us. And,' he shrugged, 'cutting a long story short, we have access to both the KGB places and the Stasi offices.' He smiled. 'Very low level but high-technology, and beyond the dreams of even J. Edgar Hoover looking for commies in Hollywood.

'We finally judged you as non-political. Neither left wing nor right wing. Thought we might be able to get you to help us, but as you got more involved and they started to use the girl against you we thought you were heading for trouble.' He shrugged. 'And of course you were. Not just heading. You were in it. In deep, deep shit. When we learned about Belinkov's latest proposition to you I thought I should get together with you.' He smiled. 'What d'you think?'

For a few moments Carling said nothing, and then he said, 'What is it you're after?'

Henney shifted in his chair and when he was more comfortable he said, 'I'd like to join the game.'

'Go on.'

'All off the record. Just you and me. A combined operation. You and me versus the KGB.'

'How did you get all this background information?'

'You mean about you?'

'Yes.'

Henney hesitated, then said, 'Let's say, a bit of experience and a lot of luck. I used to do this job in the Middle East. I found dealing with East Germans was very like dealing with Arabs.' He smiled. 'Greed and corruption are international. Maybe some day I can tell you the sordid details.'

'This sounds crazy to me. What, exactly, have you got in mind?'

'Our friends over the border want information about the CIA. They want you to provide it. I could give you information that will keep them very happy. And more important, that will do no harm to either American or British interests. We could work it out together.'

Carling shook his head slowly in disbelief. 'This *is* crazy.'

Henney smiled. 'You know as well as I do that half of what we do in this business is crazy. But I'd reckon what I've suggested isn't all that crazy. You're committed because of your girl to provide information about the CIA. Just think of what that involves compared with what I'm suggesting. It ain't gonna be all that easy getting an inside track on my lot. And if you got caught you'd be in deep, deep shit. Nobody would want to touch you. Diplomatic incident and all that jazz. Washington after your head and London wishing they could give it to them. My way, the most your people could hold against you would be doing something without an official OK.'

Carling nodded. 'I realise all that. What worries me is that it all fits in so well. Almost too well.'

Henney shrugged. 'So count yourself lucky and grab the chance. It's better than your way. Your way you don't just risk being caught playing games with the CIA but of playing ball solo with the KGB.' He paused. 'If I were you I'd be very glad to solve a tricky problem like yours in a way that keeps me totally clean.'

'What if I decline the offer?'

Henney shook his head. 'Forget it. You won't. You've got more sense than that.'

'Tell me about the other two who you said know of your contact with me today.'

'I'll tell you anything you want to know about 'em. But only after you've agreed to let me in on your game with the Russians.'

'Tell me about you then.'

'Fine. Same age as you, give or take a year. Born in Wichita Falls, Texas. Grew up in New York. My old man was a plumber and my ma sewed dresses in a sweatshop. We lived in Brighton Beach, couple of miles from Coney. I did well in school. Got a football scholarship to Boston U. Took law and when we got into the war I was recruited into OSS. When OSS folded and CIA started up I was transferred to them. Served in OSS in Italy and in CIA I've worked in Cairo, Beirut, and a stint in Damascus. Grade?' He smiled. 'I guess about the same as yours. Married, one child, a daughter. Hobbies . . .?' He shrugged. 'radio ham and playing low-grade jazz.'

Carling smiled. 'What kind of jazz?'

'Piano. Anything from Joplin to Fats Waller.'

Carling was silent for a few moments and then he said quietly, 'When do we get started? We've got a lot of planning to do.'

'I'm real glad.' The American stood up. 'Can you stay for a meal and talk?'

'Sure.'

'I'll ring room service.'

They had talked about Hank Henney's family and about Rachel and the wedding while they ate, but when the waiter had cleared away the debris of their meal and brought them coffee, Henney reached inside his jacket and brought out an envelope.

'Take a look at that. It's our first move but we don't hand it over for a couple of weeks. Don't wanna make it look too easy. Have a look. See what you think.'

It was twelve pages of an internal telephone directory of the CIA unit in West Berlin. Carling looked through it slowly and then looked at Henney.

'Real or doctored?'

'Absolutely genuine.'

'Tell me about the other two people who know about our operation.'

'The guy who knows but doesn't know the background – your background, Rachel and the rest of it – his name's Morgan. Glenn Morgan. In his fifties. Rock solid. Knows how the machinery works. The other guy is my immediate boss. It was he who agreed to having a watch put on you. His name's Kaufman. Albert Kaufman. Ex-OSS but concerned with desk operations. He's in charge of case-officers – what I guess you'd call agents. Agents for us are foreigners who work for us. The CIA guys who control them are never called agents but case-officers.' He smiled. 'All same as the KGB. Kaufman's about five years younger than us. A very cool cookie. He can clear anything we want to do.'

'What about Washington?'

'They're not in the picture. But when we've been going for a few months we'll inform them provided you agree. OK?'

'Yeah.' Carling pointed at the directory. 'That's too good for the first thing I pass them.'

'It ain't even classified as secret, George. Back home our telephone numbers are in the telephone directory.'

Carling shook his head. 'It's still too good, believe me.'

'What else can we give 'em?'

'How about a grainy photograph of your building?'

'It's just a house, for Chrissake.'

'That's fine. That's enough for a start.'

'OK. You know best.'

'When can I have the photo?'

'Tomorrow.'

'Not a real estate shot. The kind of picture an agent would take.' He smiled. 'And next time we can make it a rough sketch of the ground-floor offices.'

Hank Henney laughed. 'Anything you say, old buddy. Anything you say.'

They exchanged telephone numbers where they could be contacted at any time. They arranged codenames for places to meet and codenames for people's names they may need to refer to.

As Carling walked back to his flat it was raining heavily. He sat in the kitchen in his bathrobe with a mug of coffee. It seemed to be too good to be true. He had been well aware of the risks he had been taking in doing the deal with Belinkov, but for him he had had no choice. SIS wouldn't see it that way, for them it would be treason no matter how unimportant the information he passed to Belinkov was. They would dismiss the information he got back from Belinkov as being 'planted'. But the joint operation with Henney could only be criticised because it was not disclosed. No information on SIS was involved and the CIA material was their own choosing. What he got back from Belinkov would benefit both the CIA and SIS. Operationally he would be no more than a combined messenger and listening post. The deal with Hank Henney was the best insurance he could have.

Two days after their first meeting Henney had provided

the photograph and Carling had passed it on to Belinkov, who was delighted with the first fruits of the new arrangement. It was at that meeting that Carling raised the possibility of getting the CIA's internal telephone directory.

'There would be names and job titles. Would that interest you?'

'You mean you might be able to get a copy of an original?'

'No. I'm negotiating for an actual original.'

'And all the staff names and status?'

'Exactly.'

'That would be fantastic. Moscow would be delighted.'

'It won't be easy and if I get it I want something in return.'

Belinkov's face went from smiles to neutral. 'What is it you want?'

'I want a pass in German and Russian that means I can come and go into and out of East Berlin unhindered and no time or date limitation. And signed by your top brass.'

Belinkov looked relieved. 'No problem. I'll get it arranged by tomorrow.' He paused. 'When are you likely to get the directory?'

He shrugged. 'Two or three days' time if all goes to plan.'

'OK. I'll get the special pass done for you.'

Belinkov made no effort to conceal his excitement as he read through the directory. He had already handed over the pass that Carling had asked for. It was in German and Russian and signed by the Soviet commander of both the Russian Zone and the rest of East Germany.

It required all authorities, both civilian and military, German or Soviet, to allow the bearer to pass 'without let or hindrance' and without questioning at any time. And such authorities must render any services or assistance required by the bearer. There was a photograph of Carling's face taken by an army photographer in the open air so that there was no background.

Putting aside the directory, Belinkov said, 'We are concentrating all our efforts against the Americans now. Not only here but in the United States. We have sustained many losses of our people in America because we have not made the necessary arrangements to protect them. Too many had their controllers based at our embassy and consulates. We need people who can operate independently. Here in Europe we know what to do but the Americans are from another planet. We need to learn how to beat them.'

'What are your people hoping to get in the United States?'

Belinkov pursed his lips, thinking. 'Above all we want information on the atom bomb but we also need to know what their government is planning against us. New weapons, new devices, communications. Troop deployment. Signs of aggressive moves before they happen.'

'And what do you want from the CIA in Berlin?'

Belinkov shrugged. 'Almost anything. They will have agents over here. Who are they, what are their objectives, who controls them?'

Carling nodded. 'I'll see what I can do.'

Their daughter, Rachel, was born in a private nursing home that was solely for the use of wives of senior Soviet officers and officials. Mother and child were well looked after and Carling was able to take them home after only three days in the hospital. A nurse came to visit the new mother and baby every day for the first month.

By this time Carling was living a strange life that would have seemed bizarre to almost anyone. The house at the Tierpark he treated as his home. His rooms of Savigny Platz were just 'his place'. He spent three or four nights a week with Rachel, rather as if he were some travelling salesman who couldn't always make it home.

Despite Belinkov's dismissal of Yuri as just a messenger, Carling kept up his contact with him. Yuri was too shrewd to ask what Carling was doing for his boss. Carling kept up all his old contacts in what, since the building of the Wall, was now officially East Berlin. His work for SIS gave him virtually complete independence and at the weekly joint briefing meetings he was highly respected for his insight into what was happening on the other side of the Wall. Hank Henney too was obviously impressed by what Carling knew about the other side, but he valued most Carling's reports on his contacts with Belinkov. The Americans seemed fascinated by the Russians despite the fact that Berlin itself was living proof that ordinary people were eager to escape from communism. With both the British and the Americans Carling did his best to get over to them the fact that despite the material attractions of the West there were many people, particularly older people, who found comfort and comradeship in the atmosphere of East Berlin. East Berlin was like Berlin in the old days. Lace curtains moving gently in the summer breeze, old values maintained, a!most no major crime, and old ladies could walk alone in the streets at night without being robbed or molested. East Berlin was Berlin in the thirties, Thomas

Mann and *Buddenbrooks*. Oddly enough, the Americans seemed to understand this better than the Brits did. It was like the front covers of the *Saturday Evening Post* by Norman Rockwell that used to make them feel that all was right with the world.

CHAPTER 26

Hank Henney had an apartment near the Europa Centre. They had met there just after the Christmas holidays and Carling wondered how the American would react to what he had to say.

'Tell me, Hank, if I told you an American was passing information to Belinkov's people what would your reaction be?'

'A civilian or a serviceman?'

'Serviceman.'

'Officer or enlisted man?'

'Sergeant.'

'How valuable is the information?'

'Some secret, some top-secret.'

'How long's he been doing it?'

'Three, four months.'

'For money?'

'Money and sex. His controller is a young woman.'

'What you really want to know is would I put him straight in the slammer?'

'Would you?'

'We'd have to work it out, you and me. If we just jump on him they'd realise you could have told us. We'd do better just to ease him away from wherever he gets the information he passes to them.'

Carling nodded. 'That's what I wanted to hear, Hank.' He paused. 'The chap's name is Carmichael. Randolph Carmichael. Randy to his friends. He works in your signals group responsible for all US service communications in Berlin with a feed back to your HQ in Frankfurt.'

'That means he knows the status of all our units, troop movements, responsibilities and operational orders. Not good, old friend. Not good.'

'Think about it, Hank, and we'll talk again.'

'You got any ideas?'

'If he was one of ours we'd probably promote him to make him feel safe and then post him to another command. Maybe back home. Depends on his background. We'd keep him under close surveillance and wait until he was contacted in his new place. Photographs and meetings and so on. Then move in on him. After interrogation we could decide whether we'd turn him back on them or put him on trial. There would be no connection with his job here in Berlin.' He paused. 'Our experience is never to be in a hurry. Jump in right away and you've generally exposed your informant, and you'll almost certainly be faced with indignant denials and you can't prove a thing that would stand up in court.'

Henney smiled. 'All that Brit experience based on a hundred years of being in the business. But you're right. Our instinct would be to grab him and put him away. Not very subtle.'

Carling smiled. 'I've got the feeling you're learning fast, you guys.' He looked at Henney. 'I need a tit bit for our friends. Have you got anything?'

'Our head of mission is going back to Washington in three months' time. I could give you a bit of background on the new guy.' He smiled. 'Nothing that hasn't appeared in the papers back home.'

'They'd love that, Hank. Tell me more.'

Carling was amused at the obvious irritation of the Stasi and plain-clothes KGB officers at Checkpoint Charlie. They sometimes tried asking him what was the purpose of his visit and he would point out that they were defying the orders of their highest official in East Berlin. Sometimes one of them would make a phone call and Carling could see him reading from his document. Then the hurried return of the pass, sometimes graced by a salute.

Carling had been working with Hank Henney for nine months and the two-way traffic seemed to be satisfying both parties. The information Carling passed to the CIA man covered the organisation and personnel of the KGB in East Berlin and the major cities in East Germany. What he passed on to Belinkov was information that a competent investigative journalist could have picked up from the usual gossip of the intelligence community in West Berlin.

They had arranged a meeting that day by the bridge over the canal and as they leaned over the railing watching small boys jumping into the canal from the bridge, Carling said, 'I've got a bit of a problem, Hank.'

'Anything I can do to help?'

'I've been notified that I'm to be posted to London in three months' time. They don't know that I'm married.'

'How do you claim your marriage allowances?'

'I don't. I don't need the money.'

'So what's the problem?'

'I don't think the Russians will let Rachel and the baby

leave East Berlin. They would feel they've no hold on me.'

Henney looked at him. 'So. We put something together and get her out.'

'That would still leave the problem of concealing the fact that I'm married. My people can't check on us in East Berlin but once she was over here I couldn't cover up for long.'

'So we get her and the baby out and then you tell your people.'

'Hank, she was an East German. I'd end up in the Tower of London. You know what our people and yours can be like. It wouldn't be just a case of throwing me out. They can be real bastards. Just a word in somebody's ear. The Inland Revenue checking me out like I was a Mafia *capo*. Never park a car without you get a ticket.' He shrugged. 'I've seen it done. I know what it does to even the toughest men.'

'What's your new job?'

Carling shrugged and grimaced. 'I'd be in charge of advising the Foreign Office on policy concerning the Soviets and the Warsaw Pact countries.'

For long moments Henney seemed to be just looking down at the kids playing around in the canal, then he turned to look at Carling.

'If you'd married an American girl without telling them what would they do?'

'They wouldn't be best pleased that I'd not informed them. But they'd just accept it.'

'Would you have had to get their permission to marry?'

'Only if the girl was from the Soviet Union or a Warsaw Pact country. And they wouldn't have given permission.'

'But if it was a French girl, for instance.'

Carling shrugged. 'They'd go along with it. They'd probably check up on her background on the quiet.'

'If she had been English would they check her background?'

'Yeah. But it would just be a routine check. Politics, if any, associates and central records.'

'How about . . .' Henney half smiled '. . . you said way back that our little arrangement was crazy – so you'll say this is even crazier – how about we arrange to make your girl an American?'

'How the hell can we do that?'

Hank Henney shrugged. 'It's been done before. We get her over here, I get my fellas to create documentation for her, she takes the oath with our Consul.' He shrugged. 'And that's it. You can even go through another marriage ceremony in our zone. We've got army padres who could do it.'

Carling turned round, leaning on the railings, looking at the little boys in the canal but not seeing them. Without turning to look at Henney he said, 'Would your people really do this, Hank?'

'Of course. Just say the word and I'll get things moving.'

Carling turned his head to look at the American. 'You realise that my new job would be very different. I wouldn't be much use to your people in Berlin. I wouldn't be down amongst the day to day details. I'd just be a broad oversight of a pretty big map.'

Henney sighed. 'You're a very modest chap, George. We set great store by your opinions.' He paused. 'Anyway, we'd like to pay our debts to you for helping us so far.'

'But I won't be so useful in my new position.'

Henney shrugged. 'Who knows? We'll see.'

* * *

He had notified SIS of his impending marriage and people who knew him seemed surprised but pleased. There were the inevitable jokes about him marrying an American girl and the unit had presented them with a huge casket of Solingen cutlery as a wedding present. There had been some surprise that nobody from the unit was invited to the wedding but it was reckoned to be typical of Carling who had always been a loner. It was stressed by Carling that not even his father or his fiancée's parents would be at the ceremony.

A USA Army Jeep had exercised its right to go through Checkpoint Charlie unchallenged and the driver and his armed escort had been joined by a third uniformed officer, a woman, at a brief stop in the Nikolaiviertel. She was wearing a standard issue cape against the rain and put a small bundle on the floor of the Jeep between her feet. They were back in the American Zone fifteen minutes later.

Hank Henney had a quick meal with them after the baby had been settled in her cot. Carling had bought his young wife a white silk dress with large red poppies around the skirt to celebrate the occasion. The house they were using was one of the CIA's safe houses.

The citizenship formalities for Rachel Carling had been accomplished the next morning and in the afternoon they were married in a chapel by a USAF padre.

In the evening she read through the documents that had been created to give her a background. She was amused that because of her German accent it had been decided that she had been born in Pittsburg. Her father a teacher, her mother a musician. There was a lengthy exposition of her childhood and upbringing. She had done well at school and had become a professional musician in her teens.

*   *   *

The day after their second wedding Carling phoned Belinkov. When the Russian answered the phone he sounded tense.

'Who is that?'

'It's your friend. We need to meet.'

'What the hell's going on? Where's the woman and the child?'

'Come to Checkpoint Charlie in civilian clothes in two hours. I'll be waiting for you and I'll see you through the checkpoint. We need to talk.'

'I can't risk coming through to your side, you know that.'

'I did it daily for you, my friend. See you in a couple of hours.'

He watched the Russian walking towards the checkpoint. He had never seen him in civilian clothes before. He looked uneasy in an ill-fitting suit and a short coat that was unbuttoned and flapping in the wind.

Carling had already used his SIS card to instruct the military police guards on the West side of the Wall and he took the Russian's arm and led him to his car.

'Where are we going?'

'The Europa Centre. There's a café there where we can talk. Don't worry.'

Ten minutes later they were at a table in one of the Europa Centre cafés, but Belinkov was still on edge.

'What's going on?'

'I'm going back to London in a few weeks' time. That means I can no longer co-operate with you. I arranged for my wife and daughter to move to this side of the Wall.' He smiled amiably. 'Just a precaution, of course.

213

Apart from the fact that I won't be in a position to help you there need be no problem. Our little arrangement was useful to us both. There is no need for any recriminations on either side.'

'What are you going to be doing in London?'

'That I can't tell you.'

'I can soon find out. We have experienced people in London.'

'I'm sure you have, Nikolai.' He paused. 'I hope we can remain on good terms and I hope that any guidance I have given you has done a little to help keep our two countries maintain a little respect for one another.' He smiled. 'I'll take you back to the checkpoint, Nikolai.'

As they got out of Carling's vehicle, Carling put out his hand and Belinkov took it reluctantly. He looked up at Carling's face. 'You are a strange man, comrade. I don't understand you.'

'Don't worry, Nikolai, we should both forget we ever met. It's better that way.'

The Russian shook his head in amazement, turned his back and walked off down the road towards the museum.

THREE

CHAPTER 27

Carling sat in the sun on the bench by the lion enclosures. She had been wearing the white silk dress with the poppies and she'd taken the baby to look at the lions. He had sometimes wondered what she saw in him. He still wondered. She was so incredibly beautiful and so loving. Their time in Berlin had been the happiest days of his life. Being together without subterfuge was like being let out of prison. He would never forget the Americans' willingness to help them, and their generosity that had made it all possible. Overnight Berlin had changed from a grim city, a backdrop to the Cold War, to a city with places to walk, restaurants to eat at, shops and concerts and small dinner parties at their rented house. There had been other good days away from Berlin but it was here that it started and it was this now prosperous, bustling city that represented for him the real start of his happiness with Rachel.

He had visited all their old places. The house at the Tierpark, the apartment in the Nikolaiviertel and the rented house in the American Zone. He had even gone back to find Yuri's old place but it was now a twenty-five-storey office block.

He sighed and stood up. He had to go back to the hotel

and check out. His flight was already booked in the name of Aarons. And he'd have dinner with young Rachel at the airport. He liked to be in a busy place with lots of people when he had to say goodbye.

She looked so like her mother that he was never sure whether this made him happy or sad. The same mane of black hair, the big dark eyes, the neat nose and the full sensual mouth.

'It's funny,' she said, 'I don't remember Berlin from when I was a baby but when I come here I always feel at home, even when they had the Wall I seemed to know the place.' She reached over and touched his hand on the table. 'Are you happy?'

He smiled. 'Always happy when I'm with you.'

She laughed softly. 'Now you're giving me that famous Carling charm.' She paused. 'I mean are you happy in general? When you're not with me.'

'I miss her terribly. Every day.'

'Of course you do. I miss her too. But you've got to go on with your life.' She paused. 'You always seem so busy with one thing or another. I'm always seeing pictures of you in the papers. I'm not sure it's a good idea for you to come back here. It's a bit like picking at a scab on a wound that's beginning to heal.'

He shook his head. 'It's not like that. This place was special for both of us. I'll tell you about it one of these days.' He smiled. 'How's that man of yours?'

She laughed. 'Still pressing me to marry him but I like my freedom.'

'Where are you heading for next?'

'I've got a concert in Barcelona and then back to New York and LA.'

'Are *you* happy?'

She smiled. 'I think I'm a lot like you. I'm happy but I'm always holding my breath, hoping the Good Lord isn't about to strike me down.'

'What do you most remember of your mother?'

She frowned, thinking, then smiling. 'I remember that whenever she looked at you she was always smiling. I remember her wearing a white silk dress with big red poppies on the skirt.'

He sighed. 'I can hear them calling my flight. I'd better get on my way.' As he stood up he put his hands on her shoulders and she looked up at him, smiling. 'When shall I see you again, little girl?'

'I'm not sure. Maybe at Christmas or New Year.'

He kissed her and she walked with him to the boarding channel and he turned and waved to her as he went through the checkpoint.

She went back to the restaurant and ordered herself a coffee. She wished that she could find a man like him. He seemed to have been born knowing about all the arts. Especially music. And he was so generous. Not just with money but with himself. He didn't just care about people but he did something about it if it was in his power. And if you're an earl and quite rich and charming you have a lot of power. Her mother had told her quite a lot about him but none of it fitted in with the man she knew now. Even from what her mother had told her it sounded as if he'd treated his intelligence work as if it were just a background to his real life. When her mother had died he had seemed to come to a stop. He had sold up the mansion and the estate in Scotland and she had gone back to England with him, looking at places where he could start living again. The country house in Kent had something that seemed to appeal to him as soon as he saw it. When she asked him what it was he had smiled and said that it was the big red poppies in the garden.

CHAPTER 28

Carling stayed for the night at the Spa Hotel in Tunbridge Wells and drove up to Lake Cottage in time for breakfast. Julie and Gabby were all smiles, obviously delighted to have him back. They had already eaten but he made them sit with him as he drank his tea and went quickly through his accumulated mail.

'Any excitements while I was away?'

Julie smiled. 'Carlotta's got four teeth now.'

'That's great.' He smiled at Gabriella. 'She's going to be nearly as beautiful as her mum.' He paused. 'Where's Tim?'

'He had to go to London to see his solicitor.'

Carling nodded. 'I must do something about that.' He frowned. 'What day is it?'

'Thursday.'

Carling stood up. 'I've got to make a phone call. I'll be right back.'

As he dialled 192 he wondered if, perhaps, the number was ex-directory because of the SIS connection, but there was no problem. It was still under Mathews, Timothy. He wrote the number the operator gave him on his pad.

He turned to Julie. 'There's the number, sweetie. When

she answers you say your piece. A little bit formal but very friendly. OK?'

'OK.'

Julie dialled the number. It rang only three times before a rather breathless voice said, 'Hello.'

'This is Lord Carling's secretary speaking. Lord Carling would like to speak to Pamela Bailey, please.'

'Pamela Bailey speaking. Is this some trick for selling something?'

'It certainly is not, Ms Bailey. I'll put you through to His Lordship.'

She put her hand over the receiver, counted to ten and handed it to Carling.

'Carling speaking, Ms Bailey. I hope I'm not calling at an inconvenient time.'

'I think you've got the wrong person.' She paused. 'Are you really Lord Carling?'

'If it really worries you, you could get my number from Enquiries. It's in the book. And ring me back when you're satisfied.'

'Are you the man who talks about the arts on chat shows?'

'Yes. I'm afraid that's me. There's something I wanted to talk to you about. Could I come across to see you – or better still could you have a bite with me at the House tomorrow lunch time?'

'Where is your house?' The voice was interested but cautious.

'I'm sorry. I meant the House of Lords. We've got a debate on the film industry in the afternoon or I'd have suggested somewhere a bit more glamorous.'

A few moments of silence. 'Are you sure I'm the right person? I'm not important or anything.'

'I'm quite, quite sure, dear lady. How about you come along about noon? Say twelve-fifteen?'

'All right. I hope it isn't all a ghastly mistake.'

'Of course not. See you tomorrow.'

'Yes. Goodbye.'

He pulled a face at Julie. 'Only a *white* lie, my dear. And it's in a very good cause.'

'What did she sound like?'

'Pleasant. Matching accessories. But I'm used to all that. My committee ladies are all like that.'

'Is this so that Tim can see his son?'

'Yes.'

'What will you say to her?'

He shrugged. 'I haven't the foggiest idea. I'll have to play it by ear.'

Pamela Bailey was prettier than Carling had imagined, and livelier too. Dressed rather primly. He escorted her to the table he had booked, and as she sipped a glass of wine he discreetly pointed out the lords she might recognise.

'I feel a little bit guilty about inviting you to lunch but I felt we could, perhaps, help each other.'

She smiled nervously. 'I don't see how I could help you. Or you me.'

'Tell me about yourself. Your life and the things that interest you.'

'It's a very simple life. I'm just an ordinary housewife and my main interest in life is my son.'

'That's Tony, isn't it?'

She looked shocked. 'How on earth do you know that?'

'We both have children. I have a daughter, she's about your age. Maybe a year or two younger. She's a musician. A violinist. I don't see much of her. She's based in New York but she gives concerts all over the world.' He paused. 'So I don't see much of her. I miss her a lot.' He paused again. 'Would you miss Tony if you didn't see him much?'

'Of course I would.'

'Can I ask you something very personal?'

She shrugged. 'I suppose so.'

'Do you miss your husband – I mean your ex-husband? Tim.'

'Why do you ask?'

'Because he misses his son and I suspect he misses you a little too.'

She laughed sharply. 'He's kidding if he says that.'

'He didn't say that about either you or Tony but I know him well enough to be quite certain that he misses you both.' He paused. 'In his kind of work it tends to make men conceal their inner feelings.' He smiled. 'I was in the same business myself but a long time ago.'

'How did you come across my . . . across Tim?'

'He's been staying with me for some months.' He smiled. 'Let's say we've been exchanging notes on things that happened way back.' He paused. 'He's very good at his job, you know.'

She shrugged dismissively. 'He never told me anything about his work. He'd be away for days, even weeks, and then he'd come back without any excuse or apology. Our home was just a place to change his clothes.'

'People doing his job are trained not to talk and they go along with it so that their families don't get involved. To keep them away from any possible danger. A wife, a child, a girlfriend are always pressure points. It may not seem like it at your pleasant home in Esher where you keep things calm and sensible and your young husband seems much the same as other husbands who work in the

City or in a local business, but Tim will have been aware of the penalties for talking about his work.'

'You seem to have learned an awful lot about him, so he obviously talks with you.'

Carling shook his head. 'No. Not really. I just read between the lines and fill in the silences.'

'And I don't?'

'How could you, my dear?' He smiled. 'They ought to have short courses for officers' wives at the start. Make them part of the club.'

She nodded. 'That would have helped a lot. It really would.'

'Are you happy with your new life?'

She looked away at other tables and then back at Carling. 'You said my *new* life. I don't really have a new life. I thought I was going to make a new start but that's fallen through.' She sighed and smiled. 'I don't really have a life.'

'Was there anything you liked about Tim?'

'Of course. He didn't mess around with other women. He wasn't mean about money.' She shrugged. 'But he just didn't seem to belong to me.' She paused. 'How is he?'

'He's getting by, but he's a man who's lost his anchor. You may not have felt it was so but I suspect that you were his anchor.'

'I can't believe that. He was so independent.'

'My dear, I'm heading for my seventy-first birthday so I've been around a long time, and I can tell you that I wondered if you could have been what gave him a base. And now I've met you I know I was right.' He smiled. 'When you're as young as you two it's easy to expect too much from your partner. You're not old enough yet to value the quiet, solid virtues. But you will some day.'

He paused. 'Could be with that young man you once were in love with.' He shrugged. 'Or maybe somebody else.' He sighed. 'A pity to throw away the chances without even trying.' He paused. 'And if you both sacked your solicitors it would be a good start.' He looked at her, smiling. 'Why not come over to my place for the day on Saturday? Bring the boy, have a lazy day and do a bit of shopping at Fenwicks.'

She laughed. 'Get thee behind me, Satan.'

'Will you come?'

She looked away and then back at him. 'Yes. I'll come.'

'Good girl. Let's none of us expect too much. Just a few old friends getting together.'

She leaned back in her chair, slowly shaking her head. 'I wish my father had been like you.' She leaned forward again. 'You've made everything seem suddenly brighter.'

It had been a good day. Carling had taken Tony up to the trout farm and borrowed a couple of rods. He had shown the small boy how to recognise where the fish were and taught him how to cast his fly well out on to the pond. They had fished all afternoon. Tony had caught a two-pounder and Carling had shown him how to play the fish away from the reeds and ease it gently into the net.

When they got back to the house Carling was aware of laughter, mainly female laughter, coming from the direction of the bench beside the pond. He occupied Tony with helping him to start up the barbecue and half an hour later they were all eating sausages, frankfurters, lamb chops and burgers. With Julie, Gabby and the baby, and the others, Carling found a strange peace, despite the chatter and laughter. They were all enjoying a brief spell of happiness. All was right with their worlds. Aware that in large part it was his doing that had made it so, he wondered fleetingly if it was a good idea to intrude, even interfere, in other people's lives. Maybe the road to hell was paved with barbecued sausages, fishing rods and a young woman looking at a young man as if she'd never seen him before.

He had sent the gardener in the Rover 3-litre to pick up his two guests from Esher but he registered no surprise when Tim said that he would drive them back himself in his car.

As Carling leaned against the car's open window he smiled at them all and then said, as if it were an afterthought, 'By the way, I've got two box tickets for the Last Night of the Proms. I can't use them, maybe you two could enjoy an outing.'

He stood, hands on hips, watching them drive off into the darkness and then walked back into the house. He sat at the kitchen table drinking a glass of red wine with Delius on the hi-fi coming through the open door to the living room. He was showing Julie and Gabby the movements of the pieces on a chessboard. An hour later he did his regular late-night walk to his shack, then the pond and back to the patio. He stood there for a few minutes looking up at the sky but the moon was obscured by clouds.

Inside the house he looked at his watch. It would be late afternoon in New York and he dialled Rachel's number. But there was no response and Rachel detested answering machines.

He lay in bed reading Len Deighton's latest paperback with the BBC's World Service chatting away almost inaudibly on his bedside radio. It was still on long after he was asleep.

CHAPTER 29

When Carling came down for breakfast Julie, barely concealing a knowing smile, told him that Tim Mathews had phoned and said that he'd be back midday.

Carling was in his shack when Mathews returned. He heard the car and switched on the mains switch before leaving and locking the two locks on the door.

He didn't ask Mathews how things had gone and Mathews didn't volunteer anything.

'I'm going to Tunbridge Wells, Tim. D'you fancy coming with me?'

'Sure.'

Carling put in a cartridge of Fujicolor for processing at Camera Gear in Camden Road and then they walked down to KAC and Carling bought two dozen TDK audio tapes.

As so often when they visited Tunbridge Wells, Carling stopped for coffee at Fenwicks' restaurant. When Mathews said, 'Tell me about your time in Berlin.' Carling was taken aback. How did he know he had been in Berlin? He was quite sure that he hadn't been followed. And then he relaxed, realising that Mathews was asking him about when he was with SIS in Berlin.

'I was responsible for reporting on conditions in East Berlin. Both the military and the general population.'

'How did you get in with the Wall and the checkpoints?'

Carling smiled. 'The Wall didn't exist until later and even when the Wall went up we still had the right of free passage in uniform and in an army vehicle.'

'Did you keep up your contact with the Russians?'

Carling shrugged. 'That was part of my job. I had contact with East Germans and Russians.' He smiled. 'If you look in my file you'll see that SIS were quite pleased with my efforts.' Carling looked around at the people in the restaurant and then back at Mathews. 'Doesn't it seem crazy to you to be talking about these things in a place like this? Couples drinking coffee, families with their children. Shopping in the plastic bags alongside their chairs. People whose only worry is paying the mortgage and the milk bill?'

'It's still going on, George. Behind the scenes.'

'But doesn't it seem crazy to go so far back? Everything was different then. That was then, this is now.'

'What happened after Berlin?'

'I came back to London and was in charge of the Warsaw Pact desk.'

'Did that mean you ran active operations into the Warsaw Pact countries?'

'No. I was responsible for reporting on the politicians, the economics, the civilian population, morale and that sort of thing.'

'But you were informed about our operations in those countries?'

'Of course. Some of the operations were specifically to provide information that I needed.'

'Did your old Soviet contacts keep in touch with you when you were back in London?'

Carling smiled. 'Let's just say that they wanted to.'

'But you didn't co-operate with them?'

'No. We were in the middle of the Cold War. They were no longer our allies in a war.' He shrugged. 'It was a different scenario, a different game.'

'What did you feel about communism by then?'

'Have you ever read the Soviet constitution?'

'No.'

'That's part of the problem. It's like people criticising religion who have never been in a church.'

Mathews smiled. 'I don't see the connection.'

'OK. Let me explain. The Cold War's over, we're into glasnost and perestroika now. Agreed?'

'Yeah.'

'So what lesson do we learn from that?'

'That communism doesn't work.'

'Ah, my boy, that's the rub. Maybe all it proves is that the Soviets weren't communists.'

Mathews laughed. 'How do you make that out? That's crazy.'

'Is it? Let's go back to the Soviet constitution. When you've read it you're left with two, maybe three thoughts. First – that it is very much the same as the constitution of the United States. Secondly, you realise that both constitutions are essentially democratic and creative. And thirdly, that although the Soviets had an excellent constitution based on communism, they didn't practise what they preached. The law was abused, power-hungry men ignored all those well-thought-out intentions.' He paused and smiled. 'So why didn't communism work? It didn't work because of people. *We're* the problem. There isn't too much difference between communism and Christianity. They're both great ideas. And neither of them works. They don't work because we are a selfish, aggressive, greedy species. Wave a flag, promise victory and rewards and it's easy to start a war.

It's no longer a case of wars between great nations, but wars between tribes. You can see it in Africa, in Indonesia and Palestine . . .' he smiled '. . . and you can see it at a football match on a Saturday afternoon. Heroes in claret and blue jerseys and villains in blue and white stripes.'

'It's an interesting theory.'

'It's not a theory, my friend. I wish it was. It's fact.'

'So when did you realise that communism didn't work?'

'I never believed that it worked. No more than I believed that Christianity or Islam or any other religion worked. I helped the Russians because they were our allies and they were dying in their thousands fighting the Germans, our mutual enemies.' He paused. 'I sometimes send money to one or other of the South American countries where people are starving and abused, that doesn't imply that I approve their politics.' He stopped to sip his coffee and then put down the cup and looked at Mathews. 'You know, the problem you young chaps have is that you don't understand the people you're operating against. The latest technology and lots of dull and irrelevant facts – but no humanity.'

Mathews winced. 'Isn't that a bit sweeping?'

'Tell me, how many KGB men have you known personally?'

Mathews laughed. 'None. That's called consorting with the enemy.'

'So how do you find out what motivates them?'

'We don't need to. Like you said, we're only interested in what they do.'

Carling shook his head slowly. 'We had a poster in our offices during the war. The headline said – "Know your enemy". And it showed men in various uniforms. And somebody had put an arrow against one of the figures and scrawled in pencil – "And he likes screwing blondes". The chap who wrote those words was the most successful interrogator we ever had.'

'In what way was he successful?'

'He didn't interrogate suspects. He chatted to them. Got into their minds. Enabled us to understand what motivated them.' He smiled. 'Ask your boss. Ask Freddie Kennedy. The man I'm talking about was Kennedy's father.' He paused. 'And that's why he sent you down here to chat with me because he knew full well that if he called me into Century House he wouldn't learn a thing. He's a very shrewd man is Freddie, but I was in this business before either of you were born.'

'What did you learn by being friendly with some KGB man?'

Carling thought for a moment and then said, 'I suppose the most important thing you learned was that a KGB man didn't have his eyes close together or horns growing out of his head. He was just a man. A man who was often berated by his wife for not being around when he was needed, or not getting the heating fixed. A man who liked sitting on his small daughter's bed at night and reading her a story before she went to sleep.' He sighed. 'What you learned all too often, my friend, was that you had more in common with the KGB man than you did with the kind of people who gave you both your orders. He was recruited in much the same way as you were, the same training and the same kind of work. It slowly dawns on you that despite the propaganda and the media there isn't all that much difference between you and your opposite number in the KGB.' He smiled. 'Or in the CIA for that matter.' He looked at his watch. 'We'd better get back.'

'Does it worry you that one of the tabloids seems to be taking an interest in you?'

'No way. They know that I've got just as much money as they have when we get to the High Court. Whatever they printed I'd have a writ on their editor's desk in an hour.' He stood up. 'Come on.'

Kennedy had listened intently as Mathews gave him an outline of his conversations with Carling, and when he had finished Kennedy said, 'Tell me again what he said about his time in Berlin.'

'He just told me that he was responsible for general intelligence from East Berlin.'

'No details of his contacts over there?'

'No.'

'I was hoping you'd get more. If there's any chance of nailing him it would be from that time in Berlin.'

'Was a report done when he finished his time there?'

'Yes. But it was useless.' He paused. 'D'you want to see it?'

'Yes. It might give me a lead.'

He had sat in Kennedy's outer office with a photocopy of the Berlin report.

SUMMARY OF ROUTINE CHECK ON SERVICE PERIOD IN BERLIN OF LIEUT.-COLONEL CARLING

Given brief (see routine task file 7042)
Subject was to gain information from East Berlin and adjacent *Länder* on the following:

1. Morale of Soviet and East German armed services.
2. Morale of civil population.
3. Relationship of Soviet authorities, military and civilian, with East German equivalents.

4. Economics and production.
5. KGB and Stasi personnel and organisation.
6. Operations of item 5.
7. Media attitudes.
8. Troop movements (Soviet and E. German).
9. Student opinion.
10. Building construction (public and private).

Distribution

1. SIS Berlin
2. SIS Düsseldorf
3. SIS London
4. Foreign Office (Extracts through SIS London)

Classification: Top-Secret. Certain edited items down to 'Secret'.

Local evaluation
Lt.-Colonel Carling's work was highly praised by all concerned in SIS Berlin and the London evaluations were all favourable. It was also noted that when the subject was posted back to London the flow of information from East Berlin was not only substantially reduced but was not much more than uncorroborated gossip.

Security
Subject operated virtually independently but there was no evidence of security breaches. However, I note that there is no record of subject's marriage to an American citizen in his 'P' file nor does he appear to have claimed marriage or accommodation allowances. When I queried this locally and in London I was given no satisfactory reason for this omission. I only learned of his married status by chance from a casual comment made by a local journalist in the Berlin Press Club who asked what had happened to the wife who, it seemed, was particularly attractive.

Signed: J.T. Hooper

Mathews read the report through several times and then said to Kennedy's PA, 'Where is Freddie? I need to talk to him before I go back.'

'He's at the Imperial War Museum but he'll be back in an hour.'

'I'll wait.' He stood up. 'I'll go to the canteen and get a coffee. Could you bleep me there?'

'Of course.'

Twenty minutes later Mathews was back with Kennedy.

'I read the summary.'

'Good. I can't remember what was in it but I seem to recall that it was very favourable.'

'It was.'

'So what's the problem?'

'Why wasn't I told that Carling had been married?'

'Where is the copy of the report?'

'With your PA.'

Kennedy pressed a button on the internal phone and said, 'Bring me the document that you gave to Tim Mathews.'

Kennedy sat without speaking but clearly disturbed or angry, it was hard to tell which. He almost snatched the two pages from his secretary, dismissing her with a wave of his hand as he started reading the report. When he had finished reading it he leaned back, looking up at the ceiling. Slowly he lowered his head to look at Mathews.

'I shouldn't have let you read that report. It should have been shredded way back.' There was a long pause. 'I'll tell you what happened but before I do I want you to listen very carefully to what I say now.' He paused. 'Under no circumstances will you ever raise this . . .' he waved his hand dismissively '. . . this episode with Carling. Neither will you ever mention what I'm about to tell you with anyone but me, either inside SIS or outside.' He paused and pointed a monitory finger. 'Believe me, if you don't stick to what I say your feet won't touch. You'll be out. And you know what that means. You'll get the treatment.' He paused. 'Do you understand?'

'I guess so.'

'And you'll take this as an order?'

'Yes.'

'OK. I'm going to give you just the basics. Mainly because it's only the basics that I know myself. Nobody, apart from Carling, knows what really went on.' He leaned back in his chair, both hands palm down on his desk. 'It seems that Carling fell in love with a German girl. East German, that is. He got her pregnant. He didn't want us to know. Thought we'd disapprove. Too bloody right, of course. So he used some pal of his at the American consulate to get this girl American citizenship. And some bloody US army padre married them. When it was all done he tells us. Not the full story. He told our people that she was an American and her parents wanted her married according to American law by an American priest. Very reluctantly the brass accepted the situation, for two reasons. First, Carling was a valuable and irreplaceable asset and secondly we did our own check-up and found she was in fact East German. And what was worse, her mother was Russian. You can imagine what the media would have made of that if they got hold of it. Top SIS man marries an East German commie. And, of course, puts her in the family way.'

'Was she a communist?'

'No idea. It didn't matter. It was too late to stop it.' He paused and lined up a pencil with his blotter. 'Carling would spill all he knows about everything if the truth got out.'

'Where is she – his wife?'

Kennedy sighed. 'She died. Killed in a street accident in Berlin. Carling was working for us there at the time.'

'What happened to the child?'

'The child? Oh, yes. A daughter. I think she became a musician of some sort. Goes under her mother's name. Seems both she and Carling doted on the mother.' He sighed. 'Very sad story, really.' But there was no sorrow in his eyes nor in his voice. Mathews had seen that kind of face at the funerals of SIS men. Mourners in dark suits and bowler hats, with rolled-up umbrellas even on sunny days.

'Do you still want me to carry on with Carling?'

'Of course.' Kennedy seemed surprised at the question. 'You've really got alongside him but I don't want anything to rock the boat.' He smiled. 'I meant to ask you before – how are things going about your son?'

'The court bit is in abeyance for a couple of months.' He hesitated but went on. 'There's a chance we might get together again. But it is only a chance.'

'Well done. I hope it works out well for you, Tim. Keep me in the picture, won't you?'

'Of course.'

On the train from Charing Cross to Frant Mathews sat in the First-Class carriage with his head back against the rest and his eyes closed. He found his meeting with Kennedy disturbing. He had been suspicious right from the start that they were concealing something, so that he was being used to fish around for something that would get Carling into the High Court. But why should they want to do that when it was all so long ago? Carling hadn't had any connection with SIS or even the Foreign Office for at least ten years. He never spoke in the House of Lords and he was a cross-bencher not controlled by any party's whips. Maybe Pamela was right and he ought to get out of the business right now and find some more routine job. But he had no qualifications for a normal job. And he had seen what happened to others who rebelled and took early retirement and half-pension.

They must have battened down the hatches on Carling's marriage very successfully. There was nothing about it in his *Who's Who* entry, and no mention of a wife in the newspaper cuttings.

CHAPTER 30

As they were going to include the Carling business on the agenda they met at the safe house rather than at Century House.

Kennedy outlined to Farmer and Shelley such details as he thought they needed to know and when he had finished it was Shelley who spoke first.

'Sounds to me, Freddie, that we're wasting our time. What does the DPP say about what you've got so far?'

'I can't consult the DPP in case I could be accused of prejudicing either the case or the fact that he *does* prosecute on evidence that I have already discussed with him.'

Farmer said, 'You said you'd got top legal advice. Who was it?'

'The Solicitor-General, Sir Frank Lewis.'

Shelley frowned. 'Wasn't he in intelligence during the war?'

'After the war actually. He was an I.Corps major.' He smiled. 'Who better?'

'Was it an unofficial chat?'

Kennedy smiled. 'Let's say demi-official.'

'And what did he say?'

'He said he felt we should keep going and that Mathews had established such an unusual and close relationship with our friend that we shouldn't think of throwing it away.'

Shelley was always one for negatives. 'I still think we're wasting our time.'

Kennedy nodded to Farmer. 'What about you, Dickie?'

'We probably are wasting our time but there are several good reasons why we should keep going . . .'

'Such as?' Shelley snapped.

'Calm down, Peter.' Farmer paused to collect his thoughts again. 'First of all, if something does come out eventually we can establish that we did everything legally possible to ascertain the facts. Secondly, we might even come up with enough hard evidence to put him on trial and use the rest as substantiation. And finally, what are we wasting – one guy's salary and some expenses and a few months of time.' He smiled. 'It's better odds than Premium Bonds give you.'

Shelley wasn't appeased. 'You know, Freddie, I've got a feeling in my water that you're up to something. Are you?'

Kennedy shrugged. 'Like what?'

'Like some hidden agenda that Farmer and I don't know about.'

'You've got a Machiavellian mind, old pal.'

Shelley was flattered by the comparison as Kennedy knew he would be. 'I've been in the business nearly as long as you have and I can hear the little bells ringing. I just don't recognise the tune.'

Kennedy shrugged dismissively as if mystified by Shelley's suggestion. 'It's your item next, Dickie.'

They discussed the character and life-style of an Iranian whose front was as a buyer of bits and pieces for obsolete aircraft but who was in fact working for Gaddafi gathering intelligence on the intentions of Islamic fundamentalists operating in his neighbouring states.

As Shelley and Farmer strolled towards Victoria Station

Shelley said, 'I'd like to know what that bastard Freddie is really up to.'

Farmer laughed. 'Forget it, for Chrissake. You see problems or disasters everywhere you look.'

'And I've saved us from walking into both in my time. You mark my word, that bastard's up to something.'

Farmer grinned. 'Maybe it's that girl in cyphers.'

Back at the safe house in Ebury Street, Freddie Kennedy was telling Mathews how satisfied the committee was with his work on Carling.

Carling has been asked to open a small exhibition of paintings by a local artist at the Bayham Abbey ruins. It was in a room at the back of the old house where the caretakers now lived and sold tickets to visitors.

The paintings were undistinguished watercolours and charcoal sketches and his audience was a junior reporter and photographer from the *Courier* and seven or eight people sheltering from the sudden rainstorm outside. He found things to praise in the paintings and sketches and emphasised that all people had talents but most people were too modest to try out their latent skills. If a thing is worth doing, he said, it was worth doing badly. A photograph with a lengthy caption made the front page of that week's *Courier*.

When the visitors had left, Carling stood at the open French windows looking towards the ruins of the abbey.

'He was a spiteful man was our Henry.'

'Who?'

'Henry the Eighth. He ordered the destruction that turned the abbey into a heap of stone just to avenge himself on the Pope. Two powerful men who didn't understand each other's motives. The Tudor King who wanted his marriage dissolved because he wanted a male heir, and a Pope who thought that by refusing the dissolution he was defending the Catholic faith.' He sighed. 'But I guess we mustn't complain. Out of that bloody conflict we at least got *The Book of Common Prayer*. Not to mention the first Elizabeth.'

Mathews was looking at Carling's face. His eyes seemed to be on something far away. Carling shook his head as if he were trying to wipe out whatever had been in his mind.

'You ready to walk back, Timothy?'

'Yes.' He paused. 'Can I ask you a question?'

'Go ahead.'

'Where did you live when you came back to London?'

Carling stopped and leaned against the oak gate that led to the road. 'In King's Road, Chelsea. Three floors over the Scotch Wool and Hosiery shop.'

Carling took Mathews' arm. 'We'd better get back, I've got visitors this afternoon.' He grimaced. 'Once a year I have to listen to the bankers telling me what they did with my estate last year. Jolly chaps, and not so dumb as they appear, but talking the jargon of finance that could be Mandarin Chinese so far as I'm concerned. A few bottles of champagne and the promise of tickets for England v. Scotland at Twickenham or Wembley depending on what schools they went to, and Rollses and Bentleys back to London.' He smiled. 'Better than politicians anyway.'

Mathews was with Gabby and the baby in the garden when Julie called out to him.

'Somebody on the phone for you, Tim.'

'Who is it?'

'Wouldn't say. Said he was a friend. Got an American accent.'

Mathews used the receiver in the hall.

'Mathews.'

'Hi Tim. It's Joe.' A long pause. 'Joe Maguire. I'm in London.'

'Have a nice day, Joe.'

Maguire laughed softly. 'I know. I wanted to apologise for what happened. Can we meet?'

'How did you get this number?'

There was silence for a moment and then Maguire said, 'Somebody owed me one and I cashed it in. I'm going back tomorrow so how about we have a meal tonight.'

'Where are you staying?'

'The Hilton. The one in Park Lane.'

'What time?'

'To suit you. Seven, seven thirty?'

'OK. Seven thirty in the coffee shop.'

'Great. Look forward to seeing you.'

Mathews drove the couple of miles to Lamberhurst and used the public phone on the Down. He dialled Kennedy's direct number and it was Kennedy who answered.

'Freddie, it's Tim Mathews. I've just had a phone call at the cottage. It was Joe Maguire, the CIA guy who was my contact to meet Hank Henney.'

'How the hell did he know you were there?'

'No idea. I asked him . . . waffled about collecting on a past favour.'

'What did he want?'

'Said he wanted to apologise. I fixed to have dinner with him at the Hilton. What do you think? Shall I go?'

'Yeah. See if you can find out why they ran you out. And he picks up the tab, not you.'

'I'll contact you tomorrow.'

'Do that.'

*   *   *

Joe Maguire looked like a man from IBM. Well-cut blue suit, white shirt and decorated tie, with cuff links like silver dollars. He was sitting at a table with all the trappings of tea for two, and half stood as Mathews arrived. As Maguire waved Mathews to the seat facing him he said, 'Good to see you, Tim. D'you take milk and sugar?' he grinned. 'I'm learning how to be the perfect hostess now I'm on my own.'

'Both. Sugar and milk.' He paused. 'How long have you been in London?'

'Got here yesterday morning, go back tomorrow afternoon.'

He handed over the tea and a bowl of wrapped sugar. 'I know it's hygienic but this wrapping drives me crazy.' He looked at Mathews, smiling. 'Apologies from Langley for that cock-up. Won't happen again.'

'What was it all about?'

Maguire shrugged. 'Crossed wires, rivalries, bloody-mindedness and fingers too quick on the trigger.'

'Whose finger, Joe?'

'Hard to tell. By the time Langley had at least traced the gun somebody had wiped it clean.'

'Convenient all round.'

'Not really. We made ourselves look fools to you people and we were grateful for your guy Kennedy not pressing the point too hard.' He stood up. 'I've booked a table upstairs, let's go and eat.'

They had a table by the windows that looked over Hyde Park to the traffic on the Carriage Drive down to Knightsbridge.

After they had given their orders to the waiter Mathews said, 'Now tell me how you found out where I was and how you got an unlisted telephone number.'

'Well, finding out where you were was a process of elimination. We checked your old number in Esher and got a frosty reception from a lady but a new number – your new rooms. No response and answering machine not on. Then we thought about the reason for your trip to New York. We had words with Hank Henney who not only wasn't helpful but was positively obstructive. A bit of pressure was applied and we got the name George Carling. Lord Carling, in fact. Now when you get among the lords our embassy's the place to try.' He paused. 'Seems like your Carling guy is a quite frequent visitor to Grosvenor Square.'

'And how did you get the number?'

'I got back to NSA at Fort George Meade. They cover everything. Seven minutes flat.'

'A lot of hard work just to apologise for a cock-up.'

Maguire shrugged. 'Why not. We value the goodwill of our friends in Century House.'

Mathews snorted. 'You could have fooled me.'

'Hank Henney said you were asking him about this Lord guy. What's so special about him?'

'Why not ask Henney?'

Maguire smiled. 'Henney said he thinks you're trying to frame this guy.'

'A pretty delayed action if we were. He hasn't been in the business for at least fifteen years.'

'That didn't stop you people from putting the skids under Anthony Blunt.'

'It was a book that eventually exposed him, not SIS. They kept their side of the bargain.'

'Our guy at the embassy said he'd heard that one of your tabloids was working on an exposé of Carling.'

'There's always rumours about somebody about to be exposed as a crook or a traitor.'

'So why are you alongside the Lord?'

'You don't expect me to answer that, do you?'

'Why not? He must be important or you wouldn't have flown over to the States to talk with Hank Henney. You could have phoned him and saved the fare.'

Mathews grinned. 'I only paid one way, remember?'

Maguire ignored the crack, seemingly intent on keeping the talk to Carling.

'I think Langley have got a soft spot for your guy Carling.'

'What's that mean?'

'I think they wouldn't want him to get hurt.'

'Who says he's gonna get hurt?'

Maguire shrugged. 'Nobody.' He paused. 'So far.' He looked at Mathews for a moment before he said, 'What are you people trying to pin on him?'

'Joe. You're getting very near thin ice. You'd better back off. Carling's our man – not yours.'

For a moment Mathews thought that Maguire was going to argue and then the American said quietly, 'It's just a word to the wise, old pal. Just a hint.' He paused. 'How are things with your old lady?'

'Calming down. I see my boy now without any hassle.'

'Good – when are you coming to the States again?'

'No idea.'

'If you're coming let me know and I'll pay you back for the cock-up last time.' Maguire stood up smiling and then, his face serious, he said, 'By the way, Hank Henney sends his best wishes to friend Carling.' He held out his hand and Mathews took it without comment. Maguire stayed behind to settle the bill and Mathews took the elevator back to the ground floor.

*   *   *

Mathews dialled Kennedy's direct office number and the phone was answered immediately.

'Kennedy.'

'It's Tim Mathews. I've just left Maguire. Shall we meet?'

'Sure. I've been waiting in case you called. Where are you? I'll come over.'

'In Park Lane. At the Dorchester. OK, I'll wait for you.'

Kennedy was in white tie and tails and looked quite impressive.

'Forgive the rags, I'm going on to a late do. Tell me what happened.'

Mathews went carefully through his conversation with Maguire and when he was finished Kennedy closed his eyes, thinking. When he opened his eyes he said, 'What was your impression?'

'I got the feeling that Maguire had been sent over officially to find out what the state of the game was with Carling.'

Kennedy nodded. 'I agree. But why are they interested in Carling after all these years?'

'Maybe for the same reason that we are. They want to know something out of his past.'

'Or maybe there's something that they know that they don't want us to know.' He shifted in his chair. 'Has Maguire gone back?'

'He said he was leaving tomorrow.'

'Any idea where he's staying?'

'At the Hilton.'

'Whoever wants to protect Carling over there must be high level. After the balls-up they made when you were over there they wouldn't be letting Maguire pussyfoot around unless some top brass thought it was really necessary.'

'What did Carling do when he was over there?'

'He was our man at the embassy. Third Secretary or something like that as his cover. It was more or less a liaison job. There was so much rivalry between the CIA and the FBI, and the CIA and us that we were constantly getting crossed wires. Nothing serious but they had to be dealt with diplomatically.

'I think they leaned on Carling for information about the Soviets and the Warsaw Pact countries because he knew far more than they did. But we wanted him to keep it low level. Then it was decided to appoint an SIS guy as full-time liaison with CIA. Independent and nothing to do with the embassy who constantly protested to the FO about us having an SIS man using the embassy as his cover.

'We put up several names – at least two. The Americans said no to both and then came back and said that they would accept Carling because they valued his judgement.' Kennedy shrugged. 'So we went along with it. And that's what he did for a few years before he came back here.'

'Did he retire from SIS or was he eased out?'

'Officially he retired but he stayed on our strength because the Foreign Office wanted his advice from time to time.' He looked at his watch. 'I'm sorry, Tim, but I must go.'

Mathews had phoned the cottage to warn Julie that he would be late back but she had given him a key to the main door before he left for London.

It was 2 a.m. as he drove his car over Waterloo Bridge and headed for the A21. There was little traffic on the road after he left the suburbs and he switched on the radio. He listened for a few minutes to LBC. It was a phone-in patronised by all the usual crazies and bigots not yet asleep, and he switched it off.

The strange thing about his time with Carling was that it demonstrated why they had never got Philby into court. Except for the Albanian business they had both done more or less the same things. With all the media crap about Philby it created a background that left no doubt in the public's mind that he was a traitor. But there was no way Mathews could class Carling as a traitor. Misguided maybe, but nothing more. But the media could make him into another Philby. Like Carling said, it isn't possible to make a judgement today on what happened thirty years ago. And as Carling often said – that was then, and this is now. Mathews was glad he wasn't doing his job in those days.

Julie and Gabby had waited up for him, the baby in her carrycot on the table in the kitchen alongside the chessboard. For a few moments he couldn't speak as they made him a mug of tea, he was so moved that they should stay up half the night just to welcome him back. Despite feeling guilty at his reason for being there at all he still felt more cared for than he had ever felt before in his life. It wasn't just politeness, they obviously genuinely cared about him.

CHAPTER 31

Carling was standing at the window of Mathews' bedroom. He was sipping from a large teacup and was wearing a rather worn silk dressing gown.

'You won't believe it but it's starting to snow. Real fat snowflakes coming down in slow motion like feathers. And outside it'll be wonderfully silent. "*Stille Nacht, heilige Nacht.*" Wonderful. Shame it won't last, this time of year.'

He turned to look at Mathews who was still in bed, the tea at his bedside untouched.

'The girls tell me that you were frightfully late getting home last night. A good evening?'

Mathews smiled wanly. 'Not really. But I had a good meal at the Hilton.'

'Which one?'

'The one on Park Lane.'

'Ah, yes. The only real one. The others aren't Hiltons at all. Could be in Red China for all the use they are.' He paused and said casually. 'What do Freddie Kennedy and his pals think about your time with me? Are they happy . . .' he laughed '. . . or disappointed.'

Mathews smiled but not with conviction. 'I don't really know.'

'Somebody at the Travellers' told me that one of the rags, the *Sun* I think it was, was trying to scrape together a piece on me as the Fifth Man.' He laughed. 'Or maybe the Sixth Man. They'll probably try and cross your palm with silver sooner or later.'

'They don't know anything about me.'

'Don't be so sure. Julie says she's certain that some creep has been watching the cottage recently.' He grinned. 'Maybe Kennedy's put a tail on you as well as me.'

'I don't see me as a tail on you. Far from it.'

'And how do you see yourself?'

Mathews sighed, leaned up in the bed, and it was several moments before he responded.

'I see myself as looking from today's perspective at things that happened decades ago.'

'To what purpose?'

'To do justice to all concerned.'

'You're kidding.'

'I'm not, I assure you.'

'What you're actually doing, or supposed to be doing, is trying to establish to the satisfaction of the High Court that the things that Kim Philby and the others did during the war and after were treasonable. They couldn't do it when Philby was around and they can't do it now that he's dead. They wonder if they might do it with me as a substitute. And you're their hunting dog, their blood-hound, quartering the years.' Carling smiled suddenly and said, 'Don't take it to heart, dear boy. The more you learn about those days, the more you'll have your doubts.'

'So why don't Kennedy and the others have doubts?'

'Oh they do, my boy. They do. You've got a double role. First you're just a piece of insurance and secondly, you're on a fishing expedition. Neither you nor they know what you're looking for . . .' he shrugged '. . . but who knows – maybe you could find something.' He smiled again, 'But you have to take care to make sure you land a trout not a shark.'

'I've got a feeling you're telling me something.'

'Maybe Kennedy's trying to tell you something too.'

'Give me a clue.'

Carling opened his mouth to speak and then closed it slowly, shaking his head.

'No. It's not a game. It's people's lives that are involved.'

He turned and walked to the door turning the big brass knob slowly as he looked round at Mathews. Such a young man. What was he – thirty-four maybe thirty-five? He probably understood computers and CD-ROMS but not the human mind. He could drive a high-powered car but he couldn't skin a rabbit, he knew the words of Joan Baez's songs but not what they meant. And his heart? His heart was somewhere between his belly and his head when it should have been halfway between his eyes and heaven. Like the others he had probably read Freud's words but would never understand what he meant – that men's minds were the products of fears and instincts struggling with the cobwebs of emotions and experience.

He waved his hand to the young man and quietly closed the door behind him.

CHAPTER 32

On the drive back from Esher, Mathews realised that he was glad to be returning to the cottage. Pamela was obviously considering taking him back and making a fresh start. But he didn't belong there any more. He was a visitor. Treated with a politeness that he had never had as a husband. And even for young Tony he was an interruption to his normal life. If he asked about their daily lives it sounded as if he were probing, a tourist who didn't speak the language checking on the life-style of the natives. He was seldom there for longer than a couple of hours but it had become just a duty. A duty from which he was glad to escape. Aware that in truth nobody benefited from the time he spent there. They were as relieved to see him go as he was to leave. Everybody could get back to their normal lives for another week or so.

Carling had played the piano for them after the evening meal. Viennese songs, a bit of Fats Waller stride piano and, with a smile at Mathews, one of Chaminade's *Songs Without Words*.

After Julie and Gabby had gone to bed the two men watched an OU programme on robot technology until Carling had switched off the TV in exasperation.

'There are times when I'm in sympathy with the title of the song from the musical – "Stop the World I Want to Get Off".'

Mathews smiled, he was used to Carling's outbursts of indignation. 'Why at this particular moment?'

'We make great play on the dignity and satisfaction of being in work. Unemployment must come down. The top priority. And on the other hand we extol the virtues of technology. One robot doing the work of ten men. So ten men lose their jobs. Maybe we should call a halt to technology and say that men having jobs is more important than the economies of robot production lines.

'The government urges youngsters to study maths and science and engineering – why? Because the nation needs more scientists and engineers. What arrogance. Education is for being alive with not just for getting a job. This is getting to be like Orwell's 1984. And the opposition talk about "the workers". We're all workers now, one way or another, whether we like it or not. Over six hundred idiots calling themselves MPs. A hundred would be more than enough for what they do.'

Seeing the look on Mathews' face Carling laughed. 'I'm at it again. On the soap box.'

'Why don't you say your say in the House of Lords?'

'Waste of time.' He sighed. 'If there's one thing I've learned it's that you can't do anything on a mass basis. All you can do is a bit of good here and there with individuals. Give a chap his weekly rent money and he'll take care of it but hand it out from the state and it's not valued. It's not just doing good that counts, it's how you do it.'

Carling stood up, yawned and stretched his arms. 'I'm off to bed. Lock the back door before you go up.'

*   *   *

With the battery run down on Julie's elderly Fiesta, Mathews had driven her into Lamberhurst to the village stores. Carling insisted that the village shops should be supported where possible for all their shopping, not just when they ran out of sugar.

There were enquiries in the shops about the wellbeing of His Lordship, and when he would next be on TV, and Mathews could tell that the interest was genuine. It seemed odd that a man with such unorthodox views should be so universally liked. Maybe it would be a good idea for Kennedy to fix for him to meet someone who was not one of Carling's fans.

Back at the cottage he used his mobile phone to contact Kennedy's PA and make an appointment. Kennedy could give him twenty minutes at 4.30 p.m.

Kennedy was in an amiable mood and said, 'You're right. All that bloody casual charm works on everyone.' He paused. 'Including me.' He frowned. 'The only likely critic who comes to mind is Parsons. Sir Peter. One-time Director-General of SIS. I understand that he detested George Carling. He's retired now, of course. Has been for years. Lives somewhere in Hampstead. Great cricket fan. Wants to be near Lords.' He looked at Mathews. 'Would he do?'

'Sounds ideal. Would he see me?'

'If I hint that we're taking a hard look at George Carling he'd see you all right.' He reached for his internal phone. 'Find me Sir Peter Parsons' address and telephone number, will you?'

A few seconds later he was writing on his pad. 'How do you spell that? OK. Yes – thanks.' He hung up, tore off the page of his pad and pushed it across his desk to Mathews, leaning over to read it as he dialled the number. He said to Mathews, 'Get yourself a coffee or something while I talk to . . . ' He paused. '. . . Sir Peter. I hoped I'd get you . . . it's Freddie, Freddie Kennedy.'

Mathews took the hint and left. Half an hour later he came back. Kennedy was still on the phone and he waved Mathews to a chair. He seemed to be finalising the time and place of a meeting '. . . of course . . . ten o'clock . . . at your place, tomorrow . . .' Kennedy nodded as if his listener could see him, '. . . of course . . . yes . . . thanks for your help . . . no, not Jim, Tim . . . Tim Mathews . . . good . . . take care of yourself.' As he hung up he said, 'That OK with you? Ten tomorrow at his place?'

'Where's his place?'

'Hampstead. Wedderburn Road – it's on the piece of paper I gave you.'

'Tell me a bit about Sir Peter.'

Kennedy sniffed and loosened his tie. His hands moved to tidy the papers and files on his desk.

'He was our DG for five years. Brought in from the military, supposedly to tame the wild men of SIS. He had been a major-general on the General Staff. A gunner. Left-wingers always feel that putting a soldier in charge of SIS is a suitable revenge.' Kennedy gave a brief laugh. 'We eat them, of course. In our own peculiar way we speak the same language. Carling wasn't SIS when Parsons was DG. Carling had some mystery relationship with the Foreign Office advising on Soviet affairs. Peter Parsons saw it as going behind his back. Probably was.' He paused and sighed. 'So, back to Parsons. Good army record, sports and all that. Bright.' Kennedy waved his hands around. 'That's about it.'

*   *   *

Major-General Sir Peter Parsons MBE lived in the top flat of one of the Victorian houses in Wedderburn Road that had once been the family homes of bankers and businessmen. Pevsner would have classed them as impressive but without grace or style. You got space and bricks for your money. But they were still highly desirable residences. Not mere houses.

Parsons lived alone and everything was spic and span. A place for everything and everything in its place was his oft repeated watchword. Tall, lean, with a hawk-like face and long quite elegant limbs. His voice was high-pitched but still with the rasp of the sergeant-major he had once been. Dress was casual. Sports jacket, corduroys and Royal Artillery tie. His alert dark eyes took in Mathews and was not impressed, but he ushered him into the high-ceilinged sitting room before he left to make coffee for them both.

The few books on the shelves were mainly the reminiscences of men who went on safaris hunting animals in places like the Northern Frontier District and the Ogaden, with titles like *With Rod and Gun in the Danakil Country*.

The coffee was served on a silver salver that had been awarded to Captain Parsons RA for winning the 30 Corps middle-weight boxing championship, Bad Harzburg 1965.

'Mathews, isn't it?' He said and without waiting for an answer he went on, 'Help yourself to milk and sugar.' He sat back in the leather armchair. 'Kennedy said you wanted my views of Carling, yes?'

'Yes please.'

'Never could understand why everybody saw him as a kind of mixture of Robin Hood and Mother Theresa. Lots of charm, of course, but plenty of rascals can pile on the charm to get what they want. They all said Philby had charm. But I could never put my finger on what

Carling actually wanted. And charm or not he was an arrogant man. Saw things his way and if you didn't agree too bloody bad. He was deep. Always that brain ticking away. Didn't miss a thing. I wouldn't trust him. Not a team man. Too much the loner.'

'Did you think he was good at his job?'

'Couldn't rightly say. Was gone before I took over. Farting around at the Foreign Office when I met him.' He paused. 'The only experience I had of his work was in Germany. Called to a meeting. Some chap – turned out to be Carling – had got wind of those bloody East Germans planning to break through the Wall in fifty places and take over the whole of Berlin. Hoped to catch us with our trousers down and overwhelm us. Carling pontificated about the psychology of the East Germans and said if we moved troops and guns up to the Wall they'd know they wouldn't surprise us. That's what we did – and it worked. Not a peep out of the bastards.' He gave a sharp laugh. 'He was right that time. Got to give him his due.'

'Did you see much of him?'

'No. Just odd meetings at the FO and at Joint Intelligence meetings. Never said much but he took it all in.'

They talked to no great purpose for another half-hour and in the taxi home to Charing Cross Station Mathews came to the conclusion that Parsons' dislike of Carling was mainly because he didn't see Carling as a proper soldier. Not only 'didn't stick to the book, but hadn't even read the bloody thing'. But SIS weren't intended to be soldiers.

CHAPTER 33

Carling stood at the bench in his radio shack looking at the four stacks of typewritten sheets. There were twenty-four pages in each pile and an A4 envelope beside each one.

It had taken him two weeks to compose and type the statement, and the original had been copied at the Camden Road copying shop in Tunbridge Wells. Camden Road was named after Marquess Camden who had left the ruins of Bayham Abbey to the State in 1961. Camden Road was no beauty spot but in its long necklace of pokey shops you could find anything. If you wondered where on earth you could buy something you'd do well to head for Camden Road. He had done the copying himself so that the young lad couldn't read the top page which was entitled: 'A notarised statement by George Carling made at the offices of Buss Stone, Solicitors, Tunbridge Wells, in the county of Kent, dated—' The date had been left blank despite the fact that His Lordship would be swearing his oath in a matter of hours.

He pulled up the folding chair and wrote in long-hand the appropriate words on the three envelopes. One was addressed to his friend, the senior partner of a highly respected Mayfair solicitors, the two others to the editor of *The Times* and the Director-General of the Special

Intelligence Service. His own original was taped to the back of an oil painting of a seascape on the wall over the fireplace in his bedroom.

He tucked the three copies into a Jiffy bag, sealed it and propped it up against the monitor beside the decoding terminal next to the transmitter.

He was tempted to dust the radio equipment. It hadn't been used for so long and nobody else was allowed in his shack. He found stopping people from twiddling knobs as irritating as having people smoke in his car.

He sighed as he stood up slowly and then looked at his watch. It was 4.30 a.m. and tomorrow he'd have to go up to London and hand the package over to Arthur with his instructions.

Arthur Parrish had known him for years but while Carling was sitting on the other side of the partner's desk he must be treated as a client. An important client. He listened intently to what Carling had to say and then said quietly, 'I'll do exactly as you say, my lord.' Then he leaned forward. 'D'you really think this is necessary, George?'

Carling shrugged. 'God knows, Arthur. But I'm not prepared to take the risk. This is my piece of insurance.'

'But it's all over now. When did Philby die? Eighty-eight wasn't it? Surely nobody would rake all that up after this time?'

'There's some I haven't told you, Arthur. And yes – there are those who would dig it all up if they got wind of what was in that statement.'

'You think someone could try to kill you, George? Surely not.'

'They could make at least a million, more if they played their cards right.' He smiled. 'The going rate isn't what it used to be. It's in hundreds these days, not thousands.'

Parrish shook his head slowly. 'What a world we've made, George. All those men who died. It sickens me.'

Red sealing wax and a candle were brought in and the envelopes sealed and impressed with Carling's ring.

They had lunch together at the Inn on the Park and talked only of the pre-Raphaelite collection at Birmingham's Art Gallery. Arthur Parrish was a Birmingham man, proud of its gallery, its symphony orchestra under young Simon Rattle, who was, in his opinion, well overdue for a knighthood. Parrish was also prepared to defend Aston Villa FC from all its detractors who criticised its talented waywardness. However, like a good many alumni of King Edward's, Birmingham, Arthur Parrish went back to the city only when business made it unavoidable.

By the time the train was past Sevenoaks the suburbs had given way to a landscape of woods, sheep, hops and apple orchards. Carling had left his car at Frant Station. As he stepped down on to the platform at Frant he stood and watched the train pulling out, the guard smiling and saluting as he went past.

He was the only passenger who got off the train and he stood there long after it was out of sight. There were only two railway stations he really loved. One was Milano Centrale that made him feel that it was all a wonderful mistake and they'd run a railway line through a cathedral. The other was Frant, the small, old-fashioned country station like the one in the film of *The Railway Children.*

He turned slowly and walked to his car, acutely aware of the incredible difference between his feelings now and what he had been doing in London. He was determined not to end up like that wretched man who had died in Moscow two years ago.

They were still sitting at the table after it had been cleared and Julie had brought in the coffee things and a bottle of wine.

As Carling poured coffee for himself he said casually, 'How are things on the home front?'

Mathews hesitated and then said, 'I don't really know.'

'What's the problem?'

'I think the problem's me. I think Pamela would be willing to have me back and have another go.' He sighed. 'But I don't feel any pleasure in the thought. I don't look forward to it.' He paused. 'In fact I dread the idea. But I'm worried about Tony, and seeing him.'

'Any idea why you don't want to try again?'

'Yes. Now I've had time to think about it without the old pressures, I don't think we made a pair. We just don't fit. She won't change and I wouldn't want her to change. Why should she?' He smiled. 'I know you must have talked to her about me. Pointing out any good points I have. And that makes her see me in a different light. But that isn't love. I realise now that she never did love me, and on my side it was physical attraction and I don't even feel that any longer. I don't want to criticise her. She's OK in her own way. But she's not for me. I'm bored when I'm with her. It's like being in a play. A rather boring play.' He shrugged as he came to a stop.

'And what are you going to do about it?'

'God knows.' He half smiled. 'Any suggestions welcomed.'

'D'you mean that?'

'Yes. I really do.'

'I'm not very surprised by your analysis. I think you're right in your assessment. It would be easy to say that the break-up was her fault because of the stupid affair she had with the solicitor. But bearing in mind her rather subdued personality she must have been very unhappy to see that as a solution. And now it's you who has to make the decisions. You can't make her and Tony and yourself happy but you can leave her her dignity and you can be a useful, helping father to Tony.' He smiled. 'I'm afraid there's no prize for you, dear boy. Maybe in the future but not right now. But despite that, be generous. Generous to the feelings of a rather wounded female. Let it be very gradual, maybe.' He paused. 'I know you'll be generous financially. Let her stay in the house and things like that. Practical things are her idea of affection.'

'Do you think I'm unfair about how I feel?'

'No. Not at all. You too have a life to live.'

There was a short silence and then Mathews said, 'Am I wearing out my welcome here? Would you like me to call it a day?'

'Has Kennedy said you should leave?'

'No, he hasn't said anything.'

'If he ever did suggest you should stop would you let me know?'

'Yes, of course. But I'm sure he'd tell you first or discuss it with you.' He smiled. 'I'm sure you'd be glad to hear that they'd had enough.'

'It's not in Kennedy's hands. It's the others.'

'Which others?'

'Why do you think they put you on to me?'

Mathews shrugged. 'Just to check things over. An independent opinion.'

Carling smiled. 'They know all they need to know. You're just a piece of insurance to see what you can find out. Because if you could find something then somebody else could too.'

'I don't understand, George. I'm out of my depth. Why should they want to do that?'

'To see if they can avoid having to kill me. To stop me talking. You can tell Freddie Kennedy that I've already taken appropriate precautions. They would do better just to sweat it out. It's too late to go back over that ground. And anyway it all ended when Philby died two years ago.'

'Could you tell me what all that was about?'

Carling shook his head. 'No. There's no point in involving you.' He smiled. A grim smile. 'Anyway you're part of my insurance.'

'But what if I stumbled on this thing? I'd feel guilty about talking to you in case I caused you trouble.'

'You won't, my friend.' He smiled. 'And if I told you you wouldn't believe it. There are times when I don't believe it myself.' He stood up. 'Forget all this. Just carry on. I'm off to bed.'

As Mathews undressed slowly he realised that those few sentences from Carling had changed everything. For one thing Carling had cut him off from Kennedy. If it was as Carling had described, Kennedy could easily make some unwise move against Carling. And who were 'the others'? And what did they want to hide? And what did Philby's death in 1988 have to do with it? It had all the indications of an SIS cock-up. But craziest of all – why did Carling think they might kill him? He'd said it so casually, as if it was merely another way to solve some unidentified problem.

He hadn't sounded shocked or surprised or apprehensive when he said it. Just the flat statement of an obvious solution. Maybe the old boy's mind was beginning to wander, roaming down the corridors of time to the days when they did solve problems that way. But that was a long time ago. Like Carling said so often – that was then and this is now. Or maybe it was like Dunne's Theory of Time where memory got out of kilter.

An owl hooted from somewhere in the beech trees as Carling walked in the garden and from far away he heard the bark of a hungry vixen in search of food for her cubs.

There were long shadows on the grass from the apple trees in the orchard and he was pleased to see that there was still a light on in Gabby's place over the garage. He walked slowly up the wooden stairs and knocked on the door.

A voice from inside said, 'Who is it?'

'It's me, Gabby.'

He heard two sets of bolts drawn and then came the light from inside.

'Are you all right? Come on in. You look tired.'

She had made him a pot of tea as he sat in the wicker armchair. With the cup halfway to his mouth he said, 'Are you happy, my dear?'

'Of course I am. I love it here.'

'And how's Lottie?'

She frowned. 'It's Carlotta. I don't like Lottie.' Then she smiled. 'She's fine.' She paused. 'Would you have liked to have a child?'

'I have got a child. A daughter.'

'What's her name?'

'It's Rachel, after her mother. Her mother's dead.'

'What does your daughter do?'

'She's a musician. Plays and teaches violin. She has an apartment in New York but she travels all over the world.'

'Do you ever see her?'

'I do when she's in Europe and I can arrange to be in the same place.'

'Are you lonely without her?'

He sighed. 'I'm lonely without her mother. I loved her a lot.'

'Can I ask you something silly?'

Carling laughed. 'Try me.'

'How do you get to be an earl?'

'Oh that's easy. My father was an earl and when he died I was his only child and I became the earl.'

'Do they pay you for being an earl?'

'No. Some earls are quite poor.'

'I read a piece in the *Daily Mail* about you. It said you were very rich.'

Carling smiled and shrugged. 'I get by, my dear.' He paused. 'What would you like to be when you're older?'

'I just want to be me with the baby.' She smiled, her head tilted endearingly. 'You've made me so happy.'

'You make me happy too. You and Julie.'

'Do you want to play chess?'

'Julie tells me you're very good now.' He stood up, a little clumsily. 'But it's time I was on my way.'

At the door he kissed her on the cheek and she stood holding the door open so that the steps were lit. When he turned to wave to her she waved back and he walked slowly back to the cottage. He realised that he had said too much to Mathews but he was sick of the games they played. He had thought that when Kim died that would be the end of it. With him in his grave they could bury their guilt and their fears. But he'd been wrong. They wanted him out of the way too. And if not out of the way at least subdued by constant pressures. They were scared now that that wretched tabloid might ruin it all.

Lying in bed he tried to remember how it had all started, but his thoughts kept going to the young girl who had a baby because she wanted someone to love her. There was a flicker of summer lightning on the ceiling, and a distant rumble of thunder sent his mind to Beethoven and the fourth movement of the 'Pastoral'. A few minutes later he was asleep.

He woke just after 4 a.m., put on his dressing gown and walked to the window, opening it to the scent of the honeysuckle that he had planted himself when he first came to the cottage.

As he leaned with his elbows on the window-sill his mind went back to Mathews. He ought not have given him advice about his marriage and his domestic arrangements. His advice was only suitable for the impetuous, the desperate, the people who bled from wearing their hearts on their sleeves. And Mathews was not one of those. Neither was his ex-wife. They calculated things, weighed things up and were moved only by the negatives of anger and whether they were getting a square deal. Matching shoes and handbag, and tweeds and brogues. Good people but dangerous for a man like him to advise.

It was beginning to get light when he went back to bed. His last thoughts were that it was time he brought it all to a head.

CHAPTER 34

Carling was breaking off the deadheads of a large pink pelargonium in a terracotta pot, tossing the heads into a wheelbarrow. When Mathews joined him, offering to help, Carling stood up slowly. 'I've had enough, Tim. How about you ask one of the girls to do us some coffee.'

When Mathews came back Carling was sitting on the bench by the pond in the orchard. He put the tray between them on the bench, and Carling pointed at the pond. 'This pond is a permanent reminder of the silly things that amateur gardeners can do. When I had it put here I forgot that in the autumn it would be covered with fallen leaves from the trees.' He laughed. 'I was trying for a Renoir effect.' He sighed. 'Never mind, another lesson learned.' He paused. 'There's a team from Radio 4 coming to interview me this afternoon. A series on "Are you a Christian?" '

Mathews smiled. 'And are you a Christian?'

Carling laughed. 'I can only go along with what Clem Attlee said when asked if he was a Christian. As usual he wasted no words. "Accept the Christian ethic, can't stand the mumbo jumbo." '

'What religion were you brought up with?'

'Well, my father was staunch Church of England. Seldom went to church other than for funerals and weddings and, give him his due, didn't make me anything as my mother was a Roman Catholic.' He smiled. 'And I swear she only went because she loved the singing, and all the mumbo jumbo. I think on reflection I rather liked aspects of it too.'

'What aspects?'

'The theatricality, the visual, the showbiz, the singing, the saying of prayers for sick people in the congregation. The assurance that there was forgiveness for all us sinners. Must be very consoling to have that belief.'

'So what didn't you like about it?'

Carling snorted. 'I'd never want to be part of a faith that maintained that if a baby dies before it's baptised it goes to purgatory. What arrogance. What kind of mind can think up that sort of rubbish?' He paused. 'I've just realised. I hope you're not a Catholic, Tim. I wouldn't want to detract from anyone's faith.'

'No. I'm not anything. But not with your conviction. More indifference and laziness.'

Carling turned his head to look at Mathews. 'Something I meant to ask you. Tell me, just briefly, what your impression was of Philby before you and I talked.'

Mathews thought for a moment. 'That he was a traitor, had cost men their lives, was a drunk, an adulterer.' He shrugged. 'Just a general shit.'

Carling nodded slowly. 'Are you going to be around this evening?'

'Yes. If it's OK with you.'

'Right. I'm going to tell you what Philby was really like.'

The BBC team had stayed for tea and His Lordship was obviously a firm favourite. He had eventually said that if he had to be something he thought he would be a Jew. When pressed for his reasons he had laughed and said that he would have been a more talented pianist and musician with Jewish blood in his veins.

They had dined alone and when they got to the coffee Carling pushed aside a vase of roses so that they could see each other more easily.

'So . . .' said Carling '. . . let's talk of Harold Adrian Russell Philby.' He paused. 'Did you realise that he was awarded the OBE in the 1946 New Year's Honours List?'

'No. I didn't know that.'

'It was his thirty-fourth birthday. I wonder why it's never mentioned. And he got it for his work against the Germans. So that's where we start with the truth.'

'Was it withdrawn when he went to Moscow?'

'No. If they had done that they'd have been stirring up a real hornet's nest. Anyway they had no grounds for doing it.'

'But the media didn't take long to publish the facts.'

Carling smiled. 'They thought they were the facts but they were just part of the game but they didn't know it. They still are, and they still don't know it.' He paused. 'I'd better tell you right now that you're mixed up in something . . . something that happened way back but could still cause far the biggest scandal that SIS have ever been involved in. No matter how skilfully you talked with me you wouldn't ever find out what it's all about. Freddie Kennedy has his suspicions but nothing more. And he's getting very near the line that if he crosses over he's going to be eliminated.' He paused. 'I'm going to suggest that we do a deal, you and me.'

'What kind of deal?'

'A deal that gets Kennedy off the hook that he doesn't know he's on. I'll give you some information that he'll see as valuable enough to call off this investigation but won't do anybody any harm.'

'What if the tabloid carries on its so-called investigation?'

Carling shook his head. 'They won't do a thing. They've been told what will happen to them if they don't back off. They're a big organisation with lots of interests in the UK and the USA, they could be wiped out in a couple of months. No apparent connection with us but they'd know who had pulled the plug on them.'

'They could publish that they'd been blackmailed or pressured.'

'They're in the business of making money. They've already been squeezed a little. They'll back off all right.'

'But why should I do this? Why should I make a deal that my people may not approve?'

'Because the deal is based on you not telling them what I'm prepared to tell you.' He shrugged. 'I'll give you the titbit for Kennedy and he'll be satisfied.' He paused. 'I'm relying on the fact that when you know the real facts you won't want it to go further. You won't want to turn bad into worse.' He paused and leaned forward as if he was looking at his reflection in the polished table. Then he looked back at Mathews. 'You'll learn what only four or five living people know, of something disgraceful. The others who knew, and they were very few, are long dead. It would be a condition that you would make no notes of what I tell you and that you never discuss it with anyone but me and one other person.'

'Who is the other person?'

'Would it make a difference if I told you?'

'I don't know. Depends who it is. Do I know the person?'

'You've met him, only briefly and only once. You met him a few weeks ago in New York. His name's Hank Henney. As you know, he's ex-CIA.'

There was a long pause. Then Mathews said quietly, 'How did you know I'd met him?'

Carling shrugged. 'They keep me informed. They have an interest in what happened too.'

'Am I right in thinking all this has something to do with Philby?'

Carling seemed to be considering his answer and then he said, 'Yes. That's where it started anyway.'

'Can I have time to think about it?'

'So long as you don't consult anyone else. This is between you and me.'

'Will what you tell me make trouble for SIS?'

'No. I'm trying to avoid trouble.'

'What about CIA?'

'The same applies.'

'Can I just go over what I understand you're suggesting? Just so that I don't get any wrong ideas.'

'Sure. Go ahead.'

'You said only four or five people living now know about whatever this is. Does that include you and Hank Henney?'

'Yes. And of the other three, one has been in a coma for several months. He is to have his life-system switched off in two weeks' time. So effectively there are only two others involved.'

'Are they SIS?'

'One *was* SIS and the other is CIA.'

'What does Kennedy know?'

'Nothing. He just has a faint suspicion that I could be what he describes as the Fifth Man.' Carling smiled.

'Or it could be the Sixth Man, depending on his current workload. I'll give you something factual that will keep him happy. Nothing to do with what I propose telling you about.'

'Let me get this straight, George. You're going to tell me something that is so serious it could cause chaos to SIS—'

Carling interrupted. 'And to the CIA.'

'And the CIA. So that I don't carry on with this stuff we've been doing. You'll also give me some other thing that will satisfy Freddie Kennedy that this operation was worthwhile.'

'That's about it.'

'And if I go along with this what happens?'

'Nothing. Kennedy can feel he's done his job. And I can go back to my peace and quiet.' He paused. 'And I expect you'll get a promotion.' He sighed. 'I just want to lay these ghosts once and for all.' He paused. 'I guess you'll just have to trust me – or not, as you decide. I'll have to trust you too, not to tell anyone else what I tell you.' He paused. 'Do you want to think it over for the night?'

Mathews shook his head, sighed and said, 'No. If I ever trusted anyone it would be you.'

'OK. Have a good night's sleep and we'll talk tomorrow. To give you a fair picture of what went on way back it's going to take quite a long time. I've got to try to make you feel what it was like in the early 1960s.'

'Where were you at the time?'

'I was in New York working with Hank Henney on keeping the peace between the CIA and SIS. I was just about to be brought back to London although I didn't know it at the time. Of course . . .' Carling stood up, smiling. 'Don't let me get going. It's a long story. Let's leave it for tomorrow.'

FOUR

CHAPTER 35

In the dog days of summer 1955 when the newspapers and magazines were hard pressed for a titbit, they slipped in a piece here and there about Burgess and Maclean. But the public were not really interested. It was four years since the two spies had fled to Moscow. Questions intended to revive the public interest were tabled in the House from time to time. One of these was asked by George Wigg, a Labour MP who asked – 'Would the Foreign Secretary institute inquiries into the suggestion made in a Sunday newspaper that there is widespread sexual perversion in the Foreign Office?' Herbert Morrison, the Labour Foreign Secretary, was not a man given to witty evasions but maybe he had intended no wit when he commented – 'I can only say that perhaps I have not been long enough at the Foreign Office to express an opinion.'

The first bomb fell when KGB officer Vladimir Petrov defected in Australia and stated that Burgess and Maclean were not just failures on the run, or even merely homosexual lovers, but long-term Soviet agents who had been working for the KGB since they were recruited in their young days at Cambridge University.

A rather bland White Paper was published that admitted a few minor facts but gave very little away. This led to another more pointed question in the House from

Lieutenant-Colonel Marcus Lipton, MP for Brixton. It was the first mention of Philby, and a Third Man.

The question was brief and to the point. 'Has the Prime Minister made up his mind to cover up at all costs the dubious third-man activities of Mr Harold Philby who was First Secretary at the Washington embassy a little time ago, and is he determined to stifle all discussion on the very great matters which were evaded in the wretched White Paper, which is an insult to the intelligence of the country?'

This was a question that could not be evaded. It concerned a named individual's character and by then, the Foreign Secretary was the patrician Harold Macmillan, who dealt with the matter himself. He assured the House that no evidence had been found that Mr Philby, a former temporary First Secretary in the Washington embassy, was responsible for warning Burgess or Maclean. He added that he had no reason to conclude that Mr Philby had at any time betrayed the interests of his country, or to identify him with the 'so-called Third Man, if indeed there was one.'

The next morning Philby gave a press conference at his mother's flat. He claimed that he had been precluded from defending himself because of the Official Secrets Act. He also claimed that although he thought he must have come across Burgess and Maclean at some time he could barely remember them. Most of the journalists were won round. He had been unfairly maligned. They'd leave him in peace in future.

Having once been a foreign correspondent during the Spanish Civil War, Philby didn't hesitate when supporters inside SIS used their influence so that he was offered the job of Middle East correspondent for the *Observer* and *The Economist*, who shared his salary and expenses. What the two editors were not told was that Philby was also commissioned to act on a freelance basis for SIS with his employment as a journalist giving him perfect cover.

CHAPTER 36

Carling had hired a taxi at Gatwick to take him to Marlow. Waring had told him on the phone that he had been booked in at The Compleat Angler. The meeting would be at Waring's house on the other side of the river. At the reception desk there was a note from Waring to say that he would not be needed until mid-afternoon the next day. The envelope also contained five twenty-pound notes and a copy of a letter to the hotel that confirmed that his bill would be paid in cash with no limit on his credit.

The double bedroom was well-furnished and the windows gave a wonderful view across the Thames. He thought it was the big white house on the other side of the river that was Waring's house. The Warings had made their fortune when cotton came into its own. Charles Waring had chosen the diplomatic service and never mentioned the family business which was now into textiles of every kind. He had been a friend of Carling's father. But he wasn't Director-General of SIS in those days. The gardens of Waring's house sloped down to the bank of the river. A rowing skiff and a thirty-foot cruiser were moored alongside a wooden jetty. The late afternoon sun cast long shadows across the lawn from the poplars that lined the tennis court. The meeting was to be at Waring's house but he had been given no hint of what it was about.

It was just Waring, Houghton and Smart. And despite
Waring's assurances, Smart had had the whole house
checked for bugs. Two Field Security sergeants in plain
clothes were wandering around the grounds trying to look
like house guests. There were several cars parked on the
gravel forecourt. There was Waring's dark red Daimler
Sovereign, Houghton's white Rover 105 and Smart's
green Ford Prefect that reflected his caution. He was
a psychologist and was aware that a car could indicate
the character of its owner. The spectrum of Ford Prefect
drivers was too wide to provide any clues.

Waring had set the meeting in his book-lined study and
a table had been brought up from one of the downstairs
rooms. Waring had chosen it himself. It had to be round
so that there was no status from where you sat.

'Welcome, gentlemen,' said Waring, as he looked from
one to the other. 'Dickie Smart is going to give us his
assessment of the man's personality.' He turned to Smart.
'Go ahead, Dickie.'

'OK. I don't propose using the technical jargon of
psychology. So this is as much a portrait as an analysis.
Understood?' He looked at the other two and Waring
nodded and Smart went on. 'Philby wanted out from the
pressures that were on him. The questions in Parliament.
The press. People in SIS who suspected him and he was
aware that MI5 not only had a thick file on him but were
just waiting for a chance to nail him . . .

'The offer of working for *The Economist* and the *Observer*
seemed like a great solution. He stuck it for a time but he
missed the power and the competition that he had in SIS.
He missed London. Beirut was just a backwater. He was
like those remittance men shipped out to East Africa by

wealthy families because of the scandal they caused at home. And like them he passed his time getting drunk and womanising. He was cut off from everything that had been his life. His contacts with us were remote and he wasn't interested in the Middle East. Nobody was interested in him any more. He was a nobody. People avoided him because his behaviour was outrageous. He was desperate to be back in the action. Better the harassment of being a suspected traitor than rotting in Beirut. And even his friends in Moscow weren't interested in him any more. He had nothing to give them. He was out of the game. They kept in touch from time to time but he was no longer useful. He was an old horse put out to grass.

'When his father died he was literally alone; they had shared the house up on the hill. And he realised that his old man was livelier, more used to life in an Arab country than he was. He felt older than his father.' Smart shrugged. 'That's where he'd got to.'

'How up to date is this, Dickie?' It was Houghton who asked.

'That was how it was up to August this year when he got in touch with Henderson at the embassy. And Henderson got in touch with us.' He waved towards Waring. 'It went straight up to the DG.'

For a few moments there was silence and then Waring looked at Houghton and said, 'You'd better relate your bit, Eddie.'

'He didn't exactly get in touch with Henderson. They were at some party, a private party. Kim was very drunk but he said to Henderson that he ought to have stayed with SIS and done a flit to Moscow and worked back to London.'

Smart said, 'Could be just the wandering mind of a

drunk. A fantasy.' He shrugged. 'Even a leg-pull.'

'I said that to Henderson, he doesn't think it was. He thinks Philby was serious. Says he's desperate to be the centre of attention again.'

Waring said quietly, 'Costs nothing to find out. If it worked it would be the most successful blow to the Russians we've ever made.'

Smart sighed. 'And the trickiest. We'd never know where all the mirrors were.'

'We should judge by what he passed to us.'

Houghton nodded. 'And if we turned out to have been out-manoeuvred yet again – so what? He'd be getting nothing from us.'

'So. Do we have a try?'

Houghton smiled. 'You're dying to press the button, aren't you?'

Waring shrugged. 'I don't want to miss out on a wonderful chance.'

'What have you got in mind?'

'I think we should use Carling.'

'Why Carling?' Smart was not a man who took up ideas first time around.

'He's known Philby all through their careers. He's been under suspicion himself from time to time. So he knows what it's like. He always was tolerant towards Philby.' He smiled. 'And before you ask, Eddie, he's not queer and he's not a boozer and he's never been interested in communism or any other political ism.'

'Is that enough to satisfy Philby if he was thinking seriously about such a caper?'

'Well, there's a bit more. Apparently Henderson jokingly went along with Philby's little fantasy and asked him who he'd want as his contact at SIS. Philby thought for quite a time and then said that George Carling was the only man he'd ever trust.'

Houghton reached for the Thermos. 'Anyone want another coffee?' He looked around but nobody responded so he said, 'Would *we* trust Carling?'

Waring smiled. 'More to the point is, would Carling trust us? Would we go along with it?' He looked at Smart. 'What do you think?'

'I've only met him a few times. A strange man. Very aware, very observant. A bit on the emotional side, I'd say.' He shrugged. 'That's about all I can say.'

Houghton said, 'Where is he at the moment?'

Waring avoided the real question and said, 'He's at The Compleat Angler. He doesn't know why he's been called here and I've said I'll talk to him tomorrow.'

'What do you have in mind?'

'I want Carling, if he agrees, to meet Philby, talk this over and decide between the two of them how to handle it. It will need careful planning and even with careful planning it could easily go wrong.'

'How many people will be involved?'

'Directly, only Carling and myself.'

'And indirectly?'

'I shall consult others on what we need to get from Philby. But the people concerned will not know what it's for. And I shall see that Carling formally retires from SIS but that he gets whatever assistance he needs.'

'And if it blows up it will be Carling who carries the can.'

'Let's wait and see.' He smiled. 'Philby may have changed his mind and Carling might not want to play his part, and without him there's no show.'

*   *   *

289

As they walked back to their cars half an hour later, Smart said, 'What did you make of all that?'

Houghton laughed. 'You tell me.'

'I think the old boy wants to go out with a bang. He's only got a few years to go before he retires. Having Philby in Moscow and working for us would be a nice act to go out on.'

'Do you think Philby will do it?'

'The state he's in nothing's too crazy if it makes him important again. But what about the Russians? Do you think they'll buy it?'

'Depends on the scenario that Philby and Carling can set up. They'll be suspicious because he's never shown any inclination to head to Moscow and it's at least six years he's been in Beirut. Could have slipped out to Moscow any time he wanted.' He paused. 'What sort of stuff has he been sending back to us?'

'Nothing of any importance. I guess what we get is no more than what *The Economist* gets.'

'Ah well. I guess we won't be kept in the picture.' He laughed softly. 'Not unless it goes down the pan and then it'll be all my idea.'

Smart grinned. 'That's just standard SIS paranoia, my friend.'

The phone call from Waring came as Carling was having breakfast. The meeting was to be at 10 a.m. and Waring sounded unusually friendly. It gave him time for a leisurely walk across the bridge and past the church to the drive that gave access to the half-dozen big houses that spread out along the river bank. Waring's house was the third one along. Not the biggest of the houses but in any other part of the country it would be described as a mansion.

There was a bell on one of the stone pillars that flanked the wrought-iron gates and it was answered immediately by a young man who looked him over and smiled his recognition. 'He's waiting for you, sir. Straight down the drive.'

And sure enough Peter Waring was there at the open door under a porch covered with wisteria and clematis. He was dressed casually, a white cotton shirt and light blue slacks, his hand outstretched.

'Good to see you, George. Come on in. Let's go up to my study.'

In Waring's study there were no shelves of books and no signs of hi-fi equipment and LPs. But the pictures on the walls were surprising. Original black and white prints of photographs by Doisneau, Ansel Adams, and the Westons, father and son, Ernst Haas and Robert Capa. He turned to Waring. 'What a wonderful collection. Are you a keen photographer?'

Waring smiled. 'Keen but not good. And I do mainly portraits and landscapes.' He laughed. 'I think I love cameras as much as the pictures. A bad sign. The apparatus ought not to matter. But the feel of a Leica and a Hasselblad, the workmanship, make them works of art for me.'

'And why not? Like old Doctor Johnson is supposed to have said – "if a thing's worth doing, it's worth doing badly".'

'It makes you appreciate the real thing all the more.' Waring waved Carling to one of the leather armchairs, the kind they have in gentlemen's clubs. When they were both settled Waring said, 'I'm going to ask you to do something for me. Can I ask that whether you agree to do it or not, you never discuss what I'm going to tell you with anyone else. Nobody, absolutely nobody.'

Carling smiled. 'Sounds very serious. Yes. You can have my assurance.'

For fifteen minutes Waring went over what had happened but he didn't mention Philby's comment about Carling.

When he had finished he said, 'What do you think?'

For a few moments Carling didn't reply and then he said, 'If you were talking about anybody but Kim I'd say don't take it seriously. I'd reckon it was just the ravings of a drunk.' He paused. 'But with Kim I'd say he probably means it. He's a driven man, a man who needs to make things happen. If he had been a career soldier he'd have had a chest full of medals. He needs to matter. To be in the inner circle. To be influential and respected as perceptive and far-seeing.'

'Do you think he'd do it? Go back. And work for us?'

'I think it's possible but you'd have to accept that he'd be co-operating with the KGB too.'

'Have you had any contact with him since he went to Beirut?'

'He had a drink with me the day before he left. And I've had a couple of meals with him since. When he was on leave in London. The last time was about six months ago. He was very bitter about the Russians who hadn't been in touch with him for over a year. And the last time he had contact with them he was asked to do a list of all his contacts and movements since he was at university. He was furious about it, and said so quite openly. Said it was an insult. Which it was, of course. But he knew it was because they'd never really trusted him despite all he'd done and risked for them.' Carling smiled. 'Getting his own back on them would be a considerable incentive.'

'What do you think the problems would be?'

Carling leaned back in his chair, thinking. Then he said,

'There would be three problems. Convincing him that we were on his side. That we respected him. All that sort of stuff would be the first problem. Then there'd be the problem of setting up a scenario that would convince the Russians as to why he wanted to go back. And finally there would be the problem of communication. They'd be watching him like hawks.'

'When he was talking to him, Henderson asked Philby who he would want as his control in London and Philby said you were the only man he'd trust.' Waring paused. 'Would you do that? Take over the planning and the continuing contacts?'

'Is that what you want?'

'Yes. Without you nothing will happen.'

'What support would I get?'

'Anything you wanted you'd get.'

'And I could put together a deal with Philby without needing approval from anyone else?'

Waring hesitated for a moment and then said, 'Yes. It would be up to you.'

'What incentives can I offer him apart from the work and money? Could I suggest that if he worked with us efficiently for say four or five years, that he could come back and be publicly praised as a hero rather than a traitor?'

Waring sighed. 'That's OK. I don't want to restrict you in any way.'

'Who else knows about the scheme?'

'Houghton from covert operations and Smart, who's SIS's tame psychologist.'

'What do they know?'

'They know what I've told you, they know that I'm thinking of activating the thoughts. They know that

Philby said that you are the only SIS officer who he trusted. That's it. They won't be told whether you go ahead or not.'

'Why were they in on it so far?'

'Houghton was the one who heard the story from Henderson and Smart could give me a picture of Philby's mental condition and his personality. It was a pretty accurate picture in my opinion.'

'When do you want me to start?'

'As always – soonest.'

'I need to go back to Berlin to clear things up. It'll take a couple of days. Have you got an address for Philby?'

'Yes. He's at what was his father's house in Ajaltoun up in the hills.'

'How much do the two newspapers pay him?'

'About two thousand a year. And much the same from us. He's always pressing both sources to up his pay.'

'Are the newspaper boys satisfied with what he sends them?'

'Far from it. If it wasn't for us helping them in other directions I think they'd sack him.'

'Who's our local contact with Philby?'

'A man named Weston. Do you know him?'

Carling smiled. 'I've met him a couple of times. He gave a lecture on how to recruit and run Arab agents. Absolute rubbish, of course.' He paused. 'It's best we keep it just to you, me and Philby.'

'I agree. Let's do that. And let me say I'm very pleased and relieved that you'll have a go at this rather crazy scheme.' He stood up and walked with Carling to the door. 'I won't interfere, George. But if I can do anything to help just let me know. Any time. Day or night.' He paused. 'Let me give you a lift back to the hotel.'

'I'd rather walk.' He smiled. 'I've got a lot to think about.'

They shook hands and Waring stood, shading his eyes from the sun, as he watched Carling until he disappeared at the bend in the driveway.

Philby was no longer at his father's old house and now lived in a flat in the rue Kantari and it was there that Carling left a note with his room number at the hotel. They met the same evening and Philby was obviously delighted to see him. He was leaving Beirut the following day for a holiday with Eleanor, her daughter Annie and his own son Harry, in Jordan. He'd leave them there after a couple of days and come back alone to Beirut. They could talk about the old days.

There was a paved balcony along one side of the flat and they sat there to get the breeze that came from the sea. They had talked for an hour and Philby had drunk very sparingly. When the light was beginning to go Carling turned from the gossip of SIS and asked the vital question.

'Kim, there was a rumour came back to London that you were not too happy with your present setup. And that you were thinking of making a change. Change of status and change of locale. Was it just a rumour?'

Philby smiled the smile that had charmed a lot of people. 'Was the guy at the embassy the source of the rumour?'

'Yes.'

'Who did he talk to?'

'The DG.'

'Waring?'

'Yes.'

'Who else was told?'

'The full facts – only me. Because you mentioned my name.'

'Is this why you came to see me?'

'Yes.'

'To persuade me to do it or to persuade me not to do it?'

'Neither. Just to talk about the possibility if you really were contemplating such a move.'

Philby smiled. 'Tell me what I'm supposed to have said.'

'That you loathed your present setup. That you wish you were back in SIS. That you were amused at the idea of being in Moscow and working for SIS as well as the KGB. And that if you did it you'd want me to be your contact at SIS.'

'And what did Waring say?'

'That if I agreed to handle it he'd go along with it.'

'And you. What do you say?'

'I'll talk with you about it if you really want to do it.'

Philby shrugged. 'I was half pissed when I said it. But not so pissed I didn't mean it.' He waved his arms around. 'I'm tired of living in this shitty town. Bored with the work. Bored with the people. Bored with my life.'

'There are other ways to relieve boredom. A lot less dangerous too.'

'You've thought about it, have you?'

'I've explored the idea.'

'You know what I would want in return?'

'I think so.'

'I doubt if you do. Tell me what you think I want.'

'I think you'd want to put a limit on your time in Moscow so that you could come back to the UK as an acknowledged hero. Cleared of all past suspicions and all those who were against you proved spectacularly wrong.' He smiled. 'Something like that.'

Philby was smiling. 'You look like everybody's favourite uncle but you're quite a shrewd old bugger really. Anyway, you're right on target. I'd love to see all those bastards with their pants down.'

'What about the Russians?'

'You know it's like a sign from God. My KGB handler hasn't contacted me for a year and he turned up just a week ago. Very solicitous. What could they do to help? So I asked him. What if I wanted to move to Moscow? He said he'd talk to the people in Dzerzhinsky Square and come back to me. He was back the next day. No problem. They'd be glad to have me as a kind of consultant. Just one little thing. After I was settled in there'd be a press conference, revealing that I had always been a Soviet agent. When did I want to do it?' Philby smiled. 'I told him I'd think about it and he said they'd need a week's notice before I went, to make the necessary arrangements.'

'Do you think they trust you?'

'No. I'm sure they don't. But it would be a media coup. I would be under close supervision and I could be useful.' Philby shook his head. 'They'd never trust a foreigner no matter who he was or what he did for them.' He smiled. 'Do SIS and MI5 trust me? Of course they don't.'

'We'd have to play it very, very carefully, Kim.'

'I'm glad you think so.'

'Why not think about it overnight, and if you still feel like going ahead we could start planning tomorrow?'

'I don't need to think about it. I didn't say my bit at the embassy just to shock Henderson. I was just casting bait in the water to see if anyone took it.' He paused. 'Do you trust Waring? Do you trust SIS not to play silly games?'

'The whole operation will be in my hands. Nobody else will ever know what we're doing. Just you, Waring and me.' He paused. 'Will you be taking the family with you?'

Philby shook his head. 'No. Just me. I'll send Eleanor back to the States, at least until I've settled in.' He stood up. 'Let's go down town and I'll take you to a real Arab place.' He looked at Carling's face. 'I'm excited, are you?'

'Kind of, but I want to be cautious. Make sure we've covered every angle so that you're safe.'

'There's a balance, George. Only the two of them, SIS and the KGB, working together could bring me down. One protects me from the other.'

'Don't count on that, Kim.'

'What's that mean?'

'If one or the other finds out that they've been fooled – even if it's imaginary – there are other things they can do beyond denouncing you in the media.'

'Like what?'

And Carling realised that Kim Philby thought he was too important to be killed.

'If the Russians decided that you were playing it both ways they could just dispose of you. You know that as well as I do. OK, they don't have to shoot you, food poisoning works just as well.'

'So?'

'So we walk very carefully, both of us.'

'You reckon I can trust them about coming back and having my name cleared?'

'Yes. It might offset all the criticisms that were levelled at them in the past.' He paused. 'If they didn't come clean then I would. They know that.'

'That would be a risk for you too.'

Carling smiled. 'It's not that easy to knock off an earl

without the media looking into it. They'd have to be very desperate to do that. It's up to you and me to see that they don't get desperate.'

'How are we going to communicate once I'm in Moscow? They'll be watching me round the clock.'

'Can you do Morse?'

'No.'

'Can you read Morse?'

'No.'

'Let me think about it. When can you talk to your Russian?'

'In a couple of days.'

'I'll go back to Berlin, then London, and I'll be back at the weekend. I'll contact you here, OK?'

'That's fine.' He paused. 'One other thing to think about. The Russians will be trying to work out why I suddenly want to leave when I've shown no signs of wanting to go before.'

Carling stood up. 'I think I can cover that.'

'Tell me.'

'When I come back I'll tell you. It could mean waiting two or three months before you go but it would be a perfect reason for going.'

Philby sighed. 'Apart from all this it's good to see you again, George. I know you don't agree with some of the things I did but at least you always understood even if you didn't forgive.'

'Take care, Kim.'

'You too.'

CHAPTER 37

The defection of Golitsyn provided a solid reason for Philby's planned defection. Both Philby and Carling knew that Golitsyn would have told both the CIA and SIS all he knew about Philby. And he knew quite a lot. A few weeks later Waring had fetched Carling back from Berlin for a meeting. They had met at a small Italian restaurant in King's Road, Chelsea, and after the meal they had walked up Sloane Street towards Hyde Park.

'I've got a problem, George. There has been a lot of pressure from the old China hands to try and get a confession out of Philby. Nothing has happened because nobody who knew enough was willing to go to Beirut and face him out. There's now a strong possibility that Nick Elliott is ready to go out and tackle him. If I stop him it will create a lot of resentment. But I'm prepared to do that if you feel I should. A confrontation could have all sorts of repercussions. What do you think?'

'Couldn't be better. Let him go but don't let him know about my operation, and see that his visit is leaked so that it gets back to Moscow. But I need another few weeks. I'm still trying to work out our lines of communication with Kim.' He paused. 'Could you drag it out to the turn of the year?'

'No problem.'

'A genuine move against Philby could provide all the urgency for a move to Moscow. That's something the Russians will understand. And the thought of whisking him out from under our noses will be an added incentive.'

'OK. I'll be in touch every day. Sorry to have dragged you away.'

'I've got a few things to clear up here anyway. You realise I'll have to move back to London as soon as he goes to Moscow. But I'm not going to activate him until he's been there for two or three months. Maybe a dry run on whatever system I end up with but nothing more.'

'Do you want Facilities to find a place in London for you?'

'That would help.'

'Where do you want to be?'

'Somewhere in this area would be fine. Sloane Square, King's Road, or somewhere off Sloane Street.'

'I'll get them on to it right away. D'you want furnished?'

'Yes, please.'

When Carling got back to Berlin there was a message for him from Hank Henney, who would like to see him urgently. He arranged to meet him that evening at Henney's place.

It had been snowing for an hour as he drove across from Grunewald to Henney's flat by the Europa Centre. It was the last week in November and Berlin had been lucky to escape the heavy snow that had been sweeping across Poland towards Scandinavia. At least Beirut was warm and sunny.

Henney was fond of bamboo furniture but was wondering if his wife would approve when she arrived in a few weeks' time. When he had ushered Carling into the sitting room, Henney waved Carling to a bamboo armchair stuffed with bright cushions and walked over to a small bar. He swung round to look at Carling.

'What you want, George? Got a bit of everything here.'

'Have you got a malt?'

'Glenlivet or Glenfiddich, which you want?'

'Glenlivet, please.'

Henney poured the whisky and walked over to hand it to Carling. And as Carling took the glass, Henney sat facing him on a bamboo settee.

'Good health, George.'

Carling lifted his glass. 'And to you too, Hank.'

Henney leaned down and put his glass on a small table beside the settee.

'George. The CIA had a problem.'

'*Had* a problem?' Carling smiled. 'What happened to it?'

'They passed the ball to me to run with.'

'And you're about to try and pass it to me, yes?'

Henney sighed. 'I wanna say that the only reason I'm involved is because of my relationship with you. None of it is my doing.'

Carling frowned. 'What's it all about, Hank?'

Henney shifted around on the settee, looking embarrassed and uncomfortable. 'I had a visit from two senior people from Washington. One from Langley and one from NSA. You've heard about NSA and what they do, OK?'

'Is that the outfit at Fort George Meade in Maryland?'

'That's the one.' He paused. 'As you know, they monitor everything on air – telephones, short-wave radio, the whole shooting match.' He sighed. 'And on the side they do a bit of bugging for the CIA. Seems like one of the places they've bugged is a flat in Beirut. Your friend Philby. They showed me a transcript and played me some tapes. The stuff they showed me covered you and Philby talking about a move he was thinking of doing.' Henney looked at Carling and shrugged. 'They want in on it, George, and they've got something to offer you that will solve one of your problems.'

'Let's just slow down a bit, Hank. You say your people bugged Philby's place in Beirut – why?'

'Seems they've always seen Philby as somebody special. When Angleton was head of CIA he always said Philby would end up as Director-General of SIS. But others in the CIA saw him in those days as a bit of a loose cannon. They wanted to know what he was up to.'

'You realise that what they heard me discussing with Philby is only known to our DG, Waring, and to me?'

'Yeah, they realise that and it's treated the same way on our side. Only the top man at NSA and one of my people at Langley know about this plan of yours.' He paused. 'And me, of course. And I was only told because I know you very well and we've always co-operated with one another.'

'And what are they asking for?'

'They just want to be in on it. You in charge and me feeding in some CIA input. And sharing what comes out.'

'But Langley were constantly swearing that Philby was the Third Man or some such thing.'

'That's all water under the bridge, George. Your people in SIS were the same. They still are for that matter, aren't they?'

'And what's this solution to a problem that your people are offering?'

'It provides you with a non-physical contact means of communication from a UK base to Moscow.'

'Why so coy?'

'Because the CIA use it for contact with their agents who can't read Morse and where physical contact is impossible or dangerous. Once other people know how to do it we've lost the advantage.'

'Somebody'll break into it sooner or later.'

Henney shook his head. 'No way could anyone do that. But I'll brief you properly if we can co-operate.'

'Let me think about it overnight, Hank.' He paused. 'I'm inclined to say yes but Waring would never agree. I'd have to do it solo. And I'd want to meet your two guys and be satisfied that they'd keep this operation totally secure.'

'What stops you from saying yes now?'

Carling shrugged. 'I don't know. I guess I just need to get used to the idea that I'm here in Berlin talking about something that happened in Beirut that was supposed to be higher than top-secret. Knowing that somebody in Langley ordered somebody else to bug Philby's place. And it never entered my mind, or Philby's mind for that matter, that somebody in Washington would be listening to tapes of our talk a couple of days later.' He paused. 'Why didn't your people go straight to Waring?'

'Waring would rather call the whole thing off than let the CIA in on it. He'd be scared of all the political rows it would cause if it went wrong. What's OK as a bit of private enterprise isn't so good when it brings in foreigners.'

'Maybe he's right, Hank.'

'You know better than that. We already know what's being planned so you don't take any risk on letting us come in on it.'

'What will your people do if I say no?'

'I only agreed to approach you if they swore that they'd do nothing if you turned me down.' He shook his head slowly. 'They won't play games, George. I'll see to that. And they've no interest in rocking the boat.'

Carling knew that he didn't really have a choice. They knew what he and Philby were planning to do. They could have leaked it to the media if all they had wanted was to expose the machinations of SIS. And the fact that they were active participants gave a kind of extra validity to the whole affair.

He looked across at Henney. 'You swear you've told me the truth.'

'I swear.'

'And you'll accept that my word is final on everything, even if it doesn't suit Langley?'

'On my word, George.'

Carling shrugged. 'OK. Welcome aboard. Now tell me about the communication thing.'

'The CIA has a problem in passing instructions to agents in some foreign countries who don't read Morse. They asked for help from NSA at Fort George Meade and they came up with what we call numbers stations. We use them all over the world but particularly in the Soviet Union, the Warsaw Pact countries, China, and the Arab countries. Places where our agents are under constant surveillance. From several different base stations an operator dictates a series of numbers. Five-number groups. We use German, English, Spanish, Arabic and Russian. They are broadcast on short-wave frequencies and can be copied by the agent concerned. There is an indicator at the start of the transmission that indicates the recipient and the basis of the code. The code is generally related to a book, a novel or reference book, or in some cases a specific programme from a normal broadcast station like *Voice of America*. The message is broadcast on several days on different frequencies and at different times.' He paused and shrugged. 'It works very well.'

'Isn't it easy to monitor?'

'Not easy. But even if a monitor comes across a message he has no way of decoding it because the code is not a logical code. Virtually random.'

'What about Philby's communication back to me, to us?'

'We have a couple of dozen safe dead-letter boxes in Moscow. We'll identify them. Photographs and streets maps you can show him before he leaves. He can use them and his stuff will be passed back to you unopened with a special envelope code.'

'Could I see it in operation if I flew with you to the States?'

Henney smiled. 'We've got a base station already operating in the UK. You can see that. But remember the operator doesn't know where his agent is or who he is. He's a signals expert not an intelligence guy.'

'Where is this place?'

'It's at a small village in Oxfordshire called Barford St John.'

'How long has it been there?'

'Just over a year.'

'You cheeky bastards.' He paused. 'Why can't GCHQ pick up the traffic?'

'They can, but they can't decrypt it because it's a totally unknown and random code-base.'

'When can I see the place?'

'Any time you want.'

'Let's fly over tomorrow.'

Carling drove them from Gatwick and came off the main road at the Service Station at Ardley so that they could check the road map and have a coffee. They had to circle round on to the B4100 up to the B4031. Then it was just a few miles to the two Barford villages of St Michael and St John.

The sign by the five-bar gate said Milton Poultry Farm and a smaller line of text said, 'Wholesale and Trade Only.'

There was a cement driveway that led to what looked like a wooden office building, a fairly large garden shed. Beyond the shed was a path to the doors of a dozen long battery houses. As the men got out of the car they could hear the sound of ventilation fans. As Henney led the way to the office shed, the door was opened by a young man.

'Can I help you, gentlemen?'

'My name's Henney, I've come to see Josh.'

The young man smiled and held out his hand. 'Come right in. I was expecting you. I'm Josh Abramski.'

The small office was immaculately tidy with the usual filing cabinets, desks, chairs and an electric typewriter. There was a Pirelli calendar hung on the wall. It was November but it was showing the picture for October. A very pretty blonde facing the sun on some tropical beach. As Carling stared at it, Josh laughed. 'She's my favourite. I don't go for the November girl.' He stood with his hands on the back of the chair. 'It looks like minimum security, but it ain't. That's just part of the scenario. The back of this shed, through the door, is steel-lined on the inside. No windows, no ventilation shafts. Virtually impregnable. You like to see the works, Mr Henney?'

'Yes, please. Can you give us a rundown on it? The procedures.'

The door took two keys and two coded cards to open and the lights were on inside the room already. The walls and ceiling were painted white and a white Formica-covered shelf at waist level stretched along the whole of the longest wall. On the shelf were various pieces of equipment and above the shelf was an array of a dozen or so three-pin sockets.

Josh stood between them pointing at equipment as he described it to them.

'This, gentlemen, is an ICOM transceiver. It receives signals and can transmit signals. It covers both functions in a variety of modes. You can hear normal broadcast stations from all round the world. In FM, AM and sideband, USB and LSB. It also receives in coded Morse which is called RTTY and various codes like AMTOR and SITOR. So far as this operation here is concerned I use only USB or LSB. Upper and lower sideband.

'This, is a sophisticated tape machine. It uses normal high-grade audiotapes. It records and plays back. For recording I use this microphone. Next is this special tape-player where you can stack up to ten audiotapes. This small device is an a.t.u., an aerial tuner. The computer is used together with this radio-controlled clock. The clock is accurate to within one second in a million years. The computer software controls the time, frequency and rate of transmissions.' He smiled and waved a hand. 'That's about it.' He laughed. 'But to operate it you don't need to understand anything more than switching on or off the switches in a certain order. Any questions?'

Carling said, 'Where do your transmissions end up?'

Josh smiled and shook his head. 'You're not cleared for that, sorry.'

Henney said, 'Who dictates the tapes?'

'I do.'

'In English?'

'English and German.'

'Does it work successfully?'

'I've no idea, Mr Henney. I just carry out my instructions. There's no feedback. It's not necessary.'

'And if you're ill or something?'

'There's always a standby twenty-four hours a day. Two in fact. Either one could be here inside five minutes and our traffic schedules aren't heavy. We're on air not more then sixty minutes a day. Some days nothing at all.'

Josh played them one of the tapes and they listened to the drone of his voice as he read out the numbers of the message. When he switched off the tape he smiled. 'My voice goes through a machine after taping so that it's altered.'

Carling said, 'As a matter of interest do you actually produce eggs here?'

Abramski laughed. 'We've got eighty thousand hybrid in-lay hens and we make a good profit. But what really matters is the realistic cover it gives me.'

They talked for another ten minutes or so and then Carling and Henney went back to the car. It was cold and raining and the weather matched their subdued mood. It was a long, almost silent drive back to Gatwick but they managed to get seats on the late flight to Berlin. At Tegel they arranged to meet the next morning and they shared a taxi, which dropped Henney by the Gedächtniskirche and then took Carling on to Grunewald.

Henney had got a set of operating instructions for the numbers system. Carling had found it simple to operate after a few dry runs, and Waring had arranged for the BBC World Service broadcasts to the Soviet Union to insert a codeword in their main news that would indicate 'no-message' or a message the following day. Waring asked questions as to why it was necessary. The only outstanding item was the choice of a book that Philby could take with him as a code-base. Carling had got hold of a proof copy of a book called *The Spy Who Came In From The Cold* by John le Carré and felt that Philby would be amused by the title and interested in the contents. That would be the code-base book.

At the meeting in Beirut with Philby, Carling was shocked by Philby's state of mind. He was deeply depressed and unhappy about his life in general and seemed relieved that he would be moving to Moscow. Philby had no problem in absorbing the basics of the numbers radio scheme and was highly amused by the choice of book for the code-base.

Henney provided two sets of the details of the dead-letter boxes that were to be used. There were pictures and descriptions and brief comments, indications of nearest Metro stations and public transport. This material was not to be taken with him but would be the basis of the first coded messages he would receive in Moscow. When Carling told him about the Americans wanting to be included, Philby seemed to see it as an additional safety factor for himself. Philby disliked Americans but he obviously felt that the American interest was rather flattering. He was obviously affected by the recent savage sentence of forty-two years imprisonment on George Blake. Philby suspected that the KGB defector who had exposed Blake also knew about him. He was now in regular contact with the KGB men in the Lebanon and the particular officer who would arrange his escape to Moscow. When Carling told him of the proposed visit by Nick Elliott intended to get a confession from him, Philby agreed that the visit could supply authentic evidence to the Russians that it was time for him to get out.

They ate together the following evening in the room Carling had taken at the Mushrek Hotel on rue Makdisi.

Philby seemed to have got back a lot of his usual confidence.

'Do you think your CIA friends have bugged this room too?'

Carling smiled. 'I did a deal that there would be no more bugging here or anywhere else.'

'Will you be full time on this game?'

'Yes.'

'Won't you get bored?'

'Not when somebody's life might depend on me not being bored. Don't worry, Kim. I'll back you every way I can.' He paused. 'How do you feel about going to Moscow?'

Philby sighed and looked at his glass as he slowly swirled the brandy around before he looked up at Carling.

'It's strange. Way back when I was young Moscow was the light at the end of the tunnel. The great hope for mankind. Worth taking risks for, worth all the deception and lying. But that was twenty-five years ago.' He smiled. 'It's a bit like having a blind-date with a girl that you couldn't keep. But you knew she was a real beauty and you kept sending her love letters and bunches of roses and she said she loved you too. And twenty-five years later you're going to meet her. She's forty-five now. And married with two kids.' He shrugged and smiled. 'It'll be an interesting meeting but inevitably disappointing. She's not that girl. Probably never was. And you're not the same guy either.' He shrugged. 'But it'll be interesting.'

'What about your connections back here?'

'I shall do my best to forget them. Time will tell.'

'What about Burgess and Maclean?'

Philby smiled wryly. 'Burgess is driving them crazy. His handlers are changed every two months. Can't stand him. The booze and the young boys. They never expected him to turn up. Neither did I. It was a real shock when I heard he'd gone off with Maclean.'

'How is Maclean?'

'I gather he gets by. They don't like his arrogance but he has his uses.' He paused. 'They'll want to debrief me and that can take months.'

'They'll treat you well, Kim?'

'Maybe.' He grinned. 'Even if it's only to make SIS look like the idiots they are.'

'I always felt you rather enjoyed your time in SIS despite the politics.'

'That's very perceptive of you, George. I did enjoy it. Especially when it hurt the Germans.'

'What will you miss?'

Philby thought for a moment. 'Cricket, the Test matches. Reading *The Times*. Being on the inside. Playing Gershwin and Berlin and Jerome Kern. Pubs.' He shrugged. 'That's about it.' He paused. 'Any idea when Elliott is going to appear?'

'I'd guess sometime in the first week in January.'

'Was it his idea or Dick White's?'

'A bit of both, I think.'

It was nearly midnight when Carling walked down to the street with Philby. The streets were still busy. Beirut was a night town. The Middle-East's Paris.

As Carling waved to a taxi and it pulled up he took Philby's hand. 'I won't wish you a happy New Year but I do wish you a life that maybe you can enjoy. Like your girl in the blind date. You'll be a man with two mistresses who you love almost equally. Best of luck, Kim. I'll be thinking of you all the time.'

Philby smiled but said nothing and walked across to the taxi. Carling watched him bend to give the driver his instructions and then get into the back of the cab. He watched until the tail-lights faded into the darkness.

CHAPTER 38

———————

There had been a time when Nick Elliott was amiably disposed towards Philby. Nobody, not even Elliott himself, could define when his attitude changed. He had been head of SIS's operations in the Lebanon at one time so he knew his way around Beirut. He rented an apartment to ensure privacy for his confrontation with Philby and he wasted no time in contacting him. He phoned Kim Philby on 10 January and arranged a meeting.

Nick Elliott was a shrewd and experienced interrogator and he posed his questions with considerable skill to the man he had come to despise. But Kim Philby had spent a lifetime avoiding and deflecting questions about his life and work. When Elliott laid out a pattern of accusations Philby denied nothing. But on the other hand he confirmed nothing. The pressure was considerable. He knew they couldn't arrest him in a foreign country but there were other things that they could do and Elliott was insistent and obviously determined to get a confession, preferably in writing. Philby said that he needed a few days to think about what Elliott was proposing.

When Philby discovered that the man who was head of Beirut SIS was away for some days on a skiing holiday he was sure that Elliott would wait until he was back before making any move against him.

After his meeting with Elliott, Philby contacted his KGB handler, Petukhov, and told him what had been said. Petukhov said that he needed four or five days to make the arrangements for Philby's escape to Moscow.

Through a mistaken piece of antisurveillance trade-craft involving the carrying of a newspaper when it should have been a book, Kim Philby eventually had only an hour hurriedly to pack a small bag for his journey.

There were two Russians with him in the back of the car that took him down to the docks that night and handed him over into the care of the captain of the Soviet ship *Dolmatova*. It sailed an hour later on its long sea journey to Odessa.

Carling first heard the news of Philby's disappearance from Hank Henney and the next day it was in all the newspapers. It was a field day for the media and in the following ten days all the old stories and suspicions about Philby had been aired and embellished and exaggerated. There was no official comment from SIS but it was clear from some of the press stories that some SIS and MI5 people were feeding the media with background information.

It was April before Kim Philby browsed through the boxes of second-hand books at the shop in the Arbat and offered the owner an English shilling to pay for a tattered copy of the Russian translation of Dickens's *Oliver Twist*.

The message was in Berlin two days later. Carling had a week to prepare the first message. By June the system was working. Twice a week the numbers were read out slowly in the flat tones that the voice-analyser produced, and roughly once a month something came back from Moscow. Messages picked up from the toilets in a cinema, from cemeteries, from library books, and taped under the slats of park benches.

CHAPTER 39

Mathews looked at his watch as he sat on the bench at Frant Station waiting for Carling's train from London. It was ten minutes before it was due.

He wondered how Carling would be. He had avoided Mathews the day before and had seemed preoccupied when he drove him to the station that morning.

There were blackberries on the hedges that flanked the station platform and a small border of wilting pansies and chrysanthemums that had been planted to decorate the old-fashioned station. The sun was going down, and he could see rabbits in the field on the other side of the track.

It seemed incongruous sitting there in the quiet of the small station having listened to what Carling had told him. And Carling didn't look like a man who had been involved in such a web of deceit and subterfuge. But people involved in intelligence work never did look like spies or counterspies. Like Carling always said, they were just men. There were a few Harry Palmers and a Smiley or two, but there were no James Bonds.

Maybe Carling had told him all that he was going to tell him. Philby obviously hadn't come back, he had died in Moscow in 1988. Mathews had seen the TV news reports of Philby's burial. Full military honours, they said. Mourned by his comrades in the KGB. So the Russians hadn't rumbled him, or had they just been pretending they hadn't. Nobody from the British Embassy was at the funeral and nobody from the American Embassy either. Carling had said nothing about whether the operation had been successful. From what Carling had said the operation had gone on for some years. What kind of information did they get from the solitary man in Moscow? And what a different picture Carling had painted of Philby himself. A man who lied and deceived his colleagues and his women but who seemed to have been liked or loved or at least admired by all he came in contact with. In the pictures he had seen, Philby had a sad, melancholic face, bags under those eyes that were always half closed as if to defend his innermost thoughts. And there were similarities with Carling. That hatred of powerful people, the generosity of mind towards the downtrodden. Cambridge, the admiration of the Russians, even the piano playing they had in common. But he could sense that there was a difference. Carling was a big man, a big mind and a big heart. But Philby was a small man who believed but didn't practise what he believed. Even his flight to Moscow was to suit himself. The co-operation with Carling was a veneer that gave a patina of self-sacrifice to what was really just one more deception. One more abuse of the people around him.

Mathews saw the lights of the train as it swung round the curve into the small station. Carling was the only person to get off. He was laughing at something the guard was saying, then he waved as the train pulled out, still smiling as he approached.

'It's getting nippy, Tim. Time to wear our thermal vests.'
In the car Carling seemed to be in good spirits.
'What did you do today?'

'Took Gabby and Carlotta to the surgery in Lamberhurst so that the baby could have her inoculations. Took Julie into Tunbridge Wells and bought her a hat for her birthday next week. We remembered you by having a coffee together in Fenwicks in the shopping mall. Helped the gardener sweep up leaves in the orchard for half an hour, signed some statements for my solicitor, posted them and listened to you on *Kaleidoscope*.'

'Oh my. It was all very solemn, wasn't it? All those experts claiming that a heap of coal was a work of art because it was at the Tate. Needed Arthur Scargill there, not me.'

Mathews smiled. 'But you got your own back when you defended Andrew Lloyd Webber and *The Phantom of the Opera*.'

'What crass idiots these pseudointellectuals are. There are theatres packed full every night all round the world to hear his music and the critics hate it. They can't stand anything that so many people enjoy. That song of his – "All I Ask of You" – it's beautiful. He writes like Delius . . .' he laughed '. . . and of course the experts of those days didn't like *him*. Not until he was dead anyway. You'll notice in this country that once some artist is dead there are societies that spring up in his name. J. B. Priestley; Elgar, poor soul; Kipling – you could go on all night. Mind that pheasant,' he said, as a worn-out hen pheasant fluttered across the drive to the cottage.

After their evening meal Carling said, 'I've talked all I want to for the moment. I think you need to see what happened through other eyes than mine. I spoke on the phone yesterday to Hank Henney and asked him to come over. He's arriving tonight and he's going to stay here and I'm having a few days break from all this. I've told him he can tell you anything he knows about those days.'

'Do I really need to know any more? You seem to have covered everything.'

Carling shook his head. 'I haven't even told you half of what matters. But Hank can fill you in.' He stood up slowly and for once the energy and liveliness weren't there. He nodded to Mathews as he turned to leave the room. 'I'll see you when I get back and perhaps we can then decide what to do. If anything.'

When Mathews came down the next morning Carling had already left, taking the ancient Rover 3-litre with him. Mathews was used to the machinations of intelligence work but what Carling had been involved in was extraordinary. He could make a fortune by telling the story to a newspaper or by writing a book. God knows, a lot of people had made money out of writing about Philby without any knowledge of what had really happened. But, of course, Carling wasn't that kind of man and he wasn't interested in making money. He lived extremely modestly despite his great wealth. Even his generosity was modest. Kindness and caring for individuals rather than great causes.

Carling had left him a note asking him to pick up Hank Henney at Tunbridge Wells Station off the train from Charing Cross that arrived at 10.32. Julie, who seemed very subdued, told him that she had prepared one of the spare bedrooms for Henney.

Despite his age Hank Henney looked younger than most of the other passengers getting off the train. His face was tanned and he carried his canvas holdall as if it were empty. He didn't recognise Mathews at first but when

Mathews held out his hand the American grinned. 'Long time no see, my boy. And how are you making out these days?'

'I'm OK, Mr Henney. You look fine.'

'I'm OK. I had one of those hip replacement deals and I don't even need a stick these days.' He stopped as Mathews pointed to his car. 'My, that's a neat little thing. An MG. Looks great.'

As Mathews drove to the cottage Henney was admiring the scenery. The golds and reds of autumn leaves were at their best.

'Reminds me of Vermont. You ever been to Vermont, Timmy?'

'I'm afraid not,' he said a little tetchily. He hated being called Timmy. Made him sound like a cat.

They had a rather stilted conversation on the drive back to the cottage. When they got there it was obvious that Henney already knew Julie. But despite the bear hugs and a small bottle of Chanel No. 19 Mathews had the impression that Julie was not very impressed. She smiled a lot and she was polite, and Julie was only formally polite to people she didn't much like.

Julie had laid out a plate of sandwiches and a pot of tea for them and left them alone to talk. It was Hank Henney who got down to business.

'George Carling told me about his chats with you about the old days and asked me to come over and fill in the gaps.' He paused. 'Have you got any specific questions?'

Mathews shrugged. 'He didn't tell me how it all ended. The thing with Philby.'

'I'll tell you about that later. Have you got any questions on what he's told you so far?'

'What kind of information did Philby send back?'

'It was the basis of the deal that the information he was to pass back was general, not specific, and not likely to lead to the arrest of Soviets in the UK or the US of A.

'He warned us about the breakdown of the Soviet-Chinese talks in Moscow. He warned us in advance that in July '63 they would publicise that Philby was one of theirs and had defected and been granted asylum. He told us that Harvey Oswald had not been used way back by the KGB to assassinate Jack Kennedy. He told us in advance that Moscow would agree to exchange Greville Wynne for Gordon Lonsdale. He gave constant warnings to us, the Americans, not to get involved in Vietnam, and he warned us that Moscow were supplying arms to Hanoi. And he told us early in '67 that the Chinese were going to explode their first H-bomb, which they did the following June.

'I guess the most important thing he warned us about was that the Red Army would put down the rising in Prague in '68 with tanks and artillery.' He sighed. 'Very little of it was acted upon.'

'Why not?'

'Well, there were two problems. First and foremost was that because the operation was way above even top-secret level there was no easy way to insert Philby's material without sourcing it, into the working channels of SIS and CIA. How could you explain where you got it from? And secondly, was the lack of trust. Carling passed on Philby's stuff without comment. Said he wasn't in a position to evaluate it one way or another.'

'When did it stop?'

Henney frowned. 'End of '69, beginning of '70.'

'Why did it stop?'

'What did Carling tell you?'

'Nothing. Like I told you, I don't know the end of the story.'

Henney sighed. 'I can't blame him. It must have been a nightmare for the poor bastard.' He paused and looked across at Mathews. 'What d'you think of Carling? D'you like him?'

'I like him a lot. He's something special. I've never met anyone like him before.'

'You don't know the half of it, my friend. That's why he dragged me over to talk to you.'

'Why didn't he just tell me himself whatever it is.'

Henney said quietly. 'When I've told you you'll know why he didn't want to tell you himself.'

CHAPTER 40

After Philby had been put on show in Moscow it had been July before the system brought a response from there. There had been a couple of transmissions in June but there had been no response from Philby.

They were based in a small cottage in the grounds of the CIA cantonment in Berlin. The official sign on the outer door said simply 'No entry'. Part of the problem in the early stages was to provide a reasonable cover for both Carling and Henney. For Carling it was easier, he had always been a lone operator and cut off from the controls of SIS Berlin. For Henney the word was put around that he was now an Intelligence Co-ordinator. Nobody offered a job description nor an explanation of what it meant.

As the weeks went by there was another problem, filling in the time that used to pass when there was nothing active in their Moscow system. But by the winter of '63 both Waring and whoever it was at Langley, considered the material they got from Philby as so valuable that it justified all the time that was wasted. Waring arranged for Carling to be sent the SIS reports on the Warsaw Pact countries and East Berlin for his evaluation and comments and Henney was used for general advice on the CIA's line-crossing operations into East Germany.

The two men were nothing like each other. Henney grew up in New York. He had been a captain in the US Marines and then transferred into OSS in one of its Jedburgh teams that were dropped into Occupied France. When the CIA was eventually formed they recruited a lot of ex-OSS officers and Hank Henney was one of the first to join the fledgeling organisation. He was not fond of Brits but he not only liked Carling but admired him for his knowledge of intelligence operations and understanding of the Russians and East Germans. When he first knew Carling, the Brit was a viscount and Henney had never really understood how, on the death of his father, he suddenly became an earl. For Hank Henney earls were those arrogant fighting characters in Shakespeare's plays. For or against the King. He had asked Carling how you got to be an earl and Carling had laughed and said, 'You just find you've picked the short straw and behave like you won.' Carling had likened the House of Lords to the US Senate but Henney couldn't grasp the function of a senate where not even one member had been voted into office. Anyway, what did it matter? It was just the Brits being Brits.

By the summer of 1964 both Washington and London were pleased with the results of the Philby operation. Eager to maintain the contact as long as possible but looking forward to the day when they could announce to the world that Philby was their man all the time, not the Russians'. Both Waring and Carling were privately more cautious. Maybe their reading of Philby's character was wrong. Maybe the scenario of Philby's flight to Moscow was more courtesy of the Russians than their own. But it cost so little. Encoding the tapes was simple enough, checking them a dozen times for accuracy took hours rather than days. They relied almost entirely on Philby's judgement as to what would come back to them, and their own messages were as much to build up Philby's morale as to indicate the areas that interested them most.

With more advanced radio technology there was vague talk of moving the operation to London, but Berlin was neutral territory for SIS and the CIA, and provided all the support services they needed.

Henney had gone to see the Admin Officer in the CIA's Berlin unit to argue about non-payment of some allowances he was due when Kaufman stuck his head round the door and said he'd like a word with Henney before he left. Kaufman was in charge of the CIA's penetration operations in East Berlin.

Kaufman's parents had fled to the United States in 1934, taking their two children with them. The old man was far-sighted and could see what was going to happen to the Jews in Germany. He sold his tailoring business for a tenth of what it was worth, to a Party member, and they only had money enough for bare survival in their new country. Kaufman's father and mother had worked for long hours day after day to build up the small business they had started in Queens and when Roosevelt declared war on the Axis powers Albert Kaufman Jun. had joined up. He had served in the infantry in Italy and in France. A major by then in the US 4th Infantry Division, he had landed on Utah beach on 5 June 1944 and been still with them on the day of the German surrender on Luneberg Heath.

He was a bilingual German speaker and was posted to a CIC unit based at Kassel in the American Zone. CIC, the Counter-Intelligence Corps, were largely responsible for the denazification operations in the American Zone.

CIA had head-hunted him away from the army and he had successfully run line-crossing operations into the Russian Zone for several years. It was a toss-up as to who he hated most – the Germans or the Russians.

His office was a plasterboard construction in the main HQ building.

When he saw Henney come in he said, 'Close the door, Hank.'

When Henney took the visitors chair he saw Kaufman's hand on a buff file. It was a thin one but it had the diagonal red stripe from corner to corner that indicated that it was 'eyes-only'.

Kaufman wiped the back of his hand across his mouth and put the can of Coke to one side as he leaned forward.

'We've got a problem, Hank. I raised it in our internal meeting yesterday. They shut me up and said I was to discuss it with you.'

'What's it about?'

'I gather you're doing something with a Brit named Carling. Nobody seems to know what it's all about and I was warned not to ask you about it.' He paused. 'Tell me about Carling. Not the work you two do but as a man. Character, temperament and all that. I've heard on the grapevine that at one time he was doing a job like mine – running agents into East Germany. Everybody says he was real good.' He shrugged. 'That's all I know about him.' He smiled. 'And that he's an earl or a lord or some such jazz.'

'He's a great guy. Easy-going but knows where to draw the line. Good at his work and I've never met a guy who I admire and like so much.'

'On our side?'

'Very much so.'

Kaufman sighed and leaned back in his chair. 'Tell me about his family.'

'His father was an earl and when—'

Kaufman leaned forward waving his hand to halt the flow. 'Not that part. His present family. The wife and daughter.'

'She lived in East Berlin when Carling was recruiting agents and informants over there. Very pretty, a semi-professional musician. Younger than Carling. A good loving couple I would say. And the young daughter – also very pretty. I'd guess she'll end up a musician too.'

Kaufman shook his head slowly. 'I wish to God you'd told me that they hated one another and were thinking about getting a divorce.'

'Why the hell should you want that?'

'Because she's a problem, pal. A big, big problem I don't know how to deal with.'

'What's the problem?'

Kaufman pointed to the file in front of him. 'That – is the surveillance file covering a number of years on a Rachel Maria Aarons. Some mystery in the records of who she married. Lived in East Berlin and was having an affair with an unnamed British officer. It may have been just sex but more likely she was an informant. It was confirmed later that the guy worked out of rooms off Kantstrasse and was believed to be SIS. And his name was Carling. Also turns out she was introduced to this guy by a Soviet named Porenski. Yuri Porenski. We've got him down as KGB. When we did a bit of sniffing around on who's who in SIS, Carling was a top man on intelligence in East Berlin and the whole of the Russian Zone. Our source there said he was married but no knowledge of where or when. So our target kisses the frog and changes from Rachel Maria Aarons to Lady Carling. So far, so nothing special.

'The problem came up two weeks ago when we had a walk-in from the KGB detachment in East Berlin. We trotted him around the file on Rachel Maria Aarons and we struck what seemed like oil. Before she met Carling she was the mistress of Yuri Porenski.' He stopped and looked at Henney.

Henney shrugged. 'Not that much of a problem, Al. All in the past. She's a very attractive girl.'

'That's the problem, Hank. It's not all in the past. She's still seeing him, regularly and secretively. On both sides of the Wall.'

'How often?'

'Roughly every ten days. If it were just sex that wouldn't be so worrying but there's every indication that it isn't. Could be sex and informing. Who knows?' He paused. 'I don't know what your operation is with Carling but I'd guess that our friend Yuri Porenski is well informed.'

'Where do they meet?'

Henney pointed at the file. 'There's the file. Read it.'

'Can I take it to my place?'

'No way. It won't take you long. Read it here. I've got things to do in the operations room. Read it and think about it. Tell me what we should do.'

Henney hesitated a long time before he reached for the file and opened it. He didn't want to read it, but he knew he had to.

As Kaufman had said, it didn't take long to read it. He was used to reading such reports on a target undergoing surveillance. There were all those tatty details provided by chambermaids and cleaners that confirmed all too positively that sex took place at most of their meetings. The report also quoted informants who confirmed that the girl had been Porenski's mistress some time before Carling came on the scene. The report inevitably raised the issue of whether the introduction of Carling to the girl was part of a KGB operation. There were some indications that the meeting was fortuitous, but others that it was planned or at least assisted once the relationship developed.

Henney closed the file and pushed it away from him. He wondered how much Carling told her of their game with Philby. If she knew what they were doing and had passed it on to the Russian surely by now Moscow would have taken out Philby. Or were they so sophisticated that they'd rather know what interested London and Washington so much that they risked Philby's life in sending him to Moscow? Or maybe they had turned Philby yet again. Maybe it was just sex and maybe it was just sex for the KGB man too. She was young and very beautiful and he had been her lover before Carling, so she must find him attractive too. He closed his eyes to block out his thoughts and then Kaufman came back. He pulled up his chair and sat down.

'What do you reckon, old pal?'

'I'll need time to think about it.'

'Meantime, what do you want me to do?'

'Let me think about that too. Who else knows about this?'

'Nobody. Just me and my agent. She doesn't know the background. Wonders why I bother about a KGB man screwing a local girl.'

'What do you want to do?'

Kaufman sighed. 'Tell me, how threatening is this?'

'Could be somebody's life.'

'Who's side is the somebody on – ours or theirs?'

'Ours. Could be both.'

'A mole in place?'

'I can't say any more, Al. I'll come back to you tomorrow.' He stopped at the door and turned to look at Kaufman. 'Could your people take out this Porenski guy if it was necessary.'

'No problem, Hank.'

Henney walked to a small park near the CIA HQ and sat watching the mothers with their children in the small playground. He tried not to think of what he had to do. There was no way he could do nothing, but how much did he need to tell George Carling? Was there some way he could warn him without giving any details? He sat there for almost an hour and in the end he knew that he had no choice but to tell Carling what was going on. As he drove back to his own place he was wondering where he should do it, rehearsing how he should start and what he would suggest they should do about it. Carling would be angry as well as hurt but he would be well aware that making the wrong move could endanger Philby, if he wasn't already in trouble. It was going to be messy and there was no way to avoid it. He couldn't do it at Carling's place because the girl would be around and his own place was too crowded with his wife and kids. He'd book a private room at Kempinski's. Neutral territory.

Hank Henney didn't sleep that night.

Carling had listened, sitting quite still in the armchair facing Henney, saying nothing, asking no questions until he'd finished.

For a long time Carling just sat there in silence and then he said quietly, 'You read the reports yourself, Hank?'

'Yes.'

'You think from what you read that they were accurate?'

'I'm afraid so. I'm sorry.'

Carling closed his eyes, thinking, his hands gripping the arms of the chair. With his eyes still closed, Carling said, 'We could cut out the Russian if we moved the operation to London. Would you go along with that?'

'Yes. If it would help you, George.'

'She can't have told him anything about our operation because she doesn't know anything. I've never discussed my work with her, not even when it was routine stuff. I've seen too many men go down the river through careless talk to a mistress or wife.'

Carling opened his eyes and looked at Henney, who said quietly, 'How much will you tell Rachel about what we know?'

Carling smiled. 'Nothing. There's no point. It would make bad worse. Nothing would be gained. She'd be destroyed or wounded. And she doesn't deserve that.' He turned in his chair to look at Henney. 'I owe her a lot, Hank. I love her and I don't intend playing the injured husband. She loves me and she cares about me. The other – well, it's just that. Hormones and maybe genes but not hearts and feelings. Why should I hurt her?'

But Henney was aware of the tears glistening in Carling's big brown eyes.

He said quietly, 'You're a good man, George Carling. A very good man.'

'It's odd, isn't it? Do you know where she is at the moment?'

'No.'

Carling smiled. 'She's at your place with your family with little Rachel. They both love being with your folk.

She's virtually no relatives of her own and your family are her background. I've only got very distant relatives. Most of them I've never met so we're both rather like orphans.'

Henney stood up. 'Let me get you a drink.'

CHAPTER 41

'Was that when you both moved to London?'

'No. It was nearly six months before that happened. First, CIA Langley was agin it but they gave in after a couple of weeks' wrangling from me.'

Mathews said, 'You said first. What else was there?'

Henney sighed. 'Did George tell you about his wife's death?'

'No. I think he mentioned that she died but nothing else.'

'She was killed by a car in Berlin about three weeks before we were to make our move to London.' He paused. 'It was a hit-and-run driver. He was never caught.'

'Was it a KGB operation?'

'No. I was with her at the time. That's how I got my game leg. The car hit her first and then me but mine was a glancing blow, just enough to bust up the hip joint.' He paused. 'You can imagine what that did to Carling. He just wanted to be away from everything. Berlin, SIS, his life. But he couldn't because of the operation with Philby. Another year and we had promised Philby the option of returning and rehabilitation.'

'What happened to his daughter?'

'We took her over, my wife and I. And for the rest of the time in Berlin Carling moved in with us himself. There was no publicity about her death. I think your people and your embassy damped it down.' He sighed. 'I can remember him saying how glad he was that he'd never raised the business with the Russian. Kaufman's informant said later that the Russian hadn't even heard of her death. Still wondering why she didn't contact him. If it had been a KGB revenge operation he would have known.'

'And after this you moved to London?'

'Yeah. Carling took this place in King's Road and the family and I moved in with him and we carried on the operation from an apartment in Gower Street. It went on for just over a year. Philby was going to be brought back about six months later. He was in pretty bad shape by then.'

'Why did he never come back?'

'It was like the whole setup had got a curse on it. Waring, who was then SIS's DG and the only man who knew about the Philby operation, died suddenly of a heart attack. Playing golf at St Andrews. That meant that there was nobody Carling could pass Philby's information to because it didn't officially exist. George passed the news to Philby of Waring's death but he had apparently already read about Waring's death in the London *Times* that he got regularly in Moscow.'

'What was his reaction?'

'Very little. Said he'd carry on and see what could be done to get him back. Didn't seem in any great hurry. And that in itself worried us both. Maybe he'd been playing along with the Russians from when he left Beirut. What was clear was that it was a mess and Carling and I were holding the baby.'

'What was the CIA's reaction?'

'Panic and confusion for two or three days and then I was recalled in a hurry to Langley. A couple of days of so-called debriefing that was aimed solely at making sure that it was I who carried the can. There's an old Russian proverb that says, "Success has a thousand fathers – failure is an orphan." ' He shrugged. 'I went along with what Langley wanted. I had no choice. Had six months' sick leave to see what the medics could do with my hip joint and then they put me in charge of looking over new boys who had jumped all the routine hurdles. Assessing them for loyalty, commitment, background, booze, women and sexual deviation. And after a couple of years I was retired on an enhanced pension and told to keep my mouth shut. I was forbidden to have any contact with George. That's why when you came to see me in New York it caused so much panic.'

'What happened to the little girl, his daughter?'

Henney smiled. 'She's no longer a little girl. She's in her twenties and she's a real doll. She went to the Juilliard and she's now performing all over the world. She uses her mother's name – Aarons. George sees her quite often when she's in Europe. She stayed with us for years but her father bought her an apartment in the Village in New York. That's her base now, but she spends a lot of her time in hotel rooms. Her boyfriend's a musicologist and reviews music for the *New York Times* and is a good partner for her. But she was always daddy's girl and she takes a lot of notice of what he says.' He sighed. 'But even that relationship must be tough on him because she's the spitting image of her mother. Looks, voice, gestures – you can't help noticing it.'

'Where is his wife buried?'

'Somewhere in Berlin. I don't remember where. But the headstone's in her family name of Aarons.' He paused. 'Anything else you want from me?'

'What did Philby do in the end?'

'He seemed to lose interest in coming back. Said he'd rather stay on in Moscow. I think he'd found a new woman who was looking after him.' Henney stood up unsteadily. 'I'd like to head back home on tomorrow morning's flight from Gatwick if that suits you.'

'Of course. I'll drive you there. Julie's made up a few salad things for us. We can all eat together.'

Henney put his hand on Mathews' arm. 'Don't talk to George about any of the things I've told you. He wanted you to hear it from me. He can't bear to talk about it. Just carry on where you two left off.'

Mathews waited with Henney until his flight was called and as they shook hands he said, smiling, 'It's a bit like when Maguire escorted me on to the plane at Kennedy.'

Henney laughed. 'When the CIA panics it does it in a big way. Come and see me any time you want and thanks for your time and listening to me.' As he limped slowly away Henney turned and waved. 'Take care, boy.'

Julie was sorting out the mail on the dining-room table. There were a dozen or so letters for Carling and three for Mathews.

Mathews opened the bulging foolscap envelope and unfolded the document and the letter. He read it hurriedly, the letter first. It was from his solicitor. The decree nisi had gone through and he now had to wait three months for the decree absolute to be granted. The document registered and agreed division of the family's assets. He'd taken Carling's advice and left Pamela the house and all the things she wanted and she hadn't been upset that it hadn't worked out. She seemed as relieved as he was. The other two letters were good news too. A notification that he was promoted a grade and a statement from the bank that was better than he had expected.

Julie had seemed slightly shocked when he invited her to dinner with him at the High Rocks that evening to celebrate his divorce.

When they got back just before midnight, Carling was sitting in the kitchen with a couple of sandwiches that Gabby had made for him, and when Julie went to bed Mathews had stayed on with Carling.

'Freddie Kennedy phoned for you about ten o'clock. Wants to speak to you. I told him you had taken a couple of days' leave.' He paused. 'I thought it would give us time, you and me, to wrap things up.'

'D'you feel it's been a waste of time, all our talking?'

Carling thought for a moment or two. 'No. I don't think so. Depends what Kennedy was after.'

'I think it was just a kind of insurance so that if anything unfavourable to SIS came out in the media he could show that he'd covered everything. Nobody could criticise SIS.' He paused. 'And I think he vaguely wondered if anything *had* been going on recently between you and any Soviet contacts you had in the old days.'

'You're not far out but he'll need a small gift before he can finally close the file.' He smiled. 'I give you my permission to tell him that after I left SIS I acted as a consultant on Soviet matters for the CIA. That'll be something he didn't know. And one more reason why he won't want to keep on raking over the old ground. Explains the CIA's concern about me being harassed and leaving just a small chink for media criticism if he leaked it. Why did SIS let a man go who the CIA subsequently valued as a consultant?' He smiled. 'I've fixed with Langley that if it ever did come out they'd reveal that I gave them a week's advance warning that the Wall was going to come down. They acted on it, London didn't. Then everyone can live happy ever after.'

'Could you tell me about your meeting with the new DG after Waring died?'

Carling threw up his hands. 'An absolute disaster. Tried to suggest that I was mentally ill. Having hallucinations. Nothing I could say would convince him that any of it had happened. The only thing that made him hesitate was when I suggested he checked the source of two or three intelligence items that had been fed into the system by Waring. Where did Waring get them from? I was even interviewed personally by the Attorney-General, a much shrewder man than the DG. I sensed that he didn't intend pursuing the matter too far.' He smiled. 'But it's interesting that GCHQ and SIS and the CIA all use numbers stations even today. Nobody's found a better way of contacting agents in unfriendly countries who can't read Morse. If you're ever bored tune your short-wave radio to 15682 Mh and you'll probably hear a man's voice reading out a series of numbers in English. It sometimes plays a few notes of the song "The Lincolnshire Poacher".' He grinned. 'That was my old frequency but I didn't have any music.'

'Were you worried about Philby not getting what you had promised him?'

'Yes. And thank God the Americans offered to try and smuggle him out. But he didn't seem interested. I think he was tired and ill and totally disillusioned. It ended up with him trying to convince me that none of it mattered. But it mattered to me. So I resigned.' He laughed. 'They were so pleased, so relieved to see the back of me. Farewell parties from SIS and the Foreign Office, full of phoney bonhomie. All chaps together. It was funny, ludicrous and pathetic and now the bastards send you on a fishing expedition in the hope that they can show they're still needed despite the end of the Cold War. Such bloody hypocrites.' He grinned. 'Present company excluded, of course.'

But Mathews knew that he wasn't really excluded in Carling's thinking.

'You're sure you want me to tell Kennedy about you being a consultant for the CIA after you resigned?'

'Oh yes. By all means. It's a titbit and they always appreciate that a chap should earn a buck wherever he can. They'll be doing something similar when their turns come. The days when decent men retired from Broadway to growing roses in West Sussex are long gone.' He paused. 'You'd better have something in mind to suggest to Kennedy as your new posting.'

Mathews smiled. 'Any suggestions?'

'Yes. Investigating Stasis. What they did and what they're doing now after the German reunification. I can give you some contacts if you want.'

'I'm glad all this is coming to an end. But I shall miss being here. It's kind of become home.'

Carling shrugged. 'Come back whenever you want.'

Mathews smiled. 'Julie, Gabby, Carlotta and me. Your waifs and strays.' He laughed. ' "Send these, the homeless, tempest-tost to me . . ." ' He looked across at Carling. 'What made you trust me enough to tell me what really happened?'

'Just instinct, my boy. Just instinct.'

'And nobody would believe me anyway. It's a pity that Philby didn't get his reward.'

'I've left a full account of what happened with my lawyers. It will be published when I'm no longer around, whether it's from natural causes or otherwise.'

'Do you want me to call you and tell you what Freddie Kennedy's reactions were when I tell him about you and the CIA?'

Carling smiled and shook his head slowly. 'No. He'll be glad to close the file.'

'I wish it had been a happier ending for you.'

'There *are* no happy endings in this wretched game. Not if you're good at it. There was a poem by a man named Gosse and there was one line that said it all – "The past is like a funeral gone by".'

As Carling had predicted, Kennedy accepted his 'confession' of acting as a consultant to the CIA. It explained so much of what had happened and he had begun to lose interest in those long-gone days and the players who made them what they were. Several files were closed and Mathews was given a new posting. Not investigating ex-Stasis but as SIS liaison officer to their opposite numbers in ASIO, Australia's own intelligence service. For several years he thought fondly of Carling and his 'family' at the cottage in Kent. He married after a couple of years, a woman officer who was ASIO's anti-sabotage expert. They were not a romantic couple but they got along well together, undemanding and only mildly ambitious.

A SOVIET ODYSSEY
Suzanne Rosenberg

Toronto   New York
OXFORD UNIVERSITY PRESS
1988

CANADIAN CATALOGUING IN PUBLICATION DATA

Rosenberg, Suzanne, 1915–
  A Soviet odyssey

Includes index.
ISBN 0-19-540654-0

1. Rosenberg, Suzanne, 1915–   . 2. Women
political prisoners—Soviet Union—Biography.
3. Soviet Union—Politics and government—1936–1953.
4. Soviet Union—Intellectual life—1917–1970.
5. Canadians—Soviet Union—Biography. I. Title.

DK268.R68A3 1988   947.084′2′0924   C88-093671-1

OXFORD is a trademark of Oxford University Press
1 2 3 4 - 1 0 9 8
Printed and bound in the United States of America.

For Vicky,
and to the memory of the millions
killed under the Stalin regime

Contents

Acknowledgments

A number of people, among them Irving Layton, Earle Birney, Gerald Hallowell, Linda Schachter, Vivian Felsen, Sarah Grosberg, Lou and Helen Poch, Ruth Pressman, and Lionel and June Albert, read the manuscript in draft form, and I wish to thank them for their encouragement. I am also grateful for the grant I received from the Ontario Arts Council.

I wish to express special thanks to my devoted friends Anne and Sam Madras, whose confidence in my ability to complete the manuscript never wavered. Finally, I am most indebted to Richard Teleky of the Oxford University Press for his enthusiasm for the book, and to him and Sally Livingston for their meticulous editing.

Throughout my writing I was fortunate to have the material and moral support of my daughter Vicky and my son-in-law, Timothy Walsh.

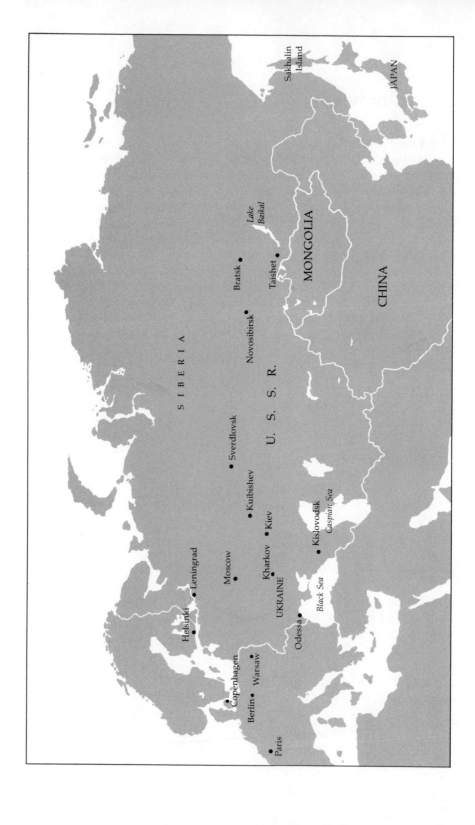

ONE

I On my tracks

In the mid-twentieth century a new wave of terror spills over into
all sections of the population. It hits hardest the intellectuals. Many
of my Moscow friends, colleagues, and family, who escaped death
on the battlefronts of World War II, are now being struck down by
it. My husband is a prisoner at Lubyanka, headquarters of the
dreaded Ministry of State Security, precursor of the KGB.

At a loss to explain such vagaries of the state, I am torn between
despair and hope, the selfish hope that I may be spared the fate
of my husband and of those many other unfortunates. My little
daughter is staying with my mother in the country. I feel stifled
within the massive walls of the building in which we occupy a single
room.

Languidly the spring day draws to a close. I long to get out into
the big city, its streets and lanes converging into breezy squares
where every stone bears witness to the turbulent and tragic past of
this country.

I dart down the ancient stairs, slip through the brick gates, onto
the newly-built Embankment. To raise my spirits the Moscow River
blows its freshness into my face.

Startled, I halt. There is the same young man standing on the corner. Tall, debonair, with good features and a beguiling smile. He has
been shadowing me day after day. Instead of feeling scared, I am
amused. He does not match the part. I speculate who he might be:
a law student making extra money, or a prospective interrogator in
training?

I board a streetcar, make my way up to the front—and turn to look.
He is there, cheery, snug against a railing. The sleuthing is quite

1

brazen. In a way it is comic; on one bus ride, the flicker of a smile passes between us. Life can be funny and grotesque, even when you walk on thin ice.

After this prepossessing young man, no doubt with a brilliant future before him, has tailed me for about a fortnight, he disappears. Having yielded no results, the sleuthing is discontinued. The next step is to send a well-briefed provocateur to trap me into a political indiscretion.

I am sitting at the Central Telegraph Office on Gorky Street waiting for a long-distance call from my brother Shurri, a lieutenant in the Far Eastern Army. Though scheduled for eleven, the call will not come through until one in the morning. I have not been inside the building for more than a few minutes when a runty man in a greasy suit ambles towards my bench and flops down on the empty seat beside me.

He prattles. I remain silent and aloof. I have a feeling that I have seen him before; for the life of me I cannot remember where. I move to the end of the bench. That only makes him bolder. He sidles closer, but his head lolls forward as though he has difficulty holding it up. Out of his pocket protrudes a copy of *Vechernaya Moskva*, which he now produces. Fluttering it in front of me, he points to an item on the back page. I glance through it and learn that Moscow's world-famous Jewish Theater has been shut down.

"What do you make of that?" he sputters. "And of the killing of its director, the shooting and arrests of the actors?"

"Nothing!" I am on my guard, aware he is out to catch me in a "thought crime."

I need only intimate in some way that I deplore the closure of the theater and the killing of its founder for him to have fulfilled his purpose: file a report to the secret police that would put me in grave trouble.

But I know the game. It is played with people of every nationality. The mother of a Ukrainian friend of mine was sentenced to ten years for just such a thought on the persecution of two Kiev actors. I am not nationalistic; I grieve for Solomon Mikhoels, but I also grieve for the non-Jewish Vsevolod Meyerhold and the Armenian Tairov, all three master spirits of the theater who have been disposed of by Stalin in various brutal ways.

I now suddenly recall where I have seen the man—at the publishing house in Zubovskaya Street for which I translate; he sat in a niche, dictating to a typist. A translator like myself, he is a salaried agent

2

of the MGB.* A common informer does not get an assignment that takes up hours of his time and requires sedulous coaching.

After my call comes through, I walk briskly out of the building and practically jog to the street corner. Red Square, which I have to cross on my way home, opens up before me, vast, frowning, crawling with shadows. I have a vision of St. Basil's breaking away from its solid foundations and sailing upwards, the cupolas vanishing behind the low-drifting clouds. Everything else in the square remains rock-firm, though mantled in darkness. I meet the stony stare of Lenin's granite tomb. The voice of the man who is following me pierces the dusk.

He shoots at me what I know is the crucial question: "Would you like to go back to Canada or live in some other Western country?"

Knowing it to be a crime even to speak favorably of anything foreign, I reply as coolly as I can: "I do not care to go to any country. I wish to stay where I am, in the Soviet Union."

I know exactly what answer to give.

Somewhat earlier, a similar question had been posed to my mother, but under quite different circumstances. It was put to her in a friendly tone, dropped casually, in the office where she worked, by Comrade Pavlov. In charge of a government cartography department, he valued her greatly for her good education and knowledge of European languages.

"Would you go to the new Palestine?" Pavlov asked cordially, as he always spoke to her.

Suspecting nothing, she replied with only that degree of caution which we knew we must exercise at all times.

"Yes, if it were a socialist state."

Unlike my mother, I give a safe answer. The man who has followed me to the Telegraph Office, pestering me with questions, could not be a satisfactory witness against me; a certain legality is observed.

I look now to see if he is still keeping in step with me. No—he has been swallowed up by the warm May night.

On a sweltering Sunday afternoon in June of the same year I have another encounter with a police spy. But this time I sense danger at once. A man of powerful physique, he has a face so coarse and depraved that I am relieved he is following me into a crowded suburban train rather than along a poorly lit Moscow street. His purpose is not to trap me into making a seditious statement, but to show me up as a woman of loose morals.

Bounding into the train after me, he elbows his way through the

_____
* Ministry of State Security (1946–53), later the KGB.

3

crowd to grab a seat across from me. Reeking of alcohol and sweat, he drops a few lewd remarks. I note the gray gabardine slacks, Ministry of State Security issue; the shirt he wears is open at the front, revealing sweaty clumps of sandy hair.

When it becomes obvious that there is little chance of luring me to a dacha where we can have "lots of fun and plenty of drinks," he gets off long before the station he named.

From the train I walk to my mother's home on the outskirts of Moscow, where my little daughter Vicky is staying. We sit around the table in the tiny quarters she now shares with my brother's family.

I do not mention the various games the security hirelings are playing with me. All our faces, even the children's, are clouded. My brother tries to cheer us up by cracking jokes. I cannot relax and enjoy the company of my dear ones. I am tense and nervous. I hardly play with Vicky at all, giving her less attention than on my previous visits. I do not know that I will not see her again for another three years, and my beloved brother never.

II Arrest

Having absorbed the daytime heat, the massive walls of the house where I live, across the river from the Kremlin, exude it into the night. June is a sultry month; Moscow has sunk into a drowsy languor, allaying my fears. I am not suspicious, dismissing the watch kept over me by the security detectives as a necessary precaution following my husband's incarceration. I am in no danger. I have never committed a disloyal action, never let drop an imprudent word.

On the last day of June at about eight in the evening, remembering I had run out of bread, I stepped out of my room, locked the door, and strolled down the dim hall. Two tall, hefty men in gray suits approached, ranging themselves in full strength before me. Both were swarthy, with the flat faces and slanting eyes that suggested Tartar origins. One of them I recognized at once as the man who ten months before had told me: "Last night we arrested your husband."

I noticed then, and now too, his long muscular arms and strong square hands.

"You're going out? Where?" he demanded.

My heart thumped with the wildest premonitions.

"To the corner bakery."

"You can go tomorrow morning," he said lightly. "We have a search warrant in your husband's name. We won't keep you long."

It was a lie. There was no search warrant. Inside his breast pocket lay the warrant for my arrest. It was dated July 1; they had come to arrest me on the evening of June 30, so the warrant would not be valid until after midnight. It was then, when the four-hour search was almost over, that the manner of the two men changed.

A few minutes earlier, after they had gone through all my belongings, missing no scrap of paper, shaking out the books, turning every piece of apparel inside out, I said: "You can see for yourselves there is nothing in my home of the least interest to state security. Could you please leave—it will take me the rest of the night to tidy up the place."

They shot me a curious glance, thinking me, I suppose, an idiot.

"Stop playing the innocent!" snapped the one who had done all the talking. The other man had hardly uttered a word. He had a lumpy, pock-marked face and a vacant stare.

Up to this moment I did not believe that I was in any danger. Now I felt wooden. Everything around me seemed to crumble away. There was only blackness, no yesterday, no tomorrow.

My mouth was parched. Mechanically I turned in the direction of the tiny improvised kitchen to get myself a drink out of a pail (there was no running water).

"Not another step! Stay where you are!"

"I'm not under arrest . . ."

"Yes you are!" He looked at his watch and, fumbling in his pocket, produced the warrant for my arrest.

I cannot remember whether I read it there and then or about twenty hours later when I faced my interrogator for the first time at Lubyanka. But the contents, word for word, are there before my eyes even today. And when, in my foolish credulity and vain hope for justice, I wrote appeals to the Supreme Soviet, which never went further than the camp commandant's office, I remembered it well enough.

In disbelief I read the two charges against me. The first was treason, specified as "espionage activities against the U.S.S.R.," and the second "anti-Soviet agitation among friends." The accusation of espionage rested on three counts: ''acquaintance with the notorious American spy Anna Louise Strong"; "a suspicious encounter with Boris Victorov, agent of an American firm"; and "arrests in Canada allegedly for distribution of communist leaflets and participation in anti-fascist demonstrations." The second charge merely cited "anti-Soviet conversations over many years."

It was around two o'clock in the morning when I was led away. Two neighbors dared stare after me. One was Georgi Mikhailov, a colleague who many years later became my husband. Our eyes met. I was afraid to utter a single word, but I knew words were unnecessary. The next morning, without fail, he would get in touch with my mother—I never suspected she was arrested the same night—and brother to tell them what had happened. The other was Vasili Stepanovich. He opened his door wide and stood there with a poignant sadness in his pale eyes. In the seven years that we had been neighbors, I had hardly exchanged two words with Vasili Stepanovich.

Often it happened to me, and I am sure it happened to others, that in a single glance the human eyes conveyed more than long hours of conversation. The look Vasili Stepanovich gave me was one of deep shame. Shame because he was a former factory worker, a member of the Communist Party, who had hailed the revolution as the greatest blessing of mankind. He was a good and upright man, poles apart from the police thugs who were taking me away from normal life, confident that I would now be buried amidst millions of others, behind the barbed wires and watch towers of the strict-regime camps.

Instead of the usual black maria, a black limousine waited for me downstairs, for some reason not in front of the house but half a block away. The limousine moved proudly through the dark streets. We did not have far to go. The car pulled up in front of the heavy iron-wrought gates on the left side of the Lubyanka building. Momentarily the gates swung open and as momentarily shut.

My two escorts led me down a narrow, bare corridor and handed me over to a guard. I was shoved into a cubby hole and frisked. Along with my bra and garters, the pins from my hair (piled on top of my head, in the fashion of the time) were taken away. Hanging breasts— I had the misfortune of being fullbreasted—falling stockings, and long dishevelled hair, besides adding to the discomforts of prison life, were meant to embarrass me and weaken my defenses in the battle with my interrogator.

I was thrust into a detention box, my eyes blinking in the glare of the 200–watt overhead bulb. The "box" was about two feet by four and had a hard, veneered bench fitted into the wall. For a few minutes there was a tomb-like silence, soon replaced by a deafening roar of the most devilish noises pummelling my ears. The box vibrated with the improvised clatter of torture racks.

Moans of torment and a wild screeching followed. I tingled with fear and bewilderment. At first I did not know what to make of it all. But after a few hours I realized it was some sort of machinery, combined, perhaps, with phonograph recordings, all meant to strike terror into the prisoner, muddle his thinking, prepare him to "confess" to his crimes, as the interrogators demanded.

"We know about your subversion against the Soviet state," my interrogator Major Porunov said, when I was ushered by the prison guard into his office. "Speak up! There is nothing you can hide from us."

The interrogator placed before me my first deposition, with his questions and my answers below each one, as he had written them down. It was a double sheet of coarse bluish-gray paper. Before signing it, I caught sight of the heading on the first page: "File No. 3868. Third Directorate, Ministry of State Security."

A second night of questioning. Major Porunov repeated the charges stated in the warrant for my arrest.

I had never been even on nodding terms with Anna Louise Strong. The name Boris Victorov meant nothing to me—nor to my interrogator. I had always avoided conversations on political topics, as did most people I knew. Never had I uttered anything that could in any way be interpreted as "anti-Soviet." The sole grain of truth in the warrant was that I had been arrested, though not convicted, in Canada. But why "allegedly" for distributing communist leaflets? It was outright lunacy; everything that followed was devoid of logic.

Was this really happening to me? Was it really I who was sitting on the prisoner's bench in the dreaded Lubyanka?

The interrogator kept shooting questions at me. What espionage assignments had I carried out? With what foreign intelligence had I been involved? Did I realize what a charge of treason meant?

Indeed I did not. I was in a state of shock. Major Porunov now handed me a blank sheet of paper and told me to write down the names of all my friends and acquaintances. I was too frightened to refuse and decided it best not to confine myself to a few names, but to make the list as long as possible.

Back to a different box with a seat instead of a shelf. I had no idea how long I had been awake. There were no windows anywhere. Soon I was taken by a guard into a small elevator. It creaked to a stop on the fifth landing.

After passing through a narrow deserted hallway I was brought into a small office with a single desk behind which sat a grubby man with a gray blob for a face; not a muscle twitched, the eyes gave no sign of life. He did not look at me when he took hold of my thumb, twisting it now to one side, now to the other, as he pressed it against an ink pad. It was a new and degrading sensation to be treated like a criminal. I could not stop the tears that rolled down my face and showed on the photographs presently taken to attach to my file, which for all time was to be kept in the vaults of the MGB.

The interrogation continued. I was told: "Only a full confession of your criminal activities against the Soviet state will save you and your child."

Unexpectedly there was a two-day break in the nightly questionings. On the third night Major Porunov surprised me with questions concerning my mother's past.

"Did your mother have Trotskyite leanings?"

I was taken aback, alarmed. What could be more perilous than to have Trotskyite leanings? Who dared even to pronounce Trotsky's name?

"No, my mother never had any such leanings!"

"How could you know, you were only thirteen at the time Trotsky was expelled from the Party, and both you and your mother were living in Canada."

I wanted to say: Then why ask the question? But I merely repeated the answer I had already given.

"Your mother, a supposed Bolshevik, left this country five years after the revolution. This in itself is an act of treason."

A harsh note crept into his voice. The accusatory statement staggered me. Though I could not for a moment imagine that my mother too was in a prison cell, that she had been arrested the very night I was, I knew my answers could have consequences, and how cautious I must be.

Years later, when I was a hard-bitten convict, I learned it was common practice for a mother to testify against a daughter, for a husband to be tricked into making incriminating statements against his wife, a sister against a brother.

"My mother left the country legally," I said, with all the calm I could muster. "She had the approval of the Soviet government to travel. She returned legally, was welcomed, in fact. "

There was a long pause. Rising from his oak and leather armchair, he stopped short, midway between his massive desk and my shaky prisoner's stool, and stormed: "So you deny your mother's Trotskyite connections?" A nasty glint settled in his eyes.

Hell, what sort of act is he putting on, I thought. In all of the later questionings I always had the feeling that we were both acting out some cheap, haphazardly concocted drama.

"What about the Trotsky picture in your Montreal home?" he now asked.

TWO

I Trotsky

The picture! I remembered it well enough. Both my parents were militant Bolsheviks who worked and fought to bring about the Revolution. In my childhood I heard Trotsky's name mentioned as frequently as Lenin's.

It was 1921, a year of famine, requisition of property, homeless children, and death. We were living in Kharkov, a city that before the Revolution and during the Civil War had been the scene of my mother's clandestine activities in support of the Bolsheviks. And now she had lived to see Kharkov the capital of the new Soviet Socialist Republic of the Ukraine. In the government she held a key post at the Commissariat of Foreign Trade.

To be closer to the downtown section of this big industrial city, we abandoned the cozy bungalow we had occupied before the revolution and moved into a single room. A number of families would now be crowded into one flat; it was the beginning of the long era of communal living.

With fuel as scarce as it was in the years that followed the revolution, the shared flat had one advantage: the more huddled together people were, the less firewood was needed to keep them warm. In the middle of our room stood a *bourjouika*, a small cast-iron stove. It took an hour of my mother's time, a box of precious matches, and a goodly amount of no less precious kindling wood to start the fire. For the heat the stove gave off we paid dearly. The long-necked black monster exhaled smoke from all its seams and pores, perhaps because the sections of the tube reaching to the chimney pot did not fit together properly.

My mother cared little for riches or comfort, although she came from a well-to-do home. She had trained herself in a life of austerity, and our dingy surroundings did not seem to bother her. Perhaps she was too immersed in the new life ushered in by the Revolution to even notice them.

Smoke hung in shreds over the room, blurring the air and covering the furniture with soot, collecting in our nostrils, causing our eyes to tear. From our comfortable old home we had brought two high-backed chairs with sea-lions mounted on the top corners and fanciful carvings on the legs, backs, and arm-rests—bourgeois reminders of our former luxury. Frowning down from the wall upon them were two enlarged photo portraits, which accompanied us wherever we moved. One was of Lenin, his eyes shrewdly but good-naturedly squinting at me, the forehead high and serene. The other was of Trotsky, anger flashing in his impatient gaze, the beard jutting menacingly. It was a time when Trotsky was still extremely popular, held in almost the same regard as Lenin.

"Your father knew Trotsky personally and fought under him." my mother said proudly.

It was two years earlier, in 1919, that my father came home late one night on furlough from the Ukrainian front. That was the only time I saw him. He was a stockily built man, with eyes like big dark cherries, neat features, and a small moustache. He appeared to be shorter than my tall, erect mother. Before the outbreak of World War I, his family had emigrated from Russia to Canada, where for long years his father, Rabbi Yudel Rosenberg, was the spiritual head of Montreal's Orthodox Jewish community.

After this brief visit, on returning to his regiment, my father was killed in battle a few miles from the city of Kharkov. He had fought on the side of the Reds in the Civil War that raged for more than three years on Russian territory.

I shall not be wide of the mark in assuming that years later, when my mother joined my father's family in Montreal, she hoped a revolutionary situation would arise in Canada. She may well have hoped too that an industrially advanced Western country would make a better job of revolution than backward, peasant Russia had.

We lived in a roomy flat in Drolet Street. On Saturday nights I would wait up until all hours in our big kitchen for my mother to come home from her weekly Canadian Communist Party meeting. I served her a glass of tea with lemon, Russian style, over which, if she was not too fatigued, we chatted about things far removed from our everyday existence.

On one such night my mother returned later than usual from her meeting. And she did a very unusual thing: she confided her troubled thoughts to me.

"Trotsky was ordered out of the Soviet Union, he's been branded a renegade," she said.

Trotsky being the greatest renegade of all—only shortly to be outdone by Zinoviev, Kamenev, Rykov, and Bukharin, Lenin's closest associates, and a couple of dozen others, later their number running into hundreds of thousands—purges and expulsions were launched in all of the communist parties.

After she had bared her heart, my mother's gaze fell on the portrait that hung next to Lenin's. She did not there and then throw the Trotsky picture into the garbage, as good Party members were doing the world over. (But eventually she did remove it, and it was this argument that saved her from one of the gravest charges that could be brought by a Lubyanka interrogator against a prisoner. But how did the interrogator know about the picture? Either an informer had reported it to the security police long before she was arrested, or the admission had been wrung from a prisoner. Either one must have been a visitor at our home in Montreal.)

The next week on returning from her meeting my mother spoke little, drinking her tea in silence. There was a perplexed look in her eyes. Fear darkened her face and snuffed out momentarily the light that drew people so forcibly towards her. It was the first time I saw my mother afraid.

Idealistic, romantic communism, as embodied in my mother's thinking, proved a potent factor in molding the moral views I have held throughout my life. It was my mother who turned me into a communist. Communism was in the air I breathed from my very early childhood.

II My revolutionary mother

The noble ideals for which my mother fought turned against her and through her against her intimates, her children, and the many persons she influenced. Poland was the home of many revolutionaries. And it was in Poland that my mother grew up. She became a radical in her teens.

To her respectable, middle-class family my mother was an enigma, an embarrassment, a source of great sorrow—and a romantic heroine.

Her father was landlord of several apartment houses in Warsaw and also one of the few Jews to have a position in a bank; her mother was the perfect lady of leisure.

My mother joined militant organizations, among them the Polish Bund, championed women's rights, and finally ended up in the Bolshevik faction of the Russian Social-Democratic Workers Party. For her beliefs she was thrown into prison and exiled for life from Poland. Proudly she claimed to have spent a few months in the same cell of the Schlüsselburg Fortress, outside St. Petersburg, that had been occupied several years earlier by Vera Figner, who plotted the assassination of Tsar Alexander II.

Exile took my mother to Paris around 1912, where she settled with her first husband and two children. There she contacted Russian emigrant revolutionary groups, attended the Sorbonne, and carried out assignments for the Bolshevik cell to which she belonged.

At the start of the First World War the European revolutionary movement split up. Russian and Polish emigrant revolutionaries had all sorts of axes to grind, but for personal reasons my mother remained aloof from the wrangling and theoretical discussions that went on among them at the time in Paris. She was either having her first marriage annulled or procuring a divorce—I do not know which. Her first husband remarried, as I later learned, raised a second family, and met his end in the furnace of Maidanek.

At the cost of separation from her two small children, my mother was able to marry my father. She rarely mentioned this part of her life to me. When, in my early teens, I plucked up the courage to mildly reproach her for having abandoned the two children of her first marriage, she paled and retorted in anger: "Do not judge until you have lived your own life."

She was right, of course. This aspect of her past was a painful subject, thereafter not touched between us.

In the early summer of 1915, the second year of World War I, having received her diploma in mathematics from the Sorbonne, she boarded an eastbound train to give birth to her third child in her parents' Warsaw home. She was in luck: the sentence of banishment that hung over her head was overlooked and permission granted to enter Poland.

A few days later Warsaw fell into enemy hands. With an infant in her arms, a bundle of wet diapers, and a few other belongings my mother fled from the city. Her destination was Kharkov, where on Party orders she was to join the Bolshevik underground and organize meetings of fighters for a revolution in Russia. The train was held up by the Germans; all passengers were ordered out and declared prisoners of war.

The story of the circumstances surrounding my birth I heard told many times. What I remember best is my mother's account of how humane and obliging the Germans were. They went out of their way to arrange sleeping quarters and procure food for her and her baby, were courteous and even apologetic. After being detained for a few days she was allowed to continue her journey.

Once in Kharkov she plunged into the work of the Bolshevik organization in the Ukraine, leaving me in the care of a nanny or with neighbors, and often disappearing for long periods. Upon her return the cellar of our house was turned into a rendezvous for revolutionaries. In the morning the house reeked of tobacco smoke. I watched my mother empty ashtray after ashtray into the flames in the kitchen stove to erase all signs of the previous night's gathering.

Kharkov was the scene of some of the heaviest fighting in the Civil War. The city kept changing hands, now captured by the Reds, now by the Whites, and at times falling prey to the Green or other marauding bands.

Bullets hissed in the air. I saw them blow off the frothy crowns of the acacia bushes that formed a fragrant hedge around the front of our home. I was startled in the night by the gunfire of sudden skirmishes, then lulled back to sleep by the soldiers' drunken chants.

My mother was hopeful and cheerful, a great optimist, a fighter, throughout her life. She would pick me up and hug me, and her rigid face, with sharply etched features and hard-set mouth, broke into smiles. She sang revolutionary songs or recited stirring poetry, often in languages I did not understand. As I listened to Schiller's "Joan of Arc" the German verse rang with the clangor of arms in my ears: *"Sieg! Sieg! Sie entflichen!"*

"Revolutionaries never give up!" my mother would exclaim. "The Reds will conquer. Kharkov is sure to stay under Soviet rule!"

A decanter of lemon-laced vodka gleamed on our dining-room sideboard and everybody helped himself. Mother called it "students' elixir" (a good many of the revolutionaries were university students) and insisted that I too take a sip—which I did, trying hard not to grimace when the liquid scorched my throat.

Grand words hovered around me and I rolled them glibly off my tongue. "Revolution," "intelligentsia," and "communism" were household terms to me from the age of two or three. Religion being the "opium of the people," my mother was furious when she caught my elderly nanny diligently instructing me in the Christian faith.

Making sure we were alone in the house, nanny would open her massive, velvet-bound Old Slavonic Gospel, which was richly illustrated, and declaim from memory story after story. To create the illusion of reading, for she was of course illiterate, she would trace the lines with her plump index finger. It was in the middle of such a session that my mother surprised us. She flew into a rage, making it clear that never again must nanny force religion on me.

After resisting the enemy for several months the Reds abandoned Kharkov. General Denikin was expected to march in with his army at any hour.

My mother carried our entire supply of food and water into the cellar.

"We may have to stay here for quite a while," she said.

Excitement gripped me. I recalled her stories about the many times she had had to hide in the past, make quick getaways through back doors. There were arrests, searches, prison sentences, exile, secret meetings with such well-known revolutionaries as Felix Dzerzhinsky, who fathered the Soviet security apparatus, and Yakir, who was later to become a distinguished general, still later to be purged. My mother's life appeared to me more than ever in an aura of romance.

A few days after Denikin marched into Kharkov my mother was seized. I awoke in time to see her prodded out by two uniformed men. Some neighbors took me into their home. People spoke in whispers. Nobody dared venture into the streets; morning after morning new bodies swung from the lamp-post across the lane in the back of the house where I now lived.

"Goodness knows if her mother will ever come back," I heard the people who befriended me say.

The day Kharkov was recaptured by the Reds, my mother walked into the house.

Breathlessly she told her story: "Twenty-five of us, all Bolsheviks, were rounded up the same night. We were held in a shed for about two days. There followed a brief trial. We were sentenced to be hanged by General Denikin's staff, with 'sixty ramrod blows to be delivered before death.'"The hanging started at dusk, which sets in abruptly in the Ukraine. And it was a pitch-black night, as only Ukrainian nights can be. The condemned Bolsheviks sat huddled behind a knoll, on the outskirts of the city, where a gallows had been erected. Crouching behind a bush, she watched her comrades, one by one, being led to their death. She was the last, and when her turn came Denikin's soldiers had forgotten about her. Afraid to stir, even

14

to breathe, she remained sitting in the grass until dawn and only then made her way into the woods.

I could not believe that the woman muffled in a dark, bedraggled shawl over a long, frayed trench coat was my mother. She looked old and haggard. Her nose seemed to have grown longer, her lips thinner; the eyes had sunk deep into their sockets.

No, this was an imposter! I darted out of the house and ran blindly through the streets. My mother's friend went after me and brought me home. A few nights later I watched my mother undress. The fresh welts of the blows dealt her by Denikin's thugs stared reproachfully at me from across her shoulders and, when she turned to face me, from her smooth white breasts.

By the end of 1920 the Civil War was, in the main, over. It ended in victory for the communist forces. But the utter collapse of the economy resulted in many years of hunger and deprivation, which took an enormous toll of the population, especially children. My own hungry childhood in the Ukraine during and after the Civil War is still vivid in my memory.

The thawing snow gleamed mysteriously at me and the wind blew in warm gusts. Famine stalked the city, mocking the festoons of bright lights in the windows of newly opened confectionery shops. Dumfounded, I stared at layer upon layer of creamy pastry and snow-white icing tapering to a pyramid adorned with rosettes and chocolate figures. Private enterprise was encouraged in 1921. Most of the new commercial ventures were started and patronized by resourceful profiteers.

Only a block away from the confectionery the winter twilight illuminated a dead boy, a few years older than myself. He lay propped against a fence, body swollen out of all proportion. His grimy trousers had slit open under the torn quilted jacket, uncovering his bloated belly and blue-veined genitals with stiff frozen hairs around them.

As I ran from the sight, the words of a neighbor, addressed to my mother only the day before, rang in my ears: "People are dying like flies, mostly children. If the bodies are not cleared away quickly, we're in for an epidemic in the spring."

My mother gave a shrug. She looked pale and worried.

I was drawn aside by the same neighbor two months later.

"You have a little brother," she told me in a half-whisper. "He was born prematurely. Goodness knows if he is going to live."

I was surprised. I did not see any connection between the grave-looking stranger who had been a frequent visitor at our home during the past year and the birth of my brother. Nor had I noticed any change in my mother's appearance. If anything, she had grown thinner, smoked more; at times I caught an apprehensive look in her eyes. I was very sensitive to my mother's moods and had a dozen tricks to lighten them. But of late nothing had worked; she remained troubled and withdrawn. I longed for her to confide in me, but she rarely did. Throughout her life she was extremely reticent, in fact far too proud to discuss her personal affairs with anyone.

Well ahead of time for visiting hours, I started out for the hospital. It was early May. The cobblestone sidewalks sparkled with sunlight. On my way I took a peek into an open bakery. There twinkling at me were buns and rolls of all shapes—glossy, sugar-coated, with golden crusts down the middle. They were not for us. We could never afford the sky-high prices of the few privately owned shops, spawn of the New Economic Policy, introduced by Lenin to spur economic recovery.

As I stood inhaling the heavenly smells, the portly Armenian who owned the bakery poked out his head, with a face as rosy and shiny as the nicest of the buns. A pleasant face, wreathed in smiles and billows of fat.

"Come on in, little girl," he said.

Timidly I crossed the threshold. Pride restrained me from ever showing that I was hungry, and now, to conceal how I ached for the rolls, I put on an air of indifference, trying to keep my eyes averted from the counters. The proprietor dug his hand into a mountain of rolls. His long meaty nose, huge ears, and tremendous midriff made him resemble a good-natured elephant. With a gracious smile and a wink of one dark eye, he held out a most appetizing golden bun.

"Take it, pretty child." He thrust it into my hand.

I thanked him in a voice I tried to keep even, and in a happy trance trotted out of the bakery. How tempted I was to take a bite of the roll. But I knew that even if it burned a hole in my hand I would not touch it.

My mother looked very pale and raised her head with difficulty from the gray pillow. There were five other patients in the ward and a strong odor of carbolic acid. I handed the roll to her. She could not have been more astonished if I had brought her a baby kangaroo. I smiled when she asked how I had come by it and begged her to eat it.

She broke off a tiny piece from the top crust, then from the whole. A few crumbs dropped into her hand; she picked them up one by one, and ate them slowly, watering them with her tears.

My brother Shurri and I grew up to be loving companions, with many views and tastes in common. But in the days following my mother's return from the maternity hospital this illegitimate child aroused a good deal of snickering among the neighbors. There were taunts and insinuations.

Who is his father? Has he turned up? Not daring to pose these questions to my aloof mother, they tried to pry the answers out of me.

Shurri's father! One day, shortly after my little brother's birth, he arrived with a valise. But a quarrel ensued, what about I do not know. My mother showed him the door. He left, never again to reappear in our lives. Years afterwards I noted the resemblance between my brother's eyes, the most beautiful in the world to me—velvety, almond-shaped, with sweeping dark lashes—and the eyes of my mother's lover who inspired me with jealousy and unreasonable hatred.

Kharkov was full of homeless, starving children who turned to thievery. Teenage prostitution was rife owing to the appearance of the new rich after free enterprise became a temporary feature of Soviet reality. My mother was pained, shocked, deeply concerned.

The cold weather had come to stay, and our stove was once again filling the room with its acrid fumes. There was little to eat but millet gruel, which yellowed our complexions, the rare bit of bread, rarer still sugar.

A friend pleaded with my mother: "You hold an important post—demand a ration, or you'll lose your children!"

"Why should my children be treated any different from others?" Lamely she added: "Everybody is starving."

After work she would pick up waifs and young prostitutes off the streets and bring them into our tiny quarters. Then she would spend much of her energy finding homes for them or getting them accepted into one of the communes for juvenile delinquents that were springing up in the country.

"You care for others more than for your own flesh and blood" was an accusation frequently hurled at my mother.

"But that is the essence of being a communist," she would argue.

Indeed, throughout her life she was so eager to help others that the needs of her immediate family rarely came first.

One evening she arrived with a beautiful young girl, heavily rouged, eyes outlined with charcoal, wearing a fur coat that was falling apart in shreds. She slept that night on our floor and woke up the next morning with a high fever. All day she tossed about and was delirious.

My mother went for a doctor. "Typhus again," he lamented.

Two weeks later my mother herself landed in a typhus ward where she stayed for almost two months, fighting for her life.

Typically Russian in their generosity, the very neighbors who had taunted me about the birth of my brother, and who had far more contempt than love for my impractical mother, turned from critics into saints. They saw me and Shurri through the difficult period while my mother was away. They cooked better food for us than my mother—how they obtained it in a time of famine I cannot tell—nursed Shurri, cleaned, and even managed to repair our stove so that it rarely smoked.

My mother came home from the hospital greatly weakened, wearing a kerchief to conceal her shorn head.

The neighbors reproached her: "Almost five years since the revolution and there is no end to our sufferings." "We must not lose our faith in communism," she would reply. "We need to be patient. Living conditions will improve."

She sincerely believed what she said. But patience is rarely a virtue of the headstrong, pipe-dreaming revolutionary.

III Travels

The decision my mother took to uproot herself and leave Soviet Russia, for a time or for good, cannot have been made lightly. It must have weighed heavily on her heart.

In the early twenties there were a number of people who took this course. They continued to support the new regime, but they preferred to live abroad. Some may have harbored minor grievances. Others saw the rise of unpleasant forces like the New Economic Policy, which was bringing to the forefront a fresh brand of bourgeoisie, or the terror unleashed by the Cheka, and perhaps felt intuitively that the ideals for which they had languished in tsarist prisons, as my mother had, and sacrificed so much—my father, his life—were being shortchanged and steered away from their original humanitarian intent.

My father's family were urging my mother to visit them, even to settle in Canada. The Commissariat for Foreign Trade, for which she worked, agreed to send her on a mission to Berlin and Paris. Anguished no doubt by the long separation from her older children, she must have clutched at this rare opportunity to see them, an opportunity, given the isolation of Russia, that might not present itself again.

Her attempts to procure a Polish visa so that she could visit Warsaw, where my half-brother lived with her parents, came to nothing. She arranged to meet her sister Augusta in Danzig, begging her to bring him with her. She was greatly distressed when her sister arrived alone.

Eager to meet the mother he hardly remembered and fearing that his aunt might not take him along, he had left early and tramped all the way from Warsaw to Danzig, arriving in that city hungry, footsore, and moneyless after we had boarded a train for Paris and Aunt Augusta was off home.

In Paris, luckily, the meeting went off smoothly with my half-sister Annette, who had the most gentle brown eyes, longlashed like Shurri's, and lived in a bright clean flat with her young husband. Shortly before our departure from France my mother took us both to a cozy restaurant for a farewell dinner. They chatted gaily, their eyes sparkled, and their faces were flushed from the garnet wine rarely absent from the tables of the eating-places we frequented in Paris.

But beneath the light-hearted chatter I sensed a growing sadness, perhaps caused by a shared presentiment that we might not meet again—and we never did. At the time we took leave of Annette, the pernicious idea of covering the territory of Europe with extermination camps—in one of which, twenty years later, Annette's only child, a boy of thirteen, would be gassed to death—was only half-maturing. Our faces therefore were but slightly clouded. We were smiling. My mother, I could see, was glad and relieved to know that Annette was comfortably settled in life.

THREE

I Canada

On a misty autumn morning our ship sailed into Halifax; from there we journeyed by train to Montreal, where we were met at Windsor Station by my Aunt Lily. She gave a start and opened her eyes wide at the sight of the child in my mother's arms.

There followed an awkward moment. My mother resented prying into her personal life. Moreover, she despised philistine attitudes to children born out of wedlock. In her letters to my grandparents there had never been a word about Shurri. Squaring her shoulders, she jerked a finger in my direction: "This is your brother's little girl." Clearly she was not going to offer explanations.

When I first saw my grandmother she looked like a queen compared to the wizened, wrinkled old grannies I knew in Russia, the few who had survived the revolution, Civil War, and famine.

Framed in the doorway stood my grandfather, a towering figure. He wore a long black robe of shiny material, from under the hem of which peered out the pointed toes of his shining black boots. His great height, the unbelievable length of his straight nose, the end of it almost touching his full upper lip, and his strangely asymmetrical eyes singled him out as a man who resembled nobody I had ever seen.

Afterwards, on being told he was a learned man, a scholar, I had a vision in my childish mind of him sitting at a huge desk and constantly pulling at his nose, which made it grow longer and longer. From the nostrils blew vapors that formed into thoughts, and these he recorded in his big golden book with a quill pen—which he indeed used. My grandfather inspired me with mingled feelings of awe and curiosity.

Lacking the courage to address him directly, I often asked Mother questions about him. She rarely answered, though once it broke from her: "He is a religious fanatic!"

Everything was done in my grandparents' Montreal home to make me feel happy and loved. But one thing was definitely missing. There was no effort to arrive at any sort of an "ideological" understanding and compromise with my mother.

She never concealed that she was a communist; rather, she constantly reminded people of it. It was not hard, therefore, to guess that a confrontation between my religious grandfather and my defiantly irreligious mother was on the cards. When it did occur, it ended in a complete break between her and my father's family.

Some time before this break, however, my grandparents seemed keen on finding a husband for my mother. She was still an attractive woman, having retained her great vivacity, proud bearing, and smooth white skin. But she scoffed at their plans. A marriage of convenience was repugnant to her.

In the background hovered one persistent suitor, a corpulent Englishman whose profession frequently took him away from Montreal. He wrote my mother long epistles, signing them, "Chartered Accountant, Graduate of Cambridge." In all weather he wore a raincoat and carried an umbrella and cane along with his satchel. On leaving he would bow himself out of my mother's presence with brisk backward steps, as though she were royalty.

"What? Marry a man just so he could support me and my children? Never!" my mother repeated proudly.

Her pride and independence were not rooted in egotism, but rather in the perpetual need to reaffirm the free woman in herself. She gave much of her time to spreading among her women friends what she considered to be the most advanced views on sex.

On Sunday afternoons she would read to them, translating at sight, chapters from Madame Kollontai's *Red Love* and Pantelei Romanov's *Without the Birdcherry*, interspersing her reading with comments on the revolutionary "glass of water" theory as opposed to the institution of marriage: having sex should be as simple as downing a glass of water.

With my mother's mind elsewhere—in the higher sphere, so to speak—ours was a very neglected home. The things that least interested my mother were cooking and housework. When she could afford it she engaged a maid or cleaning woman. But most of the time we ate cold meals; dust and cobwebs collected on the furniture and in all the corners, without our even noticing them. Not until I was much older did I realize that floors needed frequent sweeping, and furniture dusting.

What my mother most missed in Canada was a position in which she could make use of her professional training. It was not to be had. With no money and two children to support, her job hunt ended in her taking work in the needle trade in sheer desperation. This was a crushing blow to her self-esteem as an educated woman who spoke both English and French fairly well and had a diploma from the Sorbonne and also from the Kharkov College of Civil Railway Engineering.

At some point in her search, she applied for a post with the Canadian Pacific Railway Company. She was happy when sporadic assignments from that company came her way. Often she sat up all night over a folio of blueprints and next morning sang and smiled as she prepared our breakfast.

My mother was a splendid speaker, with a strong, well-modulated voice that carried to the last seat in a large auditorium. I often heard her address meetings both in the Soviet Union and in Montreal. She possessed a phenomenal memory and could recite long poems by heart in many different languages. Two of her great favorites were Mickiewicz and Lermontov. On Sunday mornings she would recite works from these poets as she did the laundry, scrubbing the clothes on the washboard to the rhythm of the verse and pausing to smoke her home-stuffed cigarettes in a long ebony holder.

I believe we were both of a strangely romantic frame of mind. I often pondered on how empty and commonplace our life in Canada was in contrast to the dramatic happenings of my Russian childhood. My mother, too, must have felt a spiritual void, which she filled by becoming ever more active in the Canadian Communist Party.

During one of our first summers in Canada my mother sent me and Shurri to a Catholic convent. It rained a great deal that summer, and I still remember the afternoon naps in the damp rooms, bare, uninviting, with stone floors and hard wooden boards to sleep on. There were no toys to play with. The life was Spartan, but the convent's atmosphere was one of kindness, tolerance, and understanding of children's feelings, with no gimmicks, no "fun," no comfort to detract from it—an atmosphere not so much of religion as of the spirit.

My brother and I were not requested to participate in the religious services or scriptural readings, out of respect for my mother's different views. Apparently we all came from poor families or broken homes. The meals served to us were frugal and the whole institution smelled of poverty. But somehow the lack of externals, the stark, massive walls within which we rested or slept in the afternoon and had our meals, the orderliness of our existence, the green grounds and the sky overhead, combined with our simple, unplanned pastimes, were conducive to thought and reflection.

The peace and serenity of the convent were in striking contrast to the uninhibited, boisterous play that went on in the streets and yards of Montreal. My mother was away for most of the day. Unable to resist the temptation of going outdoors, I would lock Shurri up in our mouse-infested toilet and dash out into the yard for as long as I could. As captain of a gang of wild kids, mostly boys, and with the skirmishes I had witnessed as a child in the Civil War vivid in my memory, I would get them to lie in ambush, waiting for the appearance of the "enemy" to make sudden sallies into their "territory."

And now a change came over me. A calm elation possessed me. There were times when I wanted to be more alone with myself, with my thoughts, longing to devote myself to some romantic ideal. The pugilistic phase was over. I abdicated my captaincy, often not even answering the doorbell when former playmates called.

My Canadian peers were too flighty and mindless for my taste. They had not the slightest interest in the problems that fascinated me. None of them had heard of Spartacus, my great hero; the name Lenin meant nothing to them. And when I held forth on the Russian Revolution, of which after all I had firsthand knowledge, they ran off to play baseball or read the comics. I succeeded in summoning a more sympathetic audience when I acted out scenes from Russia's past. Perversely enough, instead of impersonating revolutionaries, I made up little sketches about the royal families and, draped in old curtains, cast myself as a princess. My young spectators nicknamed me "Russian princess," which, surprisingly, I did not take as an insult.

Poor as we were, there were always plenty of books in our house or to be borrowed from the lending library. I recall one summer devoted solely to the French authors. I read them in alphabetical order; from Balzac and Daudet I went all the way to Voltaire, rounding off the season with Zola. I was intoxicated with the philosophical discourses in Anatole France. *Thaïs* supported me in the atheism ingrained by my mother. The line "Nothing is true except life on earth and carnal love" became a motto to me, although I had not the faintest idea what carnal love meant.

Victor Hugo's *Les Misérables* and the works of Charles Dickens made me ponder the misery of the world. I discussed the books I read with my mother, who blamed the capitalist system for all social ills. I was firmly convinced that once capitalism was overthrown, the world would be a true paradise.

To work for the overthrow of capitalism I joined the Young Pioneers and later was graduated to the Young Communist League. How seriously I took my membership in the League!

Studies of communism made life more purposeful, and I am thankful for the stimulation I received from them. But it was often in parrotlike fashion that I reeled off the communist stock phrases; on many issues, especially those concerning literature, I was greatly confused.

I recall a discussion about Shakespeare's place in literature I had with Irving Layton, who later became one of Canada's leading poets. I repeated the current communist view expounded by left-wing critics: that Shakespeare embodied the pessimism and collapse of the feudal system. At first somewhat stunned by my words, Irving soon saw how absurd they were.

"What about the exuberance and optimism of Shakespeare's comedies?" he parried.

Many figures in literature were branded "bourgeois" in Soviet Russia, among them the poets Pushkin and Lermontov. If these two freedom-loving bards were mostly seen as the exponents of bourgeois ideology, why should Shakespeare have fared any better? (Later such views were dropped and qualified as "vulgarization" of the literary heritage.)

From the age of about fourteen, most likely because of my good command of English and resonant voice, I was assigned to speak in front of large groups of workers. One of my audiences was the workers at Montreal's Northern Electric Plant. They were men well past their youth, and from their accents, good figures, and easy, pleasant manner I judged them to be Anglo-Saxons. I saw few French Canadians at the big industrial plants, and still fewer immigrants.

I would saunter into the factory yard during the meal break. With their lunch boxes and milk bottles on their laps, the workers sat on crates or logs. They welcomed the diversion of a young girl getting up to speak and telling them to unite against their bosses.

Knowing nothing of their conditions or grievances, I had three subjects to choose from: the international situation, the doom of capitalist society—"the capitalists are digging their own grave, imperialism sounds the death knell of capitalism"—and China, the latter being the most topical and the one with which I felt most at home. I would climb on top of a crate and from all sides came the greeting: "Hello, Rosie, how is China getting on?"

"Rosie" because of my pink cheeks, I was a plump, well-fed high-school girl talking to these seasoned workers about the downtrodden masses of China with the cocky assurance of ignorant youth. They listened with amusement, grinning and joking.

When the time of Depression and lay-offs set in, nobody grinned. Nor were the workers in any mood to listen to speeches—they wanted jobs. I brimmed with new hope. It was good to be a communist. I imagined I already heard the death rattle of capitalism, and that revolution in Canada was just around the corner.

II Irving

Most of the friends I made I tried to convert to communism and draw into the League. Among them was Irving, a tousled, bright-eyed boy with a jutting chin and a firm, generous mouth. When it came to political arguments, I met more than my match in him. We both enjoyed arguing immensely.

I first saw Irving when I was nine years old. Not being able to afford help, my working mother kept me away from school for a whole year to mind my little brother. One rainy morning I was keeping Shurri amused when the doorbell rang and a delivery boy came in, wheeling groceries on a small platform cart with a long handle. Irving was about twelve, and there was a haughty air about him that told me he hated his dull job no less than I resented being turned into a nanny, rather than learning at school and playing with my peers. My gaze caught the intensity in his deep azure eyes and for long afterwards I was haunted by it.

We did not meet again until a few years later, when we were both students at Montreal's Baron Byng High School.

Irving and I would often spend our evenings arguing about politics at Horn's Cafeteria on St. Lawrence Street over a single five-cent cup of coffee. There were times when I did not wish to be seen in his company because he was on the other side of the fence, so to speak, and my comrades, particularly the "leaders," regarded the relationship with disapproval. But Irving and I were in love.

Irving's sympathies lay with the socialists rather than the communists. Loud fulmination against the Second International was as much part of the life of the Canadian Communist Party and Young Communist League as it was of the communist movement all over the world.

But now there was a sudden change of directive from the Party. Members of the Young Communist League were instructed to penetrate the socialist ranks and try to wean the youth away. I was chosen to "infiltrate" the Young People's Socialist League in Montreal, whose meetings were often chaired by David Lewis, destined later to become a prominent Canadian politician. In a British accent I admired greatly, he would tell his audience that "the workers need to be educated before they take power and are able to rule."

What gibberish, I thought, education for the workers will be made possible only with a dictatorship of the proletariat, which will create economic conditions favorable enough for the common people to fill the universities. The dictatorship of the proletariat, with Stalin and men of his ilk at its head! How was I to know that only a decade or two later I would see with my own eyes thousands of wonderful people, among them my own family, crushed like insects beneath its heel?

On my birthday Irving gave me a volume of Shaw's plays and H.G. Wells' *Outline of History*. These two writers were our mentors. We were romantics, we hoped for a better world. Enchanted by his humanitarian views and faith in science, with Wells we believed that national and racial feelings would gradually vanish and that the world was heading for a single language, for harmony, understanding, and peace. These were the illusions we labored under in the early part of the century, when we would have done better to accept Lenin's appraisal of the times we lived in as "the age of wars and revolutions."

An English company was presenting *The Apple Cart* in Montreal and, knowing my admiration for Shaw, Irving bought tickets for the play. Years afterwards I found Shaw's mockeries distasteful; moreover, had he and other eminent men of letters been less supportive of Stalin, perhaps millions of lives might have been spared. But in my youth I was one of his votaries. To see a play by Shaw was a real treat, and I enjoyed every minute of it—except that my own behavior, which later gave me food for thought, cast a shadow on the evening. Not even the box of chocolates Irving produced could ease my mood.

The band struck up the tune of "God Save the King." Everybody rose; I alone sat through the entire anthem, despite hostile stares from the people around me. Later, on probing my motives, I saw that I had succumbed to a kind of childish exhibitionism. I knew then that I would not gain sympathy for my cause but would repel people from it. The idea of paying blind homage to a sovereign or a political leader has always been repugnant to me, but to show my feelings in this vulgar manner seemed equally unworthy.

Yet I had the choice. I sat through the entire anthem without any fear of consequences. Later, in Moscow, how I would have liked not to suffer the indignity of being forced to jump to my feet, as everybody did, and applaud each time the name of Stalin, or some subsequent wise father of the nation, was mentioned.

During my youth in Canada I was articulate; I had no inhibitions, no fears about voicing my thoughts. Irving and I would talk our heads off about literature, politics, and philosophy, though when it came to communism we quarrelled bitterly. I gave him a copy of Bogdanov's *ABC of Communism*, and after reading it he challenged the ideas that were so deeply ingrained in my heart. I remember my association with Irving best for our unrestrained exchange of thought, the clash and stimulation of our two minds, and also for his warmth and tolerance as opposed to my own antagonism and bigotry.

What marked my later love life was a constant suppression of thought. Neither I nor the partner to whom I gave my love dared to trust one another with our thoughts. Strangely, so strangely, there was always between us, even in the bed we shared, the shadow of the prying state security—the all-seeing eye and the all-hearing ear, as Pushkin even in his time called the secret police.

The tiny room Irving rented in downtown Montreal had a small bookcase; books were piled high on the table, too, and spilling out on the bed. He bought them second-hand with the money earned by private tutoring. From the age of fourteen I also was able to earn a little money by teaching English to immigrants. Always generous, even in those poverty-stricken days, Irving gave me richly bound books as gifts, each with a new poem of his on the front page. I took these books to Moscow, but when I was hard up I sold them to a second-hand dealer, long before my childhood friend began to publish his poetry.

After our fill of arguing at Horn's Cafeteria, we would round off the evening by taking a long walk in the somber little streets that ended abruptly in a steep mountain slope. Behind tall forbidding fences stood the villas of the rich. The rich! They will be expropriated—both Irving and I agreed on that measure. Neither a socialist nor a Bolshevik government could tolerate such indecent class distinctions. But years later I was to see even taller and more massive fences in Moscow, one close to Lenin Hills, my own neighborhood, others in Kislovodsk, Sukhumi, Sochi, Yalta, and in hosts of other places, owned by Stalin, Beria, and their many underlings; they are still in existence today, with the same fences, armed men guarding the gates, big shepherd dogs lurking behind.

Moonlight silvered the shadows and illumined the fluffy crown of a lilac tree. Irving climbed the spiked fence, helped himself to the flowers and, jumping down, handed me a huge bouquet, looking like a knight out of a fairy tale.

Back in the downtown section of Montreal, I noticed in the street light that he had a big tear in the seat of his trousers, possibly the only pair he owned. On my doorstep he blurted out that he was famished. He had not eaten anything that day and had no money. We too were so hard up that I knew there was little food in the house. If I were to take the last morsel and give it to my starving sweetheart, I would have to face my stern mother and listen to a cascade of reproaches.

Shamefacedly, angry at myself and at him for the dilemma thrust on me, I turned away and quickly vanished into the house. I felt terrible. A beautiful day was wrecked—because we were so poor. Because of our economic state, I thought bitterly, I was forced to deny food to a dear person. Would he forgive me?

Next morning Irving came to see me as though nothing had happened. He possessed that breadth of heart and mind from which trifling things were hastily dismissed. And that endeared him to me more than any other characteristic.

I owe much to Irving Layton. Through him I was able to see far beyond the world of communist ideas in which I lived. Methodically expanding his knowledge of English, he imbued me with his love of language. Even in those years, at the dawn of his poetic ambitions, he was never in the clouds, as were my mother and myself; like Antaeus he drew his strength from the earth, and was opening himself up to the realities of living. Happily our romantic love ended as it did, and Irving, much as he desired to at the time, did not follow me into the unknown in the socialist land. If he had, he would have surely ended his life in a Siberian prison camp, and Canada would never have heard of him.

III Uprooted

After distributing communist leaflets one day I found myself in the detention room of the local police station. Into the gloomy cell, with its porous cement floor, young girls and women were being shoved in one after another. From their appearance I could easily guess who they were: the police had raided a section of Montreal's notorious red-light district, close to the harbor. The arrested women kept to themselves; I was too shy to talk to them.

Mugs of murky, sugarless tea and thick square slices of well-buttered, though stale, white bread were handed out. I did not have to touch the prison fare, because my comrades brought me appetizing pie, hot coffee, and chocolate bars. I was not insulted or manhandled. When I look back at it, by comparison with my later experiences the entire arrest was more in the nature of a picnic. Almost immediately I was released on bail, and when I appeared before a judge at the Juvenile Recorder's Court the case was dismissed. It was all a trivial affair, and I would not have given it a thought had it not had repercussions.

With a presentiment of trouble, I went back to classes the next morning. I learned that I had been expelled from Baron Byng High School. I was upset mostly because I knew my mother had sent me to that school, not a commercial high, in the hope that I would go to college. How my impractical mother imagined she would be able to pay the tuition fees was anybody's guess.

My expulsion was a shock to her. Partly she must have felt that she herself was to blame. She had brought me into the communist movement, was proud of my activities, and never chided me for neglecting my school work. She now betook herself to Mr. Astbury, the principal, and pleaded with him to have me reinstated.

Mr. Astbury wanted my mother to assure him that I was not likely to get myself arrested again—in other words, that I would cease to be an active member of the Canadian Young Communist League. This she did, though she knew it to be an empty promise. Much as I loved her, I was furious: she had acted without the Party's blessing, thinking only of our personal interests. Her conduct gave me a sense of guilt. Nothing was more important to me than to meet the Party's expectations. The lofty principles of communism—how dear they were!

My case was brought up at the Board of Education and in a few days I was reinstated. Mr. Astbury called me into his office, assuring me that the teachers were well disposed towards me and pleased with my progress. This was a surprise, because truancy had become part of my life. I continued to skip lessons.

Over the years I have often thought of what I learned from my Baron Byng teachers, most of whom were Englishwomen. There is much good to be said for Soviet education. But had I had Soviet teachers who were obligated to inculcate in their students worship and total acceptance of Stalin's "wisdom," I would have resisted, inwardly of course, this imposition on my mind. I could never have become reconciled to the blind adulation of the leader, the "genius of mankind," as Stalin was called.

I remember the way my Latin teacher, whom I adored, would by little tricks of her own make us see the weakness of a Caesar, a religious dogma, or the prevailing system of values. She would flip up an American coin and with a sardonic grimace say to the class, "In God we trust—for cash." That kind of healthy skepticism was communicated to us. Yet when she said, "Do others or they'll do you!" by her very irony she succeeded, I think, in showing the nobility of the Christian maxim. Similarly, the excerpts of English prose and poetry we discussed with our literature teacher were designed to show us the fallibility of men, the magnitude and diversity of life itself.

Many choices that were crucial to keeping my self-respect as a human being, when it could have been trampled, lay ahead of me. Somehow I owe it to those two teachers, whose names I do not even remember, as well as to the great prophets and moralists of world literature, that I have refrained from adopting courses of action I would have recalled with shame today.

On the other hand, I was never in an extreme situation that would have forced me to commit an ignominious action. I did not stand ankle-deep in water in a small cell with hungry rats around me, as did an elderly fellow prisoner of mine at Lubyanka. Nor was a loaded gun pointed by a Gestapo officer at the temple of a child of mine, as happened to Roslyakova and her little boy during the Nazi occupation of Kiev. This mother of three slept next to me in a prison shed; the officer had threatened to shoot her son if she did not sign a pledge to cooperate with the Gestapo.

I was back at school, but my political life took precedence over my studies. I was arrested again during an anti-fascist demonstration and then a third time, which meant farewell to my education.

We were quite destitute after my mother lost her job during the Depression. But no matter how poor we were, she would never forego her subscription to *Pravda*, which arrived regularly at our home in Montreal. Often she translated to me articles describing Russia's achievements. To us the Soviet Union was a land of justice and equality, if not exactly milk and honey—in any event, of jobs for all who cared to work. My mother believed every word she read.

Canadian newspapers carried headlines of "Forced Labour in Russia," which my mother and other communists pooh-poohed as shameful fabrications. Yet among the small trickle of immigrants from

Russia arriving in Canada my mother ran into a woman from Kharkov, who told her that collectivization had resulted in the deaths, arrests, and deportations of thousands of hard-working peasants who were not kulaks. There was hunger in all parts of the country, and the people with jobs had less to eat than the unemployed in Canada.

My mother must have realized, as I did, that some of the reports in the Canadian press and the accounts of new immigrants from the Soviet Union were not groundless. But being devoted communists we would not admit it, or rather we knew we must not.

Yet in my own mind I was troubled by the rigidity that prevailed in the communist movement in Canada and the acceptance of all acts by the Soviet Union as infallible. I remember a doubt creeping into my mind following a conversation with a Young Communist League leader who had just returned from training at the Lenin School of Moscow. To many of my questions about life in the Soviet Union he avoided giving direct answers. His candid, broad-featured face grew clouded. I sensed that this comrade, whom I believed to be honest, preferred to leave many things unsaid.

Meanwhile a new idea on the further course of communist activities was brewing in my mother's mind. The conclusion she arrived at raised many an eyebrow among her comrades. She now believed, and was quite outspoken about it, that communists the world over, instead of putting so much effort into the futile struggle to gain power in their own lands, would do better to help build socialism in the Soviet Union, which could then become an example to the rest of the world of a flourishing new society. She was convinced of the validity of her view, but the leadership of the Canadian Communist Party was not and warned her to abandon it.

The warning came too late. My mother was in the midst of organizing a group of immigrant Canadians, mostly Ukrainians and Russians, ready to leave Canada and make their home in the Soviet Union. This was in 1931, at the height of the Depression; at that time many workers were driven to seek jobs in the Soviet Union, unemployment in their own countries being as much a motive for them as sympathy for communism. The group consisted of about forty people and their children. Unwilling to go to the socialist land empty-handed, they pooled their meager savings to buy agricultural machinery as a gift.

The Montreal group was following in the footsteps of Ukrainian immigrants from Canada who had gone back to their homeland in the early twenties and taken machinery with them. Settling on the fertile soil northwest of Odessa, they had founded the Lenin Commune, where the new enthusiasts from Canada hoped to join them. The entire repatriation scheme proved a disastrous undertaking.

On me it descended like a bolt from the blue; not until a few days before our departure did I learn of my mother's decision. I regarded Canada as my homeland. I did not want to be uprooted. At the same time, I supported the criticism the Party directed at my mother. One's loyalty was first and foremost to the Party—one of the inhuman twists that went with fighting for a cause. I wrote a letter to Party leader Tim Buck: "Canadian communists should be concerned with the struggle in their own country and not abandon it . . ." I appealed to him for advice. He never replied.

My legal status as a minor (I was only turning sixteen), combined with my love for my mother and brother, left me without a choice. My mother, unlike myself, was happy. She was going back to her communist country. She was certain an education for her children was assured there, and the future looked bright. Moreover, she had nothing to lose. Canada had treated her shabbily.

From New York, where at the Amtorg she arranged for the purchase of the machinery, my mother brought back clothes we needed badly. Among her buys was a pale green woollen spring coat with a squirrel collar, now the only coat I possessed. Her own capacious Persian lamb coat, bought ages ago in Europe, she refused to pack. It would look too "bourgeois," she claimed, in a land where all were "equally rich or poor." Both of us would freeze in the long severe winters to come.

The night before we departed from Montreal I lay awake with a strange premonition of disaster, weeping hysterically into my pillow. The good cry relieved my tensions. In the morning I felt a different person.

Once aboard the ocean liner I gave myself up to happier reflections. I thrilled to the toil of the billows, making me feel an expansion of self into the universe. I mused upon the future: I must live with an overpowering intensity of feeling, thinking, loving, doing. With these thoughts, foolish, vain, naive, I was leaving my girlhood behind me, in Canada.

As we sailed into the ports of northern Europe my mood of exhilaration faded away. Copenhagen was a cemetery of ships, a sinister reminder of the Depression. Our vessel stood at anchor. No motion, no joy. The city crouched in the lap of idleness.

Baltic ports presented an even sorrier sight, teeming with embittered people. Hundreds of men, women, and children had swarmed into the harbor to beg for food. Apparently every time an ocean liner docked it was met by the city's destitute inhabitants.

Passengers were soon pitching oranges, bread, and other eatables to the throngs below. But much that was tossed down was caught in the air by the no less famished seagulls. People on deck now wrapped up the food in neat packages with weights strung to them before dropping it down. There was far from enough for everybody. I fled to our cabin. The lunch gong sounded. In the dining-rooms the tables were laden with rich foods. I almost cried.

Sentences from Lenin and Marx condemning the capitalist system raced through my mind. Economic crises, unemployment, the impoverishment of the working-class—yes, these two great men had foreseen it all! A socialist society alone, I told myself, held out the promise of equality, of enough food and clothes for all. Had not Lenin said that under communism we would line the toilet bowls with gold? Spiritual values would take precedence over material greed. Unfettered man, proud man, intellectual man! Thus Marx, Lenin, Maxim Gorky had referred to man under socialism. A thrill ran through me. I was going to the land of socialism; I would be a zealous builder of the new society.

Such were my thoughts as our boat docked at Helsingfors, on a sunny day in late June. The city's thick-walled, craggy buildings shone with amber. In between sightseeing excursions we took refuge from the hissing north wind in the little coffeehouses at the top of the flagstone stairs descending to the waters of the Gulf of Finland.

My escort was a Finn, one of the ship's passengers. The color of his eyes, skin, and hair blended into a rugged gun-metal handsomeness. His sister had come to meet him at the pier, and throughout the day she was my chaperone; in the puritan Finland of the early thirties it was improper for a young girl to be seen alone in male company. In the streets of the Finnish capital I noticed how attractive the men were with their muted coloring and reserved manner. But the women, their calves encased in lisle stockings, their muscular shoulders broader than their hips, looked undesirable, more fit for hard work than sex.

An overnight train was taking us to Leningrad, with a stop at Belo-ostrov, the border point. The trimly buckled Finnish guard who examined our papers eyed me with more than mild surprise. In sign language he conveyed to me that I would find life no picnic on the other side. He drew himself up with that arrogance the Finns were destined to shed after the Second World War and pointed an accusing finger at the territory of the Soviet Union. His eyes became cold and hostile.

FOUR

I I am in a socialist state

We poured out of the train and set foot on Soviet soil. The Russian border guards, gawky country lads, smiled a broad welcome. They were guileless, the soul of hospitality—a far cry from the haughty, dour-faced, suspicious guards I was to encounter decades later on a train from Cologne to Moscow. It was the road traversed by Soviet officials, minor and major: from lowly peasant to arrogant urbanite.

Vasili K., a squat young man with a more refined cut of features than the guards, welcomed our group at the Finlyandsky Railway Station. He was from the Leningrad City Executive Committee, assigned to look after our needs and show us around the fabled city. Vasili had the same gun-metal coloring as the handsome Finn from Helsingfors, but he was more tense, more withdrawn, and there was a hint of caprice and weakness about his mouth and chin. The clothes he wore were typical of the government officials of the period: an ill-cut dark gray tarpaulin coat, a khaki army tunic buttoned up to the top of its stand-up collar, breeches, and army boots. He also carried a bulky dispatch case, with which it seemed he never wanted to part. There was a tight-lipped, dead earnest expression about him, and he rarely smiled.

We were installed in a cheap hotel and given a hearty breakfast of savory freshly baked bread, rather soggy, and plenty of black caviar. The latter, I must say, is an excellent morale booster, putting one in just the right all-receptive, enthusiastic frame of mind to view the achievements of the world's first socialist state.

With no sign of approaching darkness, I could not drop off to sleep on my first night in Leningrad; I was very excited. The next night

Vasili pressed me to go for a walk with him. I had forgotten the Russian I knew as a child. But silence befitted the entrancing scene of a city draped in a violet haze, the stone and granite of its stately buildings melting into the dreamy twilight. It was the magic of the "white nights" of Dostoevsky.

When the time came to say goodbye—we were to board a train for the commune in the south of the Ukraine—Vasili claimed to be in love. I sensed that he was not in love with the real me, but with some romantic vision that his imagination had conjured up in its almost morbid pursuit of forbidden bourgeois beauty.

"I read about the love I now feel in novels, but did not think it could exist," he said.

Later I was to realize, sadly, that it was mainly my "different," non-Soviet appearance, and in a way behavior too, that constituted my attraction for the men I met in the thirties. But for them or me to utter such a thought aloud would have been heresy.

I told Vasili he would get over his love. I smiled. It was nonsense! *Chepukha*!

There was no nonsense about that love when, six weeks later, Vasili turned up at the commune. From there he followed us to Kharkov, where my mother had gone on commune business. He took the revolver he carried out of its holster, clamped the weapon down on the hotel-room table, and threatened to shoot himself if my mother refused to let me go alone with him to Leningrad. Realizing that he meant what he said, and scared out of her wits, she very reluctantly agreed, but not before making him promise that there could be no talk of marriage before I was of age. Our "affair" turned out to be purely platonic and altogether one-sided.

The early thirties were very hungry years. A return to the millet of my childhood did not dampen my enthusiasm for the new order, but it did affect my health, causing skin rashes, boils, and other minor troubles. I tried not to think of food. But I craved a juicy apple and had forgotten the taste of an orange.

For a while I lived at the Oktyabrskaya Hotel near the Moskovsky Railway Station—this was arranged or perhaps wangled by Vasili—and spent a good deal of my time studying Russian. I took lessons from a prim elderly lady who, like the tiny, cluttered room in which she lived on the Petrogradskaya Storona, breathed the mustiness of the old regime. Soon I was able to make myself understood pretty well, but it took another year or more before I acquired a good command of Russian.

I made a few friends, some of them members of the old Russian intelligentsia. The great luxury of the table then was herring and potatoes boiled in their jackets. I was struck by the elegance of the tableware. There were gold-rimmed blue teacups, old silver, plates with hand-painted copies of famous paintings and the monograms of renowned Russian families. Onto these ornate plates we dropped the shrivelled skins as we ate our small hot potatoes with relish, washing down the delicacies with vodka or red wine in massive, exquisitely designed crystal goblets—another legacy of the St. Petersburg aristocrats who had fled abroad.

Vasili had managed to get me a job as a translator at the Leningrad port administrative office, a job I was not doing well at because my written Russian was poor. The work itself was quite simple: translating bills of lading from English, German, and French into Russian. I came to know a few of the top port bureaucrats; some of them had called me into their office just to take a look at the *inostranka*, the foreign girl. Then one afternoon the head of the port administration sent for me.

It was lunch hour and I was quite famished when a deputy of his, a tall man with a satanic air about him, approached and whispered that "Comrade Bronstein" desired a word with me. "But it's lunch hour . . ." Hunger tugged at my insides. "Don't worry about that," he smiled mysteriously.

Glad to escape the tedious bills of lading, I climbed cheerfully up the steep steps that led to the top man's shrine, wondering what the summons was all about. I had never laid eyes on him. I knew only that he was Trotsky's brother.

A door padded in burgundy leather bore the bronze nameplate "Bronstein." I walked in and saw on my left another door. I knocked. A voice said "Come in!" Passing through an anteroom, I stepped into an opulent suite. It was like a corner of the Hermitage— embossed tables, malachite urns, settees and couches upholstered with costly colored brocade. Every piece was genuine, all were well matched. An added luxury were two polar-bear skins on the highly polished parquet floor.

The whole atmosphere was more of a love nest than of a business office. That was my first impression, but on second thought I concluded that perhaps it was an appropriate environment for striking deals with the captains of foreign merchant ships.

Awed by the surroundings, I paused for a few seconds before catching sight of a table in the shadows at the end of the room. It was covered with a snow-white cloth and laden with platters of jellied veal, cold turkey, juicy ham framed in fat, sliced pink sturgeon, and fruit in tall cut-glass bowls. Two bottles of Russian champagne reclined in silverplate ice-buckets.

With an unctuous smile my host came towards me. The moment I saw him I felt an aversion for this man and for everything the scene represented. Gross, with a huge midriff and rolls of fat spilling over the starched white collar onto the nape of his neck, he was no answer to a maiden's prayer. The lascivious gleam in his pale eyes made me tighten inside. He had a bulbous nose, and his pink skin looked powdered. But the domed forehead commanded attention, and later, at a meeting of the harbor employees, I would see the full, sensuous mouth clamp into a firm line.

His eyes softened as he approached me, and the lust in them changed to an expression of surprise when he realized my youth and innocence. Taking my cold hand into his, he held it for a while in the hollow of his plump palm. He moved a chair for me to sit down, peeled an orange, putting it gingerly on my plate, and hovered satyr-like over me. A last glimmer of the brief, wan autumn sunlight flitted across the room.

On a corner table stood a horn gramophone. He put on a record and the strains of a foxtrot floated in the air. With a gallant gesture I found repulsive, my host invited me to dance. Not to seem rude, I went along. What a mockery the scene was! The overfed high executive taking time off his work to indulge his low pleasures, the table laden with rare, exotic foods, when people all over the land were starving.

The atmosphere of *après moi le déluge* shocked me. I said I must go, leaving practically untouched the food he had put on my plate. He escorted me to the door, to my relief pressing no advances, and cordially enough bade me goodbye.

The fate that shortly afterwards befell Trotsky's brother is well known. Had he any premonition of his end? Perhaps he did. Perhaps, too, like so many others in his position, he wished to indulge his appetites, make the most of his power while he possessed it, before his downfall and physical destruction.

I pleaded a headache and left the office a little earlier than usual. Instead of taking the streetcar, I trudged homeward. I paused on a bridge over the Neva River. A fierce wind ruffled the surface of the water. That man was no communist, I thought, he was scum. I tried to regain my composure. The proud sweep of the Admiralty spire on the opposite bank, the glow of sunset in the windows, the austere dignity of the architecture, mitigated a little the shock and disgust I had experienced in Bronstein's company.

Then my thoughts took a general turn: why were these privileges allowed in hungry Leningrad? How skimpily clad the men and women were who passed me in the street. "Fashion" was dictated by the scarcity of manufactured cloth. Young women and girls wore skirts above their knees, faded kerchiefs, flimsy jackets over cotton blouses, while many of the older women walked about in drab home-spun skirts that reached to their ankles. Almost everybody was shod in canvas shoes, poor protection against the cold of approaching winter.

As I peered into the faces of the passersby, some of the old elation returned to me. They shone with idealism and hope. Cheeks were sallow and sunken, but spirit and courage glowed. I noted especially the delicately molded features, the inspired, purposeful expressions; in years to come so many of them would disappear.

Just a few steps away from the home I now shared with Vasili's family was a small bakery. I dropped in to see if I could buy some-thing for tea. But, as could be expected, the bare counters stared mockingly at me. I knew that Vasili's mother would not let me go hungry, though I contributed little to the family budget. She would generously set before me a plate of fried potatoes with sliced pickle, treat me to a little honey for tea.

When I entered the house on Stachek Street, in the newly estab-lished neighborhood close to the Putilov Works, later named the Kirov Plant, I found Vasili locked up in his room with his former lover, Nina. I took this as a matter of course; if anything, I was glad that his romantic mood had ebbed away. The person I most admired in that household was the mother, constantly fighting to keep the family fed. Once a week she drove to a nearby village to barter old uniforms—Vasili's two brothers were army officers—vodka, soap, and other items in short supply for potatoes and honey. She queued up for bread and cereals, mostly millet, and in cooking she employed amazing ingenuity to stretch the rationed groceries. She washed, scrubbed, carried heavy loads, while her menfolk read their news-papers and books, drank vodka, and indulged themselves as they pleased. What went on in the world around her hardly mattered, and women's emancipation was an empty phrase to her.

"What made you leave Canada? Why did you come here?" I was frequently asked. The people who put these questions to me really meant: What idiot would decide of her own free will to share our existence?

I spoke sincerely when I replied that I thought ordinary people got a far better deal under socialism than in a capitalist society. They did not argue with me. But a lift of the eyebrows or a twist of the lips showed that they thought me a liar or a hopeless idealist.

Missing my mother, I said goodbye to Vasili and took a train to Migayevo, the site of the Lenin Commune with its two contingents from Canada.

Not one of the repatriates, least of all my mother, had been prepared for the hardships that confronted them. Families were lodged in sheds with no running water, no toilets. True, the commune was one of the fortunate farming enterprises to have electricity. Indeed, by the standards of the times—the very early thirties, the time of the Volga and Ukraine famines—it prospered, providing three good meals a day in the canteen for all members. Perhaps the commune owed its well-being to the astute management of Chairman Melnik, a red-headed giant who spoke to me in the broken English he had retained from his Canadian days; no doubt the tractors and harvesters brought over by the resettlers helped as well. Some time afterwards the commune was disbanded. What became of its hard-working chairman and other members I do not know; I can only guess the worst.

There was little for my mother to do at an agricultural commune. However, since educated people were in demand everywhere, the local board of education was only too happy to place her in charge of the village school, where she became the principal and taught many of the subjects.

The brief feeling of comfort and security I experienced in my mother's presence was soon replaced by a growing restlessness. The bleak village scene, especially in winter, was more than I could bear. I had to get away, out into the big world again. My mother was sympathetic.

She quickly arranged for me to stay with a family she knew in Odessa. In exchange for their hospitality, she managed to scrape together a little parcel of farm products for me to take them. It was greatly appreciated at a time when food was scarce.

II A dissident of the thirties

Gales swept the streets, snow turned momentarily into slush. A bluish gray mist hovered over the maritime city. I had been told that Odessa had the most beautiful women in all of Russia, heavy-browed, dark-eyed—*eti chorniye glaza . . . oni sveli menya s uma*, "those dark eyes are driving me crazy," ran a popular song. I now came face to face with them in Richelieu Street, huddled in fur coats that had seen better days, and later in restaurants and at the opera, wearing low necklines that revealed tempting white flesh. It was the first time I became aware of the difference between real sex and the spurious commodity purveyed in the movies and magazines of my Montreal girlhood. Chill gusts rising from the Black Sea almost blew me off my feet, they penetrated right through the flimsy Canadian windbreaker I wore. The sting of frost. I loved it. I felt exhilarated, as though riding a chariot, fleeing from the cares and uncertainties of my chaotic youth.

But I had to get down back to earth and face reality, for I was very much at loose ends. My mother had hoped I would go on with my education. She had no idea of the regulation that made enrollment at schools of higher learning practically impossible for the sons and daughters of non-working class or non-peasant parents.

I would take any job and go to evening school, I decided, but first I was determined to get a transfer, through the Youth International in Moscow, from the Canadian to the Soviet Young Communist League. To drop out of the movement was inconceivable to me. I hoped the Odessa League could help.

Morning after morning I kept returning to the building on the Black Sea esplanade where the league had its headquarters. I would pause across the street from it, turning over in my mind what to say. Finally, I plucked up my courage and made my way towards the entrance, almost bumping into a young man in his late twenties who was also going into the building.

He smiled a broad smile. "I've seen you across the street three days in a row . . . hardly a place for a date," he teased.

Tall, lithe, with his head proudly thrown back and slightly inclined to one side, his hat worn at a tilt and back from the forehead, revealing a mass of auburn curls, he was not a man to escape notice. Besides, he radiated an infectious warmth and lightheartedness. I took to him at once.

"I want to speak to the Secretary," I said trustingly. "Do I need an appointment?"

"I can introduce you, if you wish."

Once in the office I hastily stated my case.

"This comrade can do more for you than I can." The secretary pointed to my companion. "He is deputy General Secretary of the Ukrainian Young Communist League."

A few minutes later the young man who held this exalted post was walking with me up and down the Embankment, high above the

Black Sea, and chatting excitedly. When he saw me home, we continued talking indoors for a while, then went out for another stroll.

My new acquaintance, who introduced himself as Ivan Stepanovich Frolov, was staying at Odessa's exclusive Londonskaya Hotel, which overlooked the harbor. He invited me in for dinner.

We lounged against the red plush of the chairs in a cozy nook of the hotel restaurant, away from the cold nip of the Black Sea wind. Cognac and wine were served with the meal. His tongue loosened by the drinks, Ivan Stepanovich spoke about himself. He was twenty-seven, had a degree in engineering, held a high position in the government as well as in the Communist League. There were many privileges attached to his posts, but he did not give a hoot for them. After a pause, he moved his chair closer to mine, cast a glance around, and, inclining his tousled head, told me he was going to Moscow on an important mission. He would be leaving in a few days.

The minute the words "important mission" were out of his mouth, he sat up with a jerk, very sober. It was as if he had blurted out a piece of intelligence. He bit his lips and peered into my eyes without blinking, a peculiar trick he had when he was upset about something.

I noticed that he had on the same khaki tunic, breeches and calf-hugging boots that Vasili had worn, except that they were of superior quality and sat better on his tall athletic figure. I wondered why all party, Komsomol, government, and trade-union officials in the early thirties affected that military look, carried over through the twenties from the time of the Civil War. Perhaps what accounted for it was the scarcity of any but army cloth.

There was a quickness of mind and an urbanity about Ivan Stepanovich that I found quite irresistible. Every night we went to the opera. The Odessa opera house, a replica of Vienna's, was one of the most charming structures in the city. All my friend had to do was produce a card, showing the high post he held, for us to be ushered into the government box. Much as I enjoyed the company of Vanya, as I now came to call him, and was flattered by his attentions, my mind was set on one thing: getting my transfer, joining the Soviet Komsomol, and plunging into work for socialism. A romantic entanglement was the last thing I desired, and I said so to Vanya. With a violent toss of his curls he replied: "As you wish."

"But you want the transfer, I take it?" He paused. "That means we travel to Moscow together."

In Moscow Vanya's good friends, the Ukrainian poet Samborsky and his wife, put me up in their apartment in Karetny Ryad. There were many visitors, to whom Samborsky would read his poetry.

Sometimes the conversation that went on in that home, in hushed tones, puzzled me; my Russian was still faulty. I could only surmise that a common topic was the future of the Ukraine.

When I look back at that period of the early thirties, I realize that there must have been groups hoping to remove Stalin from his post or curb his lust for power. Possibly most active among them were the Trotskyites. They had little to lose, especially those whose earlier association with Trotsky was known.

I had noticed that Vanya carried about with him an attaché case crammed with papers and booklets. One evening when we were alone in the Samborsky dining-room he dug his hand into it and from the very bottom produced a book with white and gray binding.

He handed it to me. "Care to read it?" he asked casually. When I took it from him I could not believe my eyes. It was a Paris edition of Leon Trotsky's *My Life*.

Even to handle a book like that I knew to be dangerous. It could bring reprisals beyond one's wildest imaginings.

I returned it to him immediately. Apart from being frightened, I believed it wrong for a loyal communist to be carrying and handing out a book openly maligning Soviet policies. Vanya was now a greater enigma to me than ever. Why did he walk about with the banned Trotsky literature in his attaché case, something for which he could easily be stripped of his posts and jailed? Quite often now I was stunned by things Vanya said and did. The conviction grew in my mind that he was playing some dangerous game.

The mystery around Vanya deepened even more when he started to take me to visit friends of his at the Select Hotel. In frosty weather, on slippery ground, we walked down from Karetny Ryad on the Outer Boulevard, later uprooted and turned into the wide Sadovaya thoroughfare, to Petrovsky Gates, an intersection of the Inner Boulevard. There we boarded the Annyshka streetcar, which took us to Stretensky Gates. On the right-hand side of Stretenka Street were the hotel's matt glass doors, almost on a level with the sidewalk, the word "Select" traced in barely visible lettering across them. This hotel, about a quarter of an hour's walk from the main Lubyanka building, catered exclusively to the big shots in Soviet intelligence and the security apparatus. Here they stayed for weeks and sometimes months, waiting for new postings, attending refresher courses, or getting established in the expanding Moscow secret directorates.

Interrogators came here from Lubyanka for a short fling before their nightly questionings. The evenings were spent drinking vodka and dancing to the banned music and songs of the émigrés Leshchenko and Vertinsky. Anti-Soviet jokes, forbidden to be told in ordinary Soviet homes, were freely swapped. Indeed, nowhere did I run into such censure of the Soviet system and such open cynicism as among the high OGPU* officials at the Select Hotel. Vanya joined in the conversation and the laughter. He seemed to be taking a macabre delight in the double-facedness of these "guardians of the revolutionary gains," as the security officers were sometimes called.

One could not help being struck by the resemblance between Vanya and the Ukrainian anarchist Batka—Makhno, as he was known. It occurred to me that he was proud of this likeness, for he seemed to cultivate it in the way he wore his hair, in long tangled ringlets, his brisk gait, and his habit of abruptly tossing his head. He also had a way of biting his lips and dropping into a chair, seeming moody and crest-fallen, as though some plan he was hatching had fallen through, and these habits too were strongly reminiscent of Makhno. One would think that there the resemblance ceased between the cruel Makhno, chieftain of one of the worst gangs of marauders the Civil War had produced, and the chivalrous, urbane Ivan Stepanovich. Yet they shared as well a love of adventure and a readiness to gamble away human lives, including their own.

At the time of my friendship with Vanya and acquaintance with the Samborskys I was only seventeen, hardly capable of understanding what was happening around me. Later I wondered: If these opponents of Stalin had succeeded, would there have been less misery and annihilation of human life than under his rule?

Vanya had finally arranged for me to meet with Deniman of the English-speaking section of the Communist Youth International. I saw him at the Luxe Hotel in Gorky Street, where most of the Comintern members resided almost permanently. He turned out to be a short, glum person. He spoke strange words, their gist sinking into my mind only after I left the hotel: Get married, raise a family, and stay out of trouble. In a way he echoed my own growing conviction that I no longer had any heart for politics.

Once again I felt the need to be close to my mother, and I travelled back to the Ukraine. On finding myself in the peaceful little Ukrainian village where my mother taught school, I was no longer as bored and restless as I had been the year before. I had had enough adventure. But I kept my thoughts to myself. Clearly there were communists in key positions who were not at all what they seemed to be; I had seen them in those rare moments when they shed their pretence.

* United State Political Administration (1923–1934).

The mind's departure from set ideas is slow, and it is usually preceded by a period of befuddlement. It was this phase that I had now reached.

Still viewing my surroundings with bubbling enthusiasm, I found an outlet in writing long letters to Mr. Eld, a Montreal *Star* reporter whom I had once tried to convert to communism during a walk along the moonlit paths of Mount Royal. With a picture in my mind of the thousands of unemployed I had seen in the streets of Montreal, lined up for their bowl of soup, I wrote of how everybody I met had a good job. In letters almost thirty pages long I related my impressions of the Migayevo commune; I wrote of the bumper harvest, which after deliveries to the state was evenly divided among all the commune members; about the hardworking Chairman Melnik, who took no greater share than the rest.

When the commune could not find a second bookkeeper I recalled the petite, golden-haired daughter of a neighbor of ours in Drolet Street, a bookkeeper, whose fruitless job hunting I had followed sadly in the spring of 1931.

I perceived no incompatibility between the communist and humanitarian ideals and vowed to cling to both. These feelings were tied up with sadness and regret when my gaze travelled around the room my mother and brother occupied. How shabby and uninviting it looked—grubbier than any place we had lived in in Montreal. My mother had aged greatly in the short time since we left Canada. Her hair had thinned and was streaked with gray, her eyes had a strained look, and shadows nestled in the hollows of her cheeks.

There was a demand for trained specialists in all fields, and after some persuasion I convinced my mother to apply for a job in Moscow.

III We settle in Moscow

With little trouble my mother obtained a post at the Commissariat for Railways. So acute was the housing shortage that when she received an offer of a five-by-three-meter room in a communal flat she ought to have jumped at it. However, she turned it down in favor of two tiny rooms in a distant Moscow suburb, in a shanty with no washroom or running water. My impractical mother! I was dismayed, but powerless to change her mind. Two rooms, my mother argued, were better than one.

In spring and autumn we squelched through mud to reach our quarters, in winter walked in almost knee-deep snow. We had no money for furniture, but even with it, no furniture was available unless you had good contacts. We slept on beds knocked together from boards. My mother worked, designing stations for the North Railway Line, with her customary zeal and spent from two to three hours commuting in a crowded train. The money she earned barely kept us from starving.

I took a proofreader's job at a publishing house that was putting out foreign dictionaries, started a night course in typography, and began making friends. One of them was Vera Schwartz, a fellow proofreader. Fluent in English and French, she had majored in Persian linguistics at the oriental languages department of Tashkent University. Both of us found proofreading dull. Luckily, in 1935 Intourist, a new travel organization set up to attract tourists from abroad, was advertising for guides. We applied and were accepted.

The guides were regarded as propagandists for the Soviet system, and during the slack winter season time and money to advance their education were not spared.

Most of the girls I worked with were college graduates, cultivated and well-read, for whom work as a guide was not much more than an interim period for training in language skills. I was learning a great deal about art galleries, museums, and theaters. Suddenly I realized that I was much happier talking about drama, painting, and new books than about social and political affairs.

Vera and I shared these interests, and we saw a good deal of one another. Graceful, enchanting, with her elongated eyes, oval face, and exquisite small mouth, Vera looked like a figure in one of the Persian miniatures she had collected since her student days. Men were always hovering around her, and it amused me to watch her lead them on; I may have been a little envious of her popularity. Her buoyant spirits had a wholesome effect on me. She took every day as it came.

The atmosphere in her home was cozy and relaxing. Her mother was an excellent cook who managed to produce delicious meals at a time of constant food shortages. I would sit back on their sofa and enjoy the warmth of these two women, the mother looking almost as young as the daughter and just as attractive, though very different in appearance—short, blonde, blue-eyed. Vera's mother was a Russian, and it was from her late Jewish father that Vera must have inherited her dark oriental beauty and zest for life.

Vera had many suitors, but she chose to become the mistress of a Frenchman more than twice her age, the portly Havas Agency correspondent in Moscow. It was just what her mother wanted for her—

an easy life, fashionable clothes, living it up in the "high society" of the foreign press and embassies. Her lover managed to get a large apartment for Vera and some beautiful furniture. She put in much effort to introduce a "Russian" atmosphere with a samovar, embroidered towels, and corner ikons. When she showed off her new home to me I stayed for as short a time as decency permitted and was happy that the man of the house was out. To see or be seen with aliens was to court danger. We knew our friendship was over.

Then the worst happened. The Havas Agency correspondent was ordered out of the country for "immoral conduct": he had a wife in Paris. The apartment was confiscated and Vera was arrested for her liaison with a "spy." I learned from her mother that she had received the fairly mild sentence of five years in prison camp and five years' exile in Siberia. Also, it was clear that she would not be able to live in Moscow after the two terms expired. Her mother was beside herself with grief.

At about the same time, many of the women who hung around the Intourist bars—secret police informants, assigned to flirt and go to bed with tourists or embassy people and then make full reports— were also apprehended. Among them were some of Moscow's most beautiful women, also the few who wore elegant Western clothes. Their glory was short-lived. They had served their purpose. What followed was back-breaking work in labor camps and their end.

Poor Vera! It was the first time, though certainly not the last, when a close friend whom I knew to be utterly non-political was to suffer the horrors of Lubyanka, incarceration, and camp. Strangely enough, fifteen years later Vera's love life would ricochet upon me, helping to substantiate another crazy charge against me.

My work as a guide was bringing me in contact with people from all over the world. Ocean liners on world cruises docked at Leningrad for two days, after which the passengers took an overnight train to spend a short time in Moscow. For these vacationers, mostly wealthy Americans, Intourist arranged gala concerts with top performers in music, ballet, and folk dancing. The concerts were held at the marble-columned hall of the old Red Army Theater. Intourist Lincoln cars would glide to the theater entrance. From them would step out well-groomed gentlemen and expensively coiffured, bejewelled ladies. Passers-by gazed at them in disbelief and wonder, as though they had landed from another planet. (Since that day things have changed greatly:millionaire ladies dress more casually and many young Moscow girls look like fashion plates as they arrogantly pass through the widened modern streets or in their turn alight from small sedan cars.)

At these concerts I was the English announcer. Standing in the middle of the stage one night in the summer of 1935, I felt a thrill on suddenly noticing a familiar face in one of the front rows. The long jaw, the trim moustache, the high brow—at once I recognized H.G. Wells.

During the intermission there was a commotion in the audience: people were rising form their seats and hurrying towards somebody in the aisle. Elegant little books fluttered, and I assumed that everyone was seeking Wells' autograph. Happy that I had seen the writer I so greatly admired, I smiled to myself.

But the smile vanished when I walked into a side foyer and saw standing in a far corner, very much by themselves, the short, stocky Wells and a younger, lankier replica of himself, his son. Curious as to who had caused the flurry of excitement among the wealthy Americans, I stepped down into the auditorium. The center of attention were two popular American variety stars.

Tourists visiting the Soviet Union could not understand why travel was so restricted. Often the explanation was simple: the absence of transportation and the poor sanitary conditions in many cities of historical interest. I remember how exasperated the American writer Richard Haliburton was when Intourist failed to arrange a trip to Samarkand. (He was writing a book about Tamerlane; Samarkand had been the capital of his empire, and his famous tomb was there). The writer was nervously pacing the lobby of the Metropole Hotel when I had the unpleasant task of telling him that Samarkand did not come on any tourist itinerary and that no exception could be made for him.

Haliburton was having his bit of friction with Intourist when Clement Attlee, leader of the opposition and head of the British Labour Party, was also visiting Moscow. His request to see a small town outside the capital was gratified without delay. Attlee came to Moscow with his secretary, an easygoing, sprightly man of thirty-five, with a teasing ironic manner, and the secretary's courteous mother. They were three of the most pleasant and undemanding tourists I ever worked with.

The day I took Clement Attlee on a tour of Gorky Park was torrid, the air laden with gritty dust. We dropped in for lunch at one of the open-air restaurants on the Moscow River Embankment. The whole idea, I must say, was Major Attlee's. I would have suggested going back for his meal to the National Hotel, where he and his companions were staying, but one does not do too much suggesting to a future prime minister. Attlee wished to have something Russian, and because it was so very hot we ordered *okroshka*, an ice-cold soup made of *kvass*, greens, boiled eggs, and meat.

The meal unfortunately resulted in an upset stomach. Instead of seeing Moscow's façade, Attlee got more than a full view of the back yard—that is, the toilets, not easy to find in those days, most of them just holes in the ground with raised platforms and foot treads.

I found the situation mortifying and later, with tears in my eyes, complained to my fellow guides how dirty the public toilets in Moscow were. I sincerely wanted Attlee to see the best side of Soviet life. That these efforts of mine should be thwarted by the silly *okroshka* and the toilets upset me.

Fortunately the visit to Podolsk went off without misadventure. The road to the city was mostly rubble, so we kept the windows of the Lincoln shut to avoid the churning dust, and our driver steered carefully around the bumpy sections. Podolsk, the closest small town to Moscow, was the center of a fertile farming area, and it also had a number of developing industries. Attlee, who had himself been mayor of Tupney, wished to get some idea of the problems and growth of a similar Soviet area. Podolsk was the answer.

After taking us around one of the big outlying farms, the mayor had a huge lunch served in the open air, answering there and then Attlee's questions concerning the municipal management and history of Podolsk.

I was not with Attlee when he was received by Stalin or Kalinin, but I did go with him to the city hall, a red brick building on Gorky Street, where his host was Nikolai Bulganin, then chairman of the Moscow Soviet, or mayor of the capital. It is interesting now to think that both Attlee and Bulganin, each in his own time, were to be prime ministers, Attlee to retire with honor, Bulganin to be booted from his post and blotted out of the public memory.

IV Omens of the times

Forgotten foods were at last appearing in Moscow stores. Tverskaya, renamed Gorky Street after the writer's death, was being widened. Muscovites gasped at the skill with which the massive buildings were being moved back from the sidewalk. The architect Shchusev, of pre-revolutionary renown, still wearing a glittering gold and diamond tiepin, and Chechulin and Mordvinov, of the new Soviet crop, were designing the first modern hotels and apartment buildings. The palatial, marble-lined metro stations were a powerful argument for the contributions a socialist state can make towards urban beauty and the convenience of its citizens.

After a visit to the United States, Anastas Mikoyan, Commissar for the Food Industry, introduced such novelties as fruit juices and freshly canned strawberries, which graced the counters of a newly opened Dietetic Store in Arbat Street. This was the neighborhood where I lived, and with its old mansions of the Moscow gentry, among them the poet Pushkin's home, it seemed to have escaped any imprint of the new regime. Oranges, another novelty, were sold on Moscow street corners—delicious, juicy oranges with which Republican Spain paid for the arms the Soviet Union shipped to her.

Pianist Robert Casadesus played Debussy and Werner Klemperer conducted at the Conservatory on Hertzen Street before audiences better fed and dressed than they had been in twenty years. Moscow became a mecca of the world theater.

It was the year 1936, remembered by Muscovites of my generation for the sudden availability of food after the hungry years of the early thirties, for the flowering of the arts, and for its more optimistic outlook. The blood baths of 1937 and 1938 were still ahead of us, and although in 1936 too there were trials, among them the big Zinoviev and Kamenev case, the defendants in the dock were known for their deviations from the Party line, and there was still some plausibility to the charges.

The security apparatus, through its expanding spy network, had not yet achieved total control of the people's minds, and fear had not yet silenced all tongues. Perhaps this explains the candid outbursts I heard from A.G., the new chief of the Intourist guide department, who took over after the arrest of the former head.

He was so gentlemanly and attractive that many of our guides fancied themselves in love with him, myself among them. A.G. was of slight build, agile of mind and body, his dark eyes, the yellow tinge of his skin, and his lank jet-black hair revealing him to be a member of the small Chuvash nationality. One afternoon in early spring he invited me to join him for a stroll after office hours. We directed our steps towards the nearby Alexandrovsky Garden under the Kremlin wall. The garden was full of promenading couples and we were soon lost in the crowd.

A.G. began by telling me that he was happily married and had two small daughters he adored. Then, to my astonishment, he switched to political topics, speaking with a bitterness I had never encountered before.

"I'm a long-standing Party member," he began. "The principles of communism are dear to me. But what I see happening today makes my stomach turn. The worst part of it is that I can do nothing about it. I dare not even speak up. Everything seems to have gone wrong. Take the plight of the peasantry. My own parents are collective farmers. And to think that they are no better off than were the serfs. For their work they are paid in kind. They are denied identification papers, are restricted in their movements—in fact all of them are tied to the farm, just as the bondsmen were tied to the property of the landlords."

I listened with mounting fear and said nothing.

"We are supposed to be a workers' state. But who runs the state? The workers? Most assuredly not! A bunch of unscrupulous bureaucrats who will stop at nothing to stay in office."

On and on he continued in the same vein. There were always food shortages, the women were doing the hardest work, the Party was becoming corrupt with more opportunists and careerists than honest communists in its ranks.

His caustic words made me think of Vanya, who also could be very outspoken in his own sardonic way. But unlike Vanya, A.G. was not reckless, not flippant about his own and other people's lives. He would not *act*. His protest would go no further than confidences to harmless non-political persons like myself. He dared not confide in his wife for fear of bringing misfortune upon his family.

There were many more walks in the Alexandrovsky Garden. He went on talking about the seedy aspects of Soviet society, vehemently condemning the purges and trials; yet at meetings he approved these same purges and denounced the "enemies of the people."

On the ability to play a double-faced role the life and liberty of everyone now depended. It was becoming a way of survival, taking deep root in the Soviet consciousness. This make-believe was repugnant to men like A.G., and for all that it did not save him. His turn came in 1947; from my interrogator I was to learn that he was a "British agent" and received a sentence of twenty-five years.

Cold weather set in early in the autumn of 1936, with snow flurries following rain. On a blustery morning in October I boarded a train to Kislovodsk for a month's vacation. I slept through the long journey, awaking refreshed to the golden sunshine, blue sky, and healthy mountain air for which this resort in the Caucasus is famous. An Intourist hotel was being built on a hillside terrace, and I had the good luck, as a work bonus, to be accommodated in a finished wing.

Feeling on top of the world, inhaling the aroma of rose bushes, I made my way briskly down to the tiny plaza at the foot of the mountains towards which holiday-makers converged at all hours of the day. There I ran into Jessica, a free-lance journalist writing for the Intourist press center. Jessica introduced me to Victor, who stopped to speak to her, casting a few quizzical glances in my direction. Jessica knew him from the *Moscow News*, a Soviet English newspaper of which he had some years before been the editor.

We stood for a while exchanging generalities. I felt immediately attracted to Victor. He was a forceful man, with a gaze that was disturbingly assessing. It could be, I felt, very friendly or openly hostile; in the present instance, as he looked at me, it was definitely friendly.

That very afternoon he turned up at our hotel with a friend, a sandy-haired doctor as flamboyant as Victor himself. The friend became infatuated with Jessica, and over the entire month that followed we hardly saw them at all; they spent most of their time behind the closed door of Jessica's hotel room.

Victor, on the other hand, showed no ardor. I saw him every day, but always in the company of friends or work associates who, like himself, were on vacation. From what he told me, and from anecdotes about him related by friends, I was able to piece together a little of his background. He came of a middle-class family, had studied languages with tutors, completed an automobile engineering course, joined the Red Army, distinguished himself in the battles of the Civil War. In the late twenties the Party sent him on a mission to China. He was among Chiang Kai-Shek's Russian advisers, escaping prison by a hair's breadth when the Kuomintang turned against communism. I also knew that he had had talks with Stalin and admired Bukharin. At the time I met him, he had long been director of NATI, the Soviet Union's first and most important automobile- and tractor-designing center.

Sometimes I saw a frown settle on Victor's handsome face. He crinkled his forehead and narrowed his eyes, which were small compared with his powerful jowl and straight nose. I imagined—wrongly perhaps—that he was preoccupied with some problem of automobile production.

I was twenty-one and Victor was thirty-nine. Perhaps in some way he was a father figure to me, embodying the most admirable qualities of manhood, just as I believe the mother figure does of womanhood; it seems to me that these two figures, projected on our minds in our most impressionable years, help us to seek in our sex partners the human traits most familiar and dear to us. As our relationship developed, Victor came to sum up everything I valued in a man and a human being.

Limpid air, warm sunshine, the Caucasus mountains with their silvery peaks, wooded flanks, and mauve shadows, gave me a sense of timelessness. I longed to cry out: May this moment never fade! I felt Victor's nearness. His every gesture, every remark, penetrated into my being. Giddy, I seemed to be soaring in mid-air. I smiled. My eyes must have betrayed my happiness. My cheeks flamed. Our love still lay ahead of us! We wished to prolong the gentle and gradual exploration of our two personalities.

Victor was unmercenary, undemanding, dedicated to his work. He had no bank account, no dacha, no free cash, he took no bonuses for himself. He was quite content with the Party maximum of 275 roubles a month. The new acquisitive instincts, the philistinism and vulgarities that later became so prevalent were still in their embryonic stage. Whenever Victor ran across them, he could be devastatingly sarcastic.

Victor worked under Ordzhonikidze, the Commissar for Heavy Industry. Every day at the same hour we saw Ordzhonikidze on the serpentine. Like many Georgians in their middle years, he had a proud, eagle-like countenance, the long nose resembling a beak. Flanking him were his body guards, and at his side walked his wife Zinaida, more thick-set than he and perhaps slightly taller. Both husband and wife had a forthright gaze that was rare in those days.

In less than a year this "eagle" would put a bullet through his head, either to avoid arrest or because so many of the people he had worked with, and with whom he had built up the machine construction and other heavy industries, among them his own brother, were incarcerated, and many executed. Stalin shed crocodile tears over him.

Another person enjoying the mountain air of Kislovodsk was Genrikh Yagoda, the most feared man in the land, for many years head of state security and the secret police, who was later charged with the poisoning of Maxim Gorky and other black deeds. Since at the time there was no Karlovy Vary, no golden beach of Bulgaria, not even the Baltic Sea coast, at the disposal of the Party élite, it was at the sumptuous newly built villas in Kislovodsk and Sochi that the top Party and government bosses spent their vacations. Unlike the "eagle," Yagoda was never seen on the main promenade.

A few times it gave me a start to catch sight of his hatchet face, with the black dots of eyes, suddenly appear from the tall, lush grass on the side of the mountain track. Fascinated, I watched the long, thin form slink away with a faint rustling of the leaves. The reptile who devoured others was soon to be devoured himself. Yagoda's days were numbered. But so were those of most people I met on the smooth, sunlit mountain paths of Kislovodsk; it was their last vacation, their last months of freedom.

A few weeks later, back in Moscow, Victor and I went to see a movie that was the great hit of the time. It was then that I had a glimpse of the disenchantment that must have been settling in him and that prompted many of his pointed and acrid remarks. The film was *Peter I*, the first of a series extolling the strong rulers of the past.

Peter the Great was portrayed as a wise empire-builder. Simonov, Leningrad's tallest actor, had an especially strong face, and he was chosen for the part. He did his best to persuade viewers that, owing to his powerful physique, superior intelligence, and statesmanship, Peter had no match among the monarchs and politicians of Europe.

This superman treatment was repugnant to me. I was also greatly puzzled, for there were always hidden reasons for every new approach and interpretation in the arts, the ideological weaponry of the Party. Scene after scene of the glorification of Peter elicited applause from the audience. Did it touch some deep chord in the Russian heart? The longing for a strong and good tsar?

Peter's known brutality, his boorishness, the terror of his reign, were deliberately played down. Peter had ordered the death of his son Alexei, incarcerated his half-sister Sophia, banished the Old Believers, executed the Streltsi. A different Peter appears in the famous painting "Morning of the Execution of the Streltsi" by Surikov: the monarch is portrayed as small, petty, vindictive. But that picture was painted under a tsar—not under Stalin.

I asked Victor what he thought of the film.

He replied: "No tsar has ever been a hero of mine."

When Victor drove me home I did not ask him in. Neither of us was in the mood for lovemaking; an emotion more powerful than desire had been released in us. I walked into my room torn apart by what I had seen on the screen, fearful of its implications. The sad part of it was that Victor and I could not discuss the film frankly. We dared not trust one another with our thoughts, lest at some future date, perhaps under torture, they might be wrested from us as "evidence."

Yet, though we did not say it aloud, we both knew what was behind the film and why it had shocked us.

It contained the virus of a contagion that would spread and have far-reaching effects. Its purpose was to project a certain image, inculcate a precise idea for Soviet viewers, twist their mentality and turn them away from communism to nationalism, from democracy to dictatorship. Stalin was now to be identified with the great rulers of Russia. His brand of nationalism was to replace Marxist-Leninist internationalism. Patriotism and loyalty were to be the great catchwords.

In the forties I watched with even more troubled thoughts two other films, Sergei Eisenstein's *Alexander Nevsky* and *Ivan the Terrible*. They contained the same underlying message as *Peter I*. It may be argued that artistically they were notable creations. But they had a nefarious purpose that I believed should be condemned: to make audiences see Peter the Great, Ivan the Terrible, and Alexander Nevsky as the precursors of the great Stalin and also to justify the need to rule with an iron hand, to treat dissenters ruthlessly.

It puzzled and pained me that a movie director like Eisenstein, who in his *Battleship Potemkin* had focussed attention on the masses, showing sympathy for their plight and aspirations, should have veered from that humanitarian approach to glorify the Novgorod Prince Alexander Nevsky and the half-demented Ivan the Terrible. I discovered in myself a mounting contempt for artists who had not shrunk from employing their art to deify a bloody dictator like Stalin. None of the fine artistic points of *Ivan the Terrible*—not even the perpetually lauded drawings, by Eisenstein himself, of the costumes for Ivan and the boyars used in the picture—could redeem him in my eyes.

V A reprieve

Victor had many fascinating friends, to whose homes he took me. Among them was Lunacharsky's widow, Natalya Alexandrovna Rosenel. Worldly, literary, a little aloof, with luminous blue eyes, delicate features, and impeccable taste in clothes, she was an actress with the company of the Maly Drama Theater which, like the Bolshoi, overlooks the Theater (now Sverdlov) Square.

Her home on Starokonyusheny Lane, off Arbat Street, remained, as it had been in Lunacharsky's time, one of Moscow's literary salons. Natalya Alexandrovna would draw Victor away from the company for long private chats. I watched them with a jealous pang; her delicate skin glowed and silvery notes tinkled in her voice. She was a far more interesting person than I, but with youth on my side I felt secure in Victor's love.

Among Victor's most trusted friends were the sculptor Sergei Dmitrievich Merkurov and his wife Asta. They lived on the very fringe of Izmailovo Park, in the east of Moscow. Former hunting grounds of the early Romanoffs, the park was visible from the windows of the small timber cottage given to Merkurov, along with a sizeable plot of land, on Lenin's orders. This was after Lenin had signed a decree containing a long list of monuments to be erected in Moscow and other cities. The old statues of tsars and national heroes were to be torn down and replaced with new monuments of revolutionaries and revolutionary events—a true blessing for the country's sculptors.

Part of the Merkurovs' estate was taken up with an apple orchard, a vegetable garden, and a shed for animals; the family kept cows, pigs, and poultry, which made life easier—less hungry—for themselves and their friends. In addition to an indoor studio adjoining the house, there stood apart on the grounds a tall makeshift structure with a detachable roof designed for monumental works. Inside one could see apprentices perched on ladders or scaffolding, putting the finishing touches on an enormous head of Lenin or Stalin.

Of towering height, dark and bearded, Merkurov was half Armenian and half Greek, with the noble profile one sees on old Assyrian coins behind glass museum cases. His reputation as a sculptor was made before the revolution. He had studied at the Munich Academy of Arts and travelled a great deal; he loved to tell the story of how, practically penniless, he had cycled through Europe. At the time when we became friends Sergei Dmitrievich was one of Moscow's wealthiest men, owing largely to the great number of Lenin and Stalin statues he had produced, which stood in city squares all over the land.

Few places I had ever been to had the magic of the Merkurov home. Victor would heave himself out of the driver's seat of his sparkling aquamarine Graham Paige, a gift from an American car manufacturer during a trip to the United States, and ring the electric bell on the left side of the green timber gates. On a mild winter's night, with the feathery snow softly dropping in huge flakes, the car glided down the path leading to the back of the cottage. The odd assortment of statuary gave me a strange thrill. On our left, gleaming in the light of the lamp post, stood the haughty snow-mantled figure of Catherine the Great, the crown knocked off her head, while a few steps away, sprawling in the snow, lay a statue of Alexander III, divested of all symbols of power. (He was one of the few monarchs of Russia to die a natural death.) Looming directly in front was an unfinished monument to the twenty-six Baku commissars executed by the British during the Civil War; the figures were portrayed in standing and falling positions at the moment of shooting.

There was both an unreality and a sense of historical tragicomedy about the scene. I felt as though I were being torn away from the present and transported into a fabled world. From this dreamy state I was returned to reality by the barking of the dogs and the squealing of the pigs that contributed greatly to the lavish meals the Merkurovs served to their guests.

As 1936 drew to a close, the Merkurovs invited Victor and me to see in the New Year at their home. I was enjoying the luxury of a tiny room at the Novomoskovskaya Hotel, which took up a small block on the Moscow River Embankment and had a roof restaurant famous for its view of the Kremlin. A section of the ground floor was set aside for Intourist employees with no place to live.

Meeting an acquaintance in the hotel lobby, Victor introduced him to me as George M., a Comintern comrade. Pudgy, unprepossessing George had an egg-shaped head far too large for his body, but a kind twinkle in his eyes, and were he an ordinary Soviet citizen I would have responded to his friendliness. But because George was an American I gave him a wide berth. By this time I avoided tourists staying at the hotel and had also stopped corresponding with Canadian friends.

When New Year's Eve approached, George complained to Victor that he had nowhere to go. Victor suggested that he accompany us to the Merkurovs. This he did, making a perfect nuisance of himself the entire evening. Finally Victor drove him back to the hotel and returned to the party as we ushered in the first dawn of 1937 with hopes for better and less fearful days in the coming year.

One of the guests asked, "Who is that crazy American? Giving me a wink, Victor lied: "He's an agent of an American firm."

Obviously he did not want it known that the drunken and boorish George had any connection with the Comintern.

One of the counts on which my charge of espionage rested read: "Had a meeting with Boris Victorov, agent of an American firm."

A muddled informer's report handed in fourteen years prior to my arrest must have named George as Victorov—possibly confusing him with Victor—and linked him with me. This is the sole explanation I can offer for the mysterious Victorov who figured in the warrant for my arrest, unless, in his haste to concoct a charge against me, the interrogator had confused the names himself.

I was so wrapped up in my personal affairs and ambitions that I paid only rare visits to Losinostrovskoe, the suburb of Moscow where my mother and brother lived. On the Sundays I did visit, I would find them both engrossed in some mathematical problem. Although happy to see me, they could not tear themselves away from their mathematics. They covered sheet upon sheet of paper with formulas, and when they ran out of paper, which they often did, they proceeded to put down their symbols and figures on the log walls of the room. Ashtrays were always spilling over with cigarette stubs and the small kitchen table would be piled with several days of dirty plates.

My visits began with a clean-up job. The worst part was the battle with the bedbugs. The more I fought them, mostly with kerosene, the more they multiplied and the fatter they grew. If I managed to get them out of the interstices between the log walls, they crawled to the ceiling and from there dropped in a bee-line on the beds, chairs, and table.

Returning from one such visit, I found the newspapers full of the Zinoviev and Kamenov trial and the conviction of two eminent Moscow medical men, Levin and Pletnev.

Frequent guests at Merkurov's gatherings were Pletnev's assistant, Dr. Mikhailov, and his beautiful violet-eyed wife, an actress at the Maly Theater. Like Pletnev, Mikhailov was one of Moscow's leading specialists in gastric disease. He was a well-built, elegantly dressed man, his long square chin giving him a noble equine look. We knew him as a lover of English poetry, especially Byron, and an admirer of the British parliamentary tradition. His conversation flowed with easy grace, steering clear of polemical topics, his gaze often wandering in his wife's direction as though longing above all to catch her attention; his great affection and admiration for her were apparent to us all. At the time in Moscow's theater world she was greatly lauded for her portrayal of Mary, Queen of Scots, in Scribe's play *A Glass of Water*.

We feared for the life of the pleasant, loving couple because of the doctor's connection with the convicted Pletnev. And our fears were well founded: the two were arrested.

We were not unprepared for such disposal of lives. All along there had been "cases" of so-called wreckers, foreign spies and doctor poisoners. They had not yet assumed the proportions of a mass onslaught on the population, the wholesale shootings and arrests that shortly awaited us.

All the same, it amazed me how coolly we were taking these events, how Communist Party members inside the Soviet Union and in the world at large accepted them without a word of protest, a word of commiseration for the victims. The silence and acceptance were contemptible. It was like crushing beneath our own boots good and innocent human lives.

Clearly we were undergoing a deep change of personality. Soon some, though fortunately not all, proud members of the intelligentsia would turn into Stalin's apologists and obedient executors of his man-hating policies. Moscow, the entire country, was being transformed into an ugly jungle; each beast for himself, each saving his skin according to his own lights.

But hope had not yet been completely abandoned. We prayed with all our hearts that the blood baths would come to an end. And indeed the trials would be followed by a brief breathing-space, a lull and even recantations from those on high, as later happened in the case of security chief Yezhov, removed from his post for his "excesses."

There were people who tried convincing themselves that the repressive measures were justified and, most important, foolishly believed that they themselves might be allowed to go on unharassed with their own lives. Some indeed were being rewarded by stepping into the shoes of their convicted superiors.

When Bukharin was kept on as editor of *Izvestia*, the guests at the Merkurov home said it was a good omen. Victor too was reassured by this piece of news. Optimism surged. Victor went to see Bukharin and speedily wrote a lengthy article for the paper on problems in the automobile and tractor industry.

The article appeared in record time. How like Bukharin, everybody said. Bukharin, called by Lenin the Party's favorite, might yet be spared.

"If no action is taken against Bukharin," Victor proclaimed, "there will be a reprieve."

How wrong he was. How wrong we all were in thinking that silence and acquiescence would save our skins. It did not. Instead it created an atmosphere in which it was possible to bring millions to a death all the more cruel because so many of the victims were loyal supporters and dedicated builders of the Soviet system. If a firmer stand had been taken at this early stage, the entire course of history might have been less brutal. Stalin and his great admirers the world over paved the way for this great treachery and annihilation of human life.

VI The "traitors" of 1937 and 1938

The year whose coming we had welcomed with hope at the Merkurovs' was shedding its benign mask. Once it was off, 1937, and later 1938, struck out with enormous force, the blows rendered so suddenly that shock, bewilderment, and confusion gave way to naked, animal fear for one's life and the lives of one's closest and dearest.

Besides the big trials, spectacles that glued the eyes of the world to the Soviet Union, small fry by the thousands and hundreds of thousands were also being caught in the net. For the new victims, who were not top Party members, not internationally known figures, there would be no trials, no judges, only torture, death, or deportation to places where they would perish unknown and unmourned, for even to mourn them was forbidden.

When you arrived at your job you never knew who would be missing next. Department heads went as fast as the big bosses. You found their offices locked or sealed. Presently replacements were brought in. A new brand of executives! Some were recruited from the provinces and judged to be more reliable. The new bosses were hard, suspicious, and surly. Manners were brusque; beneath the high-handedness there was often a hidden insecurity and incompetence. These newcomers went about with a doglike, homeless look. Little attention was paid to them, for we were not at all certain what their fate would be. Many of them, indeed, followed their predecessors down into the overcrowded prison dungeons. Before work started there would be meetings with readings from *Pravda* or *Izvestia* about the crimes of the arrested, their involvement in plots to overthrow the government, undermine the system, restore capitalism, and other nonsense. Somebody with whom you had shaken hands just a few days before was now branded an enemy and a traitor. The "disclosures" were met with applause and votes of approval. If you did not join in the farce, you jeopardized your own safety and that of your dear ones. It was always the same vision I had at these meetings: cannibals dancing to the tom-tom of drums, clapping their hands in glee, as one after another the victims, often their own blood brothers and sisters, even their parents, were hurled into the flames.

Most people at these meetings knew the charges to be fabrications. Yet with a few exceptions—these courageous people suffered for it and were in their turn thrown into jail—all of us endorsed the resolutions condemning the "traitors."

When Stalin's name was mentioned people applauded, at first mostly out of fear, later as if in a hypnotic trance, and still later with a convenient conviction that he was the great father in whom people must put all their trust.

I hated Stalin and refused to find excuses, as other people tell me they did, for the glorification of the "leader," the need for arrests and executions. Some thought: Perhaps the trials are necessary, perhaps the defendants in the dock and those hundreds of thousands of others, declared "enemies," are in fact responsible for the ills, the backwardness, the dangers facing the country. ("The Soviet Union has wiped out its fifth column!" world communists, to their eternal shame, shouted in unison.)

Others adopted a different way of thinking: The Party is obviously doing something crazy, cruel and irrational, but one has to live with it, better still, accept it as the correct way. Such thinking was essential for those who wished to get ahead with their careers, realize their ambitions, and who craved high posts.

Later, in self-justification, these people would say that they had no idea the millions sentenced to die or rot in the prison camps were innocent. Was it possible that they really thought that? Or did they persuade themselves to think it for their own comfort?

For me to forget the people I knew in 1936, 1937, and 1938 who were shot outright, or condemned to a slow death in the camps, is equivalent to cutting out a part of my heart and brain. But even this feeling, throughout my life, I was compelled to keep to myself because it was shared only by a small minority.

Most of the people whose arrests shocked me so deeply were communist zealots, uncynical, idealistic. Their doom was sealed, for if the system was to pursue its devious course of survival, they had to make way for a new breed, the Stalin breed, power-lusting, treacherous, venal, unscrupulous.

One of the first among those I worked with to be mown down by the Lubyanka machine was the high-spirited Kurtz, a descendant of the Germans who had settled on the banks of the Volga at the time of Catherine the Great. He was a brisk, open-hearted, trustful man, bubbling over with energy, remarkably resourceful in grappling with difficulties, responsive to other people's troubles, kind and courteous.

Kurtz was the founder and later chairman of the German Autonomous Republic on the Volga banks, his energy and initiative helping to turn it into one of the most productive areas in the land. After diplomatic relations with the United States were established and the Soviet Union launched into tourism, Kurtz, who spoke German and English, was put in charge of organizing the Intourist travel agency. It was a wise choice, which paid enormous dividends to the state.

A month before his arrest I was sitting in his office adjoining the National Hotel when his plump, rosy-cheeked pregnant wife walked in. They were recently married, and I caught Kurtz's proud and tender glance on her lovely Madonna face. When he was taken away to the Lubyanka prison she, too, was incarcerated. Cruel repressive measures followed against his first wife and their sons. Having devoted his days and nights to his country, devising ways of attracting more tourists and making hard currency available for industrialization, Kurtz was doomed.

Most likely he was accused of becoming a German spy in his swaddling clothes, and later a secret agent of all the imperialists. (Think of the many contacts he could strike up with the "spies" from all over the world, disguised as "tourists," who sneaked into his office!)

A very different man from the robust, buoyant Kurtz was Axelrod, assistant editor of the *Moscow News*. Pensive, preoccupied, he rarely looked up at you when shown an article for the paper, but would poke his bony finger at a line to which he objected. Axelrod was in the last stages of tuberculosis, but he did not miss a day of work. Soon I realized that this frail, cadaverous man in his middle years was one of the most cultured persons I had ever met, simple and lovable. At the office we all knew that he had very few years to live. But even those few years were denied him, for this long-standing and highly respected communist was among the first group of persons arrested at the *Moscow News*.

Joe Zilbert, whom I met through Victor, was a general in the Soviet air force who had fought for a year in Spain. Long before, he had served under General Blücher (a Civil War hero who was later purged) and was with him and Victor in China as an adviser to Chiang Kai-shek. The Soviet advisers' lives were in danger when China broke with the Russian communists.

Joe's wife Katya, a former baroness of German descent, who had become a fervent revolutionary and Communist Party member, employed her feminine charms to persuade the German consul to engineer the Soviet advisers' flight from China. On returning from Spain, Zilbert discovered that Katya had been arrested. With her background it was easy to pin the most fantastic charges on this remarkable woman, who had rejected family and aristocratic origins to devote herself to the noble cause of equality and a good life for all. Katya, as I remember her, was the archetype of the liberated woman of the period, with sleek, dark, short-cropped hair falling in bangs over her broad forehead and a long cigarette-holder poised in her slender fingers as she spoke, intense, passionate in defending her ideas.

A few months after her arrest I met Joe Zilbert near the *Moscow*

News building on Petrovsky Pereulok in downtown Moscow. He had suddenly emerged from behind a house and after we parted hastily slipped into a courtyard, as if he wanted to keep away from exposed sidewalks. Perhaps he had acquired the habit in beleaguered Spain. In his melancholy gray eyes and the pathetic hunch of his shoulders I recognized the feeling of inescapable doom—the look of the hunted animal—that had become so familiar to me. Soon he too disappeared.

The sons and daughters of shot or arrested persons! I have seen so many of them, my own beloved daughter among them. The pain in their eyes is forever. Joe Zilbert was not yet forty when the Lubyanka steamroller passed over his body; his son Lyova was fourteen.

Joe's sister and her husband, who were childless, took in their nephew. (Nine years later, in 1947, both were arrested: they were freed in 1956, exonerated—as were Joe Zilbert and his wife, posthumously.) They dared not speak to Lyova of his parents' fate lest he become embittered and politically indiscreet. To prove that he was a Soviet patriot, he volunteered to fight in the war against Hitler when he was not yet of drafting age. He was killed in his very first battle.

Leonid Petrov was a carefree, lackadaisical kind of person. He held a non-spectacular position in the musical-instruments industry and liked to read English books. Now and then he would drop in to borrow a book from me.

Much as he loved Sima, the woman he had been living with for several years, he could not make up his mind to marry her. His excuse was that Sima, being a true city girl, would not care to live in the country, while he hoped eventually to return to his native village and get together a balalaika orchestra; he would show the world how talented Russian villagers were. "Sima would never follow me there," he claimed fretfully.

A few months went by. He had failed to return two books of mine— a well-illustrated edition of Andersen and Grimm fairy tales and a volume of stories by Edgar Allan Poe. I phoned him. There was no answer. Some time afterwards I met Sima close to the Kropotkinskaya metro station. I was shocked to see how she had aged. She was carrying a huge bundle.

"I'm going to join him," she said.

From the way she spoke and from her appearance, I guessed that she was not going to the countryside, but to quite a different place.

"You are very brave," I told her. "How much did he get?"

"Ten years . . . I'll try for a job near his prison camp. He's all I have in the world and all I care for."

VII Victor

Victor and I now spent as many evenings together as we could. Sometimes he would just drop in for an hour or two and then rush back to the big research center of which he was head. It was the style in those days for high-ranking executives to work through the small hours of the morning—decreed by Stalin.

We deliberately avoided discussion of the arrests. Nor did we talk of a life together as we had during the first months of our love. Often now he sat opposite me at the table in my long narrow hotel room, silent, drained of strength.

At such moments the world took on the quality of a horror film from which I longed to escape, only to find that I was nailed to my seat, kept there at gunpoint by two guards who stood on either side of me. Victor was with me; we were trapped.

We who always talked a great deal seemed to have suddenly lost the power of speech. Arrests, intimidation, the constant sowing of fear, the mushrooming of informers, imposed silence on all of us as a means of survival.

The heavy, oppressive armor of silence stifled, it strangled, and sometimes, if only for an hour, it had to be cast off. One form of relief was the anti-Soviet joke. But there was always sure to be an informer in the company, and some time, perhaps years, afterwards, the person who related the joke would be pulled in and given a sentence of ten years. A life finished—because of a single joke! Yet people risked it.

There were other ways of defying the imposed silence. You could be engulfed by it, yet the human mind, resourceful as it is, enabled you to converse in half-meanings, innuendoes, twisted sentences, and in this way convey your thoughts. Words could be treated in a manner so ingenious that they denoted the opposite of the intended thought, and yet they were understood. When spouted by officials they could be a jumble of meaningless stock phrases, and yet trigger off a stream of indignation, make people strain at the leash. To channel one's speech into restricted patterns of conversation was not easy. But I noticed that gradually people, myself included, were doing just that and getting to be adept at it.

But Victor and I—how could we use that trick language? More often than not we would lapse into silence. Those long, agonizing silences hung heavy in the empty air between us, and perhaps they alone saved my life; for had I been hauled off to Lubyanka in the late thirties and landed in a prison camp, I would not have survived.

A panic I had never known before seized me when for three days

Victor neither came to see me nor phoned. On the fourth night I walked across half of Moscow until I reached the house where he lived. With a pounding heart I paused in front of the entrance. Two men in plain clothes, along with the yardman, whom I recognized at once, and a fourth person I could not place were climbing the stairs, the first two with a firm step, the others trailing along. Four persons late at night, two security men and two "witnesses": an arrest! At one point the two who walked ahead threw a glance behind them. Their faces were a blank. Presently all four stopped on Victor's landing, on the fourth floor.

There were three apartments on that landing.

The men had not noticed me. I dashed down the flights of stairs and reached the yard. It was long past midnight. I stood in the shadows of a row of tall dust-bins. Most of the windows were dark. The people who lived in this newly built apartment house were either asleep or had been dragged from their beds and, after a search of their homes, hauled off to Lubyanka.

Suddenly two windows on the fourth floor came ablaze with light. I tried hard to keep calm. Were they Victor's windows? It took me a long time to figure that out. Finally, with a leap of joy, I realized what a fool I had been. The corner windows belonged to Victor. They were dark: Victor was either asleep or spending the night working at his office, as he often did. Greatly relieved, I trudged back home, arriving around three in the morning. Then from a deep sleep I was awakened by the ringing of the phone.

Victor's tone was level: "Never do that again, never!"

"Do what?"

"I saw you in the court last night . . ." There was a pause. Victor added that he would drive over to the Merkurovs' after work.

He never turned up. I stayed for a few hours and then left. Oddly enough, we who always talked so much about Victor never mentioned his name at all that evening.

Around midnight he knocked on my door. Neither of us dared voice aloud the fear in our hearts. Victor gave me a long, weary stare—devoid of all hope. Like dumb animals we let the eyes convey that all was lost, that the sword would descend. It was our last night together. Victor fell asleep but soon woke with a start and quickly left.

Another two months of freedom. We both knew that he was being shadowed and that it was best for me not to see him. We communicated through Asta, Merkurov's wife.

Victor took turns staying now with one friend, now with another, avoiding his own apartment and spending a few nights at the Merkurovs'. Neighbor after neighbor was being hauled away at night from the house on Kaptelsky Street where he lived; most of the tenants were top industrial executives. Soon after the men disappeared, the security police came to arrest the wives.

One morning Asta phoned: "Did Victor spend the night at your place?"

"No, he didn't."

My heart stood still. Asta's voice sounded flat, deceptively unemotional: "I have had no word from him for two days."

She replaced the receiver. It was not safe to pursue the conversation. We both knew too well what had happened.

A couple of days later Banovich, a friend of Victor's, phoned to say he was coming over right away. They were pals from their teens, when both fought in the Civil War. Banovich, who had lost an arm in that war, also held a post at the Heavy Industry Commissariat under Orzhonikidze, as Director of the Oil Industry Board.

"Victor was arrested a few days ago," were his first words. "I can't believe it. I simply can't believe it. Victor was absolutely trustworthy, a dedicated Bolshevik. He built up the tractor and automobile industry—from scratch."

I looked at Banovich. His florid, ugly face showed plainly how perplexed he was by Victor's arrest. He was a true friend, and yet I dared not bare my sorrow, even utter a single expression of regret. All those who had been intimate with someone arrested now feared for their own safety and that of their relatives. Silence was our sole refuge. We pretended that the arrested person never existed—and in this we became stout allies of the state's repressive apparatus, acquiescing in its policies. Nothing can bring Victor back, I told myself, he is as good as dead already. I must think of myself, my brother and mother. I shall not forgive myself if they come to harm.

Such were my thoughts in the daytime. The nights were harder to endure. I would suddenly wake up with a vision of Victor in a torture cell, pummelled, knocked about, taunted, and humiliated. And it was all the harder for him, I knew, because he was a proud man.

Banovich was pacing up and down my tiny room. I felt numb. Presently I persuaded him to sit down. I made a glass of tea.

"Could there really have been some evidence against him, grounds for his arrest?" he asked suddenly.

How many times I was to hear this same question, even ask it of myself! How could the mind resign itself to the arrest and killing of devoted communists by their own supposed comrades?

"Just listen to what I have to say!" Leaping to his feet, he burst out in staccato tones.

This was a different Banovich from the jovial friend who loved to listen to Victor's funny stories and laughed heartily at them.

"Listen to what I have to say," he repeated. "I'm not a spy, not a saboteur." He laid emphasis on every word. "No imperialist agent. I was never in any opposition, I do not want to see capitalism restored. I am an honest, hard-working communist, ready to die for my ideals. I shall never be arrested."

Wasted breath, poor Banovich.

Not having heard from him for a few days, I phoned his wife.

"Yes, it has happened," she said and hung up.

FIVE

I Attitudes among the intelligentsia

A few weeks after Victor's arrest, on a Saturday night, I went to see the Merkurovs. Some fifteen persons sat around the tea table in the spacious living room next to the sculptor's studio. There was the usual lively chat and laughter.

Clouds of steam rose from the big-bellied brass samovar, topped by a brightly coloured porcelain teapot. A hush settled around the table when I entered. The guests raised their heads from the cake plates and eyed me as though I were a ghost. One of the men, known for his biting remarks and the pleasure he took in shocking people, blurted out with a wry smile: "Well, well, what a surprise to see you, we were sure you would follow . . ." He did not finish the sentence, but the company knew well enough what he meant: I would share Victor's fate.

I do not think he was a vindictive person. He spoke out of a general bitterness. But I was stunned by his words and utterly at a loss for an answer.

Rising from her seat at the head of the table, Asta walked up to me, threw an arm around my shoulders, and guided me to a seat next to her husband. As though nothing painful had been said, the conversation interrupted by my arrival was resumed. The talk was perhaps typical of the period—veiled, noncommittal. I caught the name of the journalist Mikhail Koltsov.

"Nobody's reportage about Spain was so vivid . . ."
"Vanished as soon as he came back from the Spanish Civil War."
"And Kirshon?"

"His plays were staged across the country. Great hits . . . and then banned overnight."

"One of the first to drop out of the scene was Pilnyak, wasn't he? Just when everybody was reading his book *O'Key*, about the United States, and then those intriguing stories about Japan."

It may have been only the year before that I had seen Pilnyak in a little Caucasian restaurant in Gorky Street, a favorite haunt of Moscow writers and artists. He was arguing vociferously, in a haze of tobacco smoke and alcoholic fumes, waving his hands about so violently that they almost slashed into the faces of his two interlocutors.

The people around the table, sipping their tea and treating themselves to Asta's delicious apricot jam, spoke of the writers' arrests as unconcernedly as though these unfortunates had gone away on a holiday to the Mediterranean.

Talk about writers, even in the innocuous form it was taking, was hastily dropped when the next visitor arrived. This was Alexei Tolstoy. Redolent of pre-revolutionary luxury, he wore a loosely wrapped fur-lined *shuba* of excellent cloth, a tall beaver hat in the boyar style, and an expensive scarf. He had just published *Grain*, hailed as a true socialist-realist novel, about the prosperous life of the collective farmers.

He exuded well-being from every pore of his oversized body. So smug and arrogant! Grudging him his happiness and success, I thought of the writers who had been mentioned around the table. They were paying—or had already paid—with their lives to gratify the mad whims of a man who wielded unlimited power and in whose good graces Alexei Tolstoy had always been. His position with the Great One was secure. Even the most feeble gesture from him in defense of the persecuted writers would have been a ray of hope in the dark.

There were other towering figures in literature and the arts who could have raised their voices. But they did not. They owed too much to the new regime to imperil their positions. They had been allowed to keep the mansions in which they lived before the revolution, been given sizeable grants and subsidies to carry out grand projects in the arts, so that they were in many ways better off than under the tsar. Why jeopardize all these favors to save the lives of a few thousand of their associates?

Honest and moral Soviet writers would have liked to speak up for their confrères. But the price was too high—their own liberty, perhaps life, and retribution falling on their loved ones. What about Western men of letters? They too would pay a price—run the risk of losing their Soviet readership and, worst of all, foregoing invitations from the Soviet Writers' Union. Avowed humanists from the West were in Moscow during the trials and mass arrests. We all saw and heard them. Henri Barbusse published a paean to Stalin, and Lion Feuchtwanger condoned the show trails in his *Moscow 1937*. Romain Rolland and Bernard Shaw made little attempt to speak up against the summary dispatching of thousands of human lives. Shocking numbers of intellectuals accepted or pretended to accept the so-called evidence against the "enemies of the people" as truth. Was it possible for a single country to have bred within its borders such a multitude of traitors, spies, and "agents of imperialism"? They might have asked themselves this question.

At the time I was so deeply disturbed by what I saw happening around me, I had already begun to work in journalism. But my desire to pursue it as a career was dampened by the gross and tragic events of the late thirties. How was one to comprehend and assess such cruelty on the part of the state?

At my job I received encouragement. My senior colleagues wished me well; they edited my writing and gave me assignments that suited my taste and temperament. Journalism had its attractions—it brought you closer to the outside world, broadened your horizons. You could make interesting friends, follow up events and trends more closely. But whatever conclusions you arrived at you had to sublimate, and such compliance to the state was abhorrent to me. My back was up.

You arrived in the morning and carefully perused every line of the *Pravda* editorial. In it were the cues for your topics and how they should be presented to the reader. Whatever you contributed, regardless of your beat, had to be an enlargement and illustration of the Party stand.

I remember interviewing a Ukrainian writer and then attending the premiere of his play at the Moscow Art Theater. The work was a corny piece about a doctor and his architect girlfriend, caught up in the usual predictable situations from which they emerge successful owing to the superiority of the Soviet system over the capitalist. What galled me most, because it was so incompatible with the communist beliefs I held, was that the Soviet heroine's supreme reward was a free trip to the decadent West.

Did my review say what I really thought of the play? Not at all. I wrote what was expected of me and despised myself for it. Translation was my salvation; I switched from original writing to translation.

There were fewer arrests among painters and sculptors than within other artistic groups, perhaps because they were less of a danger to the state, having little direct contact with and influence on the public. Painters could spend years over a picture in their studios without arousing suspicion. They did not appear before audiences, rarely mingled with persons outside their circle, and so were less frequently exposed to informers.

Painting Stalin was the easiest way for the artist to establish himself. Poking his physiognomy into every picture—of women's conferences, parliamentary sessions, children's rallies, sports events, harvest festivals—was a sure ticket to fame.

But by far not every painter or sculptor was willing to peddle his talent in this manner. There was A.L., whom I frequently met at the Merkurovs' and who under one pretext or another avoided all commissions to paint the great leader. Visual artists managed to get away with it, while writers and people in the theater were forced to pay constant homage to Stalin. They could produce pots with flowers, still-lifes that brought practically no remuneration, and earn a living by designing textiles or painting theater backdrops. They had little chance of exhibiting their work and were attacked in the press for "keeping aloof from Soviet reality." Yet they stood their ground.

But the artists pampered by fame, accustomed to a comfortable life and eager for commissions from the state, lent themselves with amazing zest to glorifying Stalin. This was true of Alexander Mikhailovich Gerasimov and also of my friend Sergei Merkurov.

Gerasimov became secretary of the Soviet Artists Union and Merkurov had charge of the Arts Fund. Because of these two influential posts, the sculptor and painter often conferred on matters of Soviet art, mostly at the former's home in Izmailovo. That was where I met Alexander Mikhailovich Gerasimov.

This renowned and talented painter, whose works were on view at the Tretyakov Gallery, was of a totally unartistic appearance— stocky, pot-bellied, with a head that sat like a cannon ball on his powerful shoulders. He had puffed cheeks, shrewd small eyes, and a fleshy spatulate hand with stubby fingers. Like many Russians who knew some English, he was a great fan of Agatha Christie.

I admired his work but could not forgive him his "court portraits." Nor was I alone in this attitude. Boris Ioganson, an artist of equal stature but far less subservient, took revenge on Gerasimov in an interesting way. In his famous painting "In an Old Urals Foundry," which now hangs in the new branch of the Tretyakov Gallery devoted to Soviet art, Ioganson used Gerasimov as the prototype for the villain: the lone figure of the boss, standing apart from the exploited workers who, stripped to the waist, feed coal into the glowing furnace. The likeness was unmistakable—there was the same fleshy face, sly look in the eyes, and chubby form. Moscow painters, many of whom loathed Gerasimov, were delighted with the resemblance. Such veiled forms were not infrequently used by Soviet painters and other artists to express their revulsion for the Stalin personality cult and its zealous perpetuators.

Gerasimov had come to be so closely associated with Stalin and his rigidity towards art that after the 20th and 22nd Party congresses Soviet painters were only too happy to consign the former secretary of their Union to oblivion. Under Stalin's rule Gerasimov was the country's leading painter. His works were widely exhibited and he was held up as an example of socialist realist art.

Painters who did not glorify the great leader and Soviet achievements enjoyed no such privilege. Among them was the master craftsman Alexander Yakovlev; by his own admission he always kept the painting he did "for the soul" separate from that which provided his livelihood. He was one of the few artists in whose studio I saw no portraits of Stalin. Instead, the walls of his big, government-subsidized workshop were hung with paintings of voluptuous nudes in the Rubens manner.

At the time I knew him, Yakovlev was working on a wall-sized canvas of figures in the most startling dramatic poses. He called it "Gorky's Den of Iniquity," because the characters were inspired by the outcasts of society described in many of Gorky's writings. The canvas was half-finished when I saw it. The central figure and focal point of the entire composition was a wanton creature with titian hair; because of my own wealth of reddish auburn hair, he asked me to pose for the head, something I had neither the inclination nor the time to do.

While he painted, Yakovlev kept up a run of chatter with visitors who kept dropping in and out of his studio, and with them he emptied one bottle of red port after another. The passion he had for life showed in his lush palette. His themes and manner invariably fell out with socialist realism; it was mostly by supervising the public decoration of Moscow for holidays that he supported himself and his family.

He possessed a phenomenal memory. I saw him open a book, pass his eyes over a printed page, lay the volume aside, and reproduce word for word from memory what he had read only once. He also contrived to do exactly the same thing with the paintings of great masters. This talent had led to his involvement in a sensational court case, in the twenties, in which the defendants were charged with smuggling art treasures out of the Soviet Union and disposing of them to Western dealers. The treasures, it was revealed, were not the genuine paintings but frauds—copies made by Yakovlev, from memory, of Rubens and Snyders, which even the most astute art connoisseurs failed to distinguish from the originals.

A man who chose a different road from Gerasimov and Yakovlev was A.L. He belonged to a younger generation and sat with a melancholy detachment while the venerable painters around Merkurov's table reminisced. They were splendid raconteurs, men of great foibles, who had been members of the famous "World of Art" and "Knave of Diamonds" groups, siring trends in painting that were to be taken up thirty or fifty years later and carried forward in the West.

Never having joined the ranks of socialist realist art, A.L. barely made a living. He was representative of a group of painters and sculptors who formed a silent opposition to the regimentation of art by the state. He did not adjust, and went on painting work quite different from that demanded of him. Life was not easy for such artists, either materially or intellectually, for they were cut off from the viewing public.

II The sculptor Merkurov

Like so many Russian artists, Merkurov had passed through a phase of deep devotion to the Tolstoyan philosophy. Having in his youth visited Tolstoy at Yasnaya Polyana, he later tried to model his own home and life style on those of the renowned writer. He put into his dining-room a huge unvarnished table with long benches on either side of it, turning his home into a gathering place for the most curious characters from all walks of life, especially the arts. Although inordinate amounts of vodka, along with Georgian and other wines, were consumed by his guests, Merkurov never touched alcohol.

More than anything else, the sculptor delighted in human companionship, always picking up new friends and wrapping them in the warmth of his heart, happy to have an audience for his stories, his wit, his antics. He was a prolific sculptor, a true master—but I often wondered how much more he could have produced, with his team of apprentices, if he had given less of his time to his friends.

In his home people, their souls, their woes and idiosyncracies were accorded undisputed priority, obscuring even his sculptures, the splendid paintings that hung often askew on the walls, the antiques and bric à brac. The expensive and beautiful furniture that came from his wife's once extremely wealthy home, like a bedroom suite of Karelian birchwood encrusted with mother-of-pearl, was always in need of polish, and the costly tapestries revealed greasy stains. This indifference to things made all human beings feel at ease in the Merkurov home. As unrestrainedly as the times permitted, they could bare their souls, unleash their emotions, as Russians have always been wont to do.

And no human being was more worthy to grace that home than Asta Grigoryevna, at the time one of the few women graduates of Moscow University. Her father had owned the big drugstore on Trubnaya Square and therefore, though a Jew, was permitted to reside in Moscow. Using the screen name of Asta Grey, she had appeared in some of the very early Russian silent movies, scripted by Mayakovsky and directed by Nemirovich-Danchenko.

Merkurov was fond of telling the story of how he first saw her. He was then a widower with two young daughters.

"I was standing in the lobby of the Actors Club, chatting with friends, when I looked up. There, at the top of the staircase leading down into the lobby, stood the Juno of my imagination—a statue I had long wished to chisel in white marble. What my hands had itched to mold appeared in the flesh.

"'A Juno come to life!' I exclaimed. Like myself, my friends gasped at the perfection of form and features they beheld.

" 'This woman will be my wife,' I said to myself."

Quite a few Russians I knew claimed to have chosen their wives in this manner. Possibly Merkurov's exclamation could be traced to that passage in Tolstoy's *War and Peace* in which Andrei, lost in admiration of Natasha, promises to himself: "If she first approaches her cousin and then . . . she will be my wife." But my dear friend had not said "if"; he was an Armenian, and Russian fatalism was not to his taste.

With her crown of soft curly hair, her aquiline nose, ivory skin and slightly protruding lids—perfect for a sculptor to mold—Asta had the kind of beauty that went beyond sexual attraction. She was truly adored by both men and women.

I remember seeing Asta once in the lobby of the Bolshoi Theater talking to two younger women also renowned for their beauty. One was the famous Art Theater actress Alla Tarasova; the other was Lyudmila Tolstoya, recently married to Alexei Tolstoy. Just then the actor Maxim Shtraukh walked up to me and said, "There stands the most beautiful woman in Moscow." I looked at the three beauties and asked, "Which one?"

"Can you doubt it?" he replied. "Asta Merkurova, of course!"

When a son was born to the Merkurovs so much wine was drunk that a deep trench was dug behind the vegetable patches to bury the champagne bottles alone. A great lover of women, soon after the birth of this son Merkurov went back to his accustomed way of living, moving from one mistress to another. When I met him he was fifty-five, and his mistress, to whom I believe he remained attached to the end of his days, was twenty-six.

This mistress, who later became Merkurov's wife, was very different from Asta. For one thing, she was unattached to bourgeois morality or values; in fact she was blissfully ignorant of both. She was, however, far from a simple and straightforward Soviet "new" woman. At a time when Dostoevsky was a forbidden author she steeped herself in his work. She had a typically Russian, almost morbid, love of torturing others and herself by dramatizing the most trivial situation to the extreme.

She wielded an intense sexual power over Merkurov. A clever and intuitive person, he was aware of the symbolic implication of his choice; he was trying to come to terms with the new life and the rigid "proletarian type," as opposed to his liberal-minded, cosmopolitan wife.

He saw himself that this new love was a break with the old life and a step forward in his understanding and acceptance of the new society. He had a purely artistic explanation, too: "She is my finest sculpture. Her contours unfold from the world around me. They reverberate in every stroke of my chisel."

There was nothing new or odd about older men falling in love with younger women, setting up new homes, plunging into new marriages. But as I witnessed the new unions formed by many artists of Merkurov's stature, they seemed to fall into a recognizable pattern, created not so much by nature as by social exigencies. They reflected the conflict in the hearts and minds of men who had their roots in the old pre-revolutionary Russian culture, and the Western culture as well, yet found the communist ideals alluring. To them these ideals represented equality, brotherhood, jobs for all, government by the people: "Every cook will run the state," Lenin had said.

Merkurov and many others like him took no issue with the new order. They complied. They did not flee abroad. Indeed, they embraced communism in the way Lenin had admonished: "You cannot become a communist unless you have learned and assimilated all the culture of the world." They had gone to schools and universities where they had sought Truth, where they had themselves participated in demonstrations against tsarism. They dreamed of a new kind of human society, of happiness for all people.

Gradually, however, it had become obvious how far removed from their dream was the daily activity of Soviet society. Men like Merkurov must have seen that—but there was nothing they could do, except stop posing moral problems, cast away their doubts, and above all disentangle themselves from the burden of the old values. And who was it who shared these doubts and confusion, who held them back from wholeheartedly accepting the new order? In a good many cases it was their wives. What a relief it was, therefore, to be united with the new proletarian-thinking partner, the new wife who "looked only ahead and never back," as one friend had said to me.

I could see the struggle that went on in the heart and mind of Merkurov who, much as he may have desired it, never became totally integrated into the new establishment. He continued to harbor under his roof the children of arrested friends; he also befriended members of the Russian clergy who had served their prison terms and returned to no home, no church—most of them to be hounded, blacklisted, and later rearrested.

His guests would often be startled by the appearance of a timorous black-garbed nun at the head of the stairs leading into the dining-room. Lightly, on tip-toe, she would come down, only to hastily withdraw at the sight of people she knew she must avoid, like the gross Alexander Shcherbakov, Secretary of the Moscow Communist Party City Committee, visiting Merkurov on some matter of the arts, or the puffed-up Marshal Choybalsan, newly arrived from Mongolia to sit for his bust.

A priest would leave his hiding-place and diffidently join the company if the faces were familiar, but even so he would rarely converse, sitting in a far corner by himself. Merkurov tried to find work for these unfortunates, often paying the wages out of his own pocket. Luckily his statues of Lenin, Stalin, and other great ones brought in large sums of money.

Merkurov liked to talk about his work to anyone who was ready to listen, and I was no exception. His features lit up as he dissected a new work for me, going back many centuries into the history of sculpture to explain a fold or a curve, or revealed the secret of his own foreshortening technique in the huge monuments he was designing.

His statue of Timiryazev overlooks Nikitskiye Gates, a busy intersection at Moscow's inner boulevard; this figure of the father of Russian agricultural science is one of the early Soviet modernist sculptures. In 1941, at the outset of the war on Soviet territory, it was knocked off its pedestal by a bomb blast, the head rolling away from the torso. Along with a few helpers, Merkurov worked through the morning hours after the all-clear signal to get it back in place.

"Timiryazev is up again," he told me. "Damn the Nazis! Whatever they blast will rise again like the phoenix from the ashes."

It was in 1941, too, at a very crucial time for his country, that Merkurov further proved his loyalty to the socialist regime. At the age of almost sixty he joined the Communist Party.

Most of Merkurov's statues of Stalin showed him draped in a long army coat, which served well to give the illusion of height and dignity to the puny figure. When he began work on the colossal monuments of Lenin and Stalin commanding the entrance to the Moskva-Volga Canal, Merkurov wrote a letter to Stalin, asking him if he wished to be portrayed with or without his many regalia.

He showed me the brief reply: "Better without." I made no comment. Merkurov's face, too, was inscrutable. To talk about Stalin was to paddle in dangerous waters; Merkurov apparently felt a need for some sort of communication with the man of whom he made so many statues—mostly from photographs—and perhaps the letter helped.

Despite his numerous portrayals of Stalin, Merkurov did not enjoy the trust of the powers he courted, a trust he tried to gain at no small price to his individuality as an artist and as a human being. This I was to realize when my interrogator plied me with questions, the object of which was to extract politically defamatory information against the sculptor.

III Mikhail, 1939

Fear being my counsellor, I decided I would never marry a man as conspicuous in public life as Victor had been. I was working at the *Moscow News* when I met Mikhail, an unassuming, benevolent person to whom people in our office were in the habit of pouring out their hard-luck stories. It might have been this humane quality of empathy that first attracted me to him.

In every way he was the opposite of Victor. Overpowering physically and mentally, with high animal spirits and scathing wit, Victor had a sense of his own worth and superiority that he never bothered to conceal. Mikhail was subdued, willowy, devoid of all vanity. Where Victor was every inch a fighter for what he thought was right, Mikhail was tolerant, forgiving, and fatalistic. Possessing none of the bitterness of A.G., nor the adventurism of Vanya, Mikhail was a realist, loyally serving the socialist society. Neither did he have Victor's ambitious drive—perhaps because he was wise enough to realize the price one paid in journalism to rise to a top position.

We embarked on a long, old-fashioned courtship, untypical of the times—with the traditional flowers, evenings spent together, visits to friends and relatives. He did not rush me; I needed time to get over my feelings for Victor.

When we started our life together—with no wedding, without registering the marriage—like many other couples we had no home of our own. We could only snatch brief moments of privacy and, as during our courtship, spent our evenings out. We would sit for hours at the National Café, talking, dancing, and drinking coffee out of a tall, spindle-legged nickel urn, kept hot with a bluish-pink flame.

Sustenance for our spirit we often derived from the theater, lovingly called by the Russians "a shrine of art." Censorship was stiff and there were unequivocal directives on what to stage and what to ban. But the artistry of the productions, the acting or dancing skill— and, moreover, the possibility of reading our own significant messages into what was presented on the stage— made a theater performance an uplifting experience. Muscovites still flock to the theater with something like the fervor and hope with which Roman Catholics go to church.

When Stalin gave the Art Theater the green light to stage Bulgakov's *The Days of the Turbins*, a tremor of delight passed through Moscow's play-going public. At last a shred of political truth had seeped through to the stage, we told ourselves. For once the White Guards were portrayed as human beings. Stalin's magnanimity was lauded, and people foolishly hoped for a little more leeway. The slavish mentality had become so ingrained that nobody questioned the imposition of such interference and censorship from the top.

Few people can boast of never having had any superstitious fears. At this time in my life, in the early summer of 1939, I became prey to a recurring nightmare; I always woke with the certainty that it was an omen of some disaster to come.

I was traversing a green pasture, fresh with morning dew. On the fringe of the pasture cows and horses grazed, enjoying the luscious grass. The cows flapped their long red tongues and the horses tossed their manes. The serenity of the scene, the happy animals, and the bluest of skies filled me with a pleasant sensation, but it soon melted away. The atmosphere abruptly changed from peace to evil foreboding. The animals now fidgeted nervously. Somber shadows blotted out the sky. Gray turmoil replaced the vibrant, cheerful hues.

Before my gaze the shadows took the shape of monstrous grizzly bears drifting low overhead. They came swooping down on me and the frightened animals. I tried running away but seemed to be chained to the spot by some supernatural force. In the end I got away. Escape filled me with relief. (Nightmares I had in subsequent years brought no such relief; there was no escape.)

The year 1939, a crucial year for all Europe, brought fundamental change in the Soviet Union's international policies. It was a time of territorial expansion and concern for the safety of the country's borders. That summer, the non-aggression pact with Nazi Germany was a hard pill to swallow for all Soviet people. Political passions surfaced and clashed. Piercing the silence, some spoke their despair; a few gloated. One man I met at the Merkurovs' condemned the pact openly while another was in raptures revealing, to our horror, his adulation of Hitler.

The first was the director of a big Moscow industrial plant—work-worn, harried, obsessed, like most Soviet executives, by a fear of not meeting the exaggerated targets of the Five Year Plan: "to rival and outstrip America." He was uncynical, dedicated, harping forever on what measures must be taken to improve the living standards of the proletariat. Certain of the imminence of war, he gave much time to the organization of civil defense, boasting what good marksmen his workers were and how well they could handle a gas attack.

His opinion of the pact he repeated without end: "It is plain foolishness. Hitler *will* strike! Are we prepared? No! My plant isn't! I keep saying it needs to be re-equipped to meet war needs. Do I get support from the top people? Again no!" He was panic-stricken when the war broke out and Hitler's armies were blitzing farther and farther into Soviet territory. His "defeatist talk" earned him a prison sentence. But men as good at their jobs as he was were so badly needed that, to our great amazement, he was released.

The second man whose reaction to the pact was extreme, though not so unusual, was Vsevolod Blumenthal-Tamarin, a magic name throughout the Soviet land. In Moscow he ran an extremely popular state-subsidized one-actor theater, and there was no honor, no privilege the Soviet state did not shower on him.

On that August day of pale sunlight, when the newspapers were full of the pact and the visit of the German foreign minister, von Ribbentrop, to Moscow, my husband and I went to see actor friends of ours at their dacha. The table was set for tea in the garden. Shortly after we arrived a car pulled up and Vsevolod Blumenthal-Tamarin alighted from it; his chauffeur followed behind, lugging a crate of champagne, which he dropped on the grass close to the table.

Swiftly, with an elegant gesture, Vsevolod drew two bottles from the crate and set them down on the table. He was a pampered man: the one wine he drank was champagne, sometimes emptying bottle after bottle with no visible effects. Glasses were filled and passed around. Vsevolod raised his glass, a jubilant light in his eyes. The rest of the company lifted theirs half-heartedly, wondering what the toast would be.

It was indeed unexpected.

"Let us drink to the noble alliance of the Soviet Union and Hitler Germany, and that Britain may be wiped off the face of the earth."

He pronounced the toast in the mellow voice beloved by millions of fans, who would listen entranced to his recitals of Hamlet's and other monologues.

Scandalized, I glanced at the faces around me. They were expressionless.

"I will drink no such toast." I tossed the contents of my glass into the withered grass. Pretending not to hear me, the rest of the company swallowed the champagne at almost a single gulp, as though it were vodka.

Two years later, in 1941, the Germans reached the banks of the Istra, a picturesque hilly area close to Moscow, where many actors had their private dachas. It was here that Blumenthal-Tamarin welcomed them with bread and salt, in the tradition of Russian hospitality. The Germans, in their turn, recruited him as a radio announcer. On behalf of the Nazi command he made countless appeals to the Russian troops to surrender to the Wehrmacht. In 1945 he fell into the hands of the Soviet fighting men, and rumor had it that he was strung up there and then.

Now that I was married I spent less time with my friends and more with my husband. I would look across the table at Mikhail and watch him fill the usual four or five pages of an article for the newspaper with his distinct neat handwriting, each written page the exact equivalent of a typed sheet. I was glad he did not possess Victor's hauteur and qualities of leadership. He would remain a competent rank-and-file journalist. I would be safe with him. So I thought.

Among my friends Mikhail came to be known as the ideal husband. I hoped that if I had a daughter she might inherit his blond coloring, blue eyes, and long, slender fingers.

SIX

I War! German tanks advance on Moscow

It was a cool and cloudless Sunday—June 22, 1941. We slept late, and it was not until noon that Mikhail plugged in the loudspeaker on the wall across from our bed. Molotov was on the air: Hitler's armies had crossed the Soviet border in the small hours of the morning.

"We do not claim another nation's territory, nor shall we cede an inch of our own." These words of Defense Minister Klim Voroshilov had been repeated so often over the past few years that the Soviet people knew them by heart and drew comfort from them.

But that very day, in a matter of hours, great hunks of territory had been sliced off by the enemy. Mikhail and I dressed hurriedly and walked out into the street. Knots of bewildered people, many with tears in their eyes, crowded desolately around the black disks of loudspeakers attached to street poles to hear the news. Horror, disbelief, and puzzlement glared from their faces. Men, young and old, some in uniform, others in ordinary suits with haversacks slung across their shoulders, were hurrying to the drafting stations, accompanied by weeping relatives.

I listened to Churchill's speech at the home of friends who owned a radio set. The news that Britain was our ally, that we did not confront the Nazi war machine single-handed, was reassuring. With his penchant for vivid language, Churchill was saying that he could see Russians everywhere, in the farm fields, in the cities, framing their lips in prayer. Addressed to atheistic Russia, these words rang strange. And since the speech was censored, they never reached the ears they were meant for. Two months later I was amazed to find how true they were.

I was standing on a station platform, from which one troop train after another was departing for the front. Nadezhda, a doctor friend of mine, was leaving with the Army Medical Corps, and I had come to see her off. As she was boarding the train her mother, a shrivelled woman, old before her years, raised herself on tiptoe and made the sign of the cross over her. Glancing around, I noticed that a few other women too were crossing themselves and mumbling prayers.

Air raids started in late July. Moscow skies rocked with the sinister shapes of enemy bombers, reminding me of my nightmare. Cool weather had given way to a torrid spell abetting the outbreak and spread of fires from the numberless incendiary bombs that descended upon the city. Buildings crumbled from the direct hits of demolition bombs. That very day a bomb had barely missed the Central Committee, burying in the rubble of a nearby house Afinogenov, a playwright I very much admired.

A turquoise sky shimmered in the fiery glow of the setting sun. For a moment I was entranced by its beauty. War, danger at every step, sharpened the senses, made life more precious. It puzzled me that I should feel so light-hearted—the frivolity and buoyancy of young womanhood, dismissing all thought of misfortune, anticipating only the good things of life for oneself.

I quickened my step, eager to get home in time to cook some supper for my husband and have him eat it before he took up his nightly duty on the roof of our building, along with the other fire wardens.

A hand was laid on my shoulder. I had to throw my head far backwards to look into the eyes of the man who towered above me. It was a friend from the days I had spent with Victor in Kislovodsk. We had kept in touch. A few years earlier he had graduated from the Zhukovsky Aviation Academy and become one of Moscow's best test pilots. He was in uniform, sunbeams glancing off the blue tabs on his sleeves and collar tips.

His usual jaunty air was replaced by a morose look. He scowled as he spoke, his voice shaking: "Look, I'm an expert navigator and I walk idly about the streets of Moscow. The Germans have put most of our air force out of commission right at the outset of their attack. Many of my best comrades have come down in flames."

He clenched his big fists: "God, oh God Almighty how I itch to put my hands on the controls of a fighter or bomber. And I can do nothing about it. The situation is unbearable."

How costly in human lives, both of fighting men and of civilians, were the early months of the war. It was numbers, a human avalanche, that in the end, after months and months of severe combat, held back the German advance. Then followed the miracle of regearing all industries, the home-front directing all its effort to supply the armed forces with materiel.

Silently, perhaps thinking the same thoughts, we reached the entrance of my home and I invited my friend in to share our supper. But there was no time even to drink a glass of tea. The siren wailed. My husband rushed off to the roof, while the flyer and I, along with all the tenants, made our way into the basement, which had been hastily converted into a shelter. The building above us heaved and shook. It seemed now that at any moment we would be blown to pieces. With every blast my friend's face turned darker. How crushed he must have felt, sitting among mostly old men, women, and children, when he should have been hitting back at the enemy behind the controls of a Soviet plane. Those were bitter days.

Many years after the war my friend and I once again met by chance. I caught sight of him as I was passing through Nogin Square in Moscow. He was one of many war veterans who had come here on the celebration of Victory Day. He wore an aviation colonel's uniform, his entire chest covered with medals and other decorations. But his hair was white, his handsome face deeply furrowed, and he limped.

"Nothing ages like the years," he said, smiling.

"Like a war," I corrected him. "So you got your planes after all?"

"My plane! Just one bomber all through the war, and I cherished it more than life."

There was hardly a night now when the city was not bombed. But, apparently not having achieved the desired effect, the air raids were discontinued after a few weeks.

The Merkurovs had dug trenches in their backyard. There Mikhail and I took cover when we visited them during the early heavy bombing of the city.

Asta had greatly changed; she was no longer her usual serene self. I realized it was one thing to face a calamity for the first time, another when you had been through the experience before.

This was true of Asta. She talked on and on about World War I. Beautiful Asta had become careless about her appearance. When two journalists called to interview her husband on his proposed 100–metre statue of Lenin, which was to top the Palace of Soviets—an ambitious project, eventually dropped—Asta was wearing a soiled dressing-gown. She hurried into the bedroom to change, only to reappear in front of the callers without a skirt, attired in a silk blouse over her faded blue bloomers. Nor did the general embarrassment bother her.

Asta's mind was preoccupied with fear for her son, who was nearing drafting age. He was her only child. One member of the family, her step-daughter's husband, a man in his thirties, had already fallen in battle.

Just as Asta had her unpatriotic thoughts, I had mine. My brother Shurri, nineteen years old at the time, was a student of mathematics. Any day now, I knew, he could be drafted. In the early battles of the war, casualties were enormous, especially among the youngest of the fighting men. Many perished in their very first encounter with the enemy. Shurri had his haversack ready. He was going to enlist even before he was called up. After some arguing, I persuaded him that, with his perfect knowledge of English, he could be of greater service in the war if he trained as an army interpreter.

He enrolled as a cadet in the Army Institute of Foreign Languages, where I was now teaching. For a while he was in my class. Every time our eyes momentarily locked in a loving gaze, or I watched his tall, slightly hunched figure lose itself in the crowd of cadets as they filed out of the classroom, I felt immensely relieved. A few months later the Institute was evacuated to a city far removed from the fighting. I did not go along with the rest of the faculty but stayed behind with my husband, who was then working for the newspaper *Trud*. It was not until the end of the war that I saw my brother again.

Soviet soldiers were now marching into battle with the rallying cry "For the Motherland! For Stalin!"

Only substitute "Tsar" for "Stalin," and it was the same battle cry that had spurred the soldiers and officers of the tsarist army in the First World War. At the beginning of the war the army was still called the Red Army, presently to be renamed the Soviet Army, with the old pre-revolutionary ranks restored.

Nor was the war referred to as the Second World War, but the Great Patriotic War. There was logic behind that. First, the name indicated that it was a war against an enemy's incursion, as had been the Patriotic War against Napoleon. Second, a different name implied disassociation from the goals and aims of the allies. Both the name of the war and the battle cry were carry-overs from the tsarist regime. It was a new and unexpected tactic, very different from the Leninist ideal of international fraternization of the workers versus nationalism and patriotism.

However, in 1941, when the Soviet fighting men marched into combat with the same cries as their fathers had in 1914, they felt the warmth of their native soil and new hope sprang in the hearts of those who dared think for themselves. Surely, they thought, after the war is over, after with our blood and our dead we win victory, there will be more freedom and less repression. The people around me, still apprehensive of speaking up, exchanged hopes and little confidences, *tête à tête*, like the Jesuits of old, avoiding a third person's presence, lest he bear witness to their heretical words at some later date.

"We'll breathe freely after the war is over," my husband said to me.

''Things are bound to be different after the war,'' Merkurov repeated with assurance.

Leaving with a field hospital for the battlefront, my dear friend Nadezhda took me aside and, dropping her voice to a half-whisper, said: "There will be great changes, mark my words."

So intimidated had we all become that we dared not utter the words that were really on the tip of our tongue, such as individual freedom and democracy.

The war had a cathartic effect. It overshadowed the tragedies of 1937, 1938, and earlier years. The rancor and pain for loved ones, the innocents so needlessly sacrificed, were for a while cast out of the mind.

Yet right at the outset many cruel measures were carried out: shootings, arrests, resettlings, deportations, sometimes of whole nationalities, like the Kalmyks or the Crimean Tartars. The results were often more deaths than on the battlefield, thousands of broken homes, divided families, parentless children. Rigid labor laws were enforced and even more stringent ones were to follow, when people were jailed for one year if they were twenty minutes late for work.

War, people thought, justified everything. And how we toiled for victory! The more anguished we were by reports of the retreat of our troops, by the capture of one city after another, the more fiercely we threw ourselves into our tasks.

In mid-October of 1941 we witnessed a frantic exodus from Moscow, reminiscent of the way Muscovites abandoned their homes and all their worldly possessions before Napoleon's rape of the city. By that time, Moscow was already half-deserted. Mothers and children had been evacuated even before the air-raids started. Factories, government offices, and educational institutions were relocated eastward too.

Muscovites were hoarding groceries. By the time I got to the hoarding stage, foods everywhere had been swept off the counters as though by a whirlwind. Nothing was to be had except chocolate bars, almonds, and dried apricots. Soon these too vanished. I managed to store about fifty chocolate bars and two bags of nuts and dried fruits.

Asta Merkurova had been safely evacuated to Sverdlovsk, where her son was a student at an exclusive diplomatic college. On October 14, when German tanks had advanced to within thirty kilometers of the heart of the city, Merkurov arrived in his car, urging and arguing that my husband and I leave Moscow with him. He was not going to stay and wait for the Germans to march into Moscow, he declared, as they had into Paris more than a year before. His black eyes, usually twinkling with merriment, showed the strain and alarm of all eyes in those days. There was no transport to take his work out; he would go without it. He was ready to start that very night.

Mikhail was at the office and we waited for him, hoping that he might bring reassuring news. He had different news when he arrived. Next morning, he said, there would be massive evacuation from Moscow. We took counsel and decided it would be best for us to leave in organized fashion. We hoped that there would be some means of taking Merkurov's sculptures to a place of safety.

We remained in the city for yet another two days. On October 16 the news was more alarming than ever. I had never loved a city as I loved Moscow. And now I was to abandon her in her hour of need! I packed one suitcase with warm clothes and another with eatables. Mikhail and I set out on foot to the Kursk Railway Station, quite a long way from where we lived. When we reached the square in front of the station, it was teeming with people.

Mikhail rushed back to the city to fetch our two mothers, hoping that there would be room for them in the train carriage that had been reserved for the newspaper *Trud*.

II We flee to Sverdlovsk

On that bitterly cold October day, after sitting on their belongings in the open square for twelve hours, my mother and mother-in-law were convinced of the hopelessness of their situation.

"At a time like this, old people don't count," my mother said. "Come what may, we shall remain in our homes in Moscow. It is you who are most in danger. You must go."

It proved a wise decision. Even if we had succeeded in squeezing them into the train, these elderly women might not have survived the tough and perilous journey to Sverdlovsk in the Urals, which was our destination.

So crammed with evacuees was the train that we spent the first twenty-four hours standing on the wind-swept platform between the carriages. Later we took brief turns sitting down on the benches inside.

Our journey lasted nineteen days: normally it took forty-six or fifty hours. We learned to sleep standing up, like horses, to do without water and with little food for whole days. The German Messerschmitts were on our trail. Hearing their approach we would jump off the train, tumbling over one another, and scurry off in all directions. If there were woods we made a dash for their cover; if not, we fled into the open fields and stretched out in the frozen grass, faces buried in the icy ground.

We could count on no food except bread. When we had moved far enough inland for the enemy planes to stop their pursuit, our bread rations were delivered regularly at the stations on our way. Thus we did not starve, and for that we were thankful to the organizers of this last-minute evacuation from Moscow.

At the same time, along with people everywhere, we were experiencing our first pangs of wartime hunger, a foretaste of the deprivation we would suffer throughout the war and for several years after.

Food was on the minds of the men I travelled with and, being literary persons, they vied with one another in describing succulent roasts, *shashlik*, sturgeon baked in dough and served with piquant sauce. Their imaginations oozed with savory dishes, quite different from my dried fruits and bland chocolates, which nonetheless were speedily devoured.

Bleak, overpopulated Sverdlovsk greeted us with icy blasts and the sullen faces of the local inhabitants forced to share their homes, often just a single room, with us. That first night, when at long last we were able to lie down on the floor of an office building, I found two overfed white lice on my lace nightgown.

All available trains were engaged in transporting civilians away from the fighting zones and enlisted men and arms to the battlefields. The movement of food supplies was greatly delayed. Bloated with refugees, Sverdlovsk had nothing but bread rations to offer them.

On our very first night I saw tremendous queues outside the few central grocery stores. Bundled up, only their eyes exposed, thousands of people stood in gray clouds of vapor rising from their frozen breath. The next morning they were still there, having spent the night in the bitter frost. Large-sized tins of black caviar, the sole product in stock, were their reward. But these too were soon sold out. From then on, there were lines for hastily baked black bread tasting and looking as though it were half mixed with sawdust. I went to the farmers' market. The stalls were empty except for a few women selling milk in frozen disks. One of these I bought at an exorbitant price.

It was a very hungry New Year's Eve for us in Sverdlovsk; the spread consisted of nothing but rye bread cut in tiny elegant squares, which had been sprinkled with salt and dried in the oven. These we drank down with vodka and champagne. Among the guests with whom we saw in the year 1942, a year of agonizing defeats, were the Bolshoi opera singer Kruglikova, whose husband, a general, was fighting Hitler; the painters Ryazhsky and Ioganson; and the movie actress Valentina Serova, sex bomb of her day, who at the time was in love with General Rokossovsky, dragged from prison to a leading position in the army. This was a New Year's party at which we neither smiled nor laughed. And, like Chekhov's three sisters, the one desire and thought we all shared was to return to our beloved Moscow.

With a large sprinkling of Moscow's scientists and artistic personalities in its midst, grim, dour Sverdlovsk, was acquiring a cosmopolitan air. In all fairness it should be said that before the war, too, it boasted a musical culture of some refinement; the opera house, with its blue-gray columns, did much to relieve the monotony of the tenement-like buildings on either side of Lenin Street.

It was at the Urals Hotel on Lenin Street that many Muscovites lived or congregated. The rooms and lobby swam in a haze of cigarette smoke and alcohol. Men reeled and staggered out to return shortly with more bottles of vodka. Some of them were the brave, reckless flyers, like the Pokryshkin brothers, soon to become heroes whose very names spelled out the glory of Soviet arms. There was no denying that war had its romance and appeal: you could reach dazzling heights without the plodding that leads to accomplishment in peacetime. These thoughts ran through my mind as I watched the flyers swill their liquor, knowing that the next day or the one after they would be off on their perilous missions. The men designing and testing new weapons also lived at the Urals Hotel, but kept aloof from their dashing and carousing comrades—understandably, because they guarded some of the major secrets of the war.

On nights when my husband did not work late we went to the theater, mostly the opera. There were many patriotic productions, among them the opera *Mademoiselle Fifi*, its anti-Prussian fervor echoing our own hatred for the German invaders. Asked to write a review of the production, I called next day on Reinhold Glière, its elderly composer, who lived only a few blocks away from me on Lenin Street. He could hardly speak of his work, so dismayed was he by the Red Army defeats.

"If only I were able to do more than just write music," he said. I comforted him by describing how deeply moved the audience was by his work. Many of the spectators, I told him, were young men, who would be carrying away their impressions to the battlefront. But the composer's patriotic outburst reverberated in my own heart: "If only I could work day and night to help win the war."

The four half-idle months I spent in Sverdlovsk were a painful waste of time to me. In early March, after the Germans had suffered a major defeat at the gates of the city, my husband returned with his newspaper staff to Moscow. Soon I was able to leave Sverdlovsk. That spring the trains were almost as crowded with joyful Muscovites going back to their homes and jobs as they had been with evacuees in the autumn of 1941. It was by a miracle that I squeezed into a carriage after being pushed in from behind by two Sverdlovsk friends. The sleeve of my coat was ripped out of its armhole and all the buttons wrenched from my blouse.

III Back in Moscow

Moscow was unbelievably deserted, but a work-worn Mikhail met me at the Yaroslavsky Station in the spring of 1942. A translator's job awaited me at the Soviet Information Bureau (a kind of propaganda ministry). The head of the translation department was Alexander Antonovich Troyanovsky, one-time ambassador to Japan and also to the United States. He was immensely liked by our staff because he was so open and friendly, with nothing of the tight-laced diplomat about him.

The long-vacant office of vice-chairman of the Sovinformburo was filled by Kondakov, a man very unlike the amiable and well-wishing Troyanovsky. He came to us from a top post in the propaganda department of the Central Committee and turned out to be a conceited bully, perpetually aggrandizing himself and demeaning people on his staff. Kondakov demanded the signs of homage that an inferior was expected to pay a princely personage.

A natty, short-legged, impatient man in his late thirties, Kondakov was shockingly uncivil and had a way of unexpectedly popping out from behind a door or a corner in the hallway, his shrunken form expanding into menacing dimensions. Never on his life would he greet you first. Emitting an offensive cockiness, he waited for an obsequious bow, which he acknowledged with a tilt of his head.

I remember how disgusted I was by the imperious manner in which he conducted our weekly briefings; it clashed so with his ridiculously short figure and his flat, snubby face. The briefings were held in a luxurious, high-ceilinged hall, with wainscotted walls, crystal chandeliers, a long oak table, and red plush chairs. Before the outbreak of the war the building had belonged to the German embassy. Most of its furniture, rugs, and expensive plateware had been left behind by the hastily departing diplomats.

After everybody was assembled, Kondakov burst into the conference hall. With a sharp glance around, his jaws working in disapproval, he barked sharply: "Each be seated according to rank of office. Department heads up in front, closer to me, deputy heads in the next row, editors behind them, translator-editors at the back wall."

I would sit down on the very edge of a chair "at the back wall" as ordered, actually glad to be as far away as possible from the Caesar personage that Kondakov imagined himself to be. I stole glances at the others, watching for a sign of shock or resentment at this overt command to observe the hierarchy of rank. But the eyes of everyone I could see were blank and the faces bore that craven look of servitude which I came to recognize so well—my own too, I am certain. The late thirties had taught us a good lesson.

One morning Kondakov swept into Troyanovsky's office. A meeting of the translators was called. Castigated for our work, we in turn blamed the poor editing of the Russian articles. (Translated into English, French, and Spanish, they described the Soviet people's war effort and were designed to win friends for the Soviet Union, which they did.)

Kondakov said, "Come straight to me if you find errors. That is the way to improve our work."

His instructions seemed sensible to me. But for the moment I had forgotten the nature of the man. I have done things in my life of which afterwards I was very much ashamed. One of these things I associate with the effect Kondakov's speech had on me.

The next day, finding on my desk an article containing a few examples of what I thought was slipshod editing, I felt justified in bringing it to Kondakov. It's good for our work, I told myself. Kondakov was pleased. Nor did I have any uneasy feelings about what I did.

Not until the following day, when in the corridor I ran into Shpigel, the editor of the article. He stopped me and with his habitual doleful look—none of us looked cheerful in the war years—said, "Why didn't you come directly to *me* with your criticism? Surely we could have thrashed the matter out between ourselves."

There was no hint of accusation or animosity in his pleasant, cultured voice. But before I could reply he turned on his heel, leaving me with a sense of self-disgust.

A moment later I visualized the whole scene: I could see dignified, embarrassed Shpigel standing (Kondakov, I was certain, did not offer him a seat) before the ideology boss like a naughty boy in front of a particularly sadistic schoolmaster. I swore to myself that if ever again I had any criticism to make, or was asked to review another person's work, I would do it to his face. I hardly saw Shpigel after that—I believe he managed to get himself transferred to another job—but I was grateful to him for the lesson he taught me.

Kondakov had not held his high post for as long as a year when we were informed of his downfall. It seemed he had been caught negotiating shady deals, including the sale of coupons for Persian lamb coats and valuable property left behind by the German embassy. He was not prosecuted, merely dismissed from his post.

Many people I knew starved during the war and many died of hunger. As always, Moscow was in a privileged position. But in Moscow too quite a few did not live to see the day of victory because their bread rations were so meager

Our room on Bolshaya Bronnaya Street, close to Pushkin Square, was unheated; the basin of water I prepared before bed to wash myself in the morning froze overnight. Quite often I did not return home at all but slept at the office on a long, hard table. However, I did not go hungry. The Soviet Information Bureau being part of the Central Committee ideology apparatus, its translators enjoyed food denied to ordinary Soviet people even in peacetime. Indeed, I was astounded at the enormous rations issued in wartime to Central Committee employees.

In 1942, when I began work as a translator, in the morning and evening we were served snacks of two sandwiches, one of caviar, the other of cheese or salami, and a glass of delicious tea with a sweet roll. In the afternoon we went for our mid-day meal to the Central Committee canteen in a green building on Staraya Ploshchad. I do not want to sound noble, but I was happier when the translators, as inferior employees, were cut off from these lavish meals several months later. Even so, we were issued far bigger rations of groceries than, for example, workers in the munitions plants.

Before the war I often ate in Moscow's finest restaurants, either with tourists, when I was a guide, or as the guest of friends. I enjoyed the cuisine, the warmth, and the pre-revolutionary splendor of the Metropole and the Savoy, but never in these internationally known restaurants was I served the exquisitely prepared dishes I ate at the

Central Committee dining-room in 1942, one of the hungriest years of the war. I couldn't believe my eyes when I saw the mountain of white bread in the middle of the table, the pitcher of rich sour cream served with a borshch so full of nutrients that it alone sufficed for a meal. There was a wide choice of dishes on the menu: goose stuffed with apples, tender pork chops, beef Stroganoff, stewed fruit, ice-cream.

One day I ordered chicken croquettes, prepared by an excellent chef. After eating one, I looked around for paper napkins to wrap the other two and take them home: there were none, only snow-white linen serviettes. From then on I came to the dining-room with two glass jars, which I filled with more than half my meal to feed hungry friends.

That same year a free-lance translator, denied a ration card for herself and her small daughter, because for some bureaucratic reason her Moscow residency permit could not be renewed, died of hunger.

Engrossed in my work, worried about the news from the battle-fronts, as we all were, I hardly noticed that summer had slipped into autumn and the raw, cold weather was back.

The Germans had launched another attack on Moscow. More and more men were now being drafted and sent into the thick of the fighting. On returning home late one day, I discovered that my husband had been called up. I could bid him only a brief goodbye. Learning next morning that Mikhail was at a drilling ground near Moscow, I hurried there to have a little more time with him. There was a pinched look about him that wrung my heart. Tears filled my eyes.

"Don't cry," Mikhail said brusquely. "War is war!" After a pause he added more gently, "Compose yourself. You have your work!"

"But your knee?" My husband had a stiff knee, the result of a fall.

"The Examining Board passed me. Besides, I'm a fatalist. Whatever must, will happen."

It was the worst thing he could have said, for I abhorred a fatalistic attitude. I bit my lips, making no retort. Mikhail looked so fragile. But as I waved to him in parting and stared at the other freshly drafted men, I noticed that they had the same unmilitary appearance. They were indeed the *Opolchenye*, or People's Guard, among them quite a few middle-aged professors, some wearing the Moscow University badge. Could these men, so puny, so unwarlike, push back the "invincible" Wehrmacht?

I was soon to learn how few of them returned alive from the battlefront. My husband was among the lucky ones; after eleven months' fighting not far from Moscow, he was wounded in his bad leg, brought to the Bodkin Hospital, and operated on. And yet these men did stem the German offensive. Perhaps valor is not in the way you look but in the way you feel. And their feelings? They knew they were fighting for a just cause.

IV Involvement with the secret police

A day or two after my husband departed for the front I was called to the office phone. The peace of mind I hoped to gain by immersing myself in translation was shattered by the voice at the other end of the line. From the tone and very first words I knew I was talking to an NKVD secret-police officer.

It was in 1935, when I was twenty years old and working for Intourist, that I had first become involved with the Secret Department of the NKVD (People's Commissariat for the Interior, now KGB).

A patient, good-tempered man named Meyerovich was at the time in charge of assigning guides to individual tourists and groups. At about ten o'clock one morning he called me into his office, shut the door, and, lowering his voice, told me I was expected at Lubyanka headquarters. A pass in my name would be waiting for me at an entrance on the left side of the building.

That warm late-summer day I walked into the Lubyanka on Dzerzhinsky Square of my own free will, tingling with a foretaste of adventure, quite certain that no harm would befall me, giddy with romantic visions of being commissioned with important secret work, for I knew English like a native—an obvious asset.

After a twenty-minute wait on a polished bench of solid oak my name was called out. I approached a wicket and was handed a pass. A sentry at a massive door leading from the lobby into the main building scrutinized it along with my internal passport, and looked closely at my features to make sure they matched the passport photo.

Arriving on the floor indicated on my pass, I went down a long panelled corridor.

Young men carrying bulky folders hurried past me, almost bumping into one another. They kept their eyes averted, as I did mine; their very movements suggested a compulsion to secrecy.

I soon found myself in a spacious office with a few desks, only one of which was occupied. Behind it sat a man in his middle years with a large, heavily blotched face. The blotches flamed purple as he eyed me through the thick lenses of his glasses. How different he looked from the dashing secret-police officers I danced with at the Select

Hotel! His wispy, faded blond hair and pale face gave him an anemic look.

It seemed an effort for him to break the ice between us. He was like an actor who, out of charity, had been assigned a few lines in the prelude of a play that augured no good for anybody, including himself. He was acting out his part mechanically, with no bluff or histrionics, as later I saw others do.

"You are working with foreign tourists." He came to the point at once when he at last addressed me. "It is imperative that we know what these tourists think and what they say. Put down your impressions of them, what they tell you about themselves, and what their comments on Soviet life are. Above all we want to know their political views. Compose a report and hand it to Meyerovich, your boss."

Years later, on going over this interview in my mind, I concluded that because the reports were submitted to an official at my job, and not to an undercover man, the section for which I was asked to work was different from the network controlling those who informed on their fellow citizens.

With a fatherly air he continued: "Your assistance is going to be of great value. It is an honor to cooperate with us."

My response was enthusiastic, earnest. What would I not do to maintain the socialist country's security? I replied I was ready to perform the tasks required of me.

He slipped a sheet of paper across the desk.

"Sign this after you've chosen a code name for yourself."

The paper clinched the deal. It also contained a non-disclosure vow. Searching my mind for an appropriate sobriquet, one that would reflect my idealism, I chose the initials I.S.T., The first initial stood for "international"; what the other two represented I cannot recall— the words are buried in some deep recess of my mind. At the time I signed up I had the conviction that I was doing the correct and noble thing; to say no seemed inconceivable to me.

The man behind the desk looked abashed and so uncomfortable that throughout the conversation I was somehow aware of the incongruity of such a person within the walls of the powerful Lubyanka. Events were brewing in the mid-thirties, soon to come to a head, that were far beyond my comprehension. Later, looking back, I could see that there were still decent communists in the Lubyanka security service, who longed for an escape; and some did indeed break away, finding employment elsewhere. If they had stayed on they would have become the cold-blooded executioners of the late thirties.

What choice the man in front of me made I do not know. Meyerovich was arrested along with hosts of other Intourist employees. A few months later I quit my own job, thus dropping out of the Lubyanka picture—but not forever as I had hoped. The purges so darkened the horizons everywhere that my attitude to secret work changed radically.

The first attempt to renew contact with me dated to the end of 1939 when, after two years of free-lance journalism, I took a teaching position. Walking down the mazy corridors of the First Moscow Institute of Foreign Languages, where I taught, I was stopped by a man in a crumpled tunic worn over a pair of faded khaki breeches. In the dim light of the dilapidated building, made even dimmer by the grimy windows, I could hardly make out his features, except for a general hard and tense look.

"Keep in step with me. I have a few things to say to you."

I complied without answering.

"Write down an address, quick!"

He stated the day and hour on which we were to meet. "You realize you are not to mention this or future meetings to anyone?"

"Yes."

Only vaguely do I recollect what the rendezvous was about. My tasks were to be specified at the following meeting, which I skipped. The war broke out; it was natural for contacts to scatter and be lost track of.

Moreover, luckily, I had no permanent residency registration in Moscow because, after quitting my job at Intourist, I was forced to move out of the Novomoskovskaya Hotel. I was roomless, like thousands of other Muscovites, renting privately now a "corner," now a room or even an apartment for brief spells. I had been living that way during the closing arrests of 1938, too, and this may well explain how I escaped the fate that befell so many of my friends and co-workers of those days. A similar situation had saved other would-be victims of the persecution, especially those who had relatives abroad or had frequented the homes of arrested persons.

The man now phoning me in the war year of 1942 had a gruff, commanding voice that fully accorded with the power the secret police wielded over the citizenry. He would brook no refusal from me. But if he was different from the official who recruited me in 1935, I too was a changed person, with the searing memories of those who perished in 1937 and 1938 alive in my mind. The secret police, Lubyanka, NKVD! I wanted nothing to do with their prying and surveillance. Somehow I must shrug them off.

"I work twelve hours a day and more. I haven't time for anything else."

"Never mind your work. We meet tomorrow at seven."

Again I jotted down an address—a private place for a rendezvous.

With a choking resentment I returned to my typewriter in the cigarette-smoke-filled room at the Sovinformburo headquarters. My mind was made up: by hook or by crook I must find a way to sever all ties with the secret police.

I knew it would be hard to stand up against their pressure and possible threats, but I felt that no personal peril would be involved: it was not a time of persecution and arrests. Besides, translators were badly needed. These considerations made it easier to stick to my decision.

The address took me to a downstairs apartment in a small street behind the TASS building, about fifteen minutes' walk from where I worked. I rang the bell. A shabbily dressed, unshaven man with bloodshot cobalt eyes answered. He led me through a small shadowy hall into a musty room with a few rickety pieces of furniture, among them a round table covered with a soiled, ink-stained plush tablecloth. The man's own seedy looks fitted the surroundings. Bracing myself for what I knew would not be an easy conversation, I sat down across the table from him. I did not look my best either; I had lost about twenty pounds and my prewar clothes were anything but chic. The whole atmosphere was one of strain and gloom. The strain and gloom of war.

"You have a wide circle of acquaintances," he began. "People take you into their confidence . . . We need your services."

How to slip out of the net? "That's where you're wrong. I see nobody, lead no social life."

"You visit the homes of painters and writers . . ."

"Not any more."

"All we require is brief reports of what people say."

Damn him! "I have a poor memory . . ."

"Don't hand me that crap! There's a war on. We protect the Soviet country's security. We don't want people to wag their tongues. And if they do, we must know what they're saying. You've got to help expose the harmful elements in our society."

"I do not know any harmful elements."

"Okay, what about the people in your office?"

He was beginning to show his impatience. I knew I must alter my tactics.

"I'll think it over." I wanted to gain time.

We agreed that he would phone me in a couple of days. But it was not until a couple of weeks later that I heard from him. I pleaded illness. Soon there was another call. A new voice, more airy and casual. Again I gave the excuse of not being well. He insisted on an appointment. I did not show up. More phone calls.

The last call. Would I persist in breaking appointments and wasting the precious time of security agents? Yes, I longed to be released. The voice was insistent, truculent. I was given a new address. The man appealed to my duty as a citizen in wartime. It was no use, I mumbled, they must not count on me. There was a pause. What accent did the man have? An Odessa accent, of course. And the phrase he used—*Tak ne fontan?* ("So, no fountain?"—actually meaning "No go?") was unmistakably Odessan. He was telling me to go to hell. I was relieved. I had done it! They would strike me off their lists, leave me alone.

V We survive the war

Twice a week I was on night duty at the Yauza Hospital, a big, sprawling building of solid gray masonry overlooking the small Yauza River, which runs through one of Moscow's oldest quarters.

The chill nights, filled with moans and the sight of mangled bodies, brought me as close to the tragedy of war as I ever got. Every ward and corridor was crammed with wounded men, mostly young amputees, delivered here from the battlelines. The hospital reeked of pus and rotting flesh. The men ran us off our feet with their feeble and at times hysterical cries: "Bring the pan, Sister! Quick!" "Water, a drink of water!" "Get the doctor, I'm dying!"

Exhausted by lack of sleep, longing for the briefest of catnaps, there were nights when I performed my duties as volunteer nurse half-heartedly. I chided myself, yet could not help feeling relieved and happy when morning came at last, bringing me escape from the hospital's tomb-like atmosphere, and I could emerge into the daylight. The attitude of a co-worker of mine, who lost her only son, aged nineteen, in the war, was different. Although considerably older than myself and much weaker, she did not rest for a single minute during the long cold nights, ministering patiently to the needs of the wounded and dying. We all knew how deep was her own grief.

There were other voluntary jobs. One of them was unloading freight trains, which we did either early in the morning or sometimes late at night. The lifting of heavy crates had disastrous effects on many women. I suffered a miscarriage.

True, I had had no idea I was pregnant, as I had stopped having my period soon after the beginning of the war. All the women of my acquaintance shared that experience during the war. This was also true of prison and prison camp, with rare exceptions.

Nor when I was pregnant the second time, towards the end of the war, did I suspect it.

"You look pregnant even from the back," one of the women at the office told me then.

I have always been a great vegetable eater. Practically the only vegetable besides potatoes available in wartime was sauerkraut sold at the private market, and I had indeed been buying and consuming a good deal of it.

Therefore I replied, "Nonsense, it's the sauerkraut—it bloats you so!"

When my daughter was born, she was jokingly christened "the sauerkraut baby."

Mikhail and I had to find new living quarters but there was a permanent housing shortage. For years Moscow families waited in vain to have a room or "living space" of their own. New houses were built, but at a slow pace, and were occupied mostly by government officials and important people in the sciences and the arts. There were the fine modern apartment buildings in Gorky Street, designed by the architect Mordvinov—whom I often saw standing outside the National Café, thoughtfully surveying his own work—but they too were for the élite, or their protégés and mistresses.

An elderly friend of ours, a widow with a very small pension, offered to sell us one of her two rooms. Originally it had been one big room; a partition of thin wood now converted it into two. We jumped at the offer. Buying or selling "living space" was illegal, since all property belonged to the state. But between close friends it could be arranged.

Mikhail and I worked hard to pay off the debt, which I finally did shortly before my arrest. It was in this room that my only child was born, in August, 1945, and from this room, with a period of ten months between the two arrests, that my husband and I were dragged away by night to the Lubyanka Prison.

The house stood on the Moscow River Embankment, and we had only to cross the Moskvoretsky Bridge to find ourselves in Red Square. Visible from the Embankment where we lived were the Kremlin walls and the dizzy, flaming cupolas of St. Basil's Cathedral. The house itself was a curiously designed structure, amazing in many ways. It was built of such solid masonry that it had survived the

Moscow fire during the Napoleonic invasion, when the Kremlin palace itself, across the river, was in flames. It also escaped destruction from the direct hit of a German demolition bomb during the massive air raids in the summer of 1941. Before the Revolution it had been a cheap rooming house.

It stood next door to the Novomoskovskaya Hotel, associated with the happy days of my love for Victor. Just as it must have been in pre-revolutionary times, it remained a foul-smelling, dilapidated, bug-infested building. And it had the oddest assortment of tenants. Among them was a quixotic revolutionary who at the end of the Civil War had brought Lenin a carload of gold, American dollars, and other valuables; he handed it all over to the new Soviet Treasury, without leaving himself the money to buy a meal. There lived also, on the second and third floors, a couple of pimps who provided visitors at the hotel with prostitutes; two highly intellectual lesbians; a policeman noted for his black-market deals during the war; a famous architect; and a popular film and stage actress.

The rooms were laid out along a maze of corridors, winding and twisting in a figure eight. Families lived in single rooms, sharing washrooms and latrines that were in a frightful state of disrepair. It took several weeks of living in the house before I could find my way through its labyrinths. It struck me what a marvelous setting the place would make for detective stories, with all the innumerable little niches and dark nooks behind small staircases to stack away dead bodies. But instead of corpses, I would often come upon drunken men in these hideaway places. Snoring noisily or lying in a stupor, they presented such a common sight that people rarely took notice of them.

In the late summer of 1943 the hope of victory dawned. The bedraggled remains of von Paulus's army were tramping through the streets of Moscow. We rushed out of the office and made our way to Gorky Street to watch them pass. The German war prisoners, the men who had brought such suffering and death to the people of the Soviet Union and Europe, were a sorry sight. I looked away. I did not want to see them, and quickly returned to my work.

My husband, who had joined the Party in 1941 at the front, in the darkest days of the war, now walked about with a bright sparkle in his pale blue eyes. The battle of Stalingrad was won.

He phoned me at the office: "Do try to get home earlier tonight. I have a bottle of vodka and have brought over a few friends. We are going to celebrate the good news from the front."

I told him to start without me. With what elation we all worked in those days! We were translating more and more stories about the heroic performance of the Soviet army. It was a time when the attitude of the allies was amicable towards the Soviet Union, a state of affairs not destined to last long.

When I finally arrived home all the vodka was drunk and all the food consumed, along with the bread ration for the following day. Fortunately my husband and I were used to the most meager fare. There was an asceticism ingrained in both of us, perhaps stemming from the hardships we had known. When I opened the cupboard it was empty as though a hurricane had swept through it. My husband grinned drunkenly and blamed everything on the victory at Stalingrad.

There was a flow of refugees from Central Asia and Siberia back to Poland at the end of the war. Among them was a Jewish Polish sculptor whom I had met at Merkurov's and who had become a dear friend.

Passing through Moscow on his way to Poland, he dropped in to see me. He had a lean Christ-like face and a melancholy gaze. He never smiled; his young wife and three small children had been shot dead against a house wall by the German soldiers when they marched into Warsaw. His own escape from the Nazis, along with a large group of painters and sculptors, many of them Jewish, was carried out with the assistance of the Soviet government.

And now, as he sat at the table of my scantily furnished room, he looked more emaciated than ever. I guessed that he must have starved all through the war. The worst of it was that I did not have a crumb of food in the house. I felt so guilty at not being able to offer him even a cup of tea that the joy of his unexpected visit dissolved into a gnawing embarrassment.

I could only listen with half an ear to what he was saying, his pallor and sunken cheeks tugging at my heart. Most likely sensing the reason for my discomfort, he muttered casually and quite beside the point, "I'm used to going without food for days. What I eat, a stale heel or fancy pastry, doesn't matter to me." (Nobody I knew ate pastry during the war, and many people starved to death.) I remember him vividly for those words, as well as one other remark: "If the Soviet Union had not given asylum to so many Polish refugees when the Germans captured Warsaw, I would not be sitting here talking to you."

This was true. It was later that with his help my mother learned of the tragedy of her Warsaw family, of relatives in Paris who had not fled when the city fell into German hands. All her sisters, along with their children and grandchildren, had perished in the Nazi gas chambers.

My mother echoed the Polish sculptor's words: "How fortunate we are to be living in the Soviet Union. We enjoy the protection of the Soviet government. We owe it to its humane policies that we have not been made victims of anti-Semitism."

We all came out alive from the war. It was a miracle: on Victory Day my husband and brother were with me, and many friends too, army surgeon Nadezhda among them. In her low, throaty voice she said, "Our hospital train was bombed over and over again, yet I escaped without a scratch."

In May, 1945, visible from our windows, Red Square was a sea of rejoicing crowds. We feasted on American luncheon meat from tins my brother had saved out of his army ration, washing down the meat and other *zakuski* with tumbler after tumbler of vodka. We poured champagne and clinked glasses. We sang patriotic songs and went to sleep ecstatic with joy. The war was over. The war was over. We knew we had helped win it.

The author's mother, Helen Eve Halbère, before her second marriage, c.1910.

The author's father, Benjamin Rosenberg, c.1915.

Helen Eve Rosenberg, c.1914.

In the late 1920s.

Sergei Dmitrievich Merkurov at his studio in Moscow talking to art students, February 1936. Note Lenin's death mask on the wall, first on the left.

The author's first husband, Mikhail Zinde, with family friend in woods near Moscow, 1939.

In 1942.

On the left is the old house in Moscow where the author lived from 1943 until 1962. Next to it is the Novomoskovskya Hotel (today the Bucharest Hotel). The photograph was taken in September 1987.

Shurri Rosenberg, the author's brother,
on the Island of Sakhalin, 1947.

With daughter Vicky in Moscow, 1946.   *In 1948.*

Vicky Zinde, aged seven, then in the first grade, with Georgi Mikhailov. The photograph was taken in Moscow during September 1952, a year before the author's release from the Gulag.

Kislovodsk revisited, 1954.

Vicky, 1973.

In Leningrad, visiting with Georgi and his family.

A Saturday-night party at the author's home in Moscow.

AUTHOR'S NOTE: I did not risk taking these documents out of the Soviet Union during my trips to Canada for fear of their being confiscated by customs at the Sheremetyevo Airport in Moscow. Instead, in 1985 and 1986, I enclosed each one in a letter to my daughter. Apparently my mail was not censored, for they arrived safely.

Inner Prison of the MGB of the USSR. 3/VII 1950

Duplicate receipt No. 715

Date of Birth 1915, Warsaw.
Received from Rosenberg Suzanna Veniaminovna:

1. Bank book. Account No. 43488
   with the balance of 4702 r. 28 k. — 1 item

2. Wristwatch with metal bracelet and
   missing second hand — 1 item

Prisoner signature of S. Rosenberg
Received signature (Pankratov)

Inner Prison of the MGB of the USSR. 3/VII/1950.

Copy of receipt No. 791/D
Received from the arrested Rosenberg
Suzanna Veniaminovna:

1. Passport IX-CY No. 669384 — 1 item
2. Trade union card No. 186939 — 1 item
3. Labor Record Books — 2 items
4. Marriage Certificate No. 913 1 item
5. Secondary school graduation
   certificate in the English language 1 item

Correct (author's signature)
Received by Pankratov

Butyrka Prison, Ministry of the Interior (MVD)

Cell No.   7/IX, 1950

Receipt No. 1710

received from arrested person Rosenberg
Suzanna Benediktovna Medal: 800th
Anniversary of Moscow with certificate
No. A 687226 Medal: For Labor Valor
with cert. No. R. 238889

signature

USSR
Ministry of the Interior
Ozerlag
June 11, 1953.

7-BS

Form "A"
Not valid as residency permit
Unrenewable if lost
No. 0018918

CERTIFICATE

This is to certify that Rosenberg Suzanna Veniaminovna, born 1915, Warsaw, USSR citizenship, Jewish nationality, convicted on charges stated in File No. 3868, Third Chief Directorate, MGB of the USSR, on October 14, 1950, articles 7-35 of the RSFSR Criminal Code, sentenced to five years without subsequent deprivation of rights, having no previous convictions, served her term in places of confinement under MVD until June 11, 1953. Under the Amnesty Law of 27/III, 1953 was released on June 11, 1953 and is on her way to her chosen place of residence — Moscow.

Chief of Ozerlag,
Colonel Yevstigneyev
Section Head — Major Tsivilev.

Military Collegium of the
USSR Supreme Court.
13 October, 1956
No. 4H—011260
13 Vorovsky Street,
Moscow

CERTIFICATE

The case against Rosenberg Suzanna Veniaminovna was reviewed by
the Military Collegium of the USSR Supreme Court on September 29,
1956.

In view of the absence of a criminal offense, the decision passed by
the Special Board under the MGB of the USSR on October 14 1950 in
regard to Rosenberg S.V. was revoked and the charges against her
dropped.

For the Chairman of the Judiciary Board of the USSR Supreme Court
Military Collegium.

Colonel Semik

RSFSR   Emblem

DEATH CERTIFICATE

P-A No. 880290

Citizen Zinde Mikhail, alias Solomon, Moiseyevich
Died 07/11, 1951, February 7, nineteen fifty-one.
Aged 42
Cause of death . . . .
Death registered in the Civil Acts Registry Book on November 14,
1955. Entry No. 954.
Place of death: city, village, district region, territory, republic
. . . . :
Place of registration: Civil Acts Registry Office, Kirov District,
Moscow.

Issued on November 17, 1955.
                    In charge of Registry Office — signature.
                    Registry Office seal.

Copy made from original and notarized on September 26, 1958.

Военная Коллегия
Верховного Суда
Союза ССР

12 - марта 195 8.

№ 4Н012450/57

Москва, ул. Воровского, д. 15.

С П Р А В К А

Дело по обвинению ЗИНДЕ Михаила /Соло-
мона/ Моисеевича, до ареста – 7 сентября 1949
года – литературного работника газеты "Крас-
ный Флот", пересмотрено Военной коллегией Верховного Суда СССР 8 марта 1958 года.
Приговор Военной коллегии от 21 апреля
1950 года в отношении ЗИНДЕ М./С./М. по вновь
открывшимся обстоятельствам отменен и дело за
отсутствием состава преступления прекращено.
ЗИНДЕ М./С./М. реабилитирован посмертно.

ПРЕДСЕДАТЕЛЬСТВУЮЩИЙ СУДЕБНОГО СОСТАВА
ВОЕННОЙ КОЛЛЕГИИ ВЕРХОВНОГО СУДА СССР
ПОЛКОВНИК ЮСТИЦИИ

/ЦЫРЛИНСКИЙ/

ас

Military Collegium of the
USSR Supreme Court.
12 March 1958
No. 4H012450/57
15 Vorovsky Street,
Moscow

CERTIFICATE

The case against Zinde Mikhail (Solomon) Moiseyevich, prior to his arrest on September 7 1949 literary associate of the newspaper "Red Fleet," was reviewed by the Military Collegium of the USSR Supreme Court on March 8 1958.

In view of new circumstances having come to light, the sentence passed on April 21 1950 on Zinde M.(S.)M. by the Military Collegium was rescinded and the case owing to the absence of a criminal offense dropped.

Zinde M.(S.)M. has been rehabilitated posthumously.

For the chairman of the Judiciary Board of the USSR Supreme Court Military Collegium,

Colonel Tsyrlinsky

SEVEN

I A toast to the Russians

All through the war years we worked without a single day off, no summer vacation, no winter holiday. At the close of the war it was the men who had been wounded in battle who received the first vouchers. Rather reluctantly, because he knew he would miss his newborn daughter terribly, Mikhail went off to the Crimea, to a holiday home for war veterans.

Influenced by newfangled ideas on the parent-child relationship, I imagined that to tie my little daughter emotionally to myself was wrong. I tried not to be overaffectionate with her. Mikhail, on the other hand, who doted on her, practiced no such restraint. Indeed he loved her as only a father can his firstborn, when after years of war and hardship raising a family was in itself no common thing. So strong was their attachment that when my daughter remained parentless she dreamed about her father and longed for him more than for me. (My daughter never talks of her father to anyone but me. It is too painful. I do not think she can forget or forgive his cruel death.)

With my husband away I was seeing more of my mother, who helped me look after Vicky. It seemed to me that she still believed every word she read in *Pravda*, but I was not at all certain. It had become too troublesome, too disturbing, and moreover too dangerous to utter one's thoughts.

What went on in the minds of those I loved—my mother, brother, and husband—remained a sealed book to me. Nor did I much care to read it. I was too busy working—and work was a panacea; too busy trying to make life liveable. Whenever bitter thoughts stole into my mind I tried to brush them off, persuading myself that I must see the good sides of the socialist society: the total employment, the free education, the zest for reconstructing the ravaged economy, the imaginative flair of the artistic intelligentsia, struggling desperately, as always, to get around the rigid censorship. I still hoped that the socialist society would fulfill its goals. I closed my eyes to the ugly manifestations and implored my dear ones to do likewise.

My brother arrived from South-Sakhalinsk in the northeast for a brief vacation. It was good to have him with us; the gleam in his velvety eyes brought new warmth to our one-room home, where we had to put him up to sleep on the floor. He looked manly in his army lieutenant's uniform, but the vulnerability I remembered from his childhood glimpsed at me from the soft contours of his swarthy face and the tenuous smile in the corners of his mouth. He was now married with a daughter of his own.

We talked on general subjects in a loving and bantering way. Shurri, who had a wry sense of humor, thought it rather amusing to tell a dream he had about Stalin; for some reason he related it several times, even when we had company. As it was Stalin's custom to summon his acolytes in the middle of the night, he ordered my brother, too, to appear before him at a nocturnal hour. Clutching his pipe in his stubby fingers and waving it as he spoke, he said to him affably: "See how I toil for the people's sake. I burn the midnight oil. This is what I expect all my subjects to do. Get that? Now back to your job!" The account elicited no comment, only a polite and indulgent smile.

During the postwar years, when he was staying at our home, daily life meant experiencing one shortage or inconvenience after another. Almost every night the electricity failed or was cut off. Electric appliances were unavailable. The one-burner electric cooker we had was falling apart; an electric tea kettle refused to serve; the alarm clock kept erratic time; the furniture legs splintered.

Every time I came home from work I would find my husband and brother in the middle of a repair job; one blond and one dark curly head bent over a table littered with the parts of some household object. The two men were marvelously adept at taking things apart, but somehow never managed to put them together again. Impatiently I would scoop up all the tiny screws, electric coils, springs, and chair legs, desperately looking for a place to stow them away in our cramped quarters.

When the dismantled object was something we could not do without, I would quickly fetch Ivan Mikhailovich, our janitor and odd-job man. He would arrive groggy, reeking of alcohol, a glazed look in his eyes, but it took him no more than a minute to pinpoint the damage. And—wonder of wonders!—he was able, unsteady as he was on his feet, to fit the minutest screw into the padlock or alarm clock, to connect the coil in the cooker. To our joy the clock ticked, the padlock clicked open and shut, and the coil of the electric cooker blazed red. Ivan Mikhailovich was worth his weight in gold—in vodka rather, which he was only too pleased to receive in return for his services.

My brother left. I missed him but I knew he was planning to return to Moscow after his discharge from the army. I loved him dearly, and the thought that he would soon be living close to me with his wife and little daughter was a happy one.

I could not keep the resolution I had made to lose myself so completely in my work as to drive away all troubled thoughts, for it was clear, especially to the intelligentsia, that dark clouds were once again gathering around us.

From the loudspeaker came the thickly accented voice we knew so well. In the stumbling Russian spoken by uneducated Georgians, Stalin began his postwar address with a toast "to the Russian people." Perplexed, I wondered what effect his words would have on our life. Why had he not said "to the Soviet people"? Why was he setting the Russians above others, playing them against other nationalities of the land, as on previous occasions he had played the other nationalities against the Russians?

But the wily dictator knew what he was doing. He needed to oppose Russian identity not so much to other nationalities as to the concept of internationalism. He was paving the way for isolation from the West, for persecution of all who had the least sympathy or even tolerance for Western ideals, and finally for a vicious anti-Semitism and attack on intellectuals.

After Stalin had delivered his speech with its toast to the Russians a tremendous snowballing process was set in motion, ostensibly to boost and flatter the Russian ego.

Were this process not to have the gravest consequences for thousands of persons, it could have been put down as one more great lunacy.

Most of us chuckled when, in doing our shopping, we discovered that the names of many groceries had been "Russified." A French roll was no longer French; it was a Moscow roll. My favorite chocolate's label was changed from American Nut to Southern Nut. Swiss cheese was christened Soviet cheese.

Streets with foreign names were rebaptized. Every significant discovery and invention was claimed for Russia. Thus the wireless was invented by Popov. Architecture and sculpture owed their glory to Russians alone, as though Versailles were a copy of Peterhof, rather than the other way around. Russians were proclaimed the pioneers of aviation and the earliest discoverers of the American continent's northern territories. Priority in every field. No one would deny that the Russians are a talented people. But traditionally they had never been averse to learning a great deal from their European neighbors.

"The first elephant, too, was born in Russia," the Russians themselves joked. But the whole situation was far from funny; it assumed the gross proportions of a smoldering hatred for all that was non-Russian.

Freud's writings were not to be had for love or money. New sciences, such as cybernetics, and whole schools of learning were dismissed by Stalin as "quasi-scientific." At that time I was teaching English, which had fallen into understandable disfavor—foreign languages being so very "un-Russian."

Great minds were set to the task of devising ways of teaching these languages by Russian. They indeed came up with a solution: why bother with the spoken language and vocabulary, when you can teach the grammar rules in Russian and let it rest at that? Fortunately, as I have sometimes seen it work out to the general benefit, the Russians were not as methodical as the Germans, and the grand scheme of teaching English by Russian was not followed through to the end. The students kept complaining in hushed tones. The teachers circumvented the instructions of their superiors and somehow managed to convey a minimum of knowledge. "What madness!" we sometimes whispered to one another.

But there was method to the madness. The whipping-up of this insane xenophobia was essential in the new campaign against the intellectuals, and the "foreign" religious sects like the Baptists, Seventh Day Adventists, and other believers I would later meet in the Siberian taiga, as well as to enforce the law forbidding marriage between a Soviet citizen and an alien. Marriages contracted before the new law were declared null and void; Moscow girls who had married Britishers or Americans during the war were convicted of espionage. (One of these women, married to a Mr. Squire, was to be a cellmate of mine. She was sentenced to fifteen years and stripped of her married name.)

It was on the morning of a clear summer day in 1946 that a bombshell was delivered to us which blasted all hope for a relaxation of repressive measures after the war. This was the notorious Zhdanov decree. We picked up *Pravda* and there was the wisdom of the Party staring at us from half of the front page. Worded in the usual bullying jargon, the decree attacked the poet Akhmatova and the satirist Zoshchenko, both Leningraders.

Stalin was a champion hater. Of all cities he hated Leningrad most. It was the cradle of the revolution he betrayed. He hated Leningraders because they retained more of their idealism and integrity than did the motley, kowtowing Muscovites he surrounded himself with. In his insidious way he belittled and humiliated the city, tempting away its outstanding figures with higher salaries and better working conditions, gradually forcing it to sink from its former grandeur and importance to a gray provincialism. He did away with Kirov, head of the Leningrad party organization and a dangerous rival. He concocted the infamous "Leningrad case," killing off all of the city's leading men.

Without finishing his breakfast, my husband jumped up from his seat at the table and strode off into the garden of the tiny dacha we had rented for the summer.

Akhmatova's refined, ascetic face rose before my eyes. How it contrasted with Zhdanov's small "little fat boy" face, the features buried in rolls of flesh, and the eyes bloodshot from a surfeit of alcohol. I hardly knew Akhmatova's poetry because it rarely appeared in print, but I did know something of her fate. Her first husband, the poet Gumilev, had been shot, her second or third husband had fallen a victim of the purges, and her son was serving his third term for a "political" crime.

Mikhail returned to the porch, the pain caused by the Zhdanov decree showed on his face. I refilled his glass with steaming tea. He drank it absent-mindedly. Unable to repress my own emotions but fearful of voicing my thoughts, I scribbled a few words on a piece of paper and passed it across the table to Mikhail. I cannot now recall what comments I had made, but his face turned white. He shot me a reproving glance and tore the note into shreds. Lighting his pipe, he brought each scrap to the flame of the match and watched it burn.

Soon we were back in our Moscow home. There was more shrapnel in *Pravda*, this time against Shostakovich and other composers, to be followed by virulent outbursts against scholars and scientists.

My husband was nervously pacing the room.

"We started out with a noble idea," he muttered to himself. "But the deed rarely fits the word."

It was the nearest to censure of the system that Mikhail had ever got. I think both of us were frightened and believed it best not to discuss politics.

II Anna Louise Strong, American spy

When a newspaper item of no more than two or three lines appeared inconspicuously on the back page of *Pravda*, few readers, I am sure, took any notice of it. What it said would have been quite astonishing if people had not long ago become inured to the bizarre actions of their government. Thus it appeared that the American journalist Anna Louise Strong, who had lived for long periods in the Soviet Union, was an American spy, and had been ordered out of the country.

I did not for a moment believe the accusation. Most people who knew of her long-time loyalty to the Soviet regime, and her admiration of Stalin, must have thought it preposterous. What had she done to incur the wrath of the Great One, I wondered. But I had other matters on my mind, and soon forgot about Anna Louise Strong.

That very day, as I dropped into the office of my department chairman at the Army Institute of Foreign Languages, I was reminded of her.

"Did you know Anna Louise Strong?" asked Major Tomilin, the department chairman, who was an old friend from the days when I worked for Intourist, where he held a managerial position.

His question seemed innocent enough, and I replied offhandedly, "Yes, of course I did."

I merely meant that I knew her as a public figure. Indeed, most of the English-speaking people in Moscow had heard about or run into her at one time or another.

Major Tomilin was a man of disarming candor and charm, liked by the women and for some reason heartily disliked by the men of our faculty. He took a personal interest in other people's affairs and was always sympathetic if someone was in trouble; cordial and hospitable, he was eager for people to visit his home. It was these qualities that I admired in him. But, perhaps unwittingly on his part, he was slated to play a sinister role in my life. My charge of espionage hinged on the supposition that I had been acquainted with Anna Louise Strong, and Major Tomilin happened to be the only person with whom I had ever talked about her. I therefore assume that he was an informer—most people who had at one time or another worked for Intourist were—whose report provided the "legal" grounds for my charge. (Even so, were there no such report some other pretext would surely have been found to apprehend me.)

"Have you read the item about her in *Pravda*?" Major Tomilin inquired after a pause.

"Oh, yes," I replied as I left his office—the bell had rung for my class. I had not the slightest inclination to pursue the topic. Anna Louise Strong's expulsion from the Soviet Union was merely one of the innumerable crazy things that were happening around me, and I was not going to bother about it.

This was in the late forties. But earlier, at different periods in my life, Anna Louise Strong had claimed my attention as a journalist. I first read her in 1928, when I was thirteen; her articles on Lenin fell into my hands and I was quite carried away by her own enthusiasm for him. Later, at the *Moscow News*, I had worked for the arts and literature department under Shubin, a reticent but pleasant scholarly man who was recently married to Anna Louise Strong. Whenever I saw her heading for his office I would hastily slip out, finding anything but attractive the cold look of her aquamarine eyes.

I had often seen her, too, going in and out of the office of Mikhail Markovich Borodin, the paper's editor and a legendary figure in the early days of Soviet Russia's foreign affairs. We who worked under him knew him as a gentle, worldly-wise man. With his walrus moustache and warm brown eyes, he retained a chivalrous air even in his advanced years. Eventually he who had miraculously survived the purges of the thirties was also caught in the enormous net of people in some way connected with the "American spy."

Miss Strong's expulsion from the Soviet Union triggered off a long chain of arrests of people who either had worked with her at one time or another and knew her intimately, or who merely recognized her as a journalist and public figure and had no personal connection whatever.

Anna Louise Strong was only one of a thousand and more pretexts to nab people from all sections of the population. Branding her an American spy was an accusation that did not need to be substantiated by a single shred of evidence. It was sufficient to state it, and if Stalin saw fit to have it stated, how could it be a falsehood? This was the logic that nobody dared even question. If Anna Louise Strong was a spy, it followed that all persons who had the remotest association with her were spies too.

III The new terror

The section commander made his usual report: so many present, so many absent. I began with translation from Russian into English of newspaper material, all the time puzzling over the commander's report. Why had he cited two cadets absent when three were not in attendance? And who was the third? Yes, of course, I remembered now; it was Zhukov, who for some reason had not turned in his term paper. It would have been quite simple to inquire about him from the section commander, but some inner voice cautioned me against it.

"Zhukov has been missing my classes—does he attend yours?" I asked a teaching colleague. With a glance around the hall where we were standing, she blurted out, "No, he's been arrested." Some time later I learned about the jailing of other students.

Among the translators I knew were many people of English, American, and Spanish extraction. I had quit my job at the Soviet Information Buro a year after my daughter was born, but had remained friends with many of the translators. I was now horrified to learn of the large number of arrests in the translation department. Some of the best translators were jailed as early as 1947: Talmi, George Hanna, Julius Katser, and Hilda Kazanina, all well known for their English translations of Russian classics and Soviet fiction. The same was happening among the faculty of the Moscow Institute of Foreign Languages.

Suddenly we were reliving the agonies and fears of 1937 and 1938. The atmosphere in Moscow had become unbearably oppressive. Close to a corner column of the Bolshoi Theater I was stopped by a friend, a successful painter. I was shocked by his appearance. From a picture of elegance, a buoyant, self-confident, flirtatious man, he had turned into a ghost; he looked as if he had lost all substance and would collapse any moment at the slightest whiff of air. He could talk of nothing but the new arrests, especially the vicious attacks against Jewish intellectuals and professional people.

"I never imagined I would see it happen again. It's madness!" Greatly agitated, he enumerated the individuals who had recently been arrested. I listened but said nothing. Then suddenly I caught the name of my dear friend Nadezhda. This painter had once been in love with her and hoped to make her his wife. But instead she had married a colonel in the Red Army and had accompanied him to the front at the time of the Russo-Finnish war of 1939–1940. It was just after she had graduated from medical school, and for her gallant work as a surgeon she was decorated with the Order of the Red Star. She had come back from that war, as I well remembered, greatly chagrined by the way things were organized, resulting in the needless death of thousands of fighting men.

Nor, as I also remembered well, did she keep quiet about what she saw. Her charge—I learned from her husband—was "anti-Soviet agitation." She received a ten-year sentence. Nadezhda died in camp after having survived two wars. She left two children.

The new terror and mass arrests that started in 1947 were not a clean-up of the Party apparatus as had been largely the case in 1937 and 1938, but a form of still further intimidation of an already utterly intimidated population. This time the main targets were professional and other groups. Arrest thirty or a hundred doctors, thirty or more translators, fifty leading writers, sixty Jewish intellectuals, and you will strike fear into each of these sections of the population.

In 1938, after Yezhov was booted out of office and disappeared into the unknown, a few cases were reviewed. Some lucky individuals, after a year's interrogation, were unexpectedly released and exonerated. "Sorry we've tortured you for a year, made your family tremble with fear and disown you. You're innocent, you're free to go home and resume normal life."

Stunned, hardly believing their good fortune, these people— among them Joe F., a translator I had worked with, and a young neighbor of ours—were so scared that they never uttered a word about their prison experiences. The look of abject terror in their eyes forbade anyone to ask questions. What went on in the dungeons of the security police remained a secret. Every released prisoner had signed a pledge of non-disclosure.

To prevent the truth about the prisons and forced-labor camps from leaking out to the outside world, nobody that I knew among the victims of the 1947–1953 period was released under Stalin. The majority, if they survived, waited until 1956 for their cases to be reviewed.

The trials and purges of the late thirties, it will be remembered, received some publicity and were partially reported in the Soviet and world press. Between 1947 and 1953 there were no open trials. All the arrests and executions proceeded in an atmosphere of silence and secrecy. Every little fact, every arrest, every death sentence, was carefully concealed from the public, at home and abroad.

It is apparently to the advantage of the Party to keep silent about the mass arrests and shootings that swept the country in the late forties and early fifties, to ascribe most of the "mistakes" and "illegalities" to the late thirties in order to make it appear that there had been at the time a kind of Party strife or struggle for power. This would give the whole nightmare of terror and shootings a semblance of normality and thus indirectly minimize the guilt of the Party.

As for the 1947-1953 period, people today are expected to pretend it never happened, to bear no ill will to the security apparatus and the Party chiefs who condoned the crimes, who signed papers of executions and lists of arrested persons—"to forget." Moreover, it is permissible to strike out major events, personalities, and whole periods from the history books. Historical events are being craftily distorted. When tributes are printed in the newspapers or books written about outstanding revolutionaries and public figures who disappeared during the purges, there is usually a gap of many years in the middle of their lives, or at the end.

The utmost care is taken to hush up the fact that these persons were victims of terror, whether in the purges of 1937 and 1938 or in the new mass repressions that began in 1947. The years spent in prison and camp are omitted from accounts of their lives. If the personalities now honored were shot or died in camp, that abrupt end is never specified; the reader is free to interpret in his own way. He can indeed imagine that they were carried off by an avalanche or other natural disaster. If, however, they survived, what happened during the ten or twenty years excised from their lives? Are we to suppose that they dwelt in an enchanted wood, like Sleeping Beauty, until they were awakened by a kiss from Prince Charming—Khrushchev—and then returned to their jobs?

IV Cosmopolitanism

There are good and bad words in the Soviet lexicon, catch phrases and slogans that have a mesmeric effect. "To beat America" was a longtime slogan that summed up the economic targets of the five-year plans. (A good Party slogan.) As for "liberal" and "liberalization," they have always been dirty words—ever since Lenin spoke so contemptuously of the liberal bourgeoisie, the same liberals among the Russian capitalists who donated large sums of money to the Bolsheviks in their struggle to overthrow the monarchy and establish a Soviet regime. To this day "liberalization" is so reprehensible that no leader dares utter the word; a liberal is seen as a shilly-shallying, insecure person who can be expected to defect to the enemy at any moment.

In the late forties the words "cosmopolite" and "cosmopolitanism" were suddenly sprung upon us. They carried the same portent as "enemy of the people" in 1937 and 1938. Venom and abuse were hailed upon the "rootless cosmopolites." The Party denounced them in every newspaper as persons "without a homeland," "without kith or kin," tribeless. It was a campaign directed mostly against Jewish professionals and intellectuals. Most vociferous in this chorus was Mikhail Sholokhov, who in his articles "exposed" the Semitic origin of popular Russian writers by citing their long-abandoned Yiddish names.

One day, after work, I dropped in to see the Merkurovs. The door of the sculptor's studio was open; I entered but remained on the threshold to get a better view of his work, familiar and new. In the middle of the studio was a lifesize bust draped in wet muslin. It revealed only the bare outlines of the head; and the head seemed familiar.

A number of death masks had been added to the collection I already knew so well. This was an art at which Merkurov was extremely adept. No sooner did some important Party leader, writer, or actor pass away than the sculptor was called in to make a last imprint of the lifeless features, as he had done of Leo Tolstoy, and many years later of Lenin. I paused, as I often did, to gaze at these faces, preserved at almost the moment of death, when someone gently took me by the elbow and steered me deeper into the studio.

I turned my head and found myself looking into a face so ugly that its very ugliness was a magnet of attraction. Merkurov lumbered in through the open door. He was a burly man, nearly two heads taller than the person who was still clutching my elbow and to whom I needed no introduction, for I immediately recognized him as Solomon Mikhoels, founder and zealous architect of the famous Moscow Jewish Theater. Now I realized why the head of the bust looked familiar to me.

Throwing back the wet cloth from his work, Merkurov said pleasantly: "Sit down and keep us company. Watch me sculpt the head of a Socrates." Merkurov was not exaggerating. I often heard the Jewish actor called the "philosopher of Moscow's art world," and the "wisest, most humane person," by his Russian colleagues.

He was one of the first casualties of the cosmopolitan campaign. In the late forties his popularity, as both artist and man, cost him his life. Perhaps the reason he was not shot outright, as many of his colleagues were, can be attributed to the world homage he won as a Soviet good-will ambassador in wartime. He therefore met with a road accident, engineered by the great Stalin himself. Stalin needed to get the internationally acclaimed actor off the stage before he

111

enacted his own gory drama of hatred and death against the Jews and other intellectuals.

"Cosmopolite" was a foreign word, new to Russian ears. The man in the street had not the vaguest notion of its meaning. However, it was a well-tried practice to replace ordinary, comprehensible words with veiled expressions and niceties of language. "Cosmopolite" became a euphemism for "Jew."

At the start of this campaign against them the "cosmopolites" were more flabbergasted than anybody else. Why were they branded "rootless" and "without a homeland," when this very homeland, the Soviet Union, had been brought into existence through the dedication and efforts of a proportionately larger number of Jews than persons of any other nationality?

Soviet Jews had long ceased to think of themselves as Jews; in any event this was true of most Jews I met in Moscow. They identified themselves with the culture of the Russians and in their internal passports, which all Soviet people carry, they would have gladly put down "Russian" or any other nationality—Eskimo, Chuvash, Unti, any of them was better than "Jewish."

If such accusations as "rootless" and "without a homeland" were utterly unfounded, especially in a state that proclaimed communist society to be its ultimate goal, the stigma of being tribeless was quite justified. There was no tribal feeling among Soviet Jews. They did not live in segregated communities, as they had before the revolution and as they do at present in some cities of the world. They mingled as freely with the Russians and Ukrainians as they did among themselves.

Sadly, in 1948, 1949, and right until Stalin's death, Jews were being made aware that they belonged to a national minority open to insult and persecution. This was a period during which in the press and at meetings there was undisguised talk of excluding Jews from certain professions.

One Saturday night, at a get-together in my house, the husband of a friend of mine, a colonel who had commanded a regiment in the battle for Moscow against the invading Germans, delivered himself of the current Party line. He was not in the least anti-Semitic, but merely accepted Party policy as the gospel truth.

"In Russian schools Jews should not be allowed to teach such subjects as Russian or Russian literature," he proclaimed.

Half of the guests, including his own clever, pretty wife, were Jewish. Too fearful to start an argument, we let his remark slip by.

On Pyatnitskaya Street, close to my house on Rauzhskaya Embankment, I ran into the plump, pink-cheeked wife of a newspaperman who had worked with my husband for many years. Her pretty Slavic face lit up with a smile whenever we met. This time it was contorted with pain.

She came to the point at once: "My husband's editor told him to hand in his resignation. He said there were Central Committee orders to bar Jews from the literary field."

The same Damocles' sword that now hung over every Jew working in journalism threatened to descend on my husband's head. He knew he could be fired any day and stood little chance of getting work elsewhere.

Ostrich-like, I refused to face up to reality. "You could free-lance and make out just as well," I would say encouragingly. "Above all forget you are a Jew. We must live through it. We can! By ignoring this madness."

Krasny Flot was the newspaper for which my husband had now been working for a few years. It was published in Moscow, had a wide circulation, and was designated for the men and officers of the Soviet Navy, an arm of the service with a larger proportion of Jews than any other. It was quite likely that anti-Semitism was less popular in the navy than in the army and air force. The editor of *Krasny Flot* was an admiral in his mid-fifties whose wife—so rumor had it—was Jewish.

The campaign against "cosmopolites" was not to his liking. Possibly he was nauseated by it, as were many communists I knew. Therefore, instead of following Central Committee orders to sack the Jews on his staff, he decided to put up a fight. When pressure was exerted, he tried to offer objections, tried refusing point-blank to fire the Jewish journalists, tried stalling.

Editors all over the country had long since carried out their purges of Jewish personnel. He held out. We could pay tribute to him as a good and upright communist who stuck to his principles. Unfortunately, in the long run, his stubbornness turned out to be a greater disaster for the Jews on his staff, my husband among them, than the readiness of other editors-in-chief to abide by Party directives.

A couple of ideologues were sent down from the Central Committee to look into the situation. A Party meeting was called at which they laid down the law, making no bones about how "cosmopolites" should be treated. They warned the editor to show no leniency to the "agents of international Jewry." Ludicrous as it may seem, half of the Party members present at this meeting, and listening to these vicious attacks, were Jews themselves.

Mikhail returned around midnight. I woke up and switched on the bedside lamp. His face was ashen. He was coming apart right before my eyes. His lips moved to say something, but no sound came. Dropping into a chair, he stared past me as though I were not there at all.

Alarmed, I almost shouted at him: "Tell me what happened at the meeting."

He did not seem to hear.

I got out of bed and sat down on a chair opposite him.

"Pull yourself together, darling, or we'll all pay dearly . . ." When I pronounced these words, I did not know how prophetic they were. "Forget you are a Jew!" I repeated my pet admonition.

"How can I forget something I'm being constantly reminded of?" he answered. "You can't imagine what the meeting was like. The speeches made by the Central Committee representatives smacked of the old tsarist pogrom battle cry: 'Kill the Jews and save Russia!'"

"We must not let them hurt us!" I argued. " Don't you see that this virulence is artificially whipped up? It rebounds on the hater, turns him into a brute. Forget your nationality!"

"I can't and I refuse," he retorted.

The admiral needed no further proof than the meeting to realize he had lost his battle. I can only surmise that, after being questioned by security-police officials, it became clear to him that charges were being framed against the Jewish journalists he had refused to fire. By sticking to his guns he had rendered them a disservice; he was now well aware that their liberty and very lives were in jeopardy. Hastily he ordered their dismissal, hoping, perhaps, that he might divert attention from them, save them from their doom.

Alas, he was mistaken. A "group" case had already been fabricated against them. A few months later the very people whose interests he had defended were arrested and charged with organized anti-Soviet and Zionist propaganda.

More Jewish journalists of the *Krasny Flot* staff were arrested and killed than those working for other newspapers, where the editors-in-chief had complied with Party directives. Why did that happen? What was the logic of it? For a long time I pondered these questions, until finally I arrived at the answer.

The reason was obvious: the Party brooked no resistance to its policies; the admiral had to be punished for his disobedience. The best way to punish him was to destroy human life, destroy the very persons whose rights he dared to protect. This would no doubt teach other champions of the Jews a good lesson.

I had no way of knowing how the admiral, a man of integrity, reacted to this manner of punishment. But I know that very often such retribution added to the Party member's ideological confusion, turning brave and humane persons into cowards or making them go to pieces. The Party "logic" was to achieve just that, so that people like the admiral would think twice before embarking on a quixotic course of action.

To get our little daughter away from our hot, poorly aired room, we spent the summer of 1949 in Bykovo, a pinewood recreation spot near Moscow. Early on the morning of September 7, 1949, I was expecting Mikhail, who had spent the night in the city, to arrive with a truck to move our belongings back to Moscow.

Two men in the gray suits worn by many government officials, including the MGB, strode through the garden gate down the path towards me. With no greeting or preliminary introductions, one of them said: "Last night we arrested your husband."

I became wooden, numb. The sparkling day darkened. I knew I must show no emotion. Every word, every tear, if I dared shed it, could be interpreted as censure of the state. The men's eyes peered, searching for a sign of weakness. I tightened.

"Open your bags!"

I did as I was told, wondering if they could hear the loud beating of my heart.

They rummaged through everything. No search warrant had been produced. I dared not ask for one.

Among my papers was a manuscript of about fifty pages, which I was translating for an arts publishing house. It had to do with the restoration of old churches. One of the men picked it up.

"This we're going to confiscate," he said as he leafed through it.

"Please don't, it's only a translation I'm doing." I now spoke with emotion for the first time.

How indeed, I thought, would I explain the absence of the manuscript? I plainly visualized the fear in the eyes of the editor who gave me the translation, the horror of being mixed up with anyone who had an arrested husband.

"Okay, we won't confiscate it," said the MGB man with a magnanimous air.

Later, I concluded that the search was a put-on act, a bit of strategy on the part of my future interrogator to test my reaction to my husband's arrest. If I reacted with strong emotion and let slip some uncautious remark, I could easily be charged with lack of confidence in the security organs.

There was no greater calamity in the Stalin era than arrest. The arrested person would be struck off the list of the living, his family knowing for certain that they would never set eyes on him again. There would be no trial, no defense lawyer, no semblance of justice; communication with the prisoner during the interrogation period was forbidden, and never a clue given as to what the charges were. After conviction it could be either no exchange of letters—if the sentence, as I believe it did in my husband's case, stated "Without the right to correspond"—or only a few a year.

The family of the arrested person was at once under a cloud of suspicion. Every member was compelled to state at his office or factory that he had an arrested relative, which immediately put him in danger of losing his job. And in the end, quite often, the worst happened: other members of the family were jailed and deported to camps.

My mother was so stricken by Mikhail's arrest that she came down with a high fever. Mikhail had always been a thoughtful son-in-law, showing her the same compassion he did most human beings. She now lay in bed, her deeply creased cheeks flushed, tears trickling from her eyes onto the pillow.

Now and again she dozed off, only to wake with a moan and a shiver. I wanted to call a doctor.

"Don't," she admonished. "I'll get over it soon, the fever comes from the visions I have of Mikhail in prison. *You* don't know what prison is like, but I do from my own experience in tsarist times."

My mother had often described tsarist prisons to me. But what my imagination had conjured up—prisoners allowed to meet at mealtimes, given books to read, paper and pen to write, treated like human beings, often even with respect, by the warders—was a far cry from what I was to encounter at Lubyanka, Lefortovo, and Butyrki prisons in Moscow.

A few days after Mikhail's arrest Lenya Ivich, a friend of my husband's and a fellow journalist at *Krasny Flot*, came to see me. I knew him from the time he had been a war correspondent reporting on the fighting in the Crimea and the seige of Sevastopol. There was about Lenya, as about my husband, an air of chivalry; a deep-seated humaneness marked both men. It was a brave action on Lenya's part to risk a visit to the wife of an arrested comrade at the height of the cosmopolitan campaign of which Mikhail was now a victim.

He kept repeating: "Mikhail never said a word against the system. His loyalty was beyond reproach."

I thanked Lenya for his visit. He could say nothing to comfort me. We both knew that Mikhail was lost to the world. But what neither of us could guess, at the moment, was that Lenya's own days of liberty were running out. Shortly after this visit he was arrested as a co-defendant in the group case under which Mikhail came, on the same charge of anti-Soviet agitation and sympathy for Zionism. Both men were dead long before the ''breaches of legality'' were condemned and both were posthumously exonerated.

V "Nowhere!"

With my husband's arrest a dark chasm opened up before me. I teetered on the edge, trying hard to keep my balance, to muster the moral strength needed to go on living, working, remaining a normal person and not letting bitterness overcome me. Overnight I became a pariah. I could not blame the colleagues, friends, and neighbors who now avoided me for their own safety; on the whole, however, people proved to be more fearless and kinder than I expected. My job hung on a thread. The MGB redoubled their vigilance.

Could one blame the wives and husbands who shortly after the arrest of their spouses filed for divorce? There was my gifted friend Tina, an exquisite woman who was courted by some of Moscow's most brilliant men: she ended up with a fifth marriage, to her third husband, Nikolai. Tina had divorced Nikolai shortly after he was apprehended in 1947, and married Leonid, a journalist. Upon Nikolai's release in 1956, during the Khrushchev thaw, she remarried him. There was an element of the absurd in it. Yet was it not absurd that one never dared to question the actions of the state, but was at all times expected to laud them, no matter how erratic and criminal they were?

Political prisoners were the only persons not subject to the rigid divorce laws introduced immediately after the war to strengthen the marriage tie. A man could be callously told that his marriage had been dissolved and that his wife and children, his only link with the outside world, had disowned him. Nothing was easier for an arrested man's wife than to get a divorce by proxy—no taking of the case to court as the law required, no notifying of the other party about the pending of divorce.

A brief written statement—"My husband was arrested by the state security organs and I request a divorce"—did the trick. You were no longer an outcast, no longer bound to a "traitor," "spy," or "Zionist." You could revert to your maiden name, update the long, recurring questionnaire forms at your job, making it clear that you have severed all connections with your spouse. You were applauded for your loyalty to the regime.

This was the official stand. In fact the people around you knew that you had been forced to abandon a family member in misfortune because you hoped you and your children could go on with your lives without being harassed, without the fear of sharing the fate of your loved one.

For all that, it was not easy to extinguish the spark of goodness in human beings. Tina and Leonid kept sending Nikolai parcels and letters. A well-known stage and film actor, B.Ch., mailed packages of food to his mistress, who lived in the same hut with me and sixty other women prisoners at a Taishet camp. And in the Butyrki Prison I became friendly with the young wife of a high-ranking naval officer who intervened on her behalf—to no avail, of course, but at great risk to his own position and liberty.

During the recess periods between my classes I would retire into some inconspicuous corner of the common room. But even there the compassionate eyes of my colleagues would seek me out. There was Captain B.R., the dashing, chivalrous vice-chairman of the department, and Professor R., who taught English literature; in their long stares I read a whole gamut of emotions, which in our fearful times they dared not put into words. Could they have spoken up, they would have told me how sincerely sorry they were for me, what an outrage the mass arrests were, and how they deplored their powerlessness to help people like myself. Such messages I read not only in the eyes of my colleagues, but also in the glances of neighbors and friends.

Two or three evenings a week of that bleak, hapless winter of 1949 and 1950 I spent where most wives of arrested men went in hope of receiving the barest information about their husbands: at the Lubyanka Inquiry Office. This office was situated in a small house some five or seven minutes' walk from the Lubyanka building.

The house overlooked the narrow, busy Kuznetsky Most Street, in an old quarter of the city. A few doors down the street was Moscow's well-known bookshop selling publications in foreign languages, which tourists frequented. In my carefree days I had loved sauntering through this part of the city to pick up a dictionary or a Soviet edition of an English novel. Kuznetsky Most, meaning Blacksmith Bridge, had indeed been a bridge several hundred years ago, spanning the small Neglinka River, which was later locked into pipes.

The street itself was humped and reminiscent of a bridge. As I walked along it to the Inquiry Office I wondered if, as some claimed, deep beneath its surface the Neglinka River was making a sorry bid for freedom, gurgling and swirling in its futile struggle to break through its iron casing. I felt a little like that tiny streamlet, except that there was no fighting spirit in me and I was condemned to inaction. Meekly, like everyone else, in our common tragedy hardly even speaking to one another, I would go up to the little wicket window at the Inquiry Office, show my identity passport, give my husband's name, and each time receive the curt reply: "Under interrogation."

What we all waited to hear was "Bring a small amount of money," or "Warm clothing allowed." The former usually signified that the interrogation was going well and that the prisoner, having made it easy for the MGB, could be rewarded with the privilege of ordering cigarettes or groceries from the prison commissary. A request of warm clothing meant that the prisoner had been sentenced. It was important for the wife, husband, or other relative to call regularly at the Inquiry Office in order to get the message in time—before the convicted person was railroaded to camp.

In my case, finally, it was "Warm clothing." I was not told what my husband's sentence was or where he would serve it. Years later, when Mikhail was exonerated, I learned—or rather was able to deduce from the brief conversation I had with a KGB officer when his case was being reviewed—that he was sentenced *in camera* by a tribunal to ten years' prison, a more severe penalty than camp and a sure road to death, as indeed it was for my husband. Since neither I nor his mother, nor his sisters or brothers, ever received a single letter from him, I could well conclude that his sentence read: "Without the right to correspond."

Hastily I packed a bundle of warm clothing. We were all so very poor in those days that a warm sweater was a luxury Mikhail did not possess. My neighbor Georgi kindly gave me his. I dashed off to the Inquiry Office. The man at the wicket opened the door leading from his room into the big waiting hall and took the bundle from me. I have no idea whether he received it or not, because I never heard from him. I did not discontinue my visits to the Inquiry Office, not until rudely and impatiently the officer at the wicket said: "You're wasting my time. Your husband is no longer on my lists."

"Where can I inquire about him?"

"Nowhere!"

Waiting for two or three hours, evening after evening, at the jammed Lubyanka Inquiry Office, I would see troubled faces of all ages, old and young, including teenagers whose parents had both, apparently, been arrested. It disturbed me greatly. Everybody stood or sat in silence. It was an unwritten law not to ply one another with questions, often not even to address anyone; each carried a big enough load not to be burdened by other people's woes.

The mental anguish I was suffering manifested itself in physical symptoms. One morning in early February, shortly after I had been turned away by the officer at the wicket, my fever was so high that I had no strength to get out of bed and go to work. To obtain a sick-leave certificate my mother called a doctor from the local clinic.

It was not until evening that the doctor, a woman in her thirties, arrived. I remember her bending over me, flipping a thermometer, and hastily slipping it under my armpit; no word or question escaped from her. I noticed that she was good-looking, with an oval face, hazel eyes, and dark glossy hair visible from under her white doctor's cap.

With one hand she now held the stethoscope as with the other she threw back the covers. The moment she saw I was bleeding and wearing a pad, she covered me up roughly and quickly thrust the stethoscope back into the pocket of her smock.

"You've had an abortion," she snapped angrily. "I'll send an ambulance to take you to the hospital at once."

At that time abortion was illegal and punishable by several years of prison.

"This is February, doctor . . ." Instinctively I dropped my voice to a whisper, as one always did when speaking of an arrest. "My husband was arrested by the security organs at the beginning of September. I've had no sex since. This is just my period."

A cold look was her answer. She drew on her coat. "The ambulance will be here in less than an hour," she flung from the door. Turning to my mother, she added, "Pack her things."

The doctor's bluster woke up my little daughter, whose crib was only three or four feet from my bed. She lay awake, fear in her dark brown eyes, as though she sensed the trouble we were all in.

Why in an unpunctual land was evil so punctual? Before we could gather our wits and think how to deal with this new insane problem, the ambulance arrived. The gynecologist was a large flabby blonde approaching middle age, with a much less rigid face than the first doctor. I gave her the same explanation. She knew I spoke the truth but submitted me to a thorough examination—before my daughter's startled eyes.

After the second doctor departed, I fell into a deep, fitful slumber. I awoke feeling better, but with a smoldering hatred for all doctors. I dragged myself to work. That afternoon I was called to the personnel department and told I was fired. In later years, when I recalled the manner and hostile tone of the young man behind the desk who spoke to me, I knew I should have realized that my days of freedom were numbered.

VI My brother Shurri

A few months before I lost my job, Shurri lost his. Communication between secret sections of the army and the secret departments that exist in every office, factory, and university is rapid and efficient. My brother was regarded with suspicion; after my husband's arrest, he fell into the category of family members of arrested persons. He was hastily discharged from army service in South-Sakhalinsk, thousands of miles from Moscow, and deprived of his post as language instructor.

He returned to Moscow. His job hunt in the winter and spring of 1950 made it quite plain that there was no hope of getting any position. Every person applying for a job had to be cleared by the secret section of the personnel department. And there was one crucial question, dreaded by all who had arrested relatives, in every job application: "State if a member of your family or your spouse's family has ever been repressed."

It was recorded in the great Stalinist constitution, as it is in the current one, that all Soviet citizens have the right to a job. But this ruling did not apply to you if one of your family was or had been in the past a political prisoner. You were then blacklisted and, as in my brother's case, could not even count on an unskilled laborer's job, for labor legislation banned the employment of anyone with a college degree in a menial capacity.

My brother was jobless for eighteen months, right to the day of his death. No unemployment relief, no welfare, nothing as demeaning as charity, can exist in a socialist society. Full employment was and is the boast of socialism. But in that fearsome Stalin era, no matter how hard he tried, how humbly he begged, there was no job for Shurri. Needless to say, matters became a thousand times worse for him when my mother and I were arrested.

I saw a good deal of my brother in the months preceding my arrest. Shurri did his best to distract me from my troubles, engaging me in long discourses on linguistic themes. He had in fact used his enforced leisure to write a thesis, inspired by Marxist views, on the class essence of English idiomatic phrases.

The snows of the long winter of 1950 suddenly melted away. Spring set in with a flourish of brilliant sunshine, as Moscow spring has a way of doing. The tawny little buds swelled fast and sturdy on oak and birch twigs. Faces that had been surly all winter softened and lit up with new hope. "Look, the trees are in leaf," people said to one another.

These same words dropped from my brother's lips that early spring. I can still hear them. And the thought that he never saw the budding of another spring is all the more painful to me because his death was so purposeless, so devoid of meaning—except that it demonstrated one thing: there was a limit to what the individual was able to endure under the Stalin regime, even when he was at liberty.

What I most feared, in my cell at the Lefortovo Prison, was that my brother too might be jailed. Appalled as I was by my own plight, I found immense relief in believing that I alone was fated to bear the family cross. I was not religious, but every morning, just before reveille, on returning to my cell after the night's interrogation I repeated the prayer: "Let it be me! Oh God, if one member of our family must suffer, let it be me! Spare my mother and brother!"

In October, five months before his death, I signed a long deposition clearing my brother of suspicion. He was not a spy; I never saw him associate with aliens; he never met with foreign intelligence agents when he worked as an army interpreter during the war in the Russian north. It took all night for the interrogator to write down the answers. Gradually, as I signed sheet after sheet, the significance of that night's interrogation dawned on me. Of course, it was all a comedy. My answers could carry no weight because I was miles away from where my brother was in wartime. But they were among the twisted "legalities" that could be used either to imprison an innocent person or to prevent his arrest. Most likely my brother was to be the next culprit in our small family, his name on the dreaded list of arrests. My interrogator, aware of the silly tangle of utterly unsubstantiated charges my own case presented, decided not to get himself involved with my brother. Shurri had had a narrow escape.

In their magnanimity, the Soviet security organs had decreed that this youngest member of our "criminal" family be spared. The MGB made my handsome, upright, sincerely communist brother a gift of his liberty. Shurri, at the time twenty-eight years old, knew nothing of this, of course. He still could not find a job, belonging as he did to a family with three spies in it, and was therefore not to be trusted; indeed, he was to be treated as an outcast from the socialist society.

He was a candidate member of the Communist Party. The time had now arrived for him to be accepted as a full-fledged member. His fate was in the hands of the Communist Party District Committee in Mytishchi, the large industrial district on Moscow's outskirts where he lived. The Committee, composed mostly of industrial workers or former workers who had become Party functionaries, rose to the occasion and lost no time in expelling Shurri from the Party. They performed their duties as Soviet workers always do on orders from the higher-ups.

Nobody with so many spies in the family could be a member of the Party. In early March, 1951, all the dependable, sedate worker communists on the Mytishchi committee raised their hands. For unanimous expulsion. Knowing exactly the consequences, the stigma and ostracism that went with such a decision. My interrogator, Major Porunov, expected Shurri to live. My brother judged differently. The day he was expelled he threw himself under the wheels of a running train.

Shurri was always full of new ideas; he prided himself on his thorough Marxist approach to philosophy, literature, and linguistics, a last passion. On that final meeting of ours in June, a week before my arrest, he was airing some of these ideas. But I was too preoccupied and downcast to take in what he was saying.

VII Strawberries

June was hot and dry. I remember it well for its good harvest of sweet crimson strawberries. Indeed, in Moscow June is the strawberry month, the only time of the year when they are available, usually at high market prices. Rather than serve them to the family, Moscow housewives make the fragrant jam to which guests are treated at teatime during the cold winter months—a pleasant reminder of warm days, of the beautiful month of June.

My arrest on the last day of June is linked in my mind with crushed strawberries. I had bought a kilo of berries at the farm market not far from my house to take to my mother. Not having a fridge, I kept the berries on a big flat plate on the floor, where it was cooler. The moment the two security men in plain clothes crossed my threshold they accidentally stepped on the plate, their heavy soles reducing most of the delicate berries to a bleeding pulp.

Strawberries. My memories of the Taishet strict-regime camp too bring back to me a little incident that revolves around them. Suddenly, one day, a diminutive patch of wild strawberries appeared on the camp compound. How anything so exotic, fragile, and beautiful as these berries could have burst from the parched earth of the hot

Siberian summer is a mystery to me. To behold in the hell of our camp the tiny red berries peep out from their awning of serrated green leaves was nothing short of a miracle.

It was a situation that did not catch our jailors unawares. They knew exactly how to deal with such emergencies: there were express instructions to dig up any flowers, bushes, plants, and berries on the camp compound that could be a source of pleasure to political prisoners.

Unmindful of our jailors, the wild strawberries had rashly, thoughtlessly, ventured onto territory cut off from the outside world by barbed wire, guarded by armed warders with shepherd dogs straining at the leash and by tommy gunners pacing the small but sturdy watch towers high above the camp, their rifles at the ready.

Those of us who were fortunate enough to stand close to that little green patch could not take our eyes off the berries. We were lined up to be counted, a procedure, if everything went well, lasting for a good part of an hour. A warder who had absented himself soon returned with two rusty spades. He flung them at our ranks, one falling close to where I stood.

Giving me a cold, blank look, he commanded: "Pick it up and get busy."

"You there, too!" he yelled to another prisoner.

I longed not so much to taste the berries as to smell their fragrance. For the briefest moment I closed my eyes and that fragrance suffused me, bringing memories of Moscow, my home, my friends.

"Everybody remains standing until the whole patch is levelled and covered with earth."

I picked up the heavy spade and was soon hacking away at the amazed little berries, bent on doing the job quickly, for I knew how tiring it was for my fellow prisoners to stand in the scorching midday sun, with another eight hours of hard toil ahead of them. Soon we had the little green leaves and berries entombed beneath the crust of dry clay.

June 30 blackened into July 1. After the search many of my belongings lay in a heap on the floor in the middle of the room where they had been cast by the two secret police agents who had come to arrest me.

"Some of your bedding and clothes you can leave for your child with your next-door neighbors," the man in charge of the night's proceedings told me.

One of my most prized possessions was a Latin script typewriter, a German war trophy. There was a Russian typewriter too, borrowed from my neighbor Georgi, who stood outside my open door. I now begged to be allowed to return it to him, adding that he could help carry my things next door.

The typewriter was returned to him. My own was confiscated along with my personal letters and other papers.

"Are there any pets?"

"Yes, a cat and a tortoise."

The tortoise had disappeared under the couch while from atop the wardrobe my sleek jet Cleopatra surveyed the scene with flicking whiskers and a disdainful gleam in her green eyes.

After tying into a bundle the things that lay on the floor, Georgi carried them into the next room. There they were hastily taken in by the kindly widow to whom we owed the possession of our one-room home. It was about two o'clock in the morning. Most of the neighbors were awake, fully aware of what was going on.

"No gaping, go back to your own place," the detective, who had replaced the warrant for my arrest in his breast pocket, told Georgi. "Remove the animals too."

As he was leaving, with the pets tucked under one arm and the typewriter in his other hand, I begged: "Please take the strawberries as well." It was perhaps a crazy request under the circumstances.

Georgi smiled uncertainly, sadly. How dismal the future looked.

EIGHT

I Lefortovo Prison

After spending four days at the Lubyanka Inner Prison on Dzerzhinsky Square, in the heart of Moscow, I was taken to Lefortovo in
the far northeastern section of the city.

Steel and stone replaced the oil paint, wood panelling, and polished parquet of Lubyanka. The door clanged shut. Cold air seeped
through the grimy, ancient stone floor of the cell, nipping viciously
at my ankles. I shivered. The whitewashed walls and ceiling were a
filthy gray. An iron cot stood in the middle of the cell, fettered to the
floor. Across from it, against the wall, was a long, narrow table of
rough boards and a single rickety stool. In full view of the Judas-
hole, drilled in the cell's double-framed door, a tiny rusty sink and
a seatless, badly cracked toilet bowl huddled precariously against the
wall; the stained, dirty bowl was flushed by the water from the tap.

Slimy and falling apart, a sink and toilet were yet unheard-of luxuries, never again to be encountered in my wanderings from cell to
cell and prison to prison. I sat down on the narrow cot. The air was
clammy, with mingled odors of disinfectant, rust, and mold. A last
glimmer of the July day shot through the barred window high up at
the ceiling and winked off the steel door.

Barely having had an hour's sleep in the last few days, my head
drooped. I was about to lie down when the hatch in the door shot
open.

"No sleeping until lights out!" the guard barked.

The peep-hole slid up and down. I was watched. Just as I dozed
off in an upright position, the hatch clanged down again: "Keep your
eyes open!"

Mercifully, what seemed an eternity to me, but must have been no more than four hours, came to an end. The siren hissed. With the glare of the bulb in my eyes, I fell into slumber.

This was when I first had my prison dream. It was to recur night after night during the ten to twenty minutes of sleep allowed me before being summoned for interrogation and again in the twenty minutes after I was led back to the cell in the early morning.

In my dream I was cleared of all charges and free to return home. Joy welled in me at the sight of the familiar objects in my room, and I gazed long and fixedly at them. I walked to my desk and switched on the light of the lamp so that it fell on my unfinished translation. I picked up a pen but could not write. After sitting in a kind of trance, I rose from the desk and turned to look at my daughter, peacefully asleep in her cot.

I picked her up lovingly and hugged her. Then I put her down. The room grew dimmer. My daughter's cot was no longer in its customary place, at the wall opposite the bed my husband and I had shared. Suddenly I grew restless and uneasy about something: there was something important I had to do, but I had forgotten what. I made a great effort to remember. I remembered. I knew what I must do: return at once to my cell. The darkness grew dense; I could no longer discern the objects in the room. Nervously I groped my way to the door, slipped out, and broke into a run. I was soon back in my cell. I had returned of my own accord. The real world, as represented by my home, no longer had any meaning for me. I was shut out from it. I now had to grapple with the unreality in which I was trapped and from which I knew full well there was no escape.

A dim, dark, and silent world! Such was the secret Lefortovo Prison. I was being led from my cell to the interrogator's office on the first floor of the prison's Administration Wing. Just a few flights of stairs led down to it, yet we meandered through a warren of endless steel galleries.

"Hands behind your back!" No sooner did I step out of the cell than I linked my hands tightly behind me. "Straight ahead!" It meant I dared not turn my head or look back.

Other than these two commands there was never any verbal communication between prisoner and guard, nor between the guards themselves when they were escorting prisoners. A different language was used: a snap of the fingers and click of the tongue, sounds that rang eerily in the empty prison corridors.

As soon as this warning signal came from a guard passing with another prisoner, my escort shoved me into a niche, my eyes to the wall. A snap and a click; then an answering snap and click to say the coast was clear and we could proceed to the interrogator's office. On my way I had never once come face to face with another prisoner. But one morning, as I was being led back to the cell, a woman's shrieks reached my ears, piercing the musty air: "I am innocent, totally innocent!" she cried hysterically. "Long live Stalin!" I could feel my jailor tense. Quickly he prodded me on, deeper into the silence of the prison.

Major Porunov was sitting at his big birchwood desk when the guard brought me in. A hard stool at the door was the prisoner's place, which I now occupied. The interrogator rose and slowly approached me.

"What intelligence service have you been providing with information about the Soviet Union?" He continued in a more menacing tone: "We know Anna Louise Strong recruited you."

I gave the negative answers I now delivered night after night. After each interrogation he handed me the deposition sheets. I signed them. He wrote down my replies exactly as I worded them. They were denials of the accusations against me, clearly revealing my innocence of the espionage and treason charges. There was nothing to link me to Anna Louise Strong.

Questions concerning Boris Victorov—supposed agent of an American firm with whom, it was alleged, I had some sort of a meeting—led nowhere. Major Porunov was making no headway with my treason charge.

"You wrote letters to Canada maligning the Soviet system."

This was a shot in the dark. Every avenue was to be explored to gain a conviction.

"We have evidence that you were in touch with Mr. Franseez, a Canadian spy."

I was as mystified by this new character as I had been by the reference to Victorov.

On the following night, however, Major Porunov waved his evidence at me.

"I have here a letter sent to you by this spy . . ." I suddenly recalled that I had once received a single letter from a Toronto cousin of mine, many years before my imprisonment. The name of the cousin was Frances.

I couldn't help laughing. I told my interrogator from whom the letter was and explained that "Franseez," as he pronounced it, could be a female as well as a male name.

Major Porunov resumed his questions about my mother. I suspected nothing. I could not believe that my mother had been arrested and was in fact at that very moment in a cell at Lefortovo, not far away from my own. Even when the thought did at times force itself into my mind, I dismissed it as impossible. My mother arrested? To the last she remained loyal to the Soviet system. I thought of her advanced age, of all she had been through—the tsarist prisons, two wars, the struggle to support her children, the tragedy of having left her first two children to fend for themselves from the most tender age.

My mother had three more years to live. Major Porunov was her interrogator as he was mine. He did not spare her. He told her outright that her daughter was a spy. Night after night he plied her with questions about me. She tried her best to see through the subterfuge and lies, fighting a double battle, for herself and for me.

On being driven for interrogation from Lefortovo to Lubyanka one September night, I found a man with a big, menacing head leaning forward over the second, usually unoccupied, desk next to the one behind which sat Major Porunov, my interrogator. Behind these two men was a large window. The drapes were not drawn and I let my gaze settle on the dark glass. I wondered if the window overlooked the big Dzerzhinsky Square or the prison yard of the Lubyanka building. Behind the window was the somber Moscow night; the air circled freely, people slept in their beds, not knowing how lucky they were.

"Your husband is a dangerous criminal," rasped the stranger at the second desk. At once I shifted my attention from the window to him.

It seemed to me for a moment that the fierce black pupils of his eyes had popped out of their sockets and were whirling around the room in a frenzied dance of hatred. What a hideous face, with a twist to the thick, moist lips and a clamminess about the unhealthy skin. I shuddered to think what a man like him could do to his victim— hit out blindly with his strong fists, kick with his feet, hurl himself on the defenseless prisoner.

"Did you know that your husband was unfaithful to you, that he kept a mistress?"

He expected a response from me. I said nothing. Very often during interrogation I found myself utterly at a loss. How could I respond to the sordid lies and insults, the savage attacks and lunatic reasoning with which I was kept awake night after night, straining every nerve to fight off sleep so that I could remain in my seat and not drop on the floor from exhaustion?

That September night, however, I was jolted into full wakefulness.

I knew I was looking into the face of my husband's interrogator. Branding Mikhail a "dangerous" criminal was an ominous sign. It meant that the worst physical torture was justified in the course of the interrogation. Even the weakest of human beings have proved capable of enduring physical torture for a noble cause. But human beings were so debased, so befuddled by the lies and tricks of a Stalinist interrogator that they ceased to feel and think like normal people.

They were lost, cut off from the world, betrayed by their own ideology, crushed in mind and spirit. The big, ruthless security butcher I now saw before me might well have been my husband's murderer. The evil he represented had triumphed—and he never forfeited the protection of the socialist state. He may be living now in respectable retirement in a dacha near Moscow, enjoying a better pension than any Soviet working man, never fearing that he and others like him will be brought to justice.

II Interrogation by a general

Appeals to my interrogator to tell me what would become of my daughter, now that both her parents were imprisoned, fell on deaf ears. In the hope of extracting some information about her, I went on a hunger strike. For three days I refused all food. On the fourth I was taken down to a ward in the prison infirmary. There I was pinned down by two silent husky women and a man. A long crude rubber tube lay on the floor beside me. The very next moment it was forced down my throat.

There is a Soviet film shown frequently on Moscow television. Its heroine is Lenin's mother. When Lenin's older brother Alexander is sentenced to death for an attempt on the tsar's life, his mother has an interview with the chief of police in St. Petersburg. She is permitted to see her son. What struck me in this film was not only that she was able to do things no Soviet person was allowed, but also that wherever she went she was treated like a human being. Even the hated, feared, ruthless tsarist police, responsible for the death and stifling of so many good lives, treated political prisoners and their families like human beings.

In the prison world where I found myself, I was nothing but a captive animal to be kicked about and tormented at the will of whoever were my masters. To be suddenly hurled into an animal jungle and stripped of their humanity was the prisoners' worst horror, one that could be and was for many more fearful than death.

There was yet another horror: the complete dissolution of reality as you knew it. The rational understanding of things, which human beings have always sought, suddenly ceases to exist. You find yourself trapped in the vagueness, the utter nonsense of the accusations against you. Your mind rebels against the absurdity of an innocent person like yourself, uninvolved in politics, never in the Party, hardworking, honest, suddenly becoming the target of a powerful state apparatus.

You refuse to believe it. You try hard to find some plausibility; many prisoners in endeavoring to end the vagueness of the accusations levelled against them had even contrived to provide the so-called evidence to substantiate their conviction. To get at the truth, to perceive the logic of things. Order as opposed to chaos—was this not what the human mind craved from childhood, from the dawn of civilization?

In the avalanche of lies that descended upon me, I was overjoyed when I stumbled upon something that resembled truth. I was sitting at the prisoner's tiny table, far from the interrogator's massive desk, on the right side of the door.

From the way proceedings were going, it was apparent that there did not exist a scrap of evidence that could even remotely be linked with the charges brought against me. I was dumfounded by the utter idiocy of my case, the lack of logic, the confusion. Nothing hung together.

Both Major Porunov, my interrogator, and Lieutenant-Colonel Boyarinov, the prosecutor overseeing my case, were present at the questioning. In front of the Lieutenant-Colonel lay three fat dossiers. Hastily he was leafing through them. The interrogator, I could see, was examining me on the charge of "anti-Soviet conversations" and was getting nowhere.

Suddenly out of the blue came a question that was a ray of truth. It was put by the prosecutor who had picked it out of an informer's report in one of the dossiers. He asked it without taking his eyes off the page in front of him. Unlike Major Porunov, who seemed to enjoy his job, Boyarinov gave the impression that he was eager to get things over with as soon as possible, either because he was so very busy or because he wished to distance himself from the filth he was raking up, and the lies.

"Did you go around saying that Moscow toilets were dirty?"

Here at last was something I did say—a rational seed in the entire weird examination. Relieved, even happy, I replied: "Yes, I did, I certainly did!"

The Moscow visit of Clement Attlee, Britain's future prime minister, and his diarrhea, sprang into my mind. But somehow the absurdity of bringing toilets into the interrogation must have struck all of us; we smiled, the smile clearing for a brief moment the animosity that always hung so oppressively in the air between me and my two persecutors.

But the treason charge? Espionage against the Soviet Union for a certain state. What state? How was I to know that this was a stereotyped formula used against thousands of prisoners as innocent as myself?

I was pacing my cell, bewildered, shocked, still endeavoring to pick up some logical thread, when I recalled an incident that dated way back to my work as an Intourist guide. Perhaps it had something to do with the bringing of an espionage charge against me? I'll tell it and explain . . . For a self-destructive thought like that to have even entered my mind reveals how distraught and totally lost I must have felt.

What was this incident, which as things turned out later, helped to earn me a conviction on a milder charge? It had to do with my having spent a half hour or so in the American embassy in Moscow, in either 1935 or 1936—that is, about fifteen years before my arrest. I was assigned as personal guide to a first-class tourist. He was a certain Mr. Lush, an American who had written a book called *Six Roads to Happiness,* a copy of which he presented to me. We were out sightseeing when he said he had some business at the embassy. Rather than wait outside and make myself conspicuous, I had gone in with him. That it should have flashed back into my mind during the interrogation period was perhaps not so astonishing. What was astonishing and foolish was that I now of my own accord provided my interrogator with a "piece of evidence" he had never known existed.

The moment I related the incident he gloated; exultation twinkled in his brazen eyes. During the long nightly questionings I had frequently asked him: "How can you bring these wild accusations against me, when you possess no evidence, no proof of any kind, can produce no witnesses?"

Once he burst out: "We do not require any evidence. You will provide it yourself."

That was exactly what I had done. To cross the threshold of a foreign embassy, even as part of one's job—what could be greater proof that you were indeed a spy?

For three weeks now I had had a cellmate. Olga Manina, a Muscovite, told me right away she was a graduate of the Institute of Foreign Languages, where I had taught for a few years. She spoke vaguely of her own charges; all I remember her saying was that she had dated men from foreign embassies.

Olga was extremely vain about her looks; with her green eyes, dark hair, pale skin, and small, well-shaped nose, she was very attractive. She had a regular beauty routine, which she followed religiously. Every morning she did her setting-up exercises and tried hard with her fingertips to smooth away the lines that were settling around her eyes and mouth; in one year of prison or prison camp, as I was soon to observe, women aged ten to fifteen years. Olga would set her hair in paper curlers every night before going to bed, and she was clever at inventing substitutes for cosmetics. As she smoked she dropped the cigarette ash into an empty matchbox. On collecting a fair amount, she mixed the ash with spittle, turning it into a fine mascara that made her sweeping lashes look even longer. Chalk from the whitewashed walls of the cell served as powder, and above all Olga treasured a small red beet, which was her lipstick and rouge.

"How do I look?" Olga would ask me after she had spent about an hour on her grooming. Mirrors and glass objects were proscribed and so there was no way in which she could see the results of her beautifying efforts.

"You look like a movie star!" I told her.

Pleased, she rewarded me with a rare smile.

However, as Olga talked to me about herself, I began to have the strange feeling that she was lying, and that she had been isolated from the normal world for a longer period than she claimed. There were indeed many things about Olga that should have put me on my guard. But I was too naive, too new, to comprehend their significance. For one thing, Olga was never interrogated by night, always in the morning or afternoon—and for long days not at all—so that she was not exhausted as I was by lack of sleep. Moreover, she was allowed parcels from home and had permission to buy food and cigarettes at the prison commissary. Quite often I caught her mocking glance on me. Once or twice, from the questions my interrogator asked me, I realized that Olga had been reporting on my behaviour in the cell.

I now guessed that Olga was a spy brought in from camp to trick me into making some admission that would help my interrogator to convict me. Months later, in prison camp, I met a young woman who told me that Olga had also shared her cell at Lefortovo, watched and spied on her. Olga was a useful informer, and her snooping on others made her own life as a prisoner easier.

At a late hour, after about ten weeks of interrogation, I emerged under guard from the clammy Lefortovo walls into the cobblestoned prison yard. It was a dark, drizzly night. I swallowed a few gulps of moist air before climbing into the maw of a black maria.

After spending several hours in one of the already familiar Lubyanka boxes, I was taken up a few flights into a commodious office with armchairs upholstered in burgundy leather, a large desk, and a side table covered with a green felt pad.

Major Porunov, my interrogator, and Lieutenant-Colonel Boyarinov, the surveillance prosecutor, were present, the former standing in a far corner, the latter slumped in an armchair, his myopic spectacled eyes glued to the open page of a bulky folder. The presence of the prosecutor signified that the interrogation had attained a crucial point. A young clerk entered and took a seat at the side table. There was a fourth man in the office, his back turned to me.

The interrogation that followed surpassed all the previous ones in sheer nonsense. Somebody must have switched off the ceiling light, because the figures of my interrogator and prosecutor appeared shadowy and sketchy, like the backdrop designs on a darkened stage. The man whose back was turned to me swung around; in the full glare of the large desk lamp, his insignia told me he was a lieutenant-general.

He paced in sharp, impatient steps back and forth in front of me. And he fired at me the same question Major Porunov had kept asking at Lefortovo: did I know Anna Louise Strong? His baldness, mean eyes, and pink skin, along with an enormous paunch, recalled an ill-tempered hog.

After I repeated over and over again that I had never been personally acquainted with Anna Louise Strong, he boomed: "What about her husband? You knew him!"

"Yes, I knew Comrade Shubin. I worked for him at the *Moscow News*."

Suffering from shortness of breath, the general was now panting into my face.

"Well, well, how could you know the husband and not know the wife?" he bellowed.

I made no reply. I was stunned by the general's logic. What a farce! I had not the least idea at the time that interrogation by a general—a leading man in the Directorate—signified a turning point in the legal proceedings of my case. The charge of treason was dropped. But I was to realize this only much later.

I was taken down into the Lubyanka courtyard, hemmed in by walls and gates. A van stood out from the shadows, waiting for me; in its pitch dark I sat numb, dazed, a castaway from life.

Back in my cell in Lefortovo I experienced a sensation that perplexes me to this day. It also proves the spiritual resilience we gradually build up to preserve life and sanity when they are threatened as I felt they were.

When an agonizing blow is dealt us, we squirm and tingle with the pain and injury of it. All we want is to crawl into some hole, a place of seclusion to lick our wounds, out of the sight of our torturers. That hole becomes a haven to us.

That was the way I felt about my cell on at last finding myself in it after the almost four-hour interrogation in Lubyanka, where I had had to hold out against a blast of verbiage designed to wear me down and wrest a lying confession from me, where I had encountered an unwarranted animosity, a desire to crush me out of existence as though I were some annoying insect. If there was not a shred of honesty or justice in the way my interrogator and surveillance prosecutor were conducting the case, the general was the epitome of brutality in dispensing with human lives.

No wonder I was glad to be back in my Lefortovo cell; if only for a short while, it offered protection from my tormentors. The four damp walls smiled upon me with a warmth I had not known since I had been hauled away from home. A faint strip of dawn broke into the cell from the tiny barred window up at the ceiling. It cheered me greatly.

I did not hastily slip under the coarse prison blanket to snatch the twenty minutes of sleep allowed me after interrogation. I wished to prolong this sweet sensation of safety in my Lefortovo dungeon. I had a strong premonition of worse things to come, and I prayed that I might serve my entire term within these walls—in my cell, away from the interrogation office, where the charges against me were so senseless and the whole world was made to stand on its head instead of its feet.

How odd it seemed that the dark, damp cell had the power to suffuse me with this homey warmth, to protect me from the wanton hostility of my fellow creatures, from the pain of their blows. I realized that a little privacy for even a short time can have a salubrious effect, indeed bring one back to sanity; to think that this should have been borne in upon me in Lefortovo, one of the most awesome prisons of Europe. Interrogators at Lubyanka and Butyrki were constantly using the threat of Lefortovo to their prisoners: "I'll send you to Lefortovo and you'll turn into an old woman in no time—and sign away your mother's life."

Although that early morning before dawn, when I returned from an especially traumatic questioning, I had a warm feeling for Lefortovo, it was indeed a terrifying place—gloomier, damper, more unhealthy, and with worse food, than any other prison in Moscow. It was used mostly as a place for interrogation. Prisoners were not kept long in Lefortovo, for it required blooming health to endure even a year's incarceration there.

Every morning at six, the hour of reveille, the orderly brought in the prisoner's daily half-loaf of soggy black bread, some herb coloring for tea, and six tiny square lumps of sugar. The bread tasted awful; after two or three hours it was coated with a greenish-white mold. The main meal was a skilly of split barley with a few rusty herring tails floating in it. Day after day, it was exactly the same fare, food—if you could call it that—designed, like everything else in Lefortovo, to wear down your morale, to degrade you: if that is what you eat, you cannot be a human being.

Hence, when I was brought to Lubyanka shortly before my case was closed, the better bread, a meal of real cabbage soup and a second course of *bona fide* potatoes, the kind commonly eaten by human beings, put me in an almost euphoric frame of mind. As I ate the potatoes with an aluminum fork—a fork! I had not seen one for three months and would not see one again for almost three years!—in the tiny Lubyanka box, sitting on a shelf bed, I told myself that surely a prisoner fed the kind of food normally eaten by any other human being was going to be released. Of course, I was in a kind of trance. But such is the psychological impact of food on the mind: I really believed at the time in a happy dénouement. My hopes were up. I would be released, would walk out of the Lubyanka gates.

III My interrogator

"If I declare you innocent, I take your place," my interrogator blurted out in the semi-gloom of his office on the downstairs floor of the Lefortovo Prison. The words had slipped from him at a moment when he must have felt that he himself was trapped in a situation from which there was no more escape for him than for me. There was no escape because he had accepted the role of inquisitor, working night after night to secure my conviction when he was aware even before I was apprehended that the case against me was a fabrication.

He spoke the truth. Any leniency, any attempt on his part to see justice done, would land him in jail.

But why had he not at some point in his career changed—as others had—to a different job? It was not impossible to achieve that, especially for a man with a good legal education. He was not a born hangman, not a confirmed *chekist*, not one who could be brainwashed into thinking that persons like myself or my mother were a danger to the regime. Why then did he participate in a tragi-comedy that invariably ended in the destruction of human life?

He belonged to a generation among whom there were no political fanatics, as there had been at the time of the revolution, or in the twenties and even thirties. Ideology hardly entered at all into his work, and he rarely had the satisfaction of outwitting and eliminating ideological opponents, for the simple reason that they did not exist.

He was doing what he was, obviously, out of the most sordid motives, for paltry material gains—a better apartment, a fur coat for his wife, a vacation at an exclusive place, a privileged education and jobs for his children.

My interrogator was certainly not the worst of the lot. A doctor in camp, a prisoner like myself, told me that the hundreds of young women arriving from jails in the Western Ukraine bore the marks of their interrogator's boots, sometimes across their breasts, and sometimes over their pregnant bellies.

Major Porunov was most correct with me. I was never sent to a punishment cell. Only once did he hurl an obscenity at me. I was shocked, but presumed he did it simply to put down in the reports he handed to his superiors that he had resorted to that common "method" too. Only once did he make an offensive allusion to my nationality.

And this was at a time when in my cell I could hear strings of the typical Russian obscenities from the interrogation department on the floor below. At the top of their voices the interrogators yelled out at the prisoners the three-letter Russian word for the male organ, and it was always your mother this and your mother that—the supreme insult, dating back from the Mongol-Tartar invasion when the conquerors gloried in telling their Russian victims that they had raped their mothers. To my cell window was carried the venom slung at Jewish political prisoners: *Zhidovskaya morda*, beloved yell of the Black Hundreds and the Cossacks during the pre-revolutionary pogroms. And now it reached me from the lips of Soviet interrogators, with Communist Party membership cards firmly pinned to their breast pockets, next to their hearts. (The loss of a membership card could mean expulsion from the Party.)

Major Porunov was about my age, that is, in his mid-thirties. He was blond, ruddy, athletic, with a steely glint in his eyes, which at rare moments softened, perhaps suggesting the stirring of some scruples.

A man and a woman thrown together night after night for several hours at a stretch; there was some chemistry at work between us. Had it been a normal reality in which we found ourselves, and we met socially, we might have been attracted to one another. Instead we were trapped in a bizarre predicament from which there was no way out but for him to crush me and for me to meekly accept my fate at his hands.

The surveillance prosecutor in my case, Boyarinov, was a squat, formless man in his fifties, bullet-headed, with a small snout of a nose and scared eyes behind spectacles that were strangely askew, as was everything else about him. In sharp contrast to my interrogator, about whom there was a suave, leisurely air, the prosecutor was always tense, impatient, in a great rush.

And now too, sitting on the right-hand side of the interrogator's desk, a few yards away from the tiny prisoner's table, he was impatient to get it all over with. The accusation of "anti-Soviet agitation among friends," no matter how hard he and the interrogator endeavored to procure evidence to support it, hung in the air.

At this stage in the interrogation—and the presence of the prosecutor indicated that some decision was pending—the two men had to decide if it was to be pursued or not. Right there in front of me, they carried on a whispered conference. For all I knew, they might have decided beforehand to drop the charge, and I was now present at what legally could be termed an acquittal.

I was handed a bulky folder with a complete record of all the statements I had signed; this was in conformity with Article 206 of the Criminal Code. For more than an hour I sat perusing the depositions. There was no proof whatever of my guilt, no evidence to support it, no witnesses. The charges were utterly unfounded. I told myself that no court in any country of the world, even one where the worst lawlessness existed, could sentence me on the basis of it.

Breathing a sigh of relief, and well gratified with what I had read, I inquired: "Will there be a trial?" I had asked the question before, had indeed been turning over in my mind what I would say to the judges.

The answer was one I had already heard.

"Yes, of course, I hope you are prepared."

The interrogator was merely amusing himself at my expense. For all my naiveté, I knew I could not hope for release. Yet after I read the summary my spirits rose. Perhaps, I thought, I might be lucky enough to get a term of exile to a locality not far from Moscow. I suddenly recalled all the unfortunates I knew who for years had lived a hundred kilometers from the capital and had to sneak in, risking rearrest, to see their families and friends. I shuddered. It was a grave injustice. But people lived with it, accepted it.

"Am I correct in thinking that the charges of treason and anti-Soviet agitation against me have been dropped?"

"Yes," replied Major Porunov, smiling and looking into my eyes as though expecting to find in them gratitude for the credit due him.

He had been standing just a few steps away from me. Now he walked back to his desk, picked up a paper from it, and once again approached me.

"Read and sign this. It is the conclusion of your case. You are charged under Article 7, Section 35."

I failed at first to grasp the meaning of his words— until I read the conclusion. "The accused is charged with contacts with American and French intelligence agents." What insane grounds were there for this new charge? I could only speculate that my visit to the American Embassy with a tourist and my friend Vera Schwartz's liaison with the French Havas Agency correspondent were vaguely related to it.

I now came under a more mild political article as a "socially harmful element."

The interrogator stood over me with a benevolent smile.

"You are very lucky indeed to get off with this mild charge."

I hardly heard his words. So it was all over! There would be no trial. And I had been rehearsing speeches in my defense. What a fool I was to hope for justice.

It turned out that there was yet a third document for me to sign. After the prosecutor had waddled out of the office with his bursting briefcase, the interrogator took out of his desk a bundle of papers and placed them in front of him.

"I have here your personal papers, letters and photographs," Major Porunov said in a soft voice. "You will not need them where you are going," he purred. "You will not be allowed to take them with you, nor can they be returned to any of your family."

He rose from his seat and came as close to my prisoner's table as, I suppose, security permitted. "The usual procedure," he continued, "is for the prisoner to agree to the disposal of such papers."

A chill settled in my heart. The bundle on the interrogator's desk contained photographs and letters I treasured. But what did it matter now? What was the point in having regrets about mementos when my own life was finished?

It shocked me to hear the interrogator echo this very thought in the same honeyed tone into which he had suddenly lapsed.

"Your life is finished. It's all over for you. Forget the world you have been living in . . ."

"Dispose of everything as you please," I said indifferently, with an even stronger sensation than ever that all this was happening not to me but to another person.

Major Porunov returned to his desk and presently handed me a sheet titled "Affidavit of Burning." I signed it.

Years later I learned that it had been within my legal right to refuse to sign it. But prisoners were never apprised of an alternative. Whatever rights the prisoner had—and these were few enough—they were craftily concealed from him.

"I shall not be seeing you again. The interrogation is over."

IV Butyrki Prison

I found myself in the solitary confinement tower of Moscow's Butyrki Prison. Located on the outskirts, walled in from all eyes, far away from the Metro, Lefortovo was a top-secret prison; few were even aware of its existence. But Butyrki was well known to Muscovites as a place of detention for all criminals. In times of mass political arrests—in 1937 and 1938, and in the period beginning with 1947 right until Stalin's death—Butyrki was packed to overflowing with men and women charged with or convicted of political crimes.

With its scuffed but clean linoleum floor, fair-sized window, and freshly painted walls, my cell in this wing of the prison was quite cheerful compared with the gloom, chipped concrete, and damp of Lefortovo. The food was more palatable. The millet gruel and thick soup were inviting and savory after the herring-bone slops of Lefortovo, but ravenous as I was, there was no way I could get the oversized wooden spoon issued me into my mouth. How I struggled with it, poking sidewise, working in the tip! Having failed, I ended up lapping the prison fare with my tongue like a cat or dog. Humiliated and exhausted, I flopped down on the bunk and wept.

Next day I plucked up the courage to ask the warder for an aluminum spoon. He returned with a wooden ladle. It was small, and I was grateful.

With no books allowed, the hours, the minutes, even the seconds dragged interminably. The day seemed to stand still, confronting me with a mocking immobility, a leer. I had no idea that months later, in camp, I would think back wistfully to the peace and privacy of solitary confinement—and with regret that I had not diligently searched my mind for resources that could transform emptiness into motion and activity.

How could I not have seen, not valued the advantages of solitary confinement? Perhaps it was these gradual changes from bad to worse that enabled prisoners, in the long run, to adjust and survive in the bizarre world into which they were thrust.

Although the interrogation, according to Major Porunov, was supposed to have been closed, it was pursued sedulously during my solitary confinement. It appeared that "for lack of evidence" my case was returned from the prosecutor's office for further substantiation. I was interrogated about friends who had been apprehended in 1937 and 1938, all of whom, as the questions showed, were dead. My contacts with these "enemies of the people" were to be set down in my record as further proof that I was indeed a "socially harmful element." But there was yet another objective behind the nightly questionings: to extract compromising information about friends, co-workers, and acquaintances, even neighbors.

Major Porunov was getting impatient. His tone grew more menacing. Nervously he paced his office, demanding that I tell him what anti-Soviet thoughts my friends entertained, how they viewed the arrests. I must have heard them vilify Soviet literature and art. Such talk, he persisted, was common. My obstinacy would get me nowhere. There were hosts of other reports on what people I knew were saying.

"We trust nobody," he burst out.

Indulging in a bit of histrionics to break up the tedium of the almost six-hour nightly questioning, he let loose a spate of abuse against the intelligentsia.

"Take Moscow University professors. They are a political liability, undependable, traitors in the making."

After pausing to see what effect his words had on me, he continued: "We have on record the anti-Soviet sentiments of the intellectuals. They're rotten to the core, the whole lot."

I was shocked by what he said, knowing it to be a lie. Soviet intellectuals were dedicated, hard-working, though grossly underpaid compared to him with his high salary and the many privileges he enjoyed.

141

"We'll isolate them from the rest of society—in prisons and camps," he concluded, yawning and stretching himself.

I tried to put in a remark about the loyalty of the intelligentsia.

As though anticipating what I wanted to say, Major Porunov warned: "Don't attempt to whitewash the intellectuals. I want exposures, exposures only!"

For three months now I had been allowed no more than a half hour's sleep a night, and none whatever during the day. I often recalled the Russian proverb: "Sleep is more precious than a mother and father."

Choosing a moment when I felt most weary and had hardly any control over my drooping lids, he barraged me with questions about Merkurov. The sculptor was a big catch, and to obtain information that could discredit him would add a brilliant feather to my interrogator's cap.

"For your own good, you had better describe what anti-Soviet conversations you overheard at Merkurov's."

"I heard nobody talk against the Soviet system at his home."

"And Merkurov himself?"

"Never. He was most loyal in thought and deed."

"Don't imagine you'll get away with shielding that sly fox and his entire subversive household. I demand you tell the truth."

Whenever the word "truth" crossed my interrogator's lips, I squirmed in my prisoner's bench. Truth was as remote from him and the institution he represented as freedom and a normal life were from me.

"Why give a hang for Merkurov and his family, when *your* life is finished? You'll go to a camp from which you'll never come back." How often he reiterated these words, as though he derived satisfaction from the picture of urbanites like myself vegetating in the dark womb of Siberia.

"Forget the world you have been living in," he went on. "You are doomed, so why play the noble lady? Can you deny that anti-Soviet jokes were told by Merkurov, his family, and guests?"

"They were never told in my presence!"

Major Porunov lost his temper. "Who is Merkurov to you, that you are protecting him—a father? Look, he is enjoying his freedom, his women, the best of food, while you will rot away, lose your health, your child . . ." He stopped short and turned his head away. Did I witness some human stirring in him?

My eyes filled with tears. I was thinking of my little daughter, longing for her, fearing for her.

My interrogator had not subjected me to the torture by means of which lying accusations against their best friends were extracted from prisoners. I said nothing that could slur the loyalty of Merkurov or other friends.

Merkurov was indeed a dear person to me; he had time and again reinforced my faith in the goodness of human nature. I loved him for what he was, a man of talent and resourcefulness, a highly successful artist who never looked down his nose at another human being. I loved the tickle and French scent of his graying beard when he kissed me, as he did every friend on greeting and parting.

I could imagine what fat dossiers the MGB kept on Merkurov and other prominent artists. And although I provided no ''evidence'' against him, so perverse were the practices of the Stalinist security police that for a person facing grave political charges to speak highly of Merkurov could in itself be compromising for the sculptor.

Death, however, outwitted the security police. A few months after I was interrogated, for several nights running, about him, Merkurov passed away from a heart attack.

V Cellmates, a poem

From the solitary confinement tower at the top of the Butyrki Prison I was moved to a cell on the second floor at the end of a long wide corridor with tiled walls and a red linoleum floor. Stone at Lefortovo, parquet at Lubyanka, linoleum at Butyrki.

The cell was in a part of the prison that seemed to possess the acoustics of the Bolshoi Theater. It was resonant with sounds I welcomed happily after the muteness of solitary confinement. There was the jangling of the keys on a huge ring snapped to the warder's belt, when prisoners were escorted to and from questioning; the clatter of aluminum cauldrons, trundling back and forth in the prison hallways; even the trilling of birds departing to warmer climes. Outside a large window with a grate I caught sight of a few russet leaves and heard them being swished off the trees by gusts of wind.

It is astonishing how the little attributes of civilization, like a tea kettle, give one a sense of belonging to the human race. That is why, I mused, sitting down at the well-scrubbed wooden table in the middle of the cell, such pains are exerted to deprive the prisoner of the utensils, the technology, that played so important a role in man's transition from the brutal to the human state. Back to the brute, to the dumb animal—that was the strategy employed against the political prisoner.

It was a long time since I had seen or heard anyone speak, apart from my interrogator. Now the sight of several women sitting around the table and chatting warmed my heart. After asking a few of the usual questions directed at newcomers, the prisoners picked up the thread of their interrupted conversation.

I was astonished to catch the name of a well-known writer whom I had frequently seen at the bookkeeping office of the Soviet Information Buro during the war, when he dropped in to collect fees for articles. I remembered him as a man of unstriking but pleasant appearance and a rather happy-go-lucky air, which contrasted sharply with the harried, preoccupied look we all had during the war, or the glum, dour Ilya Ehrenburg who also dropped—rather swept—in, to cavil over the English equivalent of a word or sentence in his crisp style and have it out with the translators. The wife of the writer my fellow-prisoners now mentioned was a tight-lipped, sharp-featured Moscow Art Theater actress, who had made a brilliant career for herself. He himself had risen to the position of General Secretary of the Soviet Writers Union, which gave him power over the lives of many of his confrères—and not them alone.

"Yes, it was the Writers Union's General Secretary who turned them in, " said one of the prisoners.

"Are you sure?" asked another doubtfully.

"She herself will tell you!" The speaker pointed to a swarthy woman in her sixties, but the subject was dropped. The prisoners' animated chatter died down; a brooding silence settled in its stead. The women sat spiritlessly, each a prey to her own dismal thoughts.

I now eyed the dark-complexioned prisoner. She was small and hump-backed, apparently a cripple from birth. Her face was deeply creased and weather-beaten, yet with a dignity and hauteur that intrigued me. Dusky Russian faces mostly suggested Mongolian or Tartar ancestry. The mold of her features, however, was distinctly European, and I attributed her swarthiness to perhaps a strain of gypsy blood. That she had been a migrant most of her life I was soon to learn from Maria Alexandrovna herself.

Bit by bit, I was able to form an opinion of this woman's fate and character. When, after a three-hour nightly interrogation, she was led back into our cell by the prison guard, I was startled by the transformation in her; her eyes blazed with a mystical, almost joyous light, her hollow cheeks burned, and she held her head so high over her dumpy body that it half-concealed her hump. She was as elated and triumphant as a player who had swept all the stakes off the gambling table. This change puzzled me.

It was not until days later, when I had seen her arrive after each questioning in this very exhilarated mood, that I hit on an explanation for her irrational behaviour. Of course, it could well be said that our entire existence was irrational. I realized that what gave Maria Alexandrovna this uplift was that for once in her life her person counted for something. She was happy for a relief from her drab and wretched existence—even if it was happening in prison and would surely end in her conviction.

At last there was someone willing to listen to her views and her life story, who indeed hung on her every word. The feeling that she was a somebody after all gave Maria Alexandrovna this moment of exaltation.

With the interrogator she could talk about everything and everybody. She held forth on her beloved poet Nadson, and he was ready to discuss him with her.

"I'm a pessimist like Nadson," she told me. "I cannot conceive of any thinking person not being one." It was from her own lips that I heard her story, which she had also told at different times to other cellmates.

Maria Alexandrovna came of a well-known St. Petersburg family. I knew her surname—Lopukhina—to have been common among the old Russian nobility. About her face and whole being, notwithstanding her deformity, there was a touch of arrogance and pride that could well suggest aristocratic origins. Her sister had been a celebrated beauty and a maid-in-waiting at the Imperial court. According to Maria Alexandrovna, she herself was the least educated and pampered in the family; she was the ugly duckling.

She trained for a nurse and served with the Red Cross during World War I. A brief liaison with an army surgeon had resulted in the birth of a son. Maria Alexandrovna had been a nurse in World War II as well. But for most of their lives she and her son were homeless, half-starved derelicts. They were not idlers; they worked hard for their living. Having never acquired "housing space," and not being able to afford to rent even the tiniest living quarters privately, they roamed from town to town, penniless migrants taking whatever job came their way. "We were really gypsies," Maria Alexandrovna said. And for this reason it had taken the security police two years to fall on their tracks.

In their misery the pair clung to one another. Perhaps from his mother, the son had inherited a love of poetry, and soon he thought himself a poet. It was their undoing. He wrote a poem ridiculing Stalin. Maria Alexandrovna knew this and other of her son's poems by heart. But we did not want to hear them. It would have been dangerous even to listen to anything that denigrated Stalin. However, she managed to recite the first two lines. If I can trust my memory, they ran something like this: "A Georgian pauper sits on the Russian throne, / To throat-cutting, treachery, and torture prone."

This poem, written in his own handwriting and consisting of about fifty lines, the son had mailed to the influential head of the Writers Union, its General Secretary. He sent it anonymously, giving no intimation of his address. (He had none.) The poem was directed to the secret police and they did not rest content until they had traced the handwriting to the proper source. Both the son and the mother were arrested.

To trust the Secretary of the Writers Union with anything as self-indicting as a poem vilifying Stalin was a mad thing to do. And the interrogator had indeed tried to prove that Maria Alexandrovna's son was insane. For this reason he spent hours discussing both their lives with her. The interrogator knew he was expected to show that only a mentally deranged person could dare to blaspheme against "the greatest genius of mankind." Not that it absolved the prisoner of responsibility: he would be sentenced (Maria Alexandrovna herself received ten years) without the least clemency and ordered, perhaps, to be locked up in one of the psychiatric huts of which the infirmary-camp compounds were full.

A different kind of inmate was a round-faced, pink-cheeked girl with long amber braids. She was the same age—not yet sixteen—as I had been when I was expelled from Baron Byng High School. Her name was Galya Smirnova.

Galya was one of only a few persons I met for whose incarceration there was at least a pretext. She had attended a single gathering of an incipient children's organization joined by a few brave school kids whose parents were serving terms or had been shot for so-called political crimes. Over a period of no more than a few months these teenagers met in utmost secrecy, in small groups.

They were soon tracked down by the secret police, arrested, brutally interrogated, and sentenced to long terms. The organization was called Leninskiye Krylya (Lenin Wings) and it opposed in words only—not even in the actions for which I had been arrested in Montreal, such as the distribution of leaflets and participation in demonstrations—Lenin's ideals to Stalin's repressive policies. The organizer of Leninskiye Krylya was a boy called Felix. He was sentenced to be shot; later the sentence was commuted to twenty-five years. Though released a few years after Stalin's death, these children were never cleared of their crimes, as were other political prisoners, and have had to suffer the cruel consequences.

To keep up their spirits, my cellmates would think up all kinds of rumors, like pending amnesties, pardons on important revolutionary holidays, and other nonsense. Superstitions were rife. If you spilt water while pouring it from a kettle, a calamity was in store for you, which could indeed be. If you were called for interrogation on a Monday, an unlucky day, you could expect the worst. And so it went, on and on. Dreams were swapped every morning and diligently searched for omens. New inmates arrived with fresh rumors.

One of the strangest myths afloat at Butyrki had to do with Fanya Kaplan, the woman who had fired a shot at Lenin in 1918. Two or three prisoners I met insisted that she was alive. They assured me they had been in the same cell with women who swore they had actually seen Fanya when she was taken out for walks in the Butyrki prison yard. Some described her as a wispy, half-crazed woman; others said she looked well, adding that, needless to say, in prison you stood a better chance of surviving, even of looking well-preserved, than in the brutal conditions of the camps.

Yet it was well known that Kaplan was executed directly after her unsuccessful attempt on Lenin's life. Prisoners argued that Lenin had ordered her life to be spared; she was given a life sentence; Lenin had not wanted capital punishment for her since, after all, he had not paid with his life. That may well be true, but she was shot all right.

How can the prison legend that Fanya Kaplan was alive be explained? I know how astonished I was when it was told to me—yet I gladly accepted it as the truth, against my better judgment. I can only ascribe this to a kind of wishful thinking.

We clutched at every straw, every shred of hope. If Lenin had ordered that Fanya Kaplan's life be spared, it was because he was human. Lenin epitomized the best in the Soviet society. He could show mercy. A human heart beat in his breast. Therefore the prisoners, practically all of them totally innocent, could hope for clemency, for a general pardon. The arrests were a mistake, but after a while things would be set right again. The Soviet system was a humane system.

VI My sentence is read to me

There was no trial. My sentence was read out to me in a small elevator at the Lubyanka Prison by a major in an immaculate uniform who was the same height and looked about the same age as my interrogator. He was my last encounter with the world from which I was shut out; he smelt of fragrant soap and freedom.

He had an Armenian's hatchet face, with dark hair brushed back from a frowning forehead, and a petulant blur of a mouth. In his well-cared-for hands he clutched a folder. Hastily he opened it. It was full of loose sheets of paper. After riffling through them impatiently and finding what he needed, he reeled off the words:

"In the name of the Union of Soviet Socialist Republics you are sentenced by a Special Board to five years' imprisonment to be served in the corrective labor camps."

"Five years!" It was a harsh blow. "For what?"

The elevator kept creaking in its upward or downward course—I did not know which. The major now honored me with a glance in which I read a mixture of astonishment and annoyance. He had almost stumbled over the word "five" when he read out the sentence. Later I understood why: because five years was an unusually short sentence—a "kindergarten term," the prisoners called it. And so instead of being shocked, I suppose the major expected me to jump for joy.

Slowly the elevator pulled to a stop. With a squeamish sniff as though I were a leper and he had sullied himself by contact with me, the major drifted out, never turning his head or giving me a second glance. A few minutes later I found myself in the paved Lubyanka courtyard. I was the sole passenger in a black maria. Five years! The knowledge that Soviet political prisoners' sufferings did not end with the termination of their sentence heightened my despair.

The faces of Victor and Mikhail hovered before my gaze in the black emptiness, between the bench I occupied and the one across from me. Victor was long dead. And Mikhail? How many people had emerged alive from the clutches of the security apparatus? Practically none.

I felt remorseful. All too easily I had put both these men I loved out of my mind. Life must go on, I told myself. And now, as though in a kind of retribution, life had stopped for me. Never had I imagined that I too would be arrested. I had been so careful, so circumspect, trying never even to think thoughts that might be construed as disloyal to the regime, let alone articulate them.

Seeing so many people around me mowed down by the security machine, the one thing I dreaded and wished to avoid was their fate. Why is it that we never believe the misfortunes befalling others could overtake us? Blindly I hoped not to share the fate of Victor and Mikhail and the millions of others of whom, in my selfishness, I had tried not to think. And now I was in the same boat—though not quite, for I was not going to be shot. I would live, hateful as that life might be.

The black maria pulled up in front of the Butyrki Prison. Once inside the building we did not have far to go. The guard who escorted me paused in front of a huge door on the ground floor. In a matter of seconds I found myself in a cell for the convicted. I saw before me about twenty women, noisy and agitated, with a dozen questions on the tips of their tongues—the same ones that greeted all newcomers. My mother was among them.

"What is your sentence?" were my mother's first words.

I told her.

"Good, *you* will survive."

I looked long at her. She had aged at least ten years. She was all skin and bones but still erect. My mother had beautiful hands, rather small for her height, and the fingers were not long but perfectly shaped. The hands were still lovely, white, smooth, unravaged except for the nicotine stains. I sat down beside her on the iron cot, the tears coursing down both our faces. And I took one of her hands into mine. It fitted snugly in my clasp. As I stroked it, pity for her and impotent rage against our persecutors stuck in my throat.

She told me that with her, too, the charge of espionage had been dropped, but not the accusation of ''anti-Soviet agitation among friends.'' It was on the strength of the evidence provided by her boss Pavlov, at the cartography department for which she worked, that she was convicted on this charge. During a confrontation with him at the interrogator's office, he repeated my mother's words: "I would go to Palestine if it were a socialist country." She did not deny them.

But the most painful part of her interrogation was the reference to her capture by General Denikin in Kharkov during the Civil War. "So, you say Denikin arrested you, sentenced you to death, and you got away?" the interrogator said. "Who is going to believe a cock and bull story like that?"

He rose from his seat and approached the corner prisoner's bench where my mother was sitting, yawned, offered her a cigarette, and lit it for her. Hungrily she took a quick draw.

The interrogator yawned again and in a voice of great boredom continued, "Even as early as that you embarked on your treacherous activities against Soviet power."

Another yawn. My mother did not suspect that he was merely asking routine questions, that it was all in the day's work. How could she know?

He was now working himself up into a frenzy—perhaps to keep from falling asleep.

"What did Denikin promise you?" he thundered. "Your freedom? In return for what? For becoming an Okhranka* agent?"

My mother ought to have perceived at once that it was all a comedy. Instead she took his words seriously. His cruel accusation cut her to the quick—she had herself many a time been a victim of the Okhranka agents—and she flung the burning cigarette into his face. A mistake! Perhaps a little thing like that cost her her life. The interrogator possessed great powers: the severity of the sentence could depend on him. And had she received a sentence of five years instead of ten, she might have survived and lived out her natural span of life.

My mother and I were among the thousands of close relations sentenced and deported to camps. Since prisoners were being perpetually moved from one prison to another, and from one overcrowded camp compound to the next, close relations, owing mostly to an oversight on the part of those who drew up the lists for transports, were almost bound to meet in the course of these peregrinations.

There were, however, express orders to avoid such encounters; if they occurred, separation was to be immediately enforced. And so it happened with my mother and myself. After spending only two days together in the cell for the convicted we were separated. We said goodbye, both of us wondering if it was forever. (It was not: several weeks later we met at the Taishet transit prison in Siberia.)

My sentence read clearly: "to be served in the corrective labor camps." But already, in the cell for the convicted, there were rumors that we would be going to camps quite different from those that came under the corrective labor system. We were held to be beyond redemption. In addition to our basic sentence, our punishment included complete isolation from society for life—even from the non-political prisoners, so that we would not contaminate them—and a speedy death. The "special" camps were a new penal institution, known as strict-regime camps—and that was where we were going, though we chose not to believe it.

The warder strode into our cell and, standing with his back to the door, yelled out names from a list.

"Get ready—pack your belongings. Quick!"

We guessed that we would be leaving Moscow. Despite all the fearsome talk about the "special" camps, most of us cherished the hope that life in camp would be more tolerable than in prison. In Lefortovo

* Secret police under the Tsar.

I was taken out for twenty-minute walks in a tiny yard with high timber walls around it, always alone, the guard either walking at my side or standing a few paces away; I never caught sight of another prisoner. At Lubyanka and Butyrki prisons these short exercise periods were denied me. I was starved for fresh air, for the outdoors, and above all for work. Outdoor labor would strengthen me physically, I thought. Having led a sedentary existence and engaged only in mental work, I would at last get a taste of physical labor. It would do me good.

The thoughts of other prisoners took the same course, for we could not imagine anything so destructive to the flesh and spirit as hard labor with continual exposure, sometimes for sixteen hours and more a day, to the biting frosts of Siberia in winter and the black swarms of mosquitoes in the short, scorching summers.

On the night of my arrest, apparently on instructions from my future interrogator, the two men who searched my home allowed me to pack a valise.

"Put in some warm things, you will need them," they said.

And now as we regained possession of our bags from the prison lockers, I saw that I had packed the elegant fall coat my friend Tina had made for me out of an old English blanket she had dyed black. It had a snug seal collar and cuffs.

Snow blew into our faces when we emerged into the prison yard. Tina's coat was poor protection against the winter blast, but for a brief moment it made me feel attractive and stylish.

Among the thirty or more prisoners jammed into the van were, to our great surprise, several men. They sat huddled together on a small bench against the wall of the driver's cabin. They hardly raised their heads or shifted position when we occupied the four benches across them, defeat staring out at us from every bend and curve of their crouched figures.

Like myself, many of the women in the van had arrested husbands. Did they look as crushed as these men? How I longed to talk to them, to ask questions! Perhaps one of them had shared a cell with my husband or heard from others about him, knew what accusations had been brought against him, what his sentence was . . .

"No talking! No communication of any kind between prisoners!" was our guards' strict injunction. And we sat in the van as mute as animals, averting our gaze from one another, ashamed of having been reduced to this state of submission. We had not the guts to utter a single word. None of us!

The prison van rumbled through the dark streets of the city. The guards sat at the windows. As we drove into Komsomolskaya Square the Kazansky Station, with its quaint oriental turrets and flaming colors, loomed from the shadows. Our van veered to the left, skidding into a pitch-black lane where a few railroad cars were shunted close to what I guessed to be the Yaroslavsky Station.

The faint gleam of the headlights illuminated the figures of the men sitting across me, shoulders sagging, thin legs crossed. What humiliation, what torture had been used to crush their spirit? I longed to breathe to them a few heartening words but, fearing to enrage the guards, tightened my lips. If we were not to move our lips, even in the semi-gloom we could still communicate with our eyes. This was how I conversed with one of the prisoners, very handsome, with a sensitive face, over which now passed a succession of thoughts whose meaning I endeavored to translate into words to myself. I too spoke to him with my eyes.

He may have been a few years older than I, but we were both of that age when sexual activity advances towards its apex. It must have been a long while since we had experienced or perhaps even thought of sex. Our mute communication had no room for sexual longing, yet it was illumined by a romantic thrill, an unrealistic hope for a meeting, a chance to get to know one another.

With our eyes we conveyed the need to maintain a philosophical detachment in our plight. Months later I received a verbal message from this fellow prisoner: "Remember the inscription on King Solomon's ring!" It was delivered by an imprisoned nurse on her return to our camp after work at a male sick bay. Knowing that my husband was arrested, she took it for granted that the message was from him.

Our van pulled up at a railway siding and hastily, in the black of the night, we were loaded into a train carriage with three tiers of bunks; on the next stages of our journey we would be packed into cattle cars. We were on the train for a few days. Every morning the guards brought in our food ration for the day: a loaf of bread and a dry salted herring. Water was given to us only once a day, in a slimy, rusty pail with a big jagged hole in it. There were no mugs: we drank the water directly from the pail, spilling much of it, so that soon the floor of the unheated carriage was covered with slippery frozen puddles. Many of the prisoners suffered from upset stomachs; those who had not managed to get a drink were tormented by thirst, while others who had had their fill of water had to cope with bursting bladders. We were allowed to go to the toilet only under escort and never more than twice a day.

Such treatment was calculated to break the prisoner's morale, add to his indignity. I vowed to myself never to eat herring, though it was the sole protein the prisoner could count on—and a very rare treat, as I was to learn later. Sometimes on these journeys I refrained from eating altogether, thus reducing to a minimum the shame of relieving myself like an animal in front of the guards.

The first stop was the big city of Kuibishev on the Volga; our destination, as it turned out, was southeastern Siberia. At Kuibishev too we got off the train at an obscure sidetrack, away from the city and all eyes. We were brought into a common cell packed with about five times as many people as it could hold. There were no bunks, and several dozen women huddled on the floor, knees brought up to the chin, shoulder to shoulder, body crammed against body. How we squeezed in I cannot say, but we did.

At Kuibishev I was for the first and only time thrown in contact with people convicted on non-political charges. Soon after the war a number of harsh laws had been promulgated. One was a penalty of seven years for minor thefts, such as stealing a loaf of bread, a bushel of potatoes, or a small bag of flour. Strict laws against abortion also were enforced. Among the prisoners was a gynecologist, a mother of three, who had succumbed to the pleas of a cousin to perform an abortion. The cousin could not stand up against questioning by the police and gave away her benefactor. She now sat rocking back and forth, shaking with sobs, and repeating, "What will become of my children?"

Novosibirsk, one of the rapidly growing Siberian cities, was our next stop. Here again we arrived at a sidetrack, well hidden from the local inhabitants. The prison and transit quarters were so overcrowded that a few of us were locked up in the strict disciplinary shed. I shared the back part of this ice-cold shed with the wives of three top Leningrad Party bosses who, five years after the war, had been confronted with the insane charge of having made secret advances to Hitler and had been shot.

Outdoors it was minus thirty degrees centigrade. The wooden structure in which we were confined, with half-decayed rafters for a ceiling and just one platform of naked boards, raised about a foot above the floor, to serve as bunks, was unheated. We slept huddled against one another to keep from freezing to death. I removed my Moscow sealskin hat and tucked my cold feet into it; in the morning I found that my hair had frozen to the wall. I was to see the three companions with whom I shared the platform bed in Novosibirsk many times, later, because the four of us were bound for the Taishet camps.

They were Anna Bubnova, wife of the former chief of the Leningrad security police; Popkova, married to the editor of *Leningradskaya Pravda*; and Anna Vasilyevna Voznesenskaya, the first, long-abandoned wife of Voznesensky, rector of Leningrad University. Popkova, a tiny, homely woman, retired into her shell and hardly communicated with us at all. Anna Bubnova, on the other hand, gabbed incessantly. To me she kept saying: "I cannot understand it! The men who came to arrest me stuffed their briefcases with my foreign lingerie. What would my husband have said to that?"

Anna Bubnova was in her early forties, a robust, well-fed, handsome woman. I had noticed that prisoners who had been connected with the security bodies were better treated by the camp bosses than the rest of us. No sooner did she find herself in camp than she managed to avoid hard physical work and got a trusty's job. She was put in charge of a small sewing shop that made clothes for the camp administration and their families.

Considerably older than Anna Bubnova and of very frail health, Anna Vasilyevna was to go along with me on the general labor assignments, determined to show in camp what a good and loyal citizen she was. With all her strength and all her heart she would haul her end of the heavy logs balanced on our two shoulders, from the felling site—and she did not survive. But all this happened months later, when we met at a Taishet camp.

It was in the same cattle car in which we travelled from Kuibishev to Novosibirsk that we continued our journey to the strict-regime camps dotting the territory between Taishet and Bratsk, where later rose the pride of Soviet industrial complexes, the Bratsk Power Station. These camps were known as Ozerlag, the Lake Camps—a pretty name. But since we had long been living in a topsy-turvy world, we knew that words did not mean what they said, that like ideas they could be twisted and distorted out of all proportion.

VII Taishet, Ozerlag

At the transit camp of Taishet, in the heart of the Siberian forest belt, I was cheered by the sight of open spaces. Fresh air at last! The buffeting of the harsh Siberian gales made me feel alive again. My mood of despair snapped.

Thousands of prisoners had now been herded into Taishet, in barracks so congested that many had to sleep on the ice-cold floor under the two-tier bunks. From here, after being equipped with proper clothing to enable them to work without freezing to death, they were sent on to the Ozerlag Taishet camps. The clothes consisted of padded cotton jackets, lined pants, cumbersome oversized felt boots, footrags, and caps with earflaps, all of which had belonged to army conscripts and been written off as unwearable. The threadbare, sweat-smelling garments made the women prisoners look like scarecrows.

And yet it was not easy to transform once beautiful and cultivated women, as many of the prisoners were, into drab, downtrodden slaves. With all their resourcefulness, the imprisoned women struggled to retain some semblance of their former selves. They managed to conceal little pieces of colored cloth for scarfs or belts, and with these "touches" relieve the ugliness of their uniforms. They tried to keep clean and neat. It was a pathetic battle for their humanity and femininity.

When my turn came to change into prison clothes, along with three other young women from Moscow, I had an unexpected stroke of luck in the person of Colonel Grebelsky.

"Allow me to introduce myself: Colonel Grebelsky," the prisoner in charge of the transit-camp wardrobe announced with a chivalrous air. His manner was so very courteous that I half-expected him to say, "Nice to see you here."

Colonel Grebelsky! The name was familiar to all who read the newspapers during and shortly after the war. Whenever foreign visitors or allied commanders arrived in Moscow, the newspapers noted, "the distinguished guests were welcomed at the airport by Colonel Grebelsky and other officials of the Ministry of Foreign Affairs."

"The camps around Taishet were built and lived in by Japanese prisoners of war," Colonel—or rather, convict—Grebelsky told us. "The Japanese government sent their prisoners fine overcoats. A few have been left behind. They're as warm as toast, and certainly more suited to pretty women like you than ragged soldiers' jackets."

That is how I came by this treasure—a coat so roomy that it served as a soft bed and blanket by night and kept me warm during the dreary Siberian winters. I was questioned about this coat by our overseers and warders. Was it my personal property? No, it was prison issue. No matter how envied I was, especially by the women warders, it could not be taken away from me. On the back of the coat I sewed a gray cotton number patch, and another on the knee of my snow pants.

My Moscow clothes went back into my suitcase. I put on the Japanese coat, the decaying pants, and the crude felt boots, one two or three sizes too big, the other even larger, and both intended for the same foot. I was all set for a work detail: I was handed a shovel to clear camp paths.

Blue shadows swayed across the darkening snow. Never have I seen such beautiful skies as in Taishet, always in a dramatic upheaval of some sort, turbulent, alive. And now the sky reeled with clashing shades and colors, from a blaze of vermilion to bands of amethyst and crimson. It was good to be outdoors. I looked around at my partners and did not know whether to laugh or cry.

They were the glorious warriors of the Wehrmacht, the generals' stripes distinctly visible along the outer seams of their threadbare trousers. Bundled up to protect themselves as best as they could from the frost, they had badly frayed mufflers wound around their heads and their feet were encased in sackcloth and newspapers.

The remnants of the German Reich! They were gaunt, cadaverous, hardly able to keep erect, drained of all their former arrogance. These pitiful, unmanly Germans were now smiling playfully at me, even admiringly, for apparently I still possessed the bloom and soft contours of womanhood. The sky turned a sinister purple. There was a phantasmagoric quality about the scene. I smiled back. I was, after all, a human being, and the ritual of returning a smile in a place where no one smiled recalled the fact to me. Dusk had fallen; after shovelling a path in the snow we were taken under guard to our respective barracks. This was my last encounter with male prisoners.

Next morning the women convicts were ordered to line up in front of the barracks. We formed a marching column of about three hundred in close ranks of five abreast. The infirm and elderly, among them my mother, composed the front rows. It was a gesture of mercy to allow the aged to set the pace. And as a further kindness, when they could no longer drag their feet and dropped in the snow from fatigue, as my mother did, they were assisted into a horse sleigh in which the guards and their dogs took turns resting.

The prisoners' march: columns of convicts trudging through the deep snows of Siberia, cutting a path for the mail coaches. How familiar the scene was to people raised on the Russian classics!

"Link arms! Close in!" the guards yelled. "One step out of the ranks and we shoot without warning."

We trudged along the banks of the Angora, its polished surface gleaming with silver and coral. Beautiful Angora, the Siberians fondly call this long and turbulent stream. It was a day of azure sky, flaming sun, and merciless frost.

We gasped for breath, hardly able to keep on our feet. The short

Siberian day waned. The black gun towers and sagging barbed-wire entanglements of a camp at last loomed into view. Cheered by the thought that shelter was close at hand, we quickened our step and all but broke into a trot as the gates opened to receive us, the new penal draft.

It had grown dark. We staggered into the gloomy wooden hut. Tiny wicks floating in oil were set alight with splinters. A fire was hastily started in the rude clay stove in the middle of the hut.

The few doctors among the prisoners immediately set to work. There were about ten cases of third-degree frostbite. My mother's was one of the worst. Her beautiful fingers were an ugly magenta color; the little finger on her left hand was charcoal black. When her turn came to be treated the flesh was cleared away, and there, jutting from the flat of the darkened hand, was the finger's ivory bone.

In the dim hut where everybody was milling around, lining up for the doctor's attention, or rubbing their hands and feet with snow, I averted my gaze from my mother's fingers. I must toughen. My mother understood. She did not approach me. Bartering her bread ration for some loose shag and a scrap of old newspaper to roll a cigarette, she retired to a hut for the aged and disabled.

Camp 022, of the Irkutsk Region in Siberia, where my mother and I were now domiciled, was one of the most brutal under the Ozerlag administration. Its inmates were resigned, listless creatures, their grimy jackets riddled with forest-fire holes hanging loose from scrawny shoulders and kept together with rag belts, their wizened faces hardly visible from under the gray winter caps; they seemed strangely amorphous, unsubstantial. Their sentence was twenty years of *katorga*, hard labor. It was painful to think that *katorga*, that horror of the tsarist regime, had been reintroduced by the Soviet government. "Assisting and abetting the enemy in wartime" was the charge. We landed in this camp because Ozerlag was overflowing with newcomers. Three planks of sleeping space per person!

It was December, 1950. But for us the clock had been set back many centuries. The primitive wooden shacks, the night buckets, the almost total absence of metal except for the guns, of water taps, of water itself, of radio and newspapers, the coarse oatmeal fed us three times a day—all spoke of an assault on our humanity. Civilization had slipped away, retreated into the shadows of the mind.

I was hitched to a sleigh, which I had to load in the forest with fallen wood. At that early phase in my camp life I could still see the humorous side of things. I was in my second incarnation! A draught horse! I almost snorted as I inhaled deep breaths of the invigorating air.

The moment of levity passed. Even the pine branches were too heavy for me to lift, let alone the logs. Among the other prisoners in the forest was Lilli Semyonova, youngest and most beautiful offspring of the notorious General Semyonov who tried to stop the Red Army from capturing Siberia in the Civil War and then fled abroad. His five grown children, three daughters and two sons, were in the Taishet camps, paying with sentences of twenty-five years for the sins of their father.

Lilli gave me a helping hand. Aware that I knew English, she addressed me in that language. Her English was flawless, as was her Russian, for she was born and reared among the White Guard émigrés in Harbin, China. Lilli, who worshipped her father, questioned me about mine.

I told her he was killed in the Civil War.

"Fighting on the side of the Whites, of course?"

"No, on the side of the Reds."

If in prison and during interrogation I felt I had been cast into a freakish world, this sensation was magnified a thousandfold in Taishet.

To preserve my grip on the normal world, I clutched at a straw. It was the beauty of the forest. The forest smells, the play of light and shadows were real. I thought what a perfect etching the interlacing of snowy boughs and dark bare twigs, with random patches of pale daylight, made. Perhaps it was this involuntary comparison of nature to art that recalled to me Renoir's full-length "Portrait of an Actress." Bluish-pink, translucent, so very sunny, it blotted out the insanity around me. As I often did later with other famous paintings, I strained my memory to recall in what museum and what hall I had seen it. I now remembered the walls in the Moscow Museum of Western Art where the Renoirs had hung and, too, how upset I was to learn that, along with other Impressionist paintings, they had been removed and the famous museum closed, a casualty of the policy to keep Western influences at arm's length from the Soviet people.

NINE

I Christmas Eve

The warped door gave way easily. I entered the hut for the disabled, where my mother was quartered, and edged forward into the shadows, groping my way between the sodden log wall and the double tier of plank platforms.

Midway I paused, surprised to see that women from other sheds were assembled here in small knots. The murk was pierced by the low flame of wooden splinters. Heads were bowed in prayer. In the group close to the door were a few Lithuanians, in another I recognized a Polish girl and a prisoner she called her aunt.

Now I recalled it was Christmas Eve. Inmates had chosen this hut for their clandestine service, because there was less danger of discovery by the jailors, who did not burst in as frequently on the aged as they did on the able-bodied work force.

The praying women were Catholics, mostly from Eastern Europe and the Baltic states. There was also a sprinkling of Russian Orthodox believers; many were peasant women wearing long black homespun skirts and handkerchiefs drawn low over their foreheads. They spent their days in the Disciplinary Barracks, locked up for refusing to work for the Anti-Christ, as they called the camp commandant.

My mother was sitting on the edge of the lower sleeping shelf, leaning against a support post. I sat down beside her. She kept silent, eyeing the praying inmates with a perplexed look.

"I could never turn to religion," she said after a while. "It would mean crossing out all of my past life."

We were too downhearted, too wary of stooges, to talk openly about anything or even dwell on our sad plight. An incautious utterance could bring great disaster upon us, add years to our term, if it were reported.

However, as she went on sitting, looking so fragile that it broke my heart, she added suddenly and with vehemence: "People like myself, who had such faith in the revolution and the justice it would bring to all, must go—die, in fact—to leave the stage to a new, entirely different breed of people."

Today I know how right she was.

The gong sounded for the head count. Hastily I left with the worshippers, who had extinguished the improvised candles and like myself were now struggling through the deep, shadowy snow to reach their sheds in time for the count. To be late could earn the guards' curses or a day in the punishment cell. When I got to the front of my shed, the women were just beginning to line up. I joined them in silence.

All camp regulations, I soon learned, were designed to demean the prisoners. One of the most abusive was the head count.

Gray clouds rode the leaden sky. A vicious ground wind kept blowing the snow from under my feet, momentarily piling it up on the flank of the column. I welcomed the drifts; they put a barrier between me and the patrolling jailors. I had already begun to foster in myself a detachment, a kind of protective armor.

When the count was over I breathed a sigh of relief—alas, prematurely.

"On your haunches!" rapped a guard who replaced the counting jailor.

We squatted, after a while forced by the cramps in our legs to plump down on the icy ground.

"Stand up! Stand!"

We remained standing, hoping this last command would finish the muster. We were wrong. There now followed the most dreaded order of all.

Several guards were parading up and down the column. They wore short sheepskin coats, warm, well-fitting felt boots, and fur-lined caps.

"Lie down! Face to the ground!" Their voices cut through the frosty air threaded by the gray vapors of our breath.

We lay prone. When the counting lasted that long and prisoners were ordered to lie in the snow, it was usually in retaliation for some misdemeanor or breach of prison rules. On that Christmas Eve we were kept in the humiliating position of prostrating ourselves before our jailors in reprisal for the few scattered religious services in the camp.

But, that very evening, the horror of the head count was offset by a happy announcement: it was our barracks' turn to go to the bathing-shed. Except for the snow outside, there were no washing facilities. I had not bathed now for several weeks, not since I left the Taishet transit camp.

Like other camp structures, the bathing-shed was a squat hovel made of ill-fitting timber. A few barrels packed with snow stood by the wall. These and the wash buckets were of wood. Hot bricks were dropped into the barrels to melt the snow. With wooden dips we drew the tepid water to wash ourselves.

Our prison clothes and underwear were sent out to be fumigated, and then there was yet another delousing measure, carried out by a male barber, a prisoner, with a lathered safety razor poised for action. The older inmates let him shave their armpits and pubic hair without a murmur. I recoiled and pleaded with him not to touch me. How relieved I was when he waved me aside.

"You could not pull that one off in a German camp," said Yulya, who was behind me and with whom I shared barracks in this camp, as I would in several more.

Later, when she was washing at my side, I noticed the scarred tissue of a big burn on the back of her hand.

"I spent two years in a German camp," said Yulya offhandedly, catching my questioning glance. "The hard work was killing me. One morning in the washroom I let the hot water run and kept my hand under the scalding flow till I was certain I had got a third-degree burn. My reward was a couple of days off work."

Strangely, I was less struck by the fact of self-mutilation than by the availability of a washroom, a tap, and running water in camp. They were amenities out of reach of most Siberians, even outside the barbed wire of a prison camp.

After our bath Yulya and I were sitting across from one another at the long bare table in our barracks, sipping hot water and dunking our bread in it. A few others joined us, among them a woman in her thirties. She coughed a great deal. In the bathing shed I had noticed how emaciated she was; with her, as with other inmates, hard work had resulted in a prolapse of the female organs so that they were nestled in between her legs like oversized testicles.

Proudly she told us she had been a German general's mistress: "He treated me like a princess!" She paused. "I got twenty-five years. It was worth it."

A ravishing long-haired blonde, known as the Countess, now emerged from the shadows and sat down at the end of the table.

"Twenty-five for one general, while I had a go at the whole blasted garrison and got away with a tenner," she bragged.

For once she avoided swear words. In the short time that she slept in our barracks, she would wake us up in the morning with a string of obscenities and round off the day with just as choice an outburst. Nimbly she jumped on the bench and let the huge, hand-knitted grayish-black shawl around her naked body slip to the floor.

"Look at me!" she said, stretching herself to her full height.

Her satin-skinned, pearly pink body, with firm, rosy-nippled breasts, was an apparition of female beauty as incongruous in the murk and stench of our shed as would have been a sparkling crystal chandelier had it suddenly materialized over our heads.

A mischievous twinkle came into her eyes.

"Hut warden," she cried, "get word to the commandant, I have some important information for him—political, mind you."

She gave us a wink. "Don't worry, I'm no squealer. That's my way of getting the commandant's attention. There's not a man who won't go to bed with me."

Prisoners who had been with her in the labor camps confirmed her boast. On arriving at a camp she would immediately lure the commandant with her beauty. She never worked, thus preserving herself while other prisoners withered and aged. To avoid scandal the seduced commandant would send her off to another camp where she fared just as well. But, as it soon proved to be the case, what had worked in the labor camps got her nowhere in the strict-regime camps.

The Countess, she told us herself, had been a hooker in the Odessa harbor area; most of her clients were the men who came ashore from foreign ships. Later she made herself agreeable to occupation officers, which landed her a charge of treason.

But most of the women I met in this camp were ones who had distinguished themselves as Soviet officers in World War II or served in the Medical Corps. Among them were a few Moscow doctors. One was still wearing an army greatcoat when I first saw her, because she had been picked up at a reunion of the regiment with which she had served during the war. She was a long-standing Communist Party member, greatly shaken by her arrest and fearful to the point of hysteria of the repercussions it might have on her only daughter and son-in-law. A few days before she was apprehended she had become a grandmother.

I noticed—and with good reason, I suppose—that survivors of the Nazi camps were less despondent than the rest of us, stronger in spirit and more optimistic about our plight. One of these was also a Moscow doctor, who now wished good luck to the Countess as she swept out of our barracks. This doctor, sentenced to twenty-five years, punctuated her story with little bursts of ringing laughter and ironic gibes.

At the very beginning of the war she found herself encircled by the enemy, was captured, and, after eighteen months in a German war-prisoners' camp, worked at a hospital in occupied Crimea. Four years after the war she was charged by the Soviet security police with poisoning Russian infants in wartime. For her, a Jew, to have escaped death in the Nazi gas chambers was in itself incriminating in the eyes of the MGB. Her name was Maria Anisimovna. Prisoners were drawn to her because of her sunny disposition. Through the whole period of my captivity I was fortunate to have her as a companion; I drew courage from her.

I had apparently just fallen asleep when I was awakened by the unbolting of the door. The Countess returned, escorted by a jailor.

Her tactics had failed. A "special" camp commandant knew the penalty for cohabiting with prisoners. Seeing what she was up to, he ordered her locked up in the punishment cell.

"Get into your clothes, quick, you whore," yapped the jailor.

She cast off her shawl; teasingly, trying the jailor's patience, she slowly began to draw on her prison dress over her naked body.

I noticed that the jailor kept glancing at his watch. I had not seen a watch or heard a clock tick for more than half a year, nor would I until my release.

The Countess left. I dozed off thinking of clocks, promising myself that if I was ever released and a free woman again, I would keep as many clocks in my home as I could, a promise I eventually fulfilled. What joy to sit back and listen to the ticking of a clock! Time spurs you to get things done, regulates your life and associations. You could be master of your time. In camp you served time.

From this state of half slumber I was jolted into full consciousness by a sudden commotion. A prisoner from the camp office had arrived and was calling out names. We were leaving the *katorga* camp. Luckily my mother and I were on the same draft.

Two hours later a warder arrived: "Pack your things!"

In the middle of the night! Night was the favorite time of the state security system: arrests after midnight, nocturnal interrogations, cattle cars shunted to remote, shadowy sidetracks for the loading and unloading of prisoners, convoys of transports by night from camp to camp.

Disentangling myself from the mass of wasted bodies and gray rags on the upper shelf, I slipped down onto the damp plank floor. I took a last look at the sleeping unfortunates with whom I had spent a month in the same shed. Nightmarish creatures, ageless as though in death. The woman who had been sleeping pressed to my right side opened her eyes. Empty eyes, creased gray skin, gray rags covering her. No word, no whisper escaped from her. The *katorga* women! Meek, sexless, mouths opening only at mealtime. I never heard their stories. Their lips were sealed with terror.

II I part with my mother

Transports were the blight of the prisoner's existence. In fact, prisoners tried one hoax after another to dodge postings to new camps. They rarely succeeded, but if they did, the game was worth the candle, because it meant staying on in a place where you had already spent a few months or years, acquired friends, learned to cope with the conditions. It was change, the unknown, that was most dreaded.

The policy of the administration was to keep prisoners on the move from one camp to another, one desolate part of the land to the next, to increase the rootlessness of their lives. Normality, accustomed ways of thinking and understanding, the world as we knew it, had been knocked out from under our feet. There was, as I saw later, a vagueness and impermanence to our existence. Did we exist at all?

But at the start of camp life, with little experience to go by, the prospect of change was not at all frightening. It was therefore with a sense of relief that I left behind me the *katorga* camp and its almost four hundred mute and passive inmates. Surely, I told myself, in that camp we hit the bottom of despair, and now we could look forward to more tolerable conditions of captivity. But I was mistaken. In the new camp I came as close to my end as I ever would, and, moreover, was compelled to make the bitterest choice of my life—between survival and separation from my mother.

Our transport arrived at Camp 032 in the early morning, long before reveille. Searchlights from the guntowers swept the compound, revealing a landscape no different from the one we had abandoned the night before. There were the same smoke-blackened shanties, huddled against the icy ground, as in Camp 022. Inside were the familiar two-tier sleeping platforms and barred windows, the same stench rising in vapors from the wooden bucket that served as a latrine after the prisoners were locked up for the night. But the inmates proved to be somewhat sturdier, less resigned, of a tougher fiber, sullen but not silent.

That very morning we were rushed to the medical hut. Behind a table in a tiny office sat Major Golovko, one of the Ozerlag medical officers; "the worst bastard of the whole lot of free doctors," I heard him called. After giving my naked body a glance from under a pair of grizzly eyebrows, the major muttered to a clerk who stood at his side: "First Category." This work category, dreaded by all prisoners, pronounced me fit for the hardest physical labor.

I was assigned to a tree-felling team. A few months later, when I suffered from badly inflamed varicose veins and was running a temperature, I had a second encounter with the major. Every step I took was agony. I hoped for at least one day off after working non-stop on the felling-site for weeks. No chance. The major was sitting hunched over the table. As at the medical commissioning, he hardly looked up. His stubbly cheeks and purple nose contrasted sharply with his immaculate tunic and shining army boots, looked after by a prisoner who had the good luck to be his servant.

He dismissed me impatiently: "Everybody around here runs a temperature and all women who carry babies have varicose veins."

I rejoined the column of about a hundred and fifty prisoners ready to start on a four-mile tramp to the forest.

"Heads down! No talking!" Meekly we lowered our heads—which we would have done anyway, to avoid the sting of the wind—and we were certainly not inclined to chat. In fact, I noticed that whole days would pass without any of us exchanging even a few words.

Our column heaved forward, straggling through almost waist-deep snow, cutting a path for the convenience of the free lumberjacks and the few vehicles that would follow in our tracks later that morning. We were the human snow-ploughs.

Day in and day out of that long winter I plodded to and from the felling-site. Never on these marches did I catch sight of a human being or an animal, hear any other sounds but the commands of the guards and the snarling of their dogs. How foolish I had been to think that camp would be more tolerable than prison. In prison my mind worked; here my brain and spirit had become numb. In prison you were not as cut off from the familiar world as you were in camp. The warders who brought the smell of normal life, the hateful prison itself, the cells and corridors, the flagstone stairs of Lefortovo, the parquet floors of Lubyanka, were part of the civilized world you knew. But in camp there were only the hostile elements.

My survival now depended on learning to fell the towering pines and larches of the Siberian forest. How could I, when I had never in my life done any hard physical work? I could not even keep the saw moving at a proper angle. My partner, Adele Hermann, was a young German who had worked as an interpreter at Nazi army head-quarters on Soviet territory. She was about my age, her black eyes and bird-like face recalling Goebbels. Adele had the bizarre advan-tage over me that, raised in the Hitler Youth, she had been well trained in outdoor life and sports.

She wielded well both the crude hand bow-saw and the axe. Her movements were smooth and rhythmic, while mine were jerky and forced. The saw kept slipping out of my hand, and I cursed myself for my clumsiness. Fortunately Adele was very patient with me—though, as the German prisoners roused the animosity of the others, she would not have dared to utter a word of reproach even if she wanted.

My attitude to the forest changed. I abhorred its lofty indifference, its ceaseless mocking murmur. Danger lurked in every falling tree. If you miscalculated the direction in which the sawed tree would descend, you could be trapped into death. There had already been a few casualties.

For my poor performance I was on a penalty ration and hungry most of the time. But on returning to camp I could not drag myself to the feeding hut for my half-bowl of oatmeal. It was a battle between hunger pangs and aching muscles. Often I found my mother waiting for me. It was miserably cold in my barracks and I was glad to see that she wore, under her prison uniform, a long brown knitted coat, bought many years before in Canada. Despite the strict orders to leave all personal belongings for safekeeping in the store-room until our release, she had somehow managed not to part with this coat. Her cold hands were tucked into its capacious sleeves.

Silently she handed me her day's portion of bread, which I devoured unashamedly, knowing that the bread I ate was the sole means of her obtaining tobacco, without which life was a torture to her.

Sheer physical exhaustion was paralyzing my will to live, to retain the most elementary human habits. With no water available, we never washed the aluminum spoon with which we ate but licked it clean. I had even ceased to do that, stopped washing myself in the snow or removing my work clothes. Still wearing the sodden padded snow pants I had on in the forest I would climb up to my upper shelf and before I knew it fall into a deep sleep. At five in the morning, at reveille, I awoke unrefreshed, aching all over and filled with self-disgust.

"I know the signs," Yulya said to me. "You can't last much longer unless you're taken off the logging team."

"I don't see how that can be done," I said.

"I do. Your mother's fine knitted coat is the answer. I could tempt a trusty with it and you might be put to lighter work."

Yulya's words brought me out of the stupor in which I had now been going about for weeks. Take away my mother's coat? I could never do that! And the trusties? A privileged caste set above the other prisoners. I wanted nothing to do with them.

Soon we were squelching through the mud beneath the absurdly hot Siberian sun. Spring brought two rumors to the camp. One was that women prisoners in future would not be employed as loggers and ditch-diggers. Another concerned the launching of "Communist Hydro-Electric Projects." One of these would be the Bratsk power station, on the fringe of the Ozerlag territory. To supply it with insulation material, a mica factory was being opened close to Camp 027. It would be staffed by prisoners.

"There are bound to be drafts from the surrounding camps to 027," Yulya, always well up in camp affairs, said. "Mostly of young prisoners with good eyesight. You certainly stand a chance."

Shortly afterwards we learned from prisoners who worked in the camp office that lists for a transport to Camp 027 were being drawn up. I knew I must go and talk to my mother at once.

Her face lit up when she saw me. Did she know what I came to talk about? She looked more spectral than the other women, who also were in their late sixties. But her voice was clear and sonorous as she lapsed into her lifelong habit of rhetoric.

"The dark ages have descended on Russia," she declaimed.

I half listened to her words, trying to sort out my thoughts and to quench my anger at the choice I was forced to make. Deep down in my heart I nursed a resentment against her. Had she not, with the communist dream that brought her to the Soviet Union, got us into this trouble?

She smoothed a scrap of newspaper, dropped into it a few grains of coarse tobacco, and rolled a cigarette.

"I know what you came to talk about," she said softly. "I know, too, that your mind is made up. Yes, you must not miss the chance. By all means go to the mica camp. It's for the best."

It was far too painful to pursue the conversation. I cut short my visit and quickly left. My barracks was abuzz with the excitement of the coming draft. I could hardly believe that my lumberjack days would soon be over. But the price exacted—the cruelty of having to part with my mother—filled me with remorse. Tired as I was that night, I could not sleep. My mother's face, the lips compressed to hold back her tears, stood before my eyes.

III The need for love

It was a relief to work indoors, to sit on a bench with my elbows resting on one of the eight long plank tables arranged in two rows across the width of the factory barracks. With a short-handled blunt knife I broke loose the rock crystals and then split the mica into feather-light laminae with a long sharp one.

We worked in two shifts of one hundred and fifty women each and trudged six miles a day to and from the factory. Splitting mica was child's play compared to logging. It was absorbing work and we loved it. As with deft piercing motions I cleaved the mica, the flakes on my left-hand side grew into an iridescent mountain. I was tantalized by the mica's rainbow hues. Time flew. After our shift of ten hours I would have liked to stay on and work at the factory rather than return to the congested barracks, with its barred windows, frequent searches, and rude intrusions by the jailors.

Mica made life bearable for us in other ways too. We now saw less of the guards and jailors. They brought us from the camp and took us back. But for the duration of the shift we "belonged" to the factory manager and forelady, from whom we never heard an unkind word. These two may have been ex-convicts, as were many of Siberia's inhabitants. For this reason, perhaps, they addressed us as one human being to another, although they were scared to ask any personal questions or show the least interest in us apart from our work.

Since we no longer felled trees and battled with the elements, the three bowls of oatmeal, along with our bread ration, sufficed to still our hunger. I had begun to give thought to my appearance. Not being one of the fortunates to receive the rare food parcels allowed from home, I begged my friend Yulya for a little butter. Rather than eat it, I nourished the skin of my face with it. Yulya also presented me with a toothbrush. I worked it vigorously to strengthen my scurvied gums; my teeth were loose and a few had already fallen out.

Not for a moment did we forget the lawless and brutal way in which the state had treated us. And yet it was a comfort to know that we were engaged in useful work. The mica laminae we split would help to electrify Siberia. An existence devoid of reason and purpose, I found, was what human beings dreaded most.

The camp bosses were well aware of how we felt about mica and kept threatening us with postings to Kolyma, and other camps, if we did not increase our output. But hard as we tried, we could not meet the inflated quotas. Before long, sad days came upon us again.

The food was almost impossible to eat or digest. Gone was the oatmeal gruel to which I had grown used and even ate with relish. The soggy rye bread too had vanished. Instead we were given a bitter skilly of unripe corn and unleavened greenish bread baked of the same corn. The bread was bitter and crumbled before you could stuff it into your mouth. The camp had run out of water. We drank last winter's supply of melted snow, odorless, with a cloying sweet taste.

All summer through we worked with no days of rest, leaving the camp at dawn and returning at dark. At the head count we were plagued by black flies, which swarmed in dark dense clouds over our heads. Because of these biting pests the windows of the unventilated factory remained closed. Like pads of jet moss, the flies stuck to the panes, blocking out the daylight. The silicate haze was thicker than ever and we choked and coughed.

There were several deaths. Prison doctors who performed the autopsies told us they were blinded by the glint of the dead organs, so heavily coated with iridescent mica dust were they. And we came up against strange ironies. Two prisoners alone of our shift succeeded in filling the mica quota; the rest of us lagged far behind. These two were as different in background, education, and convictions as any two human beings could be. One was a tense, emaciated woman of forty who had a Ph.D. degree in philosophy. Before her arrest she was a lecturer in Marxism-Leninism at the Leningrad University. The other was Lilli Semyonova, with whom, after our first meeting in the forest, I stayed in the same camp for almost two years. Coached by fine tutors in languages and music, she knew nothing of the theory of Marxism-Leninism, while her acquaintance with its practice was derived from prison and camp alone. These two were our "labor heroines."

At the end of the summer I was tormented by a rash; my chest was covered with itchy bleeding sores. I went to the medical section. The same major who had ordered me back to the felling-site when I could hardly walk or keep on my feet was in charge. He pronounced the sores to be eczema.

A fortnight later we were at long last granted a day off work. A blessed Sunday all to ourselves. We could rest our aching bodies. Daylight streamed through the barred windows of the barracks, replacing the gloom of months. What luxury it was to be able to lie down or sit on our narrow bunks. We attended to our personal needs, mostly the mending of our prison garments. Since few of us possessed needle and thread, we took turns borrowing them.

The itching was driving me crazy. But for what followed after I removed my coarse black cotton brassiere, I was quite unprepared. It was crawling with lice!

Most of the other prisoners had made the same discovery. We spent half of that precious Sunday ridding ourselves of parasites. Our heads itched too. Word of our lousy state had reached the camp bosses. A few days later we were issued fine combs and on the following Sunday had our first bath in months.

Happily, we now learned that we would be allowed two off-days a month. This was a luxury indeed. However, the camp bosses in their vicious way turned these days into a veritable hell for us. They hired us out like slaves to extinguish forest fires, which raged with a mad fury that hot and dry summer, or to weed fields on farms miles away from the camp. Also, to prevent us from resting, we were assigned such meaningless tasks as hauling rubble in hand barrows from one corner of the camp compound to another.

I can remember a Sunday that ended badly for me. One of my oversize boots had slipped off my foot as we retreated from the flames of a forest conflagration we were powerless to fight. At the evening head count, a notoriously mean wardress noticed my unshod foot and had me handcuffed and sent off to the punishment cell. The next morning I was released. But even one night in the crammed wooden cell, with barely standing room for one person, made me realize what courage it took to defy the strict regime of the camp. Throughout my term I was a meek prisoner, never daring to answer back, let alone disobey prison rules.

Two off-days that summer I spent digging graves, both small trenches for five or six bodies and long ones to hold fifty or more. We guessed that the common graves were for men prisoners, who were treated more brutally than the inmates of women's camps and among whom there was far greater mortality.

We were glad when Sunday was over and we could look forward to our week at the factory. Despite the high quotas we were unable to fulfil, no matter how hard and conscientiously we toiled, and the worsening of conditions at the camp, our love affair with mica continued. Of an evening we still had some time we could call our own— no more than an hour, but it allowed us to chat a little. We were drawn closer together, and our tempers were not as frayed as when we did strenuous physical work.

There were two attitudes that crystallized among my fellow prisoners, typical, perhaps, of that harsh form of human captivity of which we were the victims. The first attitude, common among prisoners like myself, was a desperate clinging to the world we knew before our arrest, to memories of our loved ones, of friends, of the books we had read, the works of art we had seen in museums, the plays and movies that had most impressed us. They mattered greatly to us because they helped to keep that other world alive in our minds. The second attitude, mostly held by the camp veterans, was expressed by them as follows: "We know only one world, the prison world. Here we live and here we shall die. We must adapt to our captivity as best we can." I found such thinking painful and alarming, but I was compelled to admit that it was justified by the long terms to which so many of the inmates had been sentenced and the little hope they had of being released even after having served their full term—or of surviving.

In keeping with this attitude, and appalled by the harsh conditions of the strict-regime camps, many of the older inmates longed desperately to be back in the labor camps. All agreed there was a better chance of survival under the corrective system. There the state had not given up on you. You were not as completely isolated from the outside world as you were in the strict-regime—also called strict-isolation—camps. You could hope in some ways to be treated on a par with the thieves, murderers, rapists, and embezzlers, all regarded as rehabilitation material, while you were not.

Regulations were more humane in the labor camps. Prisoners were paid a few roubles for their work. And those convicted on political charges who worked by their side could not be entirely discriminated against.

In the strict-regime camps under Stalin, no matter how hard and what long hours you toiled, you received no pay, and the food consisted of nothing but oats (almost as crude in form as those fed to horses), bread, and only occasionally sugar. Labor-camp inmates were permitted to write and receive more letters than the two a year we could count on in strict-regime confinement.

Visits by relatives were practically never allowed under "strict isolation." No individual prisoners, as in the labor camps, could ever set foot outside the camp zone. Barracks were locked up by the guards for the night, from lights out to reveille. A suffocating stench rose from the huge decaying bucket, which usually overflowed in the morning with urine and excrement; windows were heavily barred and never opened. The guards were far more brutal and hostile than in the labor camps, for they were certain we would never return to the normal world.

One of the women who often spoke to me nostalgically of the labor camps was Marina Spendiarova. She had served the larger part of her sentence in them.

"My dear, you've never been in the labor camps, so you can't judge," she would say. "They're quite humane, compared to the camps we're in now!"

Prison camps humane? It was a little too much, even from Marina, actress, linguist, singer, everybody's darling, the daughter of the composer Spendiarov (after whom the opera theater in Yerevan, the Armenian capital, was named).

"The great thing about them was that there were men around," Marina went on. "I don't mean the criminal riffraff, but refined, sophisticated persons like ourselves. You pick one out, talk to him on any subject, you could fall in love. Despite our wretchedness, loving made you human, romantic, lifted you above the odious, unjust, primitive jungle around you."

No one dared contradict Marina. She was too lovable, too kind— one of the few who shared the food she received in parcels with others; too influential. She had set up a cultural brigade and did everything in her power to make life a little easier in camp for people like myself. But how could I agree with her? Corrective or "special" camps, they were all a horror, an obscenity designed to crush and destroy human beings, innocent ones at that, and in numbers never before known in history.

But Marina had struck a deep chord when she spoke of love as a humanizing factor. No matter how wretched we were, how devoid of hope, the need for love, sexual or other, was great. Among women prisoners for long years completely cut off from men, over and over again I witnessed the emergence of that need and its satisfaction, at times by a lesbian bond, but more often by a surrogate mother-and-daughter or aunt-and-niece one.

Many prisoners had been disowned by their families. Others had of their own accord severed contact with their relatives to save them from losing their jobs, being thrown out of university, or, worst of all, facing arrest. In captivity the gap left by the former normal family was filled by the adoption of "camp daughters," "nieces," or "husbands" in lesbian relationships, or in sexless "marriages."

With the strong taboo against homosexuality—it was regarded as a criminal offense, punishable by prison or camp—only the very daring among the inmates, mostly those in positions of power, like the overseers or team leaders, embarked on lesbian unions.

In our barracks were two four-bunk structures. Occupied by team leaders, they stood a little apart from the rest and were curtained off with rags to prevent prying. One of them resembled a big canopy bed; by night it heaved and rocked and rattled, but no one cared or showed the least curiosity. We were too engrossed in our woes, too listless, too shocked by the hell into which we had been cast. The lesbian couple who shared the canopy bed made no secret of their relationship. But the only time the prisoners gave it a thought was when they were disturbed by the noisy rows of these two intensely passionate women.

Though such relationships satisfied the need for sex, unfortunately, they often erupted in ugly quarrels and violence. It was generally the couple's promiscuity, and the jealousy and bitterness it caused, that made other prisoners recoil and opt for the sexless marriage, a more placid attachment, usually with one partner who was stronger in spirit, more protective and solicitous, but without the clearly defined male and female roles.

There were no smiles and no laughter in our camp, but the pleasure of the giving of oneself to another human being shone in the faces of those who lived in couples. There was a mutual dependency, as well as a tendency towards generous behavior as opposed to the bestiality of the state's secret police. To an older woman the young girl with whom she formed a close bond represented the loved one she had left behind in that other world and with whom often she had no communication, and the younger clung to her as she would to her own blood.

Such couples could be seen together, sharing their bread or, on those rare occasions when a sugar ration was issued, enjoying it with the steaming water we called "tea." In the feeding shed they sat side by side. There were tears and heartbreak when two such people were forcibly torn apart and sent off on transports.

As I saw them, these emotional bonds were a cherished reminder of family and other relationships of which the women had been part in their lives before captivity.

IV Non-Soviets

Among the inmates at Taishet were large groups of prisoners from outside the Soviet Union. They were entirely ignorant of the ways of the Soviet system. Many had been picked up right off the streets of European cities at the end of the war or in the late forties and early fifties.

There were even a few teenagers. They felt much more lost and bewildered than the rest of us. Among them were two high-school kids kidnapped in West Berlin and a defiant, beautiful Polish girl who was in and out of the punishment cell most of the time I spent in the same camp with her.

These girls did not know a word of Russian. I tried addressing one of the two Berlin teenagers, Louisa by name, in German, but she hardly responded. She was in a state of shock. A sensitive, aristo-cratic-looking girl, she could not cope with the situation in which she found herself. She went stark mad. The last time I saw Louisa she was an inmate of the overcrowded, tumble-down psychiatric hut in the Taishet hospital compound.

Among the aliens were several mistresses of men in high positions. One told me she had a long-standing liaison with Popovic, a well-known Yugoslav communist. He had been critical of the Soviet Union and provoked Stalin's wrath.

In the Taishet camps I kept meeting too the paramours of Soviet public figures—of an admiral and a general, both war heroes; of a famous actor and a writer. What better way was there to intimidate and get back at the men than to victimize the women they loved?

This selfsame blow Stalin dealt the composer Sergei Prokofiev, whom he hated and whose music the great connoisseur of all the arts termed "unsuitable for the Soviet public, mere snobbery." In 1948 Prokofiev's enchanting, Spanish-born wife Lina was thrown into prison and sentenced to twenty-five years.

Prokofiev had met her when travelling with Sergei Eisenstein and Grigory Alexandrov, for whose film, set in Mexico, he was writing the music. I had visited the Prokofievs in the late thirties at their home in the newly-built state apartment house for composers on the fringe of Sadovaya Ring. The composer, with his usual preoccupied look, was seated at the piano, his domed forehead gleaming with perspiration, oblivious to everything except the score in front of him. Lina, in a clinging black sheath—she seemed to have a predilection for black—which showed to advantage her perfect petite form, busied herself with preparing coffee; the aroma of the freshly ground beans soon pervaded the entire modest apartment. Where was she, I won-dered. Most likely in one of the Taishet camps; she must have been classed as a foreigner. And their two sons?

The prisoners from foreign countries were in many ways worse off than Soviet citizens, to whom the state's policies of repression were not unfamiliar, who were able to communicate, if only twice a year, with their families and receive parcels, and who had no language barrier to grapple with.

Of one of these aliens I have the most vivid recollection. This was Dolly—I cannot quite recall her second name. With Dolly, prima ballerina of Budapest, I spent one and a half years in Taishet. She was arrested by the secret police soon after the Soviet troops liberated her country. Dolly's mother was Hungarian and her father was Jewish.

"I rejoiced when the Soviet armies marched into Budapest and the Nazis fled," Dolly told me. "A few months earlier my father, whom I dearly loved, had been put into a Jewish prisoners' camp. I wanted to find him, hoping he was among the few lucky survivors.

"The first place I went for help was the Soviet army headquarters. A captain heard me out and was sympathetic. He offered to take me in his car to places outside Budapest where a few Jews, it was rumored, had been in hiding. Our efforts came to nothing. I could find no clue as to what happened to my father. But I went on seeing the Soviet captain; we became lovers."

Dolly paused. Her eyes saddened. "One day when I was expecting him, he never showed up. Two months later I was arrested, kept for six weeks in a Budapest jail, then after a long train journey under guard was brought to Lubyanka in Moscow. My interrogator claimed that the Soviet captain was an American spy, and I, his mistress, was assisting him in obtaining important intelligence. In my wildest dreams I could imagine no such thing. No testimony was produced to corroborate these lying allegations."

At the time I met her she had served almost all of her eight-year sentence and expected to be released in sixteen months. But Dolly's health had become so poor that we all feared for her life. Among the younger women tuberculosis was the great scourge, and Dolly seemed to have all the symptoms; she was pronounced tubercular by the medical section.

Dolly had the sweetest disposition. Perhaps for this reason she was one of the few women who had retained her beauty. Her skin was pearly, unlined; goodness of heart softened the contours of her face, shone out of her eager, wide-open round eyes. She had the look of an angel. Marina Spendiarova, who had been with Dolly in the labor camps and loved her dearly, racked her brain for a way to help her.

"We must save Dolly!" Marina cried. "To get her away from the mica dust, I shall put on a concert. Dolly will dance; she'll get a few days off for rehearsals."

Save Dolly! The call swept the entire camp, and no one who was in a position to do something failed to respond.

Our emotions and thoughts were raw, unadorned by the veneer and little stratagems that serve so effectively in the normal world when we are eager to show ourselves in the best light. Our common wretchedness made us more sensitive to the sufferings of each one of our fellow prisoners. We took Dolly's condition very much to heart. Our redoubtable Marina persuaded a camp official to permit her to get together a team of camp talent and rehearse for a show.

Although Dolly was uppermost in her mind when Marina pleaded her cause, she also hoped to make life a little more bearable for a few of us. Her plans for the evening's entertainment included a scene from *The Forest* by Ostrovsky, a nineteenth-century Russian playwright. Marina generously assigned me the lead part of Madame Sadovskaya, the rich owner of many acres of forest land.

The rehearsals soon revealed that I was no actress. Marina urged me "to enter into the role" (she knew the Stanislavsky method inside out). But the fact that Sadovskaya's troubles were much too remote from me, and my own too erosive, proved an insurmountable barrier. The part finally went to another prisoner.

Dolly was practicing the dance of the captive Maria from the *Fountain of Bakhchisarai*, fluttering across the barracks rehearsal room with airy grace, whirling, gliding and extending her shapely white arms in a prayer for freedom. Yet we saw that the strain of the rehearsals was telling on her. Too often she paused for breath; once she actually fainted and had to be carried back to the barracks.

On the evening of the performance, however, she was splendid. Maria came alive to us, less a character from Pushkin than a real person, like ourselves inexorably approaching her doom. I was grateful to Dolly that evening for the brief moment of elation her art gave me.

A nurse at the camp's medical station, a prisoner like ourselves, managed to smuggle a thermometer into our barracks. In this way we could keep track of Dolly's temperature; the high fever persisted for days. Through our camp doctors we learned that a new drug said to be very effective in treating tuberculosis had been discovered. The camp's medical section lacked the simplest of medicines, let alone wonder drugs. It was through prisoners who received parcels from Moscow, through bribery and other means, that an ample supply of this drug was procured. Dolly would be saved!

Frequently now Dolly talked to us of what she was going to do after her release. Knowing well that she would not be allowed to go back to Hungary, and not having a soul to turn to, she pinned all her hopes on the man with whom she had had a love affair in one of the labor camps.

"We thought ourselves as good as married," she said. "I hope to be reunited with him."

Everybody knew about Dolly's camp husband, a young man from Soviet Georgia, convicted on a charge of embezzling funds at his job. Dolly was separated from him when, as a political prisoner, she was shipped to the Taishet strict-regime camps. He, in the meantime, having served his term, was released. It had been arranged between them, Dolly told me, that when he got settled he would write to her so that she could join him. But long months had gone by without her having heard from him.

Marina was indignant: "He's a bastard, a cad, I knew it all along. He's got himself another woman, I'm sure. He could have at least had the decency to write or send a parcel. That would do Dolly more good than the medicine."

All of a sudden Marina's eyes lit up. "My, what a fool I've been, why didn't I think of it long ago?"

Two weeks later when the parcels were handed out, Marina collected little donations for Dolly from the prisoners, packed a parcel for her, printed Dolly's name on it, and brought it over to our barracks.

"It has no return address," Dolly remarked surprised. "Yet it must be from *him*. Who else would be sending me parcels? Perhaps he has no permanent address as yet." She offered her own explanation.

We were relieved and put in hastily:

"To be sure, that's the reason, Dolly."

Personally I do not think she was deceived. Dolly saw through our little game, but being an unusually tactful person, she did not wish to let on and disappoint us. Instead, gratitude illumined her lovely smooth face.

Dolly was taking the new medication, but far from improving, her health deteriorated. She was transported to the Taishet camp hospital, about thirty miles away, to everyone's sorrow. A week later I fell very ill and found myself in the same hospital, in the bunk above Dolly's. For her noonday meal somebody had brought her a big dish of meat, mostly enormous bones, of what animal I could not tell. In the two and a half years I was in Taishet, it was no more than twice that meat, mostly bones, was doled out to us.

Dolly nibbled at the bones with relish. "That's real meat," she said. "It's sure to give me strength."

That night I was awakened by Dolly's long fit of hiccups, after which she seemed to fall asleep. In the morning I bent over the side of my bunk to look down at her. Her white face was lifeless. I listened hard, but there was no sign of breathing. Dolly died just three months before she was due to be released.

That day there was yet another death, of a sixty-six-year-old Russian émigrée from Shanghai. In 1949, at the time the Chinese People's Republic was proclaimed, Russians who had emigrated right after the revolution were assured by the Soviet government that they were welcome to return to their native land.

"My husband and I were happy to be repatriated," this lady told me a few months before her death. "We dreamed of the day we could set foot again on our beloved Russian soil, where we hoped to live out the last years of our life. Shortly after our return, we were arrested and charged with anti-Soviet agitation. My husband died on his way to prison camp."

She was a tiny, frail lady, who spoke a quaint, old-fashioned but beautiful Russian. She had managed to make it through almost three years of captivity, never comprehending why she had been imprisoned. "It is peacetime, not war," she would say with a perplexed lift of her eyebrows.

A few days later I was back at the mica factory in Camp 027. Two prisoners, freshly arrived from the maternity camp, brought the news that Lilli's sister Tatyana had given birth to a baby boy. So there were not only deaths, but births too, in our far-flung prisonland.

It was one of the ironies of life that Tatyana, or Tata, as her sister called her, second daughter of General Semyonov who, in addition to his hatred of the Soviets, was notorious for his anti-Semitism, should have married a young Jew shortly before the arrest of the entire family in Harbin. Along with all the Semyonov offspring, he was apprehended, though he ended up with a much milder sentence—eight years to their twenty-five. Tatyana was allowed two meetings with her imprisoned husband over the years of their Taishet captivity, which accounted for the birth of their two children.

There was yet another group of prisoners at Taishet who could be classed as non-Soviets. They were women from the Baltic countries, from Latvia, Lithuania, and Estonia, which became Soviet republics in 1940. Many of the professional and well-to-do people in these countries who did not wish to live under the Soviets fled. But the Baltic Jews were trapped. They had the choice between Hitler's "final solution" and "safe harbors" in the Siberian forestland.

There were two women from Riga at Taishet with whom I became quite friendly. Both of them came from middle-class Jewish families and had already spent four years in deportation and six in prison camp. They were as close as mother and daughter, and did everything they could to keep their spirits up. Both in temperament and in appearance they were opposites. The younger, Faina, was blonde, blue-eyed, and apathetic; the older, Rabinowitz, was swarthy, thin as a reed, and full of fire. Tragedy had not crushed her spirit. She had two grown-up daughters, about whom she often talked to me. One was married in Siberia to an exile like herself, had two children, and led a wretched, poverty-stricken existence. The other, a girl of nineteen, was a prisoner in a nearby camp. Faina, Rabinowitz, and her daughter were serving ten-year sentences as co-defendants in a case of group anti-Soviet agitation. Each one's testimony on allegedly anti-Soviet utterances (one being, as Faina told me, a complaint about the high collective-farm market prices) had been used by the interrogator to incriminate the other.

V The dreaded Article 58

The state security set-up, whatever names or organizational forms it has taken, has always been regarded with fear by the citizens of the country. Throughout its history it has engaged in mass arrests, mass terror, and prying into the private lives of the citizenry. The less people know of what goes on behind the doors of that institution the happier they are. Therefore, because ignorance is bliss, the secret police have been successful in keeping concealed their methods of interrogation, their abuse of the law, their prison-camp system and executions.

Not until my own incarceration, when I was thrown into contact with other prisoners, did I have any idea of how ramified with sub-clauses was the political article 58 under which we were all charged. There were clauses on "slander" of Soviet literature, the security organization itself, the "leader of the peoples" (lese majesty). There was also the "with intent to" sub-clause 17. The adding of this sub-clause to your main charge meant that you had not committed the crime for which you were arraigned, but had had the *intent* to do so. Often this sub-clause was appended to such grave charges as treason, clause 1, and terror, clause 8, of the same article.

A fellow prisoner working with me at the mica factory in Camp 027 was the daughter of a well-known Swedish communist. Having quarrelled with her husband, she snapped at him: "I'll go to Sweden and live with my father." She loved her husband and two children and did not mean a word she said. But the MGB had gotten wind of her "intent" to leave her motherland. She was charged with treason via the mitigating sub-clause of "intent to" and was sentenced to ten instead of fifteen or twenty-five years.

My friend Tina's husband, Nikolai S., a successful architect, faced the ludicrous charge of "the purchase of a house in London," which, of course, turned him into a British spy. No "intent to" there; it was treason plain and simple, and he was sentenced to twenty-five years.

Most prisoners I met who were convicted of terrorist acts were, oddly enough, sedate elderly ladies from Leningrad, with a peculiar St. Petersburg air of good breeding about them. One of them, quite out of character, while watching over her pot of cabbage soup in a shared kitchen, muttered under her breath, "I wish that sonofabitch was dead!" A neighbor reported the remark and she was arrested, for whom else could she have meant but Stalin? After a stiff interrogation she got off with a mild sentence—eight years for "the intent to assassinate the leader of the peoples."

"A son does not answer for his father!" Stalin had said in a speech. People breathed with relief. Descendants of the former bourgeoisie or nobility, as well as the children of shot "enemies of the people" could now hope to be treated, if not on a par—because no decision could be quite interpreted to mean what it said—with the offspring of "proletarian stock," or of unimprisoned parents, then in any event far more leniently than in previous years.

But the truth was that you never knew where you stood in regard to these utterances; another utterance would come from the lips of a Stalin or a successor of his that would contradict the former one, or, worse still, a secret instruction would follow to replace the leniency by even more stringent measures. This was a well-tried policy that dated back to tsarist times and served its purpose only too well. Put a few wise words on paper to appease the public, wave the carrot, and then go back to your black deeds.

It was exactly what happened this time, too; no sooner had the enthusiasm abated around this wise utterance than a new interpretation of a law that had already been in existence was added to the long list of political offenses. Called the "member of a family" law, it allowed for not only the spouses of arrested persons but also other relatives to be packed off to prison camps. It was under this law that the grown-up daughters and sons of General Semyonov, as well as his in-laws, were arrested and sentenced. It applied, too, to the many relatives of those tried and executed in the Leningrad Case of 1949–1950, which involved almost all of the Party bosses and leading municipal executives of the city. Among the relatives were the three wives of Voznesensky and his two sons who, like the Semyonov family, were serving terms in the Taishet camps. If persons were indicted on such charges, is it any wonder that prison camps were packed with millions of inmates?

Great as the crimes of the MGB and its forerunners against its own citizenry were, perhaps there were no worse felonies than the rearrest, on the same charge, of people who had completed their sentences and been released, as well as the non-release of prisoners after they had served their full terms. Those arrested during the bloody years of 1937 and 1938 were either shot or sentenced to ten years; longer terms, especially the ubiquitous twenty-five years, were instituted during and after the war. This meant that large numbers of political prisoners would have to be released in 1947, and the slave labor force so badly needed for the post-war industrial economy greatly depleted.

An ingenious solution was to rearrest the released prisoners and, ten years later, start a new wave of terror—the 1947–1953 mass arrests—to prevent the shutting down of the camps and to provide the new building projects with penal labor. Politically, too, it was most expedient to keep the innocent victims of 1937 and 1938 in continued isolation, lest they besmirch the good name of the Party. It was killing two birds with one stone.

Many of us were plagued with the fear that we would never be set free. "You are to remain in camp pending further instructions," prisoners were told when their terms expired. To have served your term, to have survived, and then be informed that you will not be released, to see the light at the end of the tunnel suddenly extinguished, what could be more shattering? People charged under Article 58, mostly those tried by a special board *in absentia*, as my mother and I were, came under the system of unspecified sentences.

This is what we all feared—an end forever to our freedom. Our sentences could be extended over and over again so that we would never return to the normal world, never be reunited with our loved ones.

I began having the first variant of a nightmare that to this day I dread. I find myself in the overcrowded prison-camp barracks—gray vapors, gray shadowy figures, and gloom. A few days have elapsed after the end of my sentence. I am on tenterhooks, awaiting the arrival of the guard with the paper for my release. I must not miss him. I must keep my ears pricked up to catch my name when he calls it out. There is pandemonium in the barracks, all the inmates talking at the top of their voices, but I ignore them. Why hasn't the guard come yet? He was due days ago.

The guard arrives. He reads out the names of two prisoners, but not mine. They say goodbye to us. I want to address the guard and ask him: Why not me? I have served my sentence just as they have. But I dare not. I am petrified with fear. As the guard leaves, I grow very articulate. I beseech my fellow prisoners to listen to my grief, to advise me what to do to regain my freedom.

In a later variant of the same nightmare, at this point I praise the Russian people: they are the best in the world, yet treated like dirt. A man—there were no men prisoners in our camp—whispers in my ear: "This talk of yours will be reported. Watch your words or years will be added to your sentence. You'll never be released. You will die here." I am now more fearful than ever.

For about twenty years after my release I had these dreams. It was as though the fear of never being set free and dying in camp had sunk so deeply into my subconscious mind that it could not accept the reality of my freedom.

And the fears that racked us all were never more real, never better founded, than in the winter of 1953.

Early in the year news reached us of the arrest of several Kremlin doctors, most of them Jewish, on charges of poisoning. We feared that the "uncovering of the Doctors' Plot," as the newspapers termed it, could stir up anti-Semitic feeling among the guards and inside our camp. But fortunately we were spared that. My own feeling is that the Russians are no more anti-Semitic than other nationalities. The seeds of anti-Semitism, like those of any other ugly feeling, are sown by the ruling clique to gain their own selfish ends.

The screws of the camp regime were tightening. Searches were more thorough. We were threatened that photographs or letters found on our person would be confiscated. Many prisoners who had been writing the two letters allotted per year now ceased communication with their families. Supplies of the few drugs available for prisoners had run short and were not replenished.

There were several suicides. It was rumored that one of them was the eldest of the three Semyonov daughters. Another young woman in our own camp hanged herself in the outhouse. One of our prisoners had learned that her thirteen-year old son was in a Taishet camp convicted of a political crime; night after night we were awakened by her sobbing. A law existed by which children from the age of twelve upwards were to be tried for certain crimes on a par with adults and could even be given death sentences.

182

Things seemed blacker than ever. Even the exuberant Marina Spendiarova, always ready to help and cheer up others, went about with a cowed look on her mobile face. She was worried about her sister in Moscow and hesitated to write to her when the time arrived for our first letter of the year.

However, there were two women in my immediate entourage who waved aside fear and panic. They were my old companion Yulya and my Moscow doctor friend Maria Anisimovna.

"It will never get as bad as in the German camps, because we have a different ideology—communist, not fascist—and even if words are not deeds, they do matter," Yulya said wisely. "Besides, when it gets that bad," she added as an afterthought, "it is bound to get better."

Linking her arm in mine, Maria Anisimovna suggested we take a walk. For a while we trudged along in silence, inhaling the icy air, listening to the crunch of the snow. The moon rode high in the indifferent February sky, dispersing the shadows of the evening, as though to introduce a little clarity into our somber and eerie existence.

There was a true friendly warmth between us. Yet we dared not speak except in the innuendoes and hidden meanings that had become the habitual way of communicating among the people of our country.

Wanting to cheer me up, she said: "Nothing goes on forever. The tightening snaps. I believe that the Doctors' Plot may prove just that last straw that broke the camel's back."

I made no reply.

"Men do not live forever," she continued. Forever seemed like a magic word with some deep connotation when she uttered it. A message to me.

My heart gave a leap. I knew what she meant. I had had the same thought, which I dared not even verbalize to myself: Stalin is bound to die and then there may be changes, perhaps new hope for all of us innocent victims of his policies. And obviously he had gone too far with the Doctors' Plot. It was too medieval, too farcical.

Maria Anisimovna's words proved prophetic. A few weeks later, on March 5, we learned of the death of the great leader, the Father, the greatest genius of mankind, the guiding light of the international proletariat, butcher of my family and millions of others.

VI Amnesty

Three weeks after Stalin's death, news of an amnesty broke upon the startled Soviet populace. It brought little joy to the camp's inmates. Hardened criminals, murderers, armed robbers, recidivists with long terms were cited for release. But pardon for political crimes was confined to a handful of prisoners with sentences not exceeding five years.

None of the prisoners I knew well—Yulya, Maria Anisimovna, Marina, Lilli Semyonova, or my mother—could count on clemency. Out of the five hundred inmates of our camp, only nine had five-year terms. I was one of them.

Clearly though it was stated in the amnesty, our camp commandant and his staff refused to believe that even this small number of Stalin victims would be allowed to return to the normal world.

"The amnesty does not apply to strict-regime camps," these officials repeated. On no account, they reasoned, can political prisoners be set free. They will talk—if only to their close ones—about conditions in the camps, their interrogation and charges. The news will leak out, perhaps even abroad. The Party cannot allow this to happen. It will hurt its prestige.

The camp bosses warned us: "Do not build up your hopes!"

Nor did the guards and jailors imagine for a moment that we would one day walk out of the camp gates free people. And they would lose their lucrative posts? No! They wanted things to remain exactly as they were, as they had been under Stalin.

One evening in late April I dropped in at the medical section. A solitary guard was sitting on the waiting bench. He was a lad of about nineteen, with a flat peasant face twisted into the scowl that all guards wore in the prisoners' presence.

I would never have dared before to make conversation with a guard, but now, heartened by the prospect of release, I said, "I'm going to be set free and will return to Moscow."

If I had hit him over the head he could not have been more astounded.

Recovering from the shock of my words, he retorted morosely, "The likes of you will never be released!"

"Why?"

"Because you are spies, saboteurs, the worst criminals."

The doctrine of lies and hatred! At their weekly political sessions it was drummed into the guards' heads that we were too dangerous ever to be released, which, of course, justified their brutality to us.

Two months went by after the amnesty was made public. We still remained in ignorance of our fate. The waiting and uncertainty were a torment. Night after night I dreamed that I would never be set free and would spend the rest of my life in the squat, damp, wretched barracks that I shared with so many other unfortunates.

At long last I was summoned to the camp office and silently handed a "Certificate of Release," with the words "unrenewable if lost" printed in the upper right-hand corner. Other papers included several receipts from my last place of detention, the Butyrki Prison, for my typewriter, wristwatch, and two government medals, all of which, I was told, would be returned to me in Moscow. Maria Anisimovna lent me the money for a train ticket in a sleeping compartment; that meant I would not have to travel for weeks in a cattle car with former inmates of the labor camps, mostly men with long criminal records.

In the early afternoon of June 11, 1953, a warm, sunny day, I walked through the tall timber gates, out of the camp inferno, dazed and unbelieving. More than myself, the air around me seemed to celebrate my release, sparkling, spinning in playful whiffs, whispering in my ear: Rejoice! you are back in the human world, free to move about as you please. I needed time, and time suddenly underwent a transformation right before my eyes, expanding enormously, every minute swelling into an hour, languorous, deliciously long, not painfully endless as it had been in solitary confinement; throbbing with new life.

I threw a last glance at the solid prison gates. There had been no goodbyes, for the camp inmates were ordered to keep a distance from the lucky nine who had five-year terms, after we had been issued our release papers.

You are still there behind the gates, my fellow sufferers, I thought. Your crippled lives, your deaths, the pain in your eyes, will never leave me.

We squeezed into a horse cart and were driven along the bumpy dirt road to Taishet, where both the westward-bound freight trains and the trans-Siberian express stopped. On arriving I learned that the express for Moscow would be departing the next day. I was put up for the night in the crummy local hotel on the floor in a room with about ten other women.

What did it matter if I slept or not that night? I was free! In a few days I would see my little daughter who, I had learned a year before, was staying with neighbors of mine. I pictured our meeting. But would she, my friends and neighbors recognize me?

In all the three years of my imprisonment I had not looked into a mirror.

"Is there a looking-glass somewhere?" I asked the receptionist.

"Yes, down the hall, badly mildewed, but you'll be able to see yourself in it," she answered kindly.

Steeling myself for the worst, I looked at my reflection in the glass. I was appalled by the expression of my face. The inhuman experiences I had been through showed clearly in it. Remembering that I had once been a light-hearted, rather exuberant romantic, I made an effort to smile, but the result was only a freaky contortion of the features.

Just then a man, whose girth must have equalled his height, advanced towards me, fluttering a fifty-rouble bill in his chubby fingers.

"Take this, cutie," he said tipsily, "and buy yourself some sweets."

Though full of liquor, he knew me for a released prisoner and longed to show his sympathy.

I broke into laughter, the first genuine laughter in long years, waved his bill aside, and thanked him as sweetly as I could. He too, I thought, was Russia, my generous, dearly loved Russia.

Cheered by the sound of my own laughter, I took another look at myself in the mirror. Laughing had relaxed my face a little. Gradually, I told myself, time will blur the horrors I have seen. But it will not blot them out from my memory. I will laugh and smile and enjoy life again, yet always in the shadow of the crippling and needless death of millions of human beings.

In the Moscow-bound train I found myself sharing a four-berth compartment with a camp commandant and his wife. With criminals being released in such great numbers, and camps shut down, that should not have surprised me. But it took much joy out of my return journey to hear the uncouth wife address me in the same harsh Siberian accent in which the guards shouted their commands. Thankfully, the husband, deprived of his post, remained silent and glum through most of our four-day journey.

I do not believe the wife suspected I was an amnestied prisoner, because she chattered on and on about her fears of being attacked or robbed by the freed criminals, complaining bitterly about the amnesty, what a mistake it was, and that the government would live to regret it. Her husband had made good money as a camp commandant, she said, "the best-paying job he ever had." All that money, she soon confided, thousands of roubles, was sewn into the lining of her girdle. Every time she absented herself to go to the washroom or accompany her husband to the restaurant car, she removed her girdle and entrusted it to my care. "So many ex-convicts are at large . . . do keep an eye on it," she begged. I assured her I would not leave the compartment until she returned.

Most of the day, however, I avoided her company. I stood mutely in the corridor watching the shaggy Siberian forest flicker past the train window. At times I was joined by a man from a neighboring carriage. Like me he was an amnestied prisoner on his way to Moscow. This I surmised from the half-syllables in which he spoke. His face was a mask of fear.

I learned nothing whatever about his life or imprisonment; what I shall always remember about him was the shirt he wore. It was good quality, of Western cut; I could tell it by the collar and the cuffs. At some point in the prisoner's life, how and when I do not know, it had been reduced to tatters, riddled with countless holes at the shoulders and sleeves. And then it was made whole again, mended in a thousand places with a minute interlacing of thread, dyed a pleasant shade with tree bark so as to make the darning almost invisible. It must have taken the prisoner many nights of patient toil to make the shirt wearable, and enable him, on stepping out of the camp gates, to resemble the spruce and prepossessing man he must have been before his arrest. Apparently it helped to restore his shattered dignity.

Our trans-Siberian express was pulling into the busy junction of Moscow's Yaroslavsky Station. Track upon track, train after train of passengers and freight cars, many loaded with timber, perhaps felled by prisoners, and presently to be delivered to Moscow's building sites; people roaming about freely, faces more or less relaxed.

Not on a sidetrack, not in the pitch of night, but on this sunny morning of June 17, 1953, just three months after Stalin's death, our train snaked into an open platform. With hardly a murmur of parting to the grim-faced commandant and his surly peasant wife, I elbowed towards the exit, dragging behind me my battered valise. On alighting I caught a glimpse of the man with the mended shirt. The train's "hard" carriages were disgorging amnestied camp inmates by the hundreds. We two were perhaps the only politicals—still too fearful, still too constrained, to wave goodbye.

TEN

I Vicky

Clutching the loose handle of my valise, which contained the clothes I had packed on the night of my arrest, I made for the long line at the taxi stand outside the Yaroslavsky Station. Men and women were scrambling furiously to grab the rare taxi that pulled up in front. I was no match for them, but the scene was poignantly familiar. *My* Moscow.

A violet sky, with filmy clouds drifting far apart, promised a balmy day. Clock faces on each of the three railway stations flanking Komsomolskaya Square showed a quarter to eight.

Parking his car some distance from the waiting crowd, a taxi driver approached and casually inquired if I had far to go. He cocked an ear as I gave him the address.

"Thirty roubles. We won't run the meter."

This was four times the regular fare and, curiously enough, the exact sum I had in my purse. A Moscow taxi driver will in a twinkling spot a customer he can squeeze dry. He sensed immediately that I was not likely to haggle over the price.

Trailing after him as he led the way, I shoved my valise into the back of the car and plumped down beside it, the seat's steel springs prodding into my sides. We were driving down Kirov Street. It was Sunday and the traffic was light.

Stone, glass, concrete—how good they looked after the wooden hovels of Siberia. On our right we passed the Corbusier office building perched on its gray pillars, epitomizing the craving for modern art. We swung into the deserted Dzerzhinsky Square dominated by the lone towering figure of the man who founded the Cheka, then skidded across Moskvoretsky Bridge, the river greeting me like an old friend with the sparkle of a silver salute.

My own Embankment. I climbed the gray stone stairs, worn by so many feet, among them those of Napoleon's soldiers, billeted in this very building in 1812. On reaching my room, Number 171a, on the fourth floor, I put down my valise and stood waiting for someone to show up with the key; before boarding the train at Taishet I had sent a wire to the neighbors who took Vicky in.

Two women in dressing-gowns, their hair in curlers, passed by on the way to the washroom shared by goodness knew how many tenants. One of them turned to say hello.

"Why, you've hardly changed," she exclaimed and walked on. Without waiting for me to be out of earshot, she added to her companion, "I'm sure she slept with the camp commandant. That's what helped to keep her looks."

The remark was like the lash of a whip. My neighbor arrived with the key. She threw me an incredulous, almost baneful look. It was as though my return, or being alive at all, was an affront. Instead of a greeting, she blurted out hysterically: "Only don't take the child away from me!" She did love my Vicky.

On that morning of crimson sunlight, Vicky, almost eight years old now, was standing up in her bed as I walked in. Solemn face, eyes probing, intelligent far beyond her years. No flicker of joy. A dignity and aloofness about her restrained me from what I had so longed to do—crush her in my arms.

I remained glued to the spot, waiting, hoping for some response. Nothing! Her form and proud face stiffened into a question mark: So, you're back, what now?

Added to the crimes of the state in arresting and exterminating innocent people were the wounds inflicted on their children. Left practically alone in the world, after my brother's suicide, Vicky was pushed around from home to home. Taken in by compassionate neighbors, she ran away from them when she was six.

Bundled up in her heavily padded coat, fur hat, and scarf, she waddled in her stiff felt boots and galoshes across the ice-encased Moskvoretsky Bridge, past Red Square, and down Gorky Street, amidst hustling pedestrians, stopping to ask how to reach Bolshaya Bronnaya Street, off Pushkin Square, where her paternal grandmother, aunt, and aunt's daughter shared one room. On arriving there and realizing she was not wanted, she hastily slipped out unnoticed, plodded all the way back, passing her own house and stopping at the home of a friend of mine. There too she was not welcome. Back into the dark night. Her new foster parents were relieved at the return of "the little orphan."

Vicky was growing up with the stigma of a child of "enemies of the people." Tactless adults did not hold their tongues in her presence. They made it clear that she was not likely to ever set eyes on her parents. Nor was she spared the teasing of her peers: "Your mother and father are in chains! They are spies and will be shot."

Longing to disassociate themselves from their arrested parents, such children all the more eagerly proclaimed their loyalty to the socialist regime. On the day of my arrival the words "Stalin is the wisest and the best in the world" hit me in the face. They were scrawled across the wall above Vicky's cot in her childish handwriting.

"We were certain you would never return. We thought it best for Vicky to forget her parents," friends and neighbors told me.

My reunion with my daughter was indeed a miracle. It was the policy of the state to isolate released political prisoners and keep them away from their families. Such people knew too much to roam freely in socialist society or to be allowed to influence the upbringing of their children, who themselves were pressured into disowning their parents.

Traumas of separation and guilt on the part of those who all too readily abandoned their loved ones in misfortune eroded family relationships. Many mothers were less fortunate than I; belated reunions resulted in total wrecks of both their relationships with their children and their children's lives. There are bounds to the capacities of human adjustment.

Years later I was to learn from Vicky that when I turned up so unexpectedly, she did not believe I was her real mother. Perhaps it was an attitude prompted by the need to stifle the guilt she must have felt in closing her heart to me. She put me down as an imposter, reacting to my homecoming in the same way I had myself to my mother's return after her narrow escape from the death sentence passed on her by General Denikin in the Civil War.

This situation between us continued for almost three years. But I was too busy teaching, translating, and picking up the threads of life to brood over it. In prison and in camp we were hungry, desolate slaves; all normal desires were crushed in us. But now, with the first breath of freedom, I began to feel and act like a woman and human being again.

I did not want Vicky to grow up in a fatherless home, as I did. Nor had I ever shared my mother's conviction that a woman should above all value her independence and stand on her own two feet alone. I had my career and was earning more than many other women—and men. But the yearning for love, companionship, also another pair of shoulders to lean upon, propelled me into the search for a life partner.

With the male population decimated by the Stalin terror and the war, it was not easy for a woman of forty to find a husband. Moreover, I could only consider someone I was sure would make Vicky a good father.

One day Vicky tore to shreds a photograph of me. This animosity hurt, but I dismissed it as something a child would grow out of. My main concern was her education. In the face of a stubborn resistance on her part, I taught her English, engaged tutors in French and music, introduced her to the best theater, travelled with her, and converted our one room—divided up into a tiny kitchen where we ate our meals, a "drawing-room" and a bedroom—into a cozy home where we could entertain our friends, sometimes as many as ten guests sitting around our small, oval mahogany table. One afternoon, on going out to a movie, Vicky left me a note ending with the words: "I would do anything for you. I love you."

Pensive, inquisitive, studious, Vicky was treading the road to independent thought. In Chernyshevsky, Herzen, and other great Russians she sought the answers to moral questions, perusing their works from the first to the last page and over again. At one time the poet Mayakovsky was her idol. It was when a new idealism, along with a contempt for philistine small-mindedness, was gaining ground in the hopeful Khrushchev era. Sensitive to my intellectual preferences, Vicky knew I did not share her enthusiasm for Mayakovsky. She had inherited my mother's good memory and also her gift for expressive recitation; her recitals of my own favorite poets were a source of enjoyment to me. I always believed that Vicky would pursue a literary career. Instead she chose my mother's and brother's great love—mathematics.

II The living and the dead

It had, after my return, suddenly grown cold and windy. I walked behind young women in flared, belted coats of good material. Very chic! Young men swaggered in narrow trousers—something never seen or imagined in Moscow before. Many of the people I now saw in the streets I mistook for visiting tourists—until I learned that the fine spring coats were imported from Czechoslovakia. And the hip-hugging trousers, resented by the older generation and even dubbed bourgeois decadence by the writer Mikhail Sholokhov at a congress, were also among the imports from the Soviet Union's new socialist European neighbors.

I've always had a sweet tooth, which made me devour our prison camp's monthly sugar ration of 400 grams, at the rare times we got it at all, in two sittings. And now my love of sweets drove me to the famous bakery and confectionery in Stoleshnikov Street on the third day of my homecoming. I could hardly believe that I was there, feasting on gooey éclairs.

At night I was kept awake by the unaccustomed traffic noises, the strange cooing of pigeons outside my window—and the nightmares bringing back the horrors of prison and camp, making me for years and decades to come wrest myself from them in a cold sweat.

I had to piece my life together again. Special advisers at Communist Party District Committees were assigned to provide employment for amnestied prisoners. I applied to one such party functionary at the Bauman District Committee. Her face set in the stern lines of Stalinist officialdom, she told me outright that the "ideological" field, such as translation and teaching, was closed to me. She proved wrong.

Editors and publishers I had worked with, also acquaintances, shrank from accepting the reality of the release of persons like myself. Statements of mine quoted by my prosecutor and investigator from bulky dossiers revealed how many informers there were in my immediate entourage. Fears surfaced. Most likely, however, it was as hard to explain our sudden reappearance as it had been our arrest.

But the climate was changing, the pendulum swinging away from the bloody Stalin era. Friends and colleagues were now going out of their way to help me. The availability of jobs for all was one of the great gains of the Soviet system. I had more work than I could handle, books to translate and classes to teach.

People around me now began to say that had Stalin lived on, they themselves would have shared my fate. They cited instances of provocation and spying against them by the secret police. I do not know how sincere they were, for they later surprised me by a roundabout turn; they refrained from any mention of the Stalin period. It was the way a new wind was blowing.

In late September of the same year I was released, a parcel I mailed to my mother in Camp 215/023 of the Taishet District, Irkutsk Region, was returned to me. Across the wooden lid were stamped the words, "Addressee dead."

No official notice of her death. No confirmation. Under what circumstances she died, or where she was buried, I do not know. I dared not, nor do I yet dare, make inquiries. No memento, no photograph of her remained. Like myself she had signed the affidavit for the burning of her personal papers. Her file at Lubyanka, "to be kept forever", as the KGB stamp on its cover reads, is the sole proof of her having existed at all.

A few years after her death, when the jailings and shootings of millions of innocent people went by the name of "violations of socialist legality," cases were reviewed and political prisoners exonerated. Both my mother and I were cleared of our "crimes," my mother posthumously. And so was my husband. On my request my husband's death certificate was issued to me. From it I learned that Mikhail died sixteen months after his arrest. He was forty-two. On the certificate neither the cause of death nor the place were indicated, as they are supposed to be on all such documents. In their stead two blank spaces stared at me.

During an intermission at a performance of Prokofiev's ballet *Romeo and Juliet*, I ran into Marina Spendiarova. Her silver hair shone like a halo around her refined, animated face. Marina was doing most of the talking. It thrilled me to hear her musical voice not in the murk of our foul-smelling prison shed in Taishet, but amidst the red plush and gilt of the Bolshoi. Excitedly she told me she was writing, translating, singing on stage, collecting musical scores to perpetuate the memory of her father, the composer.

From her I learned that Lilli Semyonova had been released and was living in exile in Siberia. She had two children. I recalled her glowing skin, pink cheeks—flushed from tubercular fever—her exquisite features, sweet temper, and artistic gifts. Lilli was an exotic flower, cruelly transplanted to wither away in the harshness of Siberia.

Maria Anisimovna dropped in a few times. Her ringing laughter had cut through the brittle Siberian frost when she listed the preposterous charges brought against her. And now the same laughter tinkled in my room—"very cozy", she commented—as she told me she had been cleared of "poisoning Russian infants in wartime." In the mid-fifties, when Vicky and I were having dinner at the home of a friend, I was delighted to see Lina Prokofieva walk in—wearing a stylish black suit, well-groomed as usual, her cheeks flushed from the Moscow frost. We both knew of each other's experiences but somehow, as in this instance too, we never spoke of them except in the company of fellow-sufferers.

Her face with its dusky complexion and well-proportioned features showed little sign of ravage. Perhaps it was her pride that kept her from bending under the harsh captivity in the strict-regime camps.

One sunny afternoon in August Yulya came to see me. She was getting married and needed to borrow some money, which I gladly gave her. Nothing was too good to repay Yulya for her kindnesses to me in Taishet. The many years Yulya spent in German and Soviet camps had creased her skin and turned her hair gray. But she still looked pretty, though much older than her thirty years.

"There is something I would like you to know, a secret really." She paused, looking around the room and towards the door as though expecting to catch an eavesdropper.

A lengthy tale followed of a summons she had received to report to an office of her District Soviet.

"They wanted me to work for them . . . as an unpaid employee."

They, I guessed at once, were the Committee for State Security, or KGB.

"And what did you say?"

"I agreed—how could I refuse? To safeguard the security of our Soviet country is vital, don't you think?"

I had no answer for that one.

Yulya left soon after this confidence.

A few days later, to my surprise, I received a similar summons. The new beginnings! The room I entered at the District Soviet Committee smelled of fresh paint, as did the rest of the building, and was in a state of disarray, having just been moved into. Chairs and desks were askew; folders with secret files were in evidence everywhere, piled up on the windowsill, cluttered on the desks, spilling over from a chair onto the floor. The folders had names on them in bold print. I recognized a few of them, all of teachers I had worked with at the Army Language Institute. One was Senior-Lieutenant Reiber who, after my husband's arrest, suddenly began showering his attentions on me. His behavior was so crude and transparent that I did not doubt he had a special assignment to sound me on Mikhail's arrest.

In former days the man in charge of this new office would have been in grave trouble for the careless way in which the folders were exposed.

"We are going back to our old contacts, to people like you whom we trust," he said.

Half-pleadingly, he continued, "A family living in your house is expecting a visit from an American uncle." He paused. "We need information about the uncle and this family."

He was callow and inexperienced. I was both amused and infuriated. Information again! More stool pigeons at every step, more prying into the private lives of the citizens. Firmly I made it clear that I would have nothing to do with the security organs.

As I walked out of the building I thought: The monster Stalin is dead. There is a sense of relief. Some warm gusts of freedom ruffle the stagnant surface of our lives. Surely we can hope for better, freer times. But is Stalin really dead? Will he ever cease to turn the tide in his favor? The years to come held the answer to that question, and they would decide my own fate.

III The state and the individual

Two short blocks from where I lived, in the army guardhouse on Osipenko Street, the butcher Beria, recent head of the secret police and Stalin's closest workmate, was tried and executed. Only a few others were slated for the same fate.

In my home, over a bottle of dry white wine, coffee, and rum cupcakes, I was chatting with a few friends. It had suddenly become possible to express political views, a situation that obtained only for a short period.

"What do you make of Khrushchev's policies?"

"He's brought a fresh breeze, revealed Stalin's crimes against his own people, and is trying to bring the survivors of prison camps back to a normal existence," I replied.

"Do you really think that is such a good policy? Consider the way it makes us look to the rest of the world. Khrushchev is a disgrace to our country! Imagine him taking off his shoe and pounding with it on the table at the United Nations!"

Since I owed my very life to Khrushchev, I was happy to hear quite a different comment: "He has opened the road to reform. We must never return to Stalinism!"

A few years would go by, and those who had condemned Stalin would be forced to eat their words. Khrushchev's inconsistencies enabled Stalin's heirs to reascend to positions of power. The opinion that Khrushchev was nothing but a boor, that he had messed up the economy and was an embarrassment to the Soviet Union abroad, persisted. The Soviet people have always been extremely sensitive about the image their rulers and country project to the world. Most truly regard their system as a model for all nations.

To distance himself from the cynical, self-seeking opportunists, of whom there were so many within the Communist Party, Georgi Mikhailov, the man I married in 1959, liked to refer to himself as a "communist of the twenties." He identified with the idealistic type my mother represented, who craved no privileges, no power over their fellow beings, and worked honestly to build what they thought should indeed be a just and good society.

A first-generation intellectual, he owed much to the revolution and the Soviet system. This he repaid with unselfish dedication to the ideological tasks the Party set before him and with combat service from the first to the last day of the war, his many wounds reopening year after year and greatly undermining his health. He was an upright man, industrious and successful in his chosen field, and a devoted husband who, having no children of his own, doted on Vicky.

Party policies affected our lives. An orientalist by profession, Georgi had written a four-hundred-page dissertation towards the coveted Doctor of Philology degree. A portion of his research dealt with Mongolian folklore, much of which had been inspired by Genghis Khan. This bloodthirsty conqueror had become a great hero in Communist China, with which the Soviet Union was eager to establish more friendly relations. Not to offend the Chinese, my husband was urged by the Central Committee to revise his assessment of Genghis Khan and show him in a more favorable light. He refused, and it was not until a few years later, when Sino-Soviet relations remained at the same low ebb, that the censor gave him the green light to promote his book.

Living with my husband and seeing him work, I could appreciate the time and energy many Russians were giving to initiating and advancing scholars and professionals among the Asian and Mongolian nationalities. Georgi not only edited and wrote many chapters of a history of the Kalmyks, but helped other Mongolian nationalities to publish textbooks in their own language, compile grammars, and switch from the ancient alphabets to the less difficult Cyrillic letters. Often I accompanied him to conferences in these republics and was impressed by the speed with which the native population, under tsarism doomed to extinction because of syphilis and other scourges, were acquiring skills and producing their own competent and well-educated intelligentsia. Many had been educated in Moscow, where they often enjoyed preferential opportunities of enrollment in schools of higher learning.

Among the leading cultural figures of these nationalities were many victims of the Stalin terror. There was the poet David Kuguldinov, a Kalmyk, and the Mongolian poet and literary scholar Damdinsuren, a close friend of my husband's. They seemed to have no rancor, perhaps because they felt that the rapid rise of culture in their republics was a compensation for their sufferings.

Out of picture frames from which only a short while ago Stalin, Beria, and Khrushchev had been removed, Leonid Brezhnev stared at us from building façades. After leader worship had been denounced as the root of all evil it was carried to new extremes.

Politicians, scholars, scientists, and writers became maudlin over the genius of the new head of state. He lost no time in making himself twice and thrice Hero of the Soviet Union, titles with which accrue hosts of benefits; he also bestowed upon himself a marshal's baton. He had masterminded, we were told, the battle of Novorossiisk, which decided the outcome of the war. This was not easy to stomach for war veterans like Georgi. Whenever Brezhnev's face came on the screen my husband turned off the television. His outstanding contribution to victory Brezhnev recorded in two volumes, an epochal work that won him the Lenin prize in literature.

Why this literate leader—like, incidentally, Stalin and Khrushchev before him—stumbled over the pronunciation of many words, among them "communism" and "socialism," was quite puzzling and soon became the butt of many jokes. Fortunately, under Brezhnev one did not pay with a ten-year sentence for a political joke.

Still, life was becoming happier and more bearable. Many of the good programs begun by Khrushchev, such as housing construction, could not be discontinued. People in Moscow, as well as a few other lucky cities, were abandoning dingy shared flats and moving into new one-, two-, or even three-room homes of their own. More foods and consumer goods were becoming available. Faces lit up with new joy. My husband and I too were now living in far more comfortable surroundings.

Political life, however, was becoming more rigid and ominous. It was a field day for the bootlicker and the timeserver. No mention was ever made of the 20th and 22nd Party Congresses, at which Stalin's brutalities had been brought to light. It was as though they had never taken place. But this was not new to the Soviet people. What the party had said yesterday could be denied today without batting an eyelid.

Muscovites love to feast and get together. No occasion for merrymaking is missed, and family celebrations are big events. In late August, 1979, on my daughter's birthday, we were all having a grand time, the old generation along with the young. I was in exuberant spirits until a friend of my daughter's, a professor of mathematics at a military academy, said to me, "Surely the people arrested under

Stalin were guilty of some criminal act against the state." I knew this man, who was in his mid-thirties, to be an honest and well-wishing person. I did not answer. His words pointed to the latest trend in political thinking. Stalin's shadow! The clang of steel in the many-tiered galleries at Lefortovo rang into my ears the warning of silence.

A sixth sense told me that among the friends I entertained on Saturday nights, the number of informers was on the increase. In comparing observations with my daughter, I realized we shared the same conviction.

A colleague of mine who had recently returned from a visit to the United States was too open in her praise of American democracy. I drew her aside, into my kitchen, in the new condominium close to Moscow University where we now lived.

"Do watch your words," I cautioned her. "There are bound to be a couple of informers sitting around my table."

"Yes, I know, I was an informer myself," she suddenly blurted out.

I was shocked. I admired and loved this person. Her confession made me sick. I paled. She flushed scarlet.

"The arrest of a dear friend is on my conscience. She never came back from camp. God, how I hate the KGB!"

"Hush! Don't talk that way. We may be overheard."

A spate of articles, novels, and television series had now descended upon us, glorifying the deeds of the Soviet secret police, from the Cheka to the present-day KGB. Not a word about the victims. I did not know that I myself was not yet through with the KGB.

Having married a Canadian (a post-doctoral fellow at Moscow University, and a mathematician like herself), Vicky, her husband, and their three-year-old son were now in Canada. Her absence for even less than a year was a strain on my nerves. We were both obsessed by the fear that for reasons unknown visas might be withheld by the Soviet authorities. Georgi and I applied for visiting permits. We were hopeful.

An old and dear friend of mine had died about six months before, leaving a will in Vicky's favor. By Soviet standards she came into a tidy sum, close to ten thousand roubles. There was no way the assets could be taken out of the country; Soviet currency is not convertible and is of no value outside the U.S.S.R. Georgi and I had no need of the money; we had savings of our own.

Learning at the Moscow Visa Office that Soviet citizens visiting abroad could legally take out a few valuables, I made the rounds of the jewelry shops to see what I could buy. On Arbat Street I stood in line for almost an hour waiting for the shop to open after the lunch break. A youngish man in an elaborate get-up that seemed to come right out of a theater wardrobe approached me.

He addressed me as "Madame," an obsolete form that has not been in use since the Revolution, and proceeded slimily; "If you are after really fine jewelry, I can take you to a private dealer in sapphires, emeralds . . ."

"No, thank you." I cut him short. A woman standing behind me pricked up her ears. "I would be interested," she said in a half-whisper.

"It is this madame that would find what she is looking for," he persisted.

I was suspicious: in making a proposition that was obviously illegal, why was he speaking in a voice loud enough for others to hear? So that, if necessary, witnesses could be summoned?

It took some time for me to brush him off. I believe I saw through his disguise. Months later, after my experience with customs at Sheremetyevo, I recalled this incident, wondering if the man had not been a KGB plant; I am still uncertain.

At the Arbat jewelry shop I bought two rings and a brooch, the value of which did not exceed what I was legally entitled to take out of Moscow. These pieces of inexpensive jewelry would be but a token reminder of the inheritance left to my daughter.

In September, 1980, carrying the new red passports issued for the duration of a visit to a foreign country, Georgi and I were on our way to Moscow's main international airport, holding hands, exhilarated, like a newly married couple. With two pieces of luggage, mostly packed with gifts, we faced customs inspection.

It was at this point that things altogether unforeseen started to happen. My husband was told to move on, while I was detained for more than an hour, with the passengers in back of me hastily melting away and fleeing to other lines. Three customs officials, two young women and a man in his late twenties, rummaged through my things, opening and closing the brightly coloured Matryoshka nest dolls, feeling and ripping the lining of coats, emptying my handbag, carefully examining every item in it. I was both frightened and infuriated, yet dared not utter a single word of protest. There was a man hovering in the background, scowling, watching the whole procedure with eagle eyes. He had the hard, arrogant look and high-handed manner I knew so well. There was no doubt in my mind that he was KGB, probably with the rank of captain or major.

The final humiliation: I was led into a cubby-hole for a body search. It yielded nothing. The KGB was behind the entire ugly masquerade.

When it was over I was told that our plane reservations had been cancelled the day before. But at the last minute, after a whispered conversation between the KGB man and a few other officials, we were allowed to board the plane. Fortunately for us, take-off was delayed because the Soviet ambassador to Canada, who was on the passenger list, arrived late. We made it to our seats in the nick of time.

Instead of feeling elated at the prospect of seeing my daughter and her family, I wept bitterly through the entire flight from Moscow to Montreal. My husband too was upset and puzzled as to why I had been singled out to be so brutally harassed.

To bully and intimidate, to wreck their citizens' plans and lives, is the long-standing practice of the KGB. They sent out signals—an ominous signal to one Jewish emigrant and his wife. They were turned back from the airport, stripped of their exit visas, told they would never be allowed out of the country. No reason was given. Another went to a member of the U.S.S.R. Academy of Sciences who, on his way to an international conference, was ordered off the plane in Moscow and sent home without a word of explanation.

What was the message to me? Since explanations for the government's actions are rarely offered, Soviet citizens must willy-nilly rely on conjecture. The grilling I received at customs was most likely a stern warning to keep my mouth shut about the gross injustices my family and I had suffered at the hands of the secret police. At the same time, the KGB might have hoped to discover a smuggled manuscript or a piece of jewelry, or provoke an imprudent censure of their tactics, any of which would have sufficed to prevent me from boarding the plane.

The message struck home—though not in the way intended by the all-powerful secret police. I was not going to risk a second grilling, or worse, refusal of an exit visa the next time I decided to visit my daughter. After several months' stay in Canada I applied and was kindly granted permanent residence by the Canadian government.

Georgi took my decision very hard, hoping fervently I would change my mind and return to live in Moscow. For him to abandon his motherland was unthinkable. Our attachment was too deep for us to live apart. Georgi came to stay for brief periods in Canada. I made several trips to Moscow in the mid-eighties, each lasting a few months.

In early May of 1985 and 1986 I watched the Victory Day celebrations, the elaborate preparations for which can last for weeks. An atmosphere of triumph and patriotism prevails. War veterans parade through cities and villages wearing their hard-earned medals. Moscow was flooded with these gallant men and women. I saw them everywhere—in the streets, public squares, museums, and theaters.

I thought of Vicky's father and my brother Shurri. They too had been in the war. No mention of them and the hundreds of thousands of other war veterans, nor their reward—prison, death, a bullet in the back of the head from a KGB thug, the latter himself wearing medals, parading in the streets of Moscow, living off the fat of the land with no fear of ever being brought to justice.

Verdant Moscow, with well-dressed crowds of shoppers from all over the land, wide new boulevards, mauve, scarlet, and pearly white tulips swaying in the spring breeze. I was sitting in the airy, well-furnished condominium bought out of my savings twenty-four years earlier.

Georgi had had a stroke, his second. Hastily I had arrived from Canada to nurse and care for him. Vicky too had, the year before, spent her Christmas holidays with him in Moscow. My husband's condition now kept me more at home, at his bedside, than on previous visits. I was tormented by guilt, feeling partly responsible for his rapid deterioration.

A long address by the new General Secretary delivered at the Palace of Congresses in the Kremlin was being broadcast. In it acclaim was given to Stalin. At the mention of Stalin's name, the audience rose as one man, as indeed in his own time, and applauded wildly.

At Moscow movie houses and in television series, again and again, I saw Stalin's face projected on the screen and listened to inordinate praise of his wisdom and deeds.

Another visit to Moscow: slogans, catch phrases, pronouncements! The air is full of them. How familiar they are to me. I have heard them from the lips of Stalin, Khrushchev, Brezhnev. Sadly, I know only too well how casuistic words can be. Tactical utterances: you must search for nuances, fathom ambiguity. The very Party leaders, along with giants in literature and the arts, who only yesterday swore by one idea are now saying and writing practically the opposite.

True to Russian tradition, the public seeks answers in literature and art. Painting, poetry, novels, the theater, and later the cinema, have played their role in disclosing elements of truth, if not the whole truth. But the artist must watch his step. Analogy, allegory, symbols have always been his stock in trade—from Pushkin to the present day. Eagerly Moscow audiences flock to see a movie recreating the dark atmosphere of the Stalin terror. However, disguised by a Hitler moustache and a Beria pince-nez, the protagonist can hardly be identified with the true perpetrator of the crimes of the period.

Many of my Moscow friends are nevertheless ecstatic. Even a crumb of truth is better than nothing. The current wishy-washy attempts to deal with the bloody Stalin era, which took a greater toll of human lives than World War II, somehow recall to me Stalin's magnanimity in allowing the production of Bulgakov's *The Days of the Turbins* in the thirties at the Moscow Art Theater. Then too, everybody was delighted. Doddering grand personalities of Moscow's theater world were known to remark: "How wise and gracious of our dear Yosif Vissarionovich to approve the play. It's getting to be freer and freer, just like before the Revolution."

Georgi was fighting for his life. I was hopeful. He had the best medical care: weekly and sometimes daily doctors' visits from the Academy Clinic of which he was a longtime patient.

Leaning on a cane—which I bought him after phoning about a dozen Moscow drugstores before at last finding one that had some in stock—he resumed his daily constitutional. Frail, his wounded legs giving him more pain than usual, he nevertheless kept up a fast pace. Though he refused to be accompanied on these walks, his sister or I, apprehensive that he might trip and fall, would follow a few steps behind, never letting him out of our sight.

He was now hobbling towards the corner of the block, where our street, Michurinsky Prospekt, began and where a statue to Indira Gandhi had been unveiled and a square laid out in her honor. On that corner stands the University Hotel, accommodating academics and students from foreign lands.

Georgi walked through the hotel doors, perhaps with the intention of glancing at the magazines displayed on the newsstand in the lobby. Presently I saw him start back. I was close enough to hear the doorman's words, flung at all Soviet people who try to go into a hotel reserved for visitors from abroad: "You're not allowed in! Entrance only for foreigners."

My husband turned away. Outrage at this treatment flamed on my face. But Georgi admonished: "Pay no attention to such trifles. Think of the good we have achieved."

I pressed his arm.

"Yes, yes, I will try."

Think of the good that has been achieved. How many times have I tried to do just that. See the Soviet experience in historical perspective, I tell myself. But the perpetual lies, the blood of the victims, of my loved ones and so many others, cannot be shunted aside by positive thinking. Can I forget and forgive? Never! Nor forgive the long silence, or the hypocrisy of the present day.

Yet I try to be fair. I repeat to myself the magic words: Economic security. The right to a job. These outweigh many of the freedoms that democracies claim for their citizens. I keep meeting people, friends, who are sincerely socialist in their views and deeds, working for the public good first and for personal gain second. Yes, and I must not forget my Soviet women friends, indeed all of the country's women. They can be proud of what they have made of their lives, acquiring skills and professions that render them indispensable to society, leading as productive an existence as the men, possessing the same sense of self-worth.

After Georgi passed away before my eyes in July 1986, I fled to Canada. But Moscow as always remained in my heart and my thoughts. In my dreams I saw her green avenues, rushing crowds—and the faces of my own generation, grim, deeply lined. On all my visits I could not tear my gaze away from them in the Moscow Metro. They were part of me, dear and close, for with them I had shared so many hardships, losses, pain. Surly clerks whose rudeness I had endured for decades had their place in my memory, too. Bolder youths—not carefree but intent—sat glued to their university textbooks or world classics. Riding the Metro I had also watched them, searching their faces for the idealism of my own youth. And then there was the constantly baffling ideological see-sawing of the Party and government bosses that had been so integral to my Soviet existence.

Years of life in Canada could not get Moscow out of my system. Nor could I forget my friends, happy now to be living comfortably in two- or three-room flats of their own, not minding the absence of bedrooms, or having to convert the couches sat on in the daytime into beds by night.

Now it is August, 1987—thirteen years away from the twenty-first century, which I fervently hope will be less brutal and tragic than the twentieth. I arrive in Moscow on a Friday night. The cool air is a relief after the heat of the Canadian summer.

In teeming rain I make my way to Arbat Street. Here I lived before my first marriage, on the contiguous Gogolevsky Boulevard. Here I shopped, ran into friends, spent Saturday night dancing and drinking wine at the Praha Restaurant, where gypsies shimmied and, with their soul-stirring, passionate songs, brought tears to the eyes of my Russian escorts.

On my previous visit to Moscow, the year before, Arbat was being transformed into a promenade, with old-fashioned wrought iron lamp-posts; former mansions of the nobility, half-concealed by scaffolding, were being restored. And now, besides the architectural face-lift, the street presented a scene so new to Soviet life and so reminiscent of nooks in Western cities that I had the feeling of not being in Moscow at all. Everywhere were little knots of young people who, though not entirely uninhibited, behaved far more casually than I had ever seen them do before. Poets were reciting their verse, painters trying to sell their pictures and offering to paint portraits for the passing crowds. A breath of freedom. Yet I could not help noticing the large number of "archangels," as, like its predecessors, the KGB has been christened by the people.

To my trained eye groceries and bakeries seemed more poorly stocked than the year before, and there was more queuing up.

"Who cares if we have shortages so long as we can get the books we want to read and the newspapers and magazines at last print the truth?" a friend says. There is a new sparkle in her eyes, a new happy look that I have never seen before. Her father was a victim of the Stalin terror. At last, she feels, she can speak openly of her deep wound and the sufferings of her whole family.

Despite the shortages, I find the table at the home of a neighbor laden with choice dishes. The spread is a credit to Muscovites' ingenuity in the perpetual hunt for foods in short supply.

The conversation around the table is as much a surprise as the Arbat scene. Historians are busy, I am told, writing articles on Bukharin, Zinoviev, and Kamenev—all three shot—to at least partly clear them of their "crimes." Daringly I drop the name of Trotsky. The air grows electric with an almost palpable bewilderment, then clears momentarily like a thundercloud pierced by rippling sunlight. We recall Trotsky's theory of permanent revolution. Time has proved him wrong.

A man who holds a high academic post—and whom I knew always to stress his wholehearted support of every Party policy, also to sing the praises of Stalin and later Brezhnev—suddenly reveals qualms of remorse: "We knew that most of the people shot or deported to camps in Siberia were innocent. But what could we do? Stick our necks out, lose our own freedom or even life?"

A lull in the conversation. The same man continues: "Most of those responsible for the crimes under Stalin are dead."

Convenient self-deceit! Nazi criminals who operated from 1939 to 1945 are being hunted down and brought to trial, while the Soviet Communist Party members who signed and counter-signed thousands of lists of people to be shot and arrested, and the secret police assassins who executed their orders, are presumed to be dead.

Such hypocrisy has its harmful effect on Soviet youth, who squirm at the lies and half-truths fed to them daily. I read the report of a trial held in one of the Soviet Caucasian republics. The offenders are young men, some even teenagers, charged with car theft, trafficking in drugs, and burglary. They want a taste of the good and easy life, they say.

"Where did you acquire such pernicious ideas in our socialist society?" the judge inquires. He does not have to wait long for an answer. Insolently the young offenders fling at him: "Where did those who set themselves up as an example to us acquire their villas, their Mercedes cars, their diamonds?"

Young people, as well as many of my own generation, long desperately to know the truth. Alas, the glaring contradiction within Soviet society is that there are millions who have become so accustomed to lies and lying that they would go to any lengths to continue living in the old way. The truth is feared.

Truth! *Pravda*! Russia has been the land of truthseekers, *pravdaiskateli*. Among the truthseekers were some of the greatest and noblest minds the country has produced. But perhaps truth was so diligently sought because it was, and still is, so rare.

EPILOGUE

This happened at the beginning of our century, just after the celebration of the New Year. The day was bitterly cold. Snow lay deep and hard on the ground. The Russian landowner's family felt dull after the Christmas and New Year merrymaking.

Annoyed by the boredom, the landowner hit on an idea to liven up things a bit.

"Fetch Ivan," he commanded one of the servants.

Ivan arrived. He paused in the doorway, crumpling his cap in his hand.

"How would you like to own twenty-five *desyatins* of land?"

The family and servants pricked up their ears. They knew the landowner was a great joker. Curious, they waited to hear Ivan's answer.

"I would like nothing better," replied the peasant. "But how will I get the land, when I have no money to pay for it?"

"I'll give it to you free—on one condition."

"And what is that?"

"See that hill over there?"

Ivan nodded.

"Remove your bast shoes and footcloths. If you can stand barefoot on it for twenty-four hours, the land is yours."

"That I'll do, because I want the land badly. But I too have a condition to make."

"And, pray, what is that?"

"Light a fire a little distance from the hilltop so that I can watch the flame."

"Very well," agreed the landlord. "But we won't use up more than just one pile of firewood."

The pile to which the landowner pointed seemed big enough to Ivan, and he nodded assent.

Hour struck after hour. The family kept staring out of the window, amazed to find Ivan still standing there in his bare feet. A wind rose, it was getting frostier, but Ivan did not stir. He seemed glued to the spot. Twenty hours had gone by. He was still on the hilltop, never taking his eyes off the flame.

The last log was fed into the fire. At the end of the twenty-second hour, the flame died out. Ivan fell flat on the ground. A servant ran out to see if Ivan was dead. Ivan was alive, unharmed, except for his feet. He was brought to the village hospital and there his feet were cut off.

Hearing the story, the doctor asked: "Why in Heaven's name, Ivan, did you do a foolish thing like that? Twenty-two hours out in the cold in your bare feet! In such weather! You must be mad!"

"Doctor, I would have stood on the icy ground all of the twenty-four hours," said Ivan. "And the land would have been mine. If only the flame were alight. Watching it was what gave me courage."

Will the flame be rekindled? People like myself who had faith in the dream of a new society have been destroyed and betrayed over and over again.

Index

Yezhov, Nikolai, 58, 109
Young Communist League, 24, 25,
   26, 29, 31, 40
Young Pioneers, 24
Young People's Socialist League, 26
Yulya, 161, 167, 168, 183, 194

Zhdanov, Andrei, 104–5
Zhukov, 108

Zilbert, Joe, 61–2
Zinde, Mikhail, 1, 4, 76–7, 79, 80,
   82, 84, 88, 91–2, 101, 115, 119, 193,
   194
Zinde, Vicky, 4, 97, 101, 189–91, 196,
   198
Zinoviev, Grigory, 11, 49
Zola, Emile, 23
Zoschenko, 105